"How can I in good conscience ruin your good name?"

"Whatever happens to my name, it is mine to ruin, not yours." Vivian tilted back her head to look at Oliver. "I am responsible for myself. Surely 'tis not dishonorable for you to take what is freely given." She smiled faintly and went up on tiptoe, so that her lips were barely a breath away from his. "I do not intend to marry for love or money or family duty. And I have never met another man I wanted except you."

"Vivian . . . oh, God, Vivian. Vivian." He kissed her lips, her cheeks, her throat, interspersing her name with his kisses. "This is madness."

She giggled girlishly and, pulling away from him, reached up to pull off the stylish turban she had worn to conceal her hair. Pins came popping loose, and her hair tumbled down over her shoulders in a glory of orange-red flame. She was a vision, he thought, wild and free and beautiful, and it occurred to him that no man could ever truly possess her. She was, as she said, her own, and however much he might curse himself for it, Oliver knew he could not resist her lure.

Vivian smiled and held out her hand to him. Throwing aside his doubts, Oliver reached out and took it.

She led him up the stairs to her bedchamber.

Turn the page for rave reviews of the sparkling Willowmere series by Candace Camp

An Affair Without En

Praise for the Willowmere series

A Gentleman Always Remembers

"An intensely passionate and sexually charged romance . . . A well-crafted, delightful read."

—*Romantic Times* (4 stars)

"A delightful romp set in the Regency period. Ms. Camp has a way with truly likeable characters who become like friends. The action pops . . . and the relationships are strong."

—Romance Junkies

"Where the Bascombe sisters go, things are never dull. Author Candace Camp delivers another witty, heartwarming, and fast-paced novel."

—A Romance Review

A Lady Never Tells

"This steamy romp . . . will entertain readers."

—*Publishers Weekly*

"Four unconventional American sisters and three aristocratic bachelor brothers set the stage for the first novel in Camp's Willowmere trilogy. With a bit of mayhem, humor, misunderstandings, and enough sensuality to please any reader, this consummate storyteller writes a well-crafted and enchanting tale."

—*Romantic Times* (4½ stars)

"Superbly written and well paced, *A Lady Never Tells* thoroughly entertains as it follows the escapades of the Bascombe 'bouquet' of Marigold, Rose, Camellia, and Lily in the endeavor to make their way in upper crust London Society."

—Romance Reviews Today

"*A Lady Never Tells* carries an allure that captures the reader's attention. Ms. Camp brings a refreshing voice to the romance genre. The touch of elegance mingled with the downright honesty of the main characters takes your breath. . . . One of those rare finds you don't want to put down."

—Heide Katros

"Filled with humor and charm . . . Ms. Camp keeps *A Lady Never Tells* from becoming a clichéd romp with her fine writing. . . . Fans of Quinn and Laurens will enjoy the first book in the Willowmere series."

—A Romance Review (4 roses)

And for the delightful works of Candace Camp

"A storyteller who touches the heart of her readers time and again."

—*Romantic Times*

"When it comes to writing sexual tension, it doesn't get better than this."

—The Romance Reader

"A double helping of romance."

—*Booklist* on *Mesmerized*

"Will leave you breathless with laughter."

—*Affaire de Coeur* on *Suddenly*

Also by Candace Camp

A Lady Never Tells
A Gentleman Always Remembers

Now available from Pocket Star Books

CANDACE CAMP

AN *Affair* WITHOUT END

POCKET **STAR** BOOKS
New York London Toronto Sydney

Pocket Star Books
A Division of Simon & Schuster, Inc.
1230 Avenue of the Americas
New York, NY 10020

First Pocket Star Books paperback edition April 2011

Cover illustration by Alan Ayers
Hand lettering by Ron Zinn

Manufactured in the United States of America

10 9 8 7 6 5 4 3 2 1

ISBN 978-1-4391-1799-6
ISBN 978-1-4391-5772-5 (ebook)

For Pete

Acknowledgments

As always, I owe thanks to a number of people who contribute greatly to my books: my wonderful agent, Maria Carvainis—I couldn't do this without you; my great editor, Abby Zidle, who is always there to hear my problems with a character or story and who, best of all, always has a solution; my husband, Pete Hopcus, for his support (and nudges); and, of course, my daughter, Anastasia Hopcus, who takes time out from her teen witches, demons, and super-powered beings to explore plot possibilities with me.

Chapter 1

London was cold, damp, and dirty.

And Lady Vivian Carlyle was delighted to be there.

As the liveried footman lifted his hand to help the lady down from her carriage, Vivian paused for an instant in the open doorway, her vivid green eyes alight with anticipation. It was still January, too early for the event to be truly fashionable, and Lady Wilbourne was not known for exciting parties. But none of that was important. All that mattered was that Vivian was back in London and going to a ball, with the whole long Season stretching out before her.

She stepped down from the carriage and swept up the front steps into the house. She had barely handed her cloak to a footman when Lady Wilbourne, a small, energetic woman who reminded Vivian of a sparrow, spotted Vivian and bustled forward, both hands held out in greeting, her eyes shining.

"Lady Vivian! I am so pleased you could attend."

"I arrived in town only yesterday," Vivian told her. "Please forgive me for not responding earlier."

"Don't think a thing of it." Lady Wilbourne waved off the apology with an airy disregard. They both knew that Vivian's presence at her ball would raise Lady Wilbourne's position as a hostess for the rest of the Season. "I am so glad that you made it back in time. I am sure it must be hard to leave Marchester. Such a magnificent house."

Vivian smiled. Marchester, known familiarly to her family as the Hall, was considered one of the grand old homes of the country, but truthfully it was a drafty old pile of stones, and during the winter the family largely kept to the newest wing of the house, avoiding the vast great hall and public rooms of the original medieval castle. She loved it; the sight of it never failed to bring up a rush of pride in her. But for comfort she would take the London house any day.

"I trust you left your father well?" Lady Wilbourne went on. "Such a lovely man. And Lord Seyre? Dare we hope that your brother will make an appearance in town this Season?"

Vivian suppressed another smile at the mention of her older brother. Gregory, the fifth Marquess of Seyre, was perhaps the most sought-after matrimonial prize in England. It was not every day that a future duke happened along, and it was considered a stroke of luck that he was also a pleasant-natured young man of better-than-average looks. Unfortunately for all the matchmaking mothers and daughters of the *ton,* however, Gregory was a shy and studious sort who rarely visited London and who avoided flirtatious young women like the plague.

"The duke is quite well, thank you," Vivian assured her. "As is Seyre, but I doubt that Seyre will travel to London. He was ensconced in the library the last time I saw him."

Lady Wilbourne frowned in the same puzzled way that most did when mention was made of Gregory's predilection for books and studies, but she said only, "Such an intelligent young man."

She steered Vivian around the room, making sure that her guests saw her in close conversation with the Duke of

Marchester's daughter, and all the while she chattered about the upcoming Season. Was the new fashion for lower waists here to stay, did she think? Would Lady Winterhaven be able to surpass the fabulous ball she had given last year? And had she heard that Mrs. Palmer's youngest daughter had chopped off her long blond hair, leaving her with a cap of curls scarcely long enough to wind a ribbon through?

"It's said she looks charming, a veritable cherubim, as it were—or is it *seraphim,* I always get such things confused—but, really, such a willful child. Everyone hoped that she would have the same success the eldest girl had—she married a count, after all, and I suppose it couldn't be helped that he was Italian. But I fear this one looks to be a handful. I've heard that Mrs. Palmer is considering holding her back another Season so that she will at least not look like a boy in a dress."

"Mm. Oh, look, there is Lady Ludley." With some relief, Vivian spotted her friend talking to an older woman near the edge of the dance floor. "I must speak to her. And no doubt you must see to your guests." She threw one of her charming smiles at her hostess, murmuring a compliment about the party, and smoothly eased out of the woman's grasp.

Vivian would have been glad to escape Lady Wilbourne's flow of chatter in any case, but it was with real pleasure that she approached Lady Charlotte Ludley. Charlotte had been her friend since they were still in short skirts and had come out the year after Vivian had made her debut. But while Vivian had remained determinedly single all the years since, Charlotte had married Lord Ludley in her second Season and was now the proud mother of a lively brood of boys.

"Charlotte, how wonderful to see you. You are not usually here this early."

"Vivian!" Charlotte gave a delighted smile and held out

her hands to her friend. "Indeed, no, Ludley had to come to London, and I could *not* stay home, even though we will be here for two weeks only. Come, have you met Lady Farring?"

They exchanged the usual pleasantries for a few moments, then excused themselves from the other woman and strolled farther away from the dance floor.

"I am so happy to see you!" Charlotte squeezed Vivian's hands.

"And I, you. Please, do not tell me you really mean to leave in two weeks?"

"I fear Ludley's business will take no longer."

"So the rest of your family is not here? Camellia and Lily? I am so looking forward to their first Season."

"They will come later, I am sure. Hardly anyone is here yet. Indeed, I quite feared that you would still be at Marchester."

"I could not bear to stay away any longer," Vivian confessed. " 'Tis almost five months since I was last in London. I think it's the first Little Season I've missed since I came out." Not everyone cared so much for the social whirl that sprang up in London each fall, but Vivian enjoyed the Little Season almost as much as the elegant full Season.

"I could scarcely believe you stayed at Halstead House with your uncle for so long—especially since there was an outbreak of measles."

"It was ghastly. I had to tend to Sabrina, and you can imagine how much I enjoyed that." Vivian rolled her eyes drolly. Sabrina was the young woman her uncle had married after his first wife died. She was only a few years older than Vivian herself, and their relationship was rocky at best. "But I could not leave them in the lurch that way. And I did at least have the satisfaction of seeing Sabrina come all over in spots."

"That would have been worth any price. And there was

more excitement at Willowmere, I understand. I don't know why I am never there when these things happen."

Willowmere was the country estate of Charlotte's family. It was only a few miles from Vivian's uncle's house, and it was on Vivian's frequent summer visits to her aunt and uncle that she and Charlotte had become friends. The sprawling old house was now the residence of Charlotte's cousin, the ninth Earl of Stewkesbury—and of his set of American cousins. The four girls, all named after flowers—and nothing like the delicate creatures their names implied—had arrived at the end of the last Season. With their blunt speech and easy manner, it had been clear that they were not ready to face London society yet, and the earl had whisked them up to Willowmere to prepare them for their debuts.

Like Charlotte, Vivian had found the young women refreshing and charming. Though it was clear that the Bascombe sisters would need some polishing to get along in the *ton,* Vivian had readily agreed to sponsor them this Season, and she had grown even closer to the girls during the time she had spent at her uncle's house.

She laughed now, recalling the events of the preceding autumn. "Things do tend to happen wherever the Bascombe girls go. If it isn't kidnappers popping up, it's French balloonists falling from the sky. Indeed, I found Marchester sadly lacking in excitement after being around your cousins for a few months."

"Tell me, which did you miss more—Camellia's and Lily's escapades or your exchanges with Stewkesbury?" Charlotte's eyes twinkled.

"Stewkesbury!" Vivian grimaced. "As if I would miss *his* sniping."

The last thing she intended to admit to her friend was that more than once while she was at her father's house, she had found herself thinking of some particularly clever remark she could make to the earl, only to remember a moment later, with a distinct sense of disappointment, that Stewkesbury was not there.

"And here I thought it was usually you sniping at him."

Vivian let out an inelegant snort. "I would not have to snipe at him if the man didn't insist on being so stiff-necked and self-righteous."

Charlotte shook her head, making a sound that was half laugh, half sigh. "And Oliver is never so stiff-necked as when you are about."

"Then you see what I mean." Vivian shrugged. "The two of us simply cannot get along."

"Yes, but what is odd, I think, is how much the two of you seem to *enjoy* not getting along."

Vivian glanced at her friend, startled, and found Charlotte watching her with a knowing expression. "I haven't the faintest idea what you're talking about."

"Mm. Yet if I remember correctly, you admitted only a few months ago that you once had a *tendre* for Oliver."

Color bloomed along Vivian's cheekbones. "When I was fourteen! Good heavens, I hope you don't think I am still carrying some sort of . . . of schoolgirl infatuation with the man."

"No. I am sure not. If you were interested in a man, I feel certain you would act upon it."

Vivian tilted her head to the side thoughtfully. "I suppose I would . . . *if* there were such a man."

"And if you were aware how you felt."

"I beg your pardon?" Vivian's eyes widened with surprise. "Are you saying . . . do you think . . ."

Charlotte simply waited, her eyebrows faintly raised in interest as she watched her usually articulate friend fumble for words.

"I am not interested in Oliver," Vivian said at last. "And, believe me, I know my own feelings."

"Of course."

"I will admit," Vivian went on candidly, "that Stewkesbury is a handsome man. That much is obvious."

"Of course," her friend agreed soberly.

"There is nothing to mislike in his face or form."

"No, indeed."

"He is intelligent, if often provokingly narrow in his thinking. He rides well. He dances well."

"It goes without saying." Charlotte's eyes danced, though she kept her lips pressed firmly together.

"I am sure that he is as eagerly pursued by marriage-minded young ladies as is my brother."

"Mm."

"But I am not marriage-minded. And I am not foolish enough to think that there is any possibility of romance between Stewkesbury and me."

"Still, I cannot help but notice that you seem . . . happy . . . when you and Cousin Oliver are engaged in one of your clashes."

Vivian's lips curved up faintly. "Sometimes it *is* rather fun."

"Even though you dislike him."

"I don't dislike him," Vivian protested quickly.

"No?" Charlotte cut her eyes toward Vivian slyly.

"Of course not. Why, there is no one I would trust more if I needed help." She paused, then added judiciously, "Though he would, of course, make a perfect nuisance of himself afterwards telling me how foolish I had been."

Her friend chuckled. "Indeed he would."

"But the two of us? We are as unlikely as oil and water."

"I am sorry to hear it. For I believe that the two of you

will be thrown together a great deal this Season, what with your sponsoring Lily and Camellia."

"I shouldn't think it will be a problem." Vivian dismissed the idea with an airy wave of her hand. "I am sure Stewkesbury will be up at Willowmere most of the time, as he usually is."

"I would not count on that," Charlotte said drily, glancing over Vivian's shoulder.

An instant later a deep male voice said, "Lady Vivian. Cousin Charlotte."

Vivian's face went suddenly hot, and her hands cold. "Stewkesbury!"

Stewkesbury strode purposefully across the floor, a tall, lean man in black breeches and jacket, his shirt blazingly white and decorated with a conservative fall of ruffles down the front. His white linen neckcloth was tied in a simple arrangement and centered by a pin of onyx. Neither on the cutting edge of fashion nor lagging behind it, his attire was of the finest quality and cut, but with no hint of flash or ostentation. His thick, dark brown hair was cropped close, more for the sake of convenience than for any attempt at fashion. He could not claim the male perfection of face that was his brother Fitz's, but he was, as Vivian had said, a handsome man, with firm, even features and level gray eyes.

He had seen his cousin and Lady Vivian the moment he stepped into the ballroom. Indeed, he thought, it would have been hard to miss Lady Vivian. She was dressed in rich black satin overlaid with a filmy material of the same color, a stark contrast to the pale white skin of her shoulders and elegantly narrow neck above it. Her flame-red hair burned like a beacon.

It was one of the many annoying things about the woman, he thought. She never blended in, never entered a room quietly. She was always immediately, flamboyantly *there*. He started across the room toward her, wondering as he did so how she managed to make a simple black ball gown look so thoroughly elegant, yet also seductive. Vivian Carlyle was never anything but stylish and tasteful, clearly a lady, but there was always something about her that made one think of secret, illicit passion. Oliver was not sure if it was the way her lips curved up in a slow smile, her green eyes lighting as if only the person she looked at shared in her humor, or perhaps it was the way the delicate hairs curled upon the milk-white skin of her slender neck, or maybe the way she carried herself, without stiffness or shyness, her curvaceous body pliant and soft.

Whatever it was, Oliver was certain that only a dead man could look at Vivian and not imagine, at least for an instant, having her in his arms, that soft skin beneath his hands. Certainly he had found himself thinking it on more than one occasion, and Oliver was certain that he was more immune to the lady's charms than most. After all, he had known her when she was a gawky girl, all sharp angles and giggles and mischief, that wealth of fiery hair tamed into bright orange braids down her back. She had been the bane of his summers down from Oxford, always up to some trick or other with his cousin. She still had the ability to annoy him as almost no one else could. God knows why he had agreed to let her sponsor his American cousins this Season. No matter how high a place she held in London society, it could not be worth the aggravation of dealing with her daily.

Oliver had been expecting to see her at any time for the past week. The social life that London offered was like food and drink to Vivian. Where others might grow weary during the exhausting round of activities that constituted the Season, Vivian thrived on it. He knew that she rarely stayed away from the city longer than a month or two. It had been most unusual for her to spend as much time as she had this fall at her uncle's—or, he should say, at her uncle's and at Willowmere, for it had seemed that every time he turned around, she was there in his house, the scent of her perfume in the air, her laughter echoing from some hallway, or sitting at his table, her eyes alight with laughter as she verbally sparred with him. The house had been so much quieter since she left for Marchester, so much calmer and somehow emptier.

It went against his grain, he told himself, to give up that calm, that quiet, and voluntarily place himself in Lady Vivian's path. But he was not one to shirk his responsibilities, and right now he was responsible for his newfound American cousins and their first Season. He had to watch over them, and that meant, perforce, watching over Lady Vivian—especially now that Eve, who would have been their chaperone, had married his brother Fitz and would no longer be in constant attendance on the girls.

Lily would manage just fine. She was already engaged and safely out of the politely cutthroat competition of husband-hunting that marked the Season, and she seemed much more attuned to the social activities—the parties, the shopping, the theatergoing and obligatory calls, the pervasive gossip—than did Camellia. It was the straightforward, blunt-speaking, so very *American* Camellia who was likely to go awry, to argue or to break a rule—not with any ill will or purposeful disobedience, but simply because the tenets of the beau monde were as incomprehensible to her as Sanskrit. The good thing about Lady Vivian was that, even though she was the daughter of a duke, she was rather like Camellia and therefore able to understand and predict Camellia's actions. The unfortunate thing was that, being like his cousin, she was as likely to join Camellia in some mad undertaking as to dissuade her from it.

His lips tightened at the thought. The only thing for it, he knew, was to keep a close eye himself upon both Cousin Camellia and Lady Vivian. It would mean a great deal more parties and social interaction than he liked, as well as spending far too much time around a woman who tried his patience. But he saw no way around it. He could not abandon his cousin; for all her unruly behavior, Camellia was sincere and honest, an innocent, really, among the far more sophisticated and lethal members of the *ton*. So he would attend the parties. He would put up with Vivian Carlyle. And, he promised himself, he would make a dedicated effort to get along with the woman, no matter how she might fray his nerves.

That resolve was tested the moment Vivian turned to greet him and he received the full impact of her dress up close. The heart-shaped neckline was low and wide, skimming over her breasts and leaving much of her chest and shoulders bare. The rich satin hugged her form, and the jet bugle beads that adorned the neck seemed designed to draw one's eye to the swelling of her creamy white bosom. Desire slammed through him, fierce and immediate, and only years-long training kept his face expressionless.

"Stewkesbury." Vivian smiled at him in that way she had, a way that hinted of secrets and laughter.

Oliver was aware that Vivian considered him a hopelessly dull sort, and he often had the faint suspicion she was laughing at him, which made him even more unbending in her presence. Now, in response to her greeting, he gave her a punctiliously correct bow.

"How nice to see you," Vivian told him. "Are Lily and Camellia with you?"

"No. I drove down alone last week. The Bascombes are coming later with Fitz and Eve. I am sure it will not be long before they arrive." Despite his best efforts, his gaze kept returning to Vivian's bosom. *Damn the woman—the way she is dressed is bloody distracting.*

"I am surprised to find you here alone," Vivian went on. "I know how infrequently you are wont to visit London."

He wasn't sure why her assumption irritated him, but it did. "On the contrary, my lady, I am often in the city. I don't know why people persist in thinking that I am always stuck away up at Willowmere."

"Because no one ever sees you."

"I am in London. I simply do not spend my time at parties."

"Ah, I see." A smile twitched at the corner of Vivian's mouth. "No doubt you are occupied in far more useful activities."

There it was again, he thought—the amusement at his staid personality. Sometimes he imagined how delightful it would be to do or say something outrageous, just to see the surprise flare on Vivian's face. But, of course, that would be an entirely silly thing to do, so he said only, "I am usually here on business."

His cousin, who had been watching their exchange, spoke up for the first time. "Oh, Oliver, surely that does not take up all your evenings as well. You might at least go to a dinner or a ball or two."

Vivian glanced at Oliver, her eyes glinting a little. "I suspect, dear Charlotte, that your cousin finds such things as balls or dinners tedious. Isn't that true, Stewkesbury?"

"Not at all," he responded drily, meeting Vivian's glance with something of a challenge in his gray eyes. "I find them much too stimulating for someone of my sedate nature. I might be utterly overcome."

Vivian let out a little laugh. "Now *that* is something I should like to see. I have always wondered what it would take to overcome you."

"Ah, Lady Vivian, you should know that 'tis easily done. You have accomplished it on many an occasion."

Vivian hesitated, looking faintly surprised. Then she furled her fan and reached out to tap him lightly on the arm with it, her eyes twinkling. "A very pretty compliment, my lord. I am shocked."

"You do not think me capable of it?"

"Oh, no, you are capable enough. You forget, I have heard you talk to others. But I would not have thought you willing to hand a compliment to me."

He raised his brows. "What a picture you hold of me, my lady. Do I appear such a boor?"

"No, not a boor. But not capable, perhaps, of polite flattery."

It was Oliver's turn to look surprised. Polite flattery? Could Vivian possibly think that he was not aware of her beauty or her powerful effect on men? Did she not realize that even now, as he stood here, chatting, carefully keeping his features composed, his nerves tingled with an awareness of her? That her perfume teased at his senses and his very blood hummed? He presumed she had chosen her dress and styled her hair, dabbed a scent behind her ears, in the hope of eliciting this exact response. She must know how men reacted to her. The only possible reason for her surprise was that she did not expect him to react as a man.

The idea galled him. Did he appear so sober, so boring, to her?

"Dearest Vivian," he said, his tone taking on a sharper edge, "I suspect you would be surprised what I am capable of."

Her eyes rounded a little, and he had the satisfaction of knowing that his words had taken her aback. Ignoring his cousin's indrawn breath of surprise, he went on, extending his hand to Vivian, "Perhaps, my lady, you would favor me with this dance?"

What in the world has come over the man? For an instant, Vivian could only stare at Stewkesbury in astonishment. It wasn't as if he had never asked her to dance or even that he had not paid her a compliment. She was sure that there had been other times, other places, when they had taken a turn on the dance floor together or when Oliver had said that she was looking lovely that evening or some such thing. But those compliments, those invitations to dance, had always been polite, expected, simply part of the world in which they lived. Just as he had offered his arm to her at a dinner party because she was the highest-ranking female present, he had no doubt escorted her onto the floor after he had dutifully danced with Charlotte or some other female relative or the hostess of the party.

But something about tonight was different. Something in his eyes, in his tone when he spoke to her. The compliment he had paid her had not been extravagant, but neither had it been the bland, customary acknowledgment of her looks that one heard at every turn. It had been . . . almost flirtatious. And his words before his invitation to dance had carried a dare. Indeed, his very invitation to her seemed almost a challenge.

Well, a challenge was certainly something Vivian never turned down.

Her lips curving up into a smile, she placed her hand in his. "Of course, my lord. I would be honored."

They took their place on the dance floor. Couples were forming around them, and Vivian realized that they were taking up the position of a waltz, not a cotillion or a country dance. She faced him, aware of a heightening of nerves inside her. Had she ever waltzed with Oliver? She could not remember doing so. Of course, the dance was no longer considered so shocking; it was even done in country assemblies now. She had danced it with many men over the years. There was no reason to feel this faint sense of unease.

Yet, she had to admit, Oliver had always had the ability to intimidate her a little. That was a rare quality, she reflected, for at twenty-eight years of age, she was a woman who knew her own mind and in general did mostly as she pleased. Wealthy in her own right and the only daughter of a duke, she was under no man's control. She had spent the last decade being pursued by many men, but none had ever won her over, and she was certain by now that none ever would. She enjoyed a light flirtation now and then, and she had a wealth of admirers from whom to choose when she wanted an escort to a play or a ball. But she could just as easily decide not to take any of them, as she had tonight. In short, Vivian felt she could hold her own with any man.

But Oliver . . . somehow Oliver was a little different. Perhaps it was that she had known him when she was young and unsure of herself, and he had seemed to her far older and more mature. Perhaps it had been the adolescent yearning she had felt for him—not only unreciprocated, but unnoticed. Or perhaps it was simply that he was the sort of man who was invariably, maddeningly correct—in words, in action, even in thought. She had once heard Fitz complain of the 'burden of perfection' that having Oliver for a brother had placed on him, and she knew what he meant. The Earl of Stewkesbury set an imposing standard, and she could not help but feel a niggling doubt sometimes that his side of any argument was, if not necessarily right, certainly the most *correct.*

Of course, that he *could* intimidate her did not mean Vivian intended to *allow* him to. She lifted her chin a fraction as she looked up into his face. His eyes held an expression that she could not quite read, and she felt the oddest little flutter in her stomach. At that moment, the music started up, and he took her hand in his, the other going to her waist as he moved closer to her.

The sensation in her stomach increased, and suddenly Vivian felt flushed, almost embarrassed at being this close to him. She glanced away, concentrating on her steps as they moved into the music. It was silly, she told herself, to feel so disconcerted at dancing a waltz with Oliver. She had known the man *forever,* after all. While it was as close as one could get to being held in his arms, nothing in his demeanor was loverlike. It was like dancing with her brother . . . except that it wasn't at all like dancing with her brother.

She was intensely aware of the way his hand curved around hers, of the way his fingers felt against her waist. Even though the material of her dress lay between her skin and his, the touch felt curiously intimate. The masculine scent of his cologne teased at her senses. She could not help but remember how giddy she had felt when she was in his presence when she was younger.

Vivian lifted her face to look at him, unaware of the slow, dreamy smile that curved her lips and lit her eyes. Oliver's hand tightened on her waist, and he pulled her almost imperceptibly closer, but then he turned his head away quickly, and his fingers relaxed their grip. As he looked out over the other dancers, a frown started between his eyes.

He glanced around, then said, "We seem to be the object of a number of gazes." His eyes returned to her, and his frown deepened. "No doubt 'tis the gown you're wearing."

Vivian came crashing quickly back into the present. *How could I have thought Oliver was any different?* She scowled back at him. "My gown? You think people are staring at us because of my gown? I take it you do not mean because it is so fashionable."

His mouth tightened. "It exposes rather more of you than is quite decent."

Vivian's eyes flashed. "There is nothing improper about my dress, I assure you. Mrs. Treherne's neckline is a good deal lower than mine."

"You wish to be compared to Mrs. Treherne?"

"I don't *wish* to be compared to anyone," Vivian retorted. "It was you who commented on the appropriateness of my dress. I was merely pointing out that there are a number of women here whose gowns are no more decent than mine, and I don't see anyone staring at them."

"That is because they don't look as you do in yours."

Vivian stared at him, nonplussed. "I scarce know whether to take that as a jab or a compliment."

He looked faintly surprised. "I'm not sure that I meant it as either."

She could not help but let out a little laugh. "Really, Stewkesbury, you are quite hopeless. Have you never looked in the mirror and seen that you are not old?"

It was distinctly unfair, she thought, that a man should have such compelling pewter-colored eyes, not to mention a smile that could suddenly light his face so that one's heart turned in one's chest . . . and yet be so unwaveringly staid.

His face stiffened. "Are you saying that one has to be old to expect certain standards of—"

"No, I am saying that no young man has ever criticized me for exposing too much of my bosom."

Color rushed into Oliver's face, and a light flared briefly in his eyes. "Vivian! Have a care what you say. Not everyone knows you as I do. There are those who would take your free sort of speech quite the wrong way."

"But I know you never will." Vivian sighed. It was useless to get upset over what he said. Oliver was simply being

Oliver, after all. She cocked her head a little to one side and smiled up at him. "Please . . . let us not argue, especially over something as inconsequential as my gown. The music is too lovely, and I am too happy to be back in London."

"Of course." He gave a brief nod of his head. "I did not intend to argue with you." He paused. "How was Marchester? Did you enjoy your visit home?"

"Yes." The lackluster tone in her voice was clear even to Vivian, and she went on hastily, "I could scarcely imagine being anywhere else at Christmas. 'Tis home, after all."

"And that means a great deal," Oliver agreed.

Vivian suspected that it meant far more to him than to her, but she did not say so. "I am always happy to see Papa and Gregory."

"How is Seyre? Still buried in his books?"

Vivian chuckled fondly as she nodded. "And in his correspondence. Gregory receives letters and packages from all over the world—gentlemen farmers in America, managers of tea plantations in Ceylon, explorers from around the globe. He is mad for plants at the moment, and I think he is going to build another greenhouse."

"Yes, I have talked with him now and then about crops. He has some interesting ideas."

Vivian grinned. Few besides her brother and Oliver would term such a conversation interesting. "I think that experimenting with the farms is one of the few things that reconciles him to inheriting the title someday. Of course, most of the tenants think him mad—harmless and good, but a trifle touched in his upper works."

"I am sure his people are most fond of him."

"Yes, they are—but I don't believe they think he will be quite a proper duke, not the way Papa is."

"They prefer your father?"

"You needn't be so surprised."

"I'm sorry." Oliver looked somewhat abashed. "I didn't mean—"

"That the duke is a little wild? The sort who hies off to London instead of inspecting his lands? Who has never gone over an account book in his life?" Vivian chuckled at the earl's rueful expression. It was clear Oliver did not approve of her father, but of course he was far too polite to admit it. "The truth is, yes, they feel Papa is precisely what the Duke of Marchester should be. Not that they would prefer someone like my grandfather, of course, whom everyone agrees was a proper libertine. But Papa is just the right blend of charm and arrogance. A duke, after all, isn't supposed to care. Or to worry."

"Mm." Stewkesbury seemed to have nothing to say to that statement.

For a few moments, they were silent as they twirled around the floor. It was easy, Vivian found, to follow Oliver's steps; his hand at her waist guided her firmly without pushing or tugging. One could always be sure with Stewkesbury, Vivian thought, and while that might not make him terribly exciting, it was a very good thing in a dance partner. Actually, she supposed, it was a very good thing in many ways. Especially, she mused, when he had a firm yet mobile mouth and wide shoulders . . . and that charming stray bit of hair that curled against his neck.

"I am surprised you stayed so short a time at home," Oliver said after a moment, breaking into Vivian's reverie.

"Oh!" She glanced at him, wondering with embarrassment if he had noticed her eyes straying assessingly over him. "Well . . ." She shrugged. "I love Gregory and Papa, but there's little to do at the Hall. I found it too cold for walking or riding—though little deters Gregory from riding.

The Hall had to be decorated for Christmas, but Falworth and Mrs. Minton had that well in hand. They are quite able to run the entire place without my advice, as they do the remainder of the year. And Gregory is usually stuck away in the library or the study or his greenhouses."

"I would think that after your time at Halstead you would have found it restful."

Vivian smiled. "Yes, but while I cannot wish for a repetition of the measles and all the rest, it was never dull there."

"That is true, at least since my cousins arrived at Willowmere." The earl gave a rueful smile. "Before, as I remember, it was rather peaceful."

"I could have endured the boredom at home, but then my brother Jerome and Elizabeth and their brood of hellions came for Christmas."

Oliver grinned, and the movement changed his face, suddenly making him look far younger and turning his gray eyes almost silver. "You are not a doting aunt, I take it."

Vivian could not help but smile back at him. At moments like this, when Oliver was warm and open, his face alive with humor, it was impossible not to like him. Indeed, it made her want to do or say whatever it took to keep that look on his face. "I think not. But my niece and nephews are less than lovable children. If they were not whining and sniveling, they were running about the halls, screeching. However, that was only part of it. Jerome and Elizabeth cannot bear each other's company—which would be all right, I suppose, if only they would keep themselves apart. But they seemed determined to inflict themselves on each other—and on us."

"I thought they were a love match."

"So they were . . . at one time. But I have known a number of marriages of sheer convenience that were more pleasant than their 'love match' after the first year or two." Vivian saw no need to explain the basis for the couple's falling out; she felt sure that Oliver knew as well as she of her brother Jerome's string of London mistresses.

"But surely they left after a time?"

"Thank goodness. Then Papa decided to invite a number of his friends for a few weeks of cards and conviviality. As that sort of party generally entails as much port drinking and general revelry as cardplaying, I decided I would be more comfortable in London. Besides, I was eager to get started on the Season with Lily and Camellia."

Stewkesbury's brows pulled together. "The devil. Your father shouldn't have invited his lot there with you at home. A drinking party with a gentlewoman in the house! What was he thinking?"

Vivian stiffened. Her father had not been the best of fathers; she would admit that. But she loved him and would not stand by to let others criticize him. "It *is* his house, after all."

Oliver grimaced. "That does not make it right. It's all of a pattern—to have raised you the way that he did, bringing in his latest para—" He stopped, apparently realizing that the topic he was broaching would not be considered fit for a lady. "That is to say, he did not always have a care who he allowed around his children."

His words made Vivian bristle even more. Naturally Oliver would not decry that her father had spent most of his time in London, leaving his motherless infant daughter to the care of nannies and governesses for much of her life. What bothered him was the inappropriate lifestyle her father had lived, that he had brought home groups of his friends, sometimes including one of his mistresses.

"Whom Marchester brought home is no concern of yours," Vivian shot back. "Nor is the manner in which he raised his children."

She stopped abruptly, jerking her hand from his. Startled, Stewkesbury, too, came to a halt as the other couples whirled about them.

"Vivian! The devil! What are you doing?" he hissed, glancing around. "You can't just stop in the middle of a dance."

"Can't I? I believe I just did." Whirling, Vivian walked off, winding her way through the other dancers.

Stewkesbury stood for a moment in stunned disbelief, then strode off the floor after her.

Chapter 2

Oliver caught up with Vivian at the edge of the dance floor. Wrapping one hand firmly around her arm, he steered her away from the crowd to an empty chair.

"Let go of me!" Vivian protested. "What are you doing?"

"Saving us from gossip, I hope." He thrust her down into the chair as he bent over her, doing his best to fix a solicitous expression on his face. "Try to look as if you felt faint."

"I don't feel faint. I feel furious."

"You'll recover," he replied unfeelingly. "Now, wilt a little in your chair and look as if you were overcome by the exertion of the waltz—unless, of course, you wish to have half the *ton* speculating as to what is going on between us to make you stalk off the floor like that."

She would have liked to jerk her hand away and give him a piece of her mind, but Vivian was wise enough in the ways of the *ton* to know that Stewkesbury spoke nothing less than the truth. She had committed a social solecism by leaving the floor in the middle of a dance. It would only make it worse if she was seen arguing with Stewkesbury now. It would set all the gossips' tongues to wagging, and while she did not care overmuch what others might say about her, she knew that any bit of gossip about her and Oliver would affect Lily and Camellia, and she certainly did not want to make the Bascombe sisters' task any harder than it was already.

So she contented herself with sending him a glare from beneath her lashes as she slumped in the chair, raising one hand to her forehead.

"Don't overdo it," he told her. "Or I shall have to employ your smelling salts."

"I don't carry smelling salts."

"I'm sure you don't. Still, I imagine I could borrow some."

"You are the most annoying man." Vivian dropped her hand and gave him a hard look. "Why don't you just go away?"

"I can scarcely leave you in your weakened state. I beg your pardon—did you just growl?"

"Don't be absurd." Vivian sighed. "I don't know how you are able to always say exactly the thing that will make me the angriest."

"Apparently it is quite easy." He turned to glance out over the room. "Ah, here comes Charlotte, looking suitably concerned."

"Dearest Vivian," Charlotte said as she crossed the last few steps to them. "Are you ill?" She bent to take Vivian's hand in hers, murmuring, "Fighting again?" She cast a laughing glance up at Stewkesbury.

"We were not fighting." Oliver frowned at her. "I was—"

"Lecturing," Vivian supplied. "And I walked away so I wouldn't *start* fighting."

"I could see that you were both doing an admirable job of not fighting." Charlotte grinned. "Well, fortunately for you, almost everyone was looking at Lord Dunstan and Mrs. Carstairs, who were dancing much too close together. I think I was nearly the only person who saw Vivian storm off the floor."

"It wasn't that dramatic," Vivian said with a grimace.

"Of course not. Even Aunt Euphronia said you were only giving yourself airs."

"Good Gad." Stewkesbury blanched.

"No! Is she here?" Vivian exclaimed, sitting up straighter and glancing around.

"Yes, but I'm happy to say that Lady Wilbourne invited Colonel Armbrister and his wife, so Aunt Euphronia is now firmly ensconced with them in the card room, enjoying a spirited game of whist." Charlotte turned to Oliver. "I think you could safely leave Vivian in my hands now."

"Yes. *Appearances* have been served," Vivian added, whipping open her fan and plying it, not looking at the earl.

He glanced at her, his mouth tightening, then swept the two women a polite bow. "Very well. I shall take my leave of you. Lady Vivian. Cousin Charlotte."

Vivian turned her head to watch Stewkesbury walk away. "Most of your relatives are enchanting, Charlotte, but that man . . ."

Charlotte chuckled. "The two of you are like oil and water."

"More like fire and tender, I'd say. I don't know how we shall manage the next few months, being thrown together so much."

"Mm." Charlotte studied her. "Yes, I would say it should be quite . . . interesting."

A little to her surprise, Vivian found the rest of the evening curiously flat even though she danced with several other men, none of whom offered a word of criticism regarding her dress, her family, or anything else. Indeed, most of them spent their time spouting compliments, some sincere and some so extravagant as to make her want to giggle. But however pleasant it might be to hear flattery, the truth was it did not spark her interest. She supposed she must be becoming jaded . . . or perhaps her tiff with Stewkesbury had simply spoiled her mood.

She did not speak to Stewkesbury again, though she spotted him once or twice across the room. He was generally engaged in conversation with some gentleman or another, though once she saw him dancing with Charlotte and another time with Lady Jersey. Vivian could not help but approve of his choice there. Not even Vivian's influence could guarantee Camellia and Lily a voucher for Almack's, of which Lady Jersey was one of the patronesses. As Lady Jersey was known for being something of a stickler, it would certainly help to firmly plant it in her mind that the Bascombes were the very proper earl's cousins.

The next time they met, Vivian thought, she would mention it—though she had to admit that, given the way she and Stewkesbury usually managed to antagonize each other, he would probably take her praise entirely the wrong way. She could not help but smile as she thought of the way the two of them had fussed all through the dance. As she looked back on it, it seemed a trifle foolish the way they had squabbled all through the lovely waltz—especially given that she had been enjoying dancing with him. Who would have thought that being in Oliver's arms as they whirled about the floor would have felt so . . . well, intriguing.

"I hope that smile is for me," a masculine voice murmured.

Vivian returned to the present with a start and looked at the man standing in front of her. She had been chatting with him when she had caught sight of Stewkesbury dancing with Lady Jersey. Well, chatting was not quite right—Alfred Bellard had been telling her a long and uninteresting story of his chance meeting with an old chum from school, which was precisely why she had been glancing about the room and caught sight of Oliver.

She could hardly tell the man that not only had her smile

not been for him but that she hadn't heard what he had said for the past few minutes. Fortunately, Vivian had been deflecting the hopes of young men for some years, and she had grown adept at it. With a snap she unfurled her fan and raised it, glancing across it flirtatiously.

"Now, sir, you know I cannot tell you that. Perhaps I was merely thinking of something else."

He raised his hand to his heart, as accustomed as she to this meaningless social back-and-forth. "You are most unkind, my lady. Pray give me some small crumb of your favor."

"As if you desire even a crumb of my favor," Vivian retorted. "When I saw myself that your eyes were all for Miss Charleford this evening." She had seen him talking to Sally Charleford not too long before, and there was no harm in redirecting his interest that way.

"Untrue, untrue," he said, but she could almost see the wheels turning as he contemplated this display of interest on his part—and whether he liked the girl more than he had realized.

Vivian let out a little laugh and made another light remark, then deftly removed herself from the conversation. She made her way through the crowd, giving a smile or a nod when someone managed to catch her eye. It occurred to her that perhaps she was more tired from her trip than she had realized. Perhaps she should simply go home and get a good night's sleep. She would need all her energy when the Season got into full swing.

Vivian began her good-byes, making sure to take her leave of Charlotte and the hostess, and strolled out into the foyer to get her cloak from the footman. As she turned to allow the servant to lay the cloak over her shoulders, she saw the Earl of Stewkesbury walking toward her.

She could not hold back a giggle when Oliver hesitated,

his face a mingling of surprise and apprehension. "No, there's no need to avoid me," she told him. "I shall not bite, I assure you."

Stewkesbury smiled, faintly abashed. "It takes a man of sterner mettle than I to face a lady's wrath."

"My wrath has completely dissipated. Did you not know that your words leave my head almost as soon as they enter?"

He let out a little huff of laughter. "Always have to have the last word, don't you, my lady?"

"I find it's generally more fun," Vivian agreed. "Come, Stewkesbury, let us cease our warfare. I scarce remember what we tussled about, as is usually the case."

"Of course." He gestured toward the footman and waited for the man to bring his greatcoat and hat. "In the spirit of reconciliation, I hope you will allow me to see you to your carriage."

"That is kind of you." Vivian knew that her coachman would be waiting for her nearby, watching for her emergence from the house. But men always liked to think that a lady could not make her way without assistance, and allowing Stewkesbury to help her would aid in smoothing over any hard feelings left from their contentious waltz.

So when the earl shrugged on his coat, a rather subdued garment sporting only one shoulder cape, she put her hand on his arm and walked with him out the front door. They paused, glancing around for Vivian's carriage. Just as Vivian spotted her trim vehicle, a shriek pierced the night.

Vivian jumped, startled, and beside her the earl was thrown so off-balance that he let out a low oath.

"Crimey!" the footman standing at the base of the steps exclaimed, in his excitement sinking back into the Cockney accent of his youth.

All three of them, as well as most of the coachmen in the area, swung to look in the direction of the scream. A short distance up the sidewalk, a woman clutched at her throat as the figure of a man ran away, melting into the shadows. Another man ran past the woman and followed the disappearing figure. The woman sank to her knees, letting out another howl.

Stewkesbury was down the steps in an instant and running to her. Vivian followed close behind him, trailed by the Wilbournes' footman. The earl crouched beside the woman, taking her arm to steady her. "Madam, are you all right?"

"No! No!" she cried, clutching at him. Wildly she waved an arm behind her. "He took my diamonds!"

Both Vivian and Oliver looked in the direction she pointed, but all they could see was the dimly lit street stretching into the darkness. "I'm sorry; I'm afraid he's gone."

This remark sent the woman into more wails. "No! He cannot get away! Oh, what will I do? What will I tell Charles? Those were his grandmother's jewels!" She burst into tears, covering her face with her hands.

Oliver shot Vivian a harried glance.

"Lady Holland." Vivian, recognizing the woman, stepped forward and leaned down. "Please, you must get up. You'll ruin that lovely cloak." Vivian reached out to take the woman's arm to tug.

Oliver's brows rose in amazement as those mundane words seemed to penetrate Lady Holland's emotional storm. She nodded and gulped, then wrapped her hand around Vivian's arm and began to pull herself to her feet. Quickly Oliver grasped her other arm and hauled her up.

At that moment the man who had given chase to the thief came trotting back, panting. "Sorry . . . my lady . . ." he gasped out. "I tried . . . but I couldn't . . . catch up with him. Fast little dev—um, man."

"You are Lady Holland's driver?" Oliver asked, and the man nodded.

"Yes, sir. I went after him, but . . . I'm sorry."

"I am sure you did all that could be expected."

"I don't know as his lordship'll say that," the man responded gloomily.

"Did you see what happened?" Oliver went on. "Did you get a look at the man?"

The driver shook his head. "No, I saw her ladyship coming, and I was climbing down, see, and going around the carriage to give her ladyship a hand. Then I heard something funny, and her ladyship screams. There was footsteps off and runnin'. I ran around the carriage and took off after him. Heard his footsteps, got a sight of his back 'fore he hit the shadows. He was a fast one. Little."

Oliver nodded. "Well, get back atop. We'll put Lady Holland into the carriage and escort her home." As the man responded to the authority in Oliver's voice and started back toward his carriage, the earl turned to Vivian. "Why don't you get Lady Holland settled in the carriage? I shall tell your coachman to follow us and take you home from there."

"Yes, of course." Vivian turned back to the other woman. "Come, let us get into your nice warm carriage? It's far too cold out here for my taste, even with a cloak on."

Lady Holland nodded, still sniffling, and allowed Oliver to hand her up into the carriage before he left in search of Vivian's coachman. Vivian sat down beside the older woman, picking up the lap robe and laying it across them both, carefully tucking it in around Lady Holland. Lady Holland smiled wanly and wiped the tears from her cheeks. A pleasant-looking middle-aged woman, she looked rather the worse for wear now. She was pale, with a livid scratch where the diamonds had been torn from her neck.

"Charles will be so furious."

"At the man who stole your necklace," Vivian said

soothingly. "Not at you. He will be glad that you were not injured in the robbery."

Lady Holland appeared as dubious as the coachman had about their lord's reaction to the thievery. "He didn't want me to wear them tonight. He told me it was too dangerous, what with all these robberies that have been taking place. But I insisted. I mean, after all, what good are diamonds if one never wears them?"

"My sentiment exactly."

"Yes, but Charles is a man. And so terribly practical. But really, it's not as if he doesn't drop that much any night at the tables. I told him he lost far more than that at faro, and I said I was going to wear them no matter what he wanted. And now he'll blame me . . ." She finished in a wail, and by the time Stewkesbury swung back into the carriage, she was in a full spate of tears again.

Oliver raised his eyebrows at Vivian, and it was all she could do not to grin. Pressing her lips firmly together, she turned to Lady Holland, patting her soothingly on the back. "There now, it's been a perfectly horrid evening, hasn't it? But soon we'll have you back home and safe, won't we, Stewkesbury?"

"Yes, of course. There's no danger now, my lady."

"It was so awful!" Lady Holland slowed into little hiccupping sobs. "I was just walking to the carriage, and all of a sudden, he was right there in front of me!" She gave an expressive shudder, but the tears had stopped.

"What did he look like?" Oliver asked.

The woman gazed at him vaguely. "Why, I don't know. Just ordinary, I suppose. Does it matter?"

"I wouldn't be surprised if Lord Holland wishes to engage a Bow Street Runner to try to find the thief and the jewels. It sounds as if they were quite valuable. A description of the thief would help the Runner find him. Was there anything distinctive about him? A scar? What color was his hair?"

"I—I'm not sure. It happened so quickly . . ."

"Just close your eyes for a moment, Lady Holland, and relax," Vivian suggested. "Now, think about the moment when he appeared in front of you. Was he as tall as Lord Stewkesbury?"

"No." Lady Holland shook her head. Then she opened her eyes, looking rather pleased with herself. "No, not nearly that tall, just a bit taller than I am. So he must have been a medium sort of height. And I remember his hair now. I mean, well, I don't remember it because I didn't see it. He had on a cap pulled low, and I couldn't see his hair. Most of his face was in the shadow of the cap, as well."

After a few more minutes of questioning Lady Holland, they came up with as good a description of the man as they were likely to obtain—a man of medium height with an ordinary face, dressed in the rough clothes of a laborer, hair color and eye color unknown. If a Bow Street Runner or anybody else could catch the thief from that description, Vivian reflected, it would be little short of a miracle.

But Lady Holland at least seemed calmer, and by the time they reached her house, she seemed content enough to let her maid whisk her upstairs and cosset her. Lord Holland was not at home, so Oliver had to be content with relating what had happened to the butler.

"I hope she will be all right," Vivian commented as they left the house and walked down the steps to where her carriage awaited. "Frankly, she seemed less upset over the robbery than having to tell her husband about it."

"I don't know the man. All I've ever heard regarding him is that he's an inveterate gambler."

"So Lady Holland said." Vivian glanced around. "Where is your carriage?"

"I sent him home. It seemed foolish to have two carriages trailing us around town. I shall escort you home and walk from there."

"Don't be silly. No need for you to walk. I shall tell Jackson to stop by Stewkesbury House first."

"I shall see you home first," Oliver replied firmly.

"Stewkesbury . . ."

"Lady Vivian . . ."

His tone was such a perfect imitation of hers, his expression so quizzical that Vivian had to chuckle. "Very well. I know I shall never shake you from your idea of your duty."

"I am glad to hear that you don't think I would let you ride home by yourself after what just happened to Lady Holland."

"Of course not. Though I cannot believe that someone is going to leap inside my coach as it rolls along and steal my bracelet from me." She reached out to take his hand to step up into her carriage, and the ruby-and-diamond bracelet on her wrist winked in the light from the streetlamp.

"I would not count on it. The chap who took Lady Holland's necklace seemed quite audacious to me."

"It was bold, wasn't it? Lady Holland mentioned that there had been other robberies."

Oliver nodded as he swung into the carriage behind her and sat on the opposite seat. "So I've heard. Lord Denmore was complaining about it at the club the other day. He was robbed as he left a gambling club a few weeks ago." Amusement lit Oliver's face for a moment. "He seemed especially outraged because he'd won that night. They took his winnings and his ruby stickpin. Fortney's wife was robbed the other evening, too, though I'm not sure of the particulars."

"Do you think the thefts are all the work of the same person?"

He shrugged. "I have no idea. Although . . . most of them seem to involve jewels, which may mean they're connected."

"Hmm. I shall have to ask Mr. Brookman."

"Who?" Oliver frowned. "What are you talking about?"

"My jeweler. He's finished resetting a gem I bought from him a few months ago. I shall ask him what he's heard about these thefts. If jewels are being stolen, they must be selling them. Who is more likely to have heard about it than a jeweler?"

"The devil." Oliver's scowl deepened. "Don't start snooping about in this."

Vivian quirked an eyebrow at him. "Really, Stewkesbury, are you trying to tell me what I can and can't do?"

"No, I know very well that you *can* act on any mad notion that comes to you. What I sincerely hope is that you will have the good sense not to do so."

"My sense is very good, thank you," she retorted. "And I am not planning on doing anything. I am merely going to ask a few questions."

"Asking questions can be dangerous, particularly when you ask them of the wrong person."

"I doubt very much that my jeweler is going about grabbing people's jewelry." Vivian's lips quirked at the idea of the slender, artistic Mr. Brookman running through the streets yanking baubles off women's necks.

"Probably not, but if I know you, you won't stop there," Oliver replied darkly.

"I am not going to do anything. I wish you would stop acting as if I hadn't any brains inside my head."

"I didn't say that," he protested.

Vivian sighed. "You didn't have to. It's clear what you think. You act as if I'm still that sixteen-year-old girl running about Willowmere, playing mad pranks. I assure you that

I am not. I make my own decisions. Why, before much longer, I will be living in my own home, with my—"

"What!" The earl stiffened, staring at her with such shock that it was almost ludicrous.

Vivian suppressed her sudden urge to giggle. "I have my business manager looking for a house in London."

"Do you mean—are you suggesting that you intend to move into your own home? Alone?"

Vivian could no longer hold back the laughter bubbling up in her. "Oh, Oliver! How you look! It isn't so bizarre. It makes a great deal of sense, you know."

"How? What are you thinking? Good Gad, Viv—" The youthful nickname slipped out in his shock. "It makes no sense whatsoever! Really, you cannot have thought."

"I have thought. I have thought about it a great deal. It is much more reasonable than staying in that huge house by myself. Papa does not spend as much time in London as he used to, so I am usually alone. It would be better to have a much smaller house and fewer servants. A cozy but stylish place. And, frankly, I would prefer not to have to endure Jerome and Elizabeth whenever they come to town. Not only do they quarrel until I want to scream, they also try to draw me into their argument, to take one side or the other, which is something I will *not* do."

As Stewkesbury struggled to find words to answer her, the carriage arrived at Carlyle Hall, and Vivian opened the door and stepped down. The earl scrambled out after her and went up the steps to her front door. When a footman opened the door to admit Vivian, Oliver followed her into the house.

"Stewkesbury! Whatever are you doing?" Vivian protested, a twinkle in her eyes. " 'Tis scarcely appropriate for you to be here this late, the two of us alone."

"No doubt," Oliver agreed grimly. "But I cannot leave when you are proposing this—this—why, it is the most nonsensical thing I have ever heard from you. And I can tell you that is saying a great deal."

Vivian rolled her eyes. "Very well, then, if you must. At least come into the drawing room to harangue me instead of standing out here in the foyer. Michael, bring Lord Stewkesbury a bottle of port. I am sure this will be thirsty work."

"No. I don't want any port," Oliver told the footman tightly before he followed Vivian into the drawing room, with some effort holding his peace until they were away from the footman. Taking up his position at the mantel, he turned and fixed Vivian with a stare. "Tell me you are jesting, that you are telling me this to upset my equanimity."

Vivian let out a little laugh. "Really, Oliver, I do not go about rearranging my life in order to upset you. I don't understand why you are over the boughs about this. Grown children often move into their own homes. Why, Fitz is buying a house in London, is he not?"

"Fitz is married!"

"But even if he were not . . . if he had bought a town house last year, for instance, you would not have quibbled. You did not when Royce moved into his own home."

"Of course not. That has nothing to do with—"

"Oh, no." Vivian's eyes flashed, vivid and green. "It has everything to do with it. If I were a man, you would not act this way."

"Of course not. If you were a man, there wouldn't be a problem."

"There is no problem now—except in your head. I should like a house of my own. As I told you before, there are ample good reasons for it. I am of an age, and I am quite capable of purchasing it. I am not dependent upon Papa; my aunt Millicent left me a very nice inheritance."

"I am sure she did, as well as stuffing your head with a lot of bizarre notions."

"They are not bizarre!" Vivian flared up. "She was a forward-thinking woman who corresponded with some of the finest minds of the day. Edward Gibbon. Herder. Mary Wollstonecraft. William Godwin."

"Radicals all," he muttered, then shook his head, holding up his hands. "We are straying from the point. It is not your aunt who is at issue—or your ability to purchase a house. It is the propriety of it."

"Your watchword!" Vivian said scornfully. *"Propriety."*

"It is all very well for you to disdain propriety," he shot back, his color rising. "But I can assure you that it rules the world you live in."

"Has it never occurred to you that perhaps that world is wrong?"

"Of course it has. That isn't the point."

"Then pray tell, what is the point?" Vivian threw her arms wide.

"The point is what your life would be if you thwart those rules. A good name lost is the very devil to get back."

Vivian stared at him, slack-jawed. "I have no intention of 'losing' my good name. I'm talking about having my own home, not becoming a courtesan!"

He closed his eyes, a pained look crossing his face. "Vivian . . ."

"Well, that is how you are behaving. I am not proposing anything scandalous. It isn't as if I'm a young girl making her come-out. I am a grown woman, a veritable spinster, in fact."

"You are scarcely a spinster."

"I am eight-and-twenty. Even my grandmother has given up on my making a good match. She is simply praying now that I don't go mad and do something utterly unsuitable."

"One can understand her position."

"It is not unheard of for an unmarried woman to establish her own household."

"It is if her father is still alive—when she already has a home with him—any number of homes, in fact. You have an unmarried brother, as well."

"What difference does that make?" Vivian took a step forward, setting her fists on her hips and glaring at Stewkesbury. "Why must a woman live with her father or her brother?"

He, too, moved closer, his face settling into an equally mulish expression. "So he can take care of her! Support her. Protect her."

"I have just established that I do not need anyone to support me. As for the rest of it . . . my father is not even in the house with me. Or Seyre. If anyone takes care of me or protects me, it is the servants, and I plan to continue to have servants."

Oliver grimaced. "Don't pretend to be obtuse. It isn't merely physical protection, and you know it. It is the protection of his name."

"Do you think that everyone will forget who my father and brother are just because I move out of Carlyle Hall?"

"Of course not." He clenched his jaw, his teeth grinding together. "It isn't that you literally need his protection or that you cannot manage well enough on your own. Obviously you are quite capable of that."

"I don't know why you say that as if it were a bad thing."

"It isn't—I don't—oh, bloody hell. You twist everything around so I scarcely know what we are talking about." He swung away, then turned back. "The problem is that what you propose is blasted unconventional."

"*I* am unconventional."

"I know." He flung his hands out to the sides as she had done moments earlier, an uncharacteristically dramatic gesture for him. His gray eyes were silver in their intensity. "That only makes it worse. It isn't as if we were talking about some sedate, sensible spinster who is going to set up a household with her widowed cousin or some such person as chaperone. You already do all sorts of things no one else does. You push the rules to the limit."

"Then no one will be surprised by my move."

"They may not be surprised, but they will be shocked. They will talk."

"They already talk. A number of people are shocked by me—as you should well know."

"Yes, but what is perhaps a little shocking, a trifle titillating, in a young woman residing in her father's home is far worse than that when she is a woman living on her own."

"It isn't as though I plan to completely flout all the rules. I will have a companion. A chaperone, if you will. I'm sure Katherine Morecomb will come live with me."

"Your cousin?" His brows flew up. "That wisp of a woman? Why, she wouldn't be able to dissuade you if you decided to stand on your head in the middle of St. James."

"I should think not, for then I should be quite mad and incapable of being reasoned with."

He shot her a dark look. "Don't think you can divert me with a flippant remark."

"Of course not. Nothing could divert you," Vivian retorted.

"Blast it, Vivian, don't you realize what people will think? What they'll say? They'll talk about your free and easy manner; they'll recall every gown you wore that pushed the edges of decorum." His eyes flickered to the neckline of her black gown, but he pulled them hastily away. "And then they'll speculate on why a woman who has a perfectly grand home should want to live by herself. In no time at all you will be branded a loose woman."

Anger sizzled through Vivian. "So that is what you think of me."

"No—," he started to protest, but Vivian cut him off with a sharp wave of her hand.

Her eyes blazed at him as she went on quickly, "I thought you had changed somewhat, but I can see that I was wrong. You are still a sanctimonious prig."

His nostrils flared, and a ridge of red stained his cheekbones. "It does not make me a prig because I point out that your dress shows entirely too much of you."

"By your standards!" Vivian came closer. She was vivid, glowing in her anger.

"By anyone's standards. There wasn't a man there tonight who could take his eyes off you."

"Don't be absurd. I looked . . . fashionable."

"You looked delectable."

She stopped, her eyes opening wide, her mouth rounding into an *O*. Oliver was looking at her in a way she'd never before seen, his eyes hot with anger, but with a different sort of heat, as well. He wanted to kiss her, she thought with astonishment . . . then realized, with even more surprise, that her insides were suddenly warm and liquid. She wanted him to kiss her, too.

In the next instant, all thought left her head entirely as Oliver took a long step forward, looped his arm around her waist, and pulled her to him, bending down to take her mouth with his.

Chapter 3

Vivian went still, riveted to the spot. Oliver's lips were warm and firm on hers yet somehow as soft as velvet, and the sensation they sent through her was like nothing she had ever before felt. She had been kissed by others, but none had ever sent pleasure sweeping through her, hot and demanding. None had ever made her feel as if everything inside her were rising up to meet his kiss. Her skin tingled. Her breath caught in her throat.

Without thinking, almost without volition, her arms went up and around his neck, and she swayed closer to him, her body pliant and yielding. He wrapped his other arm around her, pulling her into him, curving his body around her in a way that was both protective and possessive. His lips moved against hers, opening her mouth to him, and his tongue swept inside. A tremor shot through Vivian at this new delight, and she dug her hands into his shoulders.

At last he raised his head, breaking the seal of their kiss. He stared down for an instant into her face, his eyes dark and intense. His face was flushed, his mouth soft and reddened from their kiss. She could hear the harsh rasp of his breath. Vivian gazed back at him, too stunned to speak. He leaned almost imperceptibly toward her, and Vivian was certain he was about to kiss her again. But then he caught himself.

He took a quick step backward. "Oh, God. Vivian." One hand came up, sinking back into his hair. "I—I'm sorry." He shook his head. "I should never have—please forgive me."

Then he turned and strode out of the room as if the hounds of hell were nipping at his heels.

How could I have let this happen? Oliver charged out of Carlyle Hall and down the steps. Waving an impatient hand at the coachman waiting for him, he turned and hurried up the sidewalk. The last thing he needed was a slow carriage ride in Vivian's luxurious coach, which no doubt still smelled of her rich perfume. No, he needed a good walk to clear his head. To clear—dear Lord, to clear everything from him. Desire was still pulsing through him, strong and insistent; it paid no heed to the more rational caution that had finally penetrated his brain.

His long legs ate up the blocks that lay between Vivian's abode and his own while his thoughts ran madly through the last few minutes, struggling to understand how he could have let go of all reason and sanity in such a way. He had kissed Vivian Carlyle! And not just kissed her—he had grabbed her and yanked her to him as if she were a tavern wench, had sunk his mouth into hers and taken it in a thorough—and, yes, he would admit it, pleasurable—way. That he had enjoyed it wasn't the point. What man wouldn't enjoy kissing such a vital, beautiful, incredibly sensual woman? But a gentleman, a man of honor and sense such as himself, should have had more control. However alluring she was, whatever madcap things she did, she was a well-bred young woman, a lady. Kissing a woman like that involved promises and expectations—the sort of things that could never come to fruition with Lady Vivian.

He had been mad, absolutely mad, to act the way he had. He could not excuse it. He could hardly believe it. And he knew, darkly, that it was all somehow Vivian's fault.

Oliver stalked up the steps to his home, brushing past the doorman in an uncharacteristically brusque way. However, there was no escaping the small black-and-white dog that bounded down the stairway as if he had springs on his feet and launched himself straight at Oliver's chest. Fortunately Oliver was accustomed to such a greeting from the animal, whose practice it was to sit in the oriel window at the front of the house and keep watch for Oliver to come home.

"Hello, boy, good Pirate," he murmured, smiling down at the scruffy dog in an affectionate way that would have surprised a number of people. He scratched the mutt in the certain spot behind his ears that was guaranteed to make Pirate close his eyes in ecstasy. Still holding the dog, Oliver started down the hall to his study. Halfway there, he registered the voices in the room beyond the study, usually designated as the smoking room. He stopped, surprised. A woman's light laugh drifted out, followed by the murmur of a male voice.

"Fitz!" Oliver walked past his study toward the smoking room just as an attractive blond woman left it.

"Stewkesbury." She smiled at him, holding out her hand. She was slender as a reed, which the elegant lines of her dark blue carriage gown accentuated. Her hair, piled up in a simple coil atop her head, was a pale golden blond, and her face was delicately lovely.

A tall man with the thick, dark hair and light-colored eyes that were a hallmark of the Talbot family followed her out the door. "Hallo, Ol. Finally came home, eh?"

With a sharp yap, Pirate jumped down from Oliver's arms and ran a mad dash around the couple, leaping and twirling and yipping with delight as if he had not just performed the same dance of greeting only an hour before.

"Eve. Fitz." Oliver beamed as he stepped forward to shake his brother's hand and to kiss Fitz's new bride on the cheek. "I didn't expect you this evening."

"We made good time, and you know the ladies I was traveling with. No easy pace for Eve or our cousins."

"Of course not. I'm very happy to see you. Where are the girls?"

"Even Camellia and Lily admitted to being tired after driving all the way from Willowmere," Eve said lightly. "They went to bed early. In fact, I was about to retire myself and leave Fitz to wait up for you. So if you gentlemen will excuse me . . ."

Oliver bowed and moved into the smoking room, leaving his brother to conduct a protracted good-bye with his wife in the hallway. They had been married three months now, but no one had yet seen any diminution of their affection. By the time Fitz joined him, Oliver had already opened a bottle of port and poured them each a glassful. He turned to hand his brother a glass, and a smile once again crossed his face.

"By heavens, it's good to see you. I feel as if I've been rattling about in this house by myself."

Fitz grinned. "I would think you would welcome some peace and quiet after the last few months."

Oliver tilted his head to one side, considering. "You know, I think I have grown accustomed to the noise and disruption, even missed it."

They settled down in the deep wingback chairs in front of the fireplace and sipped their drinks, comfortable with each other as only brothers can be, a lifetime of habit and closeness behind them. Pirate, after a few sniffs around their chairs, whirled a few times on the rug in front of the fire and curled up to sleep.

"How was the journey?" Oliver asked after a moment.

"No Bascombe incidents?" Since their American cousins had arrived, it seemed as if something untoward was always happening.

The corners of Fitz's mouth quirked up. "Not a thing. It was remarkably peaceful. Makes one almost uneasy."

"The calm before the storm, you mean?"

"I cannot help but wonder. There hasn't been a kidnapping attempt or blackmail threat in three months now. We made the journey quickly. Neither Lily nor Camellia seemed inclined to comfort, and, of course, Eve never complains." Fitz smiled fondly at the thought of his wife.

"Of course."

"Lily was positively champing at the bit to get to London. It's been almost a month now since she has seen Neville. Camellia hated leaving the country, I think—you know her, she prefers riding to soirees and balls, but she was willing enough, knowing how eager her sister is. They mean to storm the milliners and mantua-makers, I gather. Lily and Eve are waist-deep in the plans for Lily's trousseau, and even Cam seems interested in acquiring a few new gowns for the Season."

"A few!" Oliver let out a grunt. "Lady Vivian intends to lead the charge, no doubt, and I can assure you that it will take a wagon to carry the load home. 'Tis a good thing the farms earned well last year."

"You can grumble all you want; I know you don't begrudge the girls their gowns and fripperies."

"No, you're right. They are remarkably levelheaded, really, when it comes to money. I never dreamed when they arrived that they expected so little of me."

"They have a different sense of responsibility, I think." Fitz paused, a smile playing about his lips. "Remember how they expected to do chores around the house when they arrived in return for your taking them in?"

"Yes. I can well imagine what Bostwick would have done if they had started sweeping floors and emptying ash cans." Oliver took a swig of his drink, shaking his head. "Does Eve really think they are ready for a Season?"

Fitz shrugged. "She thinks Lily will rub along well enough. She's already engaged, in any case. Camellia . . . well, she has her own sort of charm, and there will be those who love her. But one never knows what she'll take it into her head to do."

Oliver smiled and glanced over at the dog stretched out in front of the hearth. "Like bringing home a dirty, flop-eared stray."

Fitz's eyes followed his brother's gaze. "Exactly."

"I wouldn't worry so much if it were not Lady Vivian who will guide them through the *ton*. With her frivolous nature and outrageous conduct, it'll be a wonder if she doesn't land herself in a scandal. How can she keep two naïve American girls from making a misstep?"

"Lady Vivian is adept at managing to skirt scandal." Fitz's eyes twinkled. "Remember the time she came to Lady Berkeley's rout with that monkey on her shoulder?"

"How could I forget?" Oliver retorted drily. "The creature ran up the draperies and jumped from window to window. The footmen couldn't get it down."

"Made that party the talk of the Season. Once Lady Berkeley recovered from the vapors, I'm sure she was ecstatic about the whole thing."

"Perhaps." Oliver grimaced. "I saw Lady Vivian at the Wilbourne ball tonight. She was the cynosure of every eye."

"She usually is."

"Too dashing by half. She isn't even married. What single young woman wears black—and with a bodice that exposes her shoulders and a great deal of her chest, as well?"

"She's scarcely a girl at her first come-out," Fitz pointed

out reasonably. "One would hardly expect her to wear white and pastels for ten years."

"That's just the beginning. Do you know what mad thing she's taken it into her head to do?" Since his question was rhetorical, Stewkesbury rolled on, "She wants to buy a house in London and set up her own household. Says Carlyle Hall is too large, and her father's rarely there."

"Mm. I imagine that will raise a few brows. Still, if she has a chaperone—doesn't that cousin of hers, a wisp of a woman, follow her about sometimes?"

"Oh, yes, Vivian intends for Mrs. Morecomb to act as her companion and chaperone. You know very well that the woman could not put a stop to any mad start Vivian seized upon."

Fitz shrugged. "Probably not. But if you think about it, it's little different from the way Lady Vivian's lived the past few years. As you said, the duke spends less time here than he used to. Half the time he's in Brighton or off to one of his houses. And Seyre avoids London like the plague. So she's actually been living on her own for some time now."

"You're as bad as she is. Clearly her father is not doing his duty by her as he should. She shouldn't be left on her own in the city. Not, of course, that she will allow that the man is anything less than an ideal father," Oliver added darkly.

"She is quite loyal." Fitz eyed his brother with some interest. "It is unusual, but I'm sure she will carry it off. Vivian's never been involved in a real scandal, and people have become accustomed to her eccentricities."

"Yes, but what is considered an acceptable eccentricity in a duke's daughter will not be so easily tolerated in plain Miss Bascombe, an American born out of a scandalous elopement and having her first Season. We cannot hope that Vivian will control any of Cam's wilder notions. She's more likely to join Cam than to forbid her to do it."

"Eve will be here. I'm sure she will keep both of them from their wilder starts."

"I wonder if anyone could do that. Especially a newlywed. And didn't you say that you intended to set up your own household?"

Fitz nodded, his eyes glinting a little with laughter. "The only answer is for you to get married and then your wife can be in charge of bringing Cam out."

Oliver snorted. "I am not marrying to make an easier path through the season for Camellia."

"You should get married." Fitz grinned. "It's a marvelous state."

The earl rolled his eyes. "There's nothing worse than a reformed bachelor."

"You can hardly fault a man for wishing the benefits of love on his brother."

"I believe we were talking about marriage, not love," Stewkesbury retorted.

Fitz shrugged. "Isn't that what you want in a marriage? 'Twould be a difficult road, I'd warrant, to be fast-tied to a woman without love."

"Not if a man chooses wisely. I will allow that everything is roses and sunshine with you and Eve. No doubt your marriage will be as happy as it will be long. But Eve is an intelligent, responsible, pleasant-tempered woman who would be a good wife whether there is love or not."

"I notice you give all the credit to her." Fitz laughed, then tilted his head to one side, considering. "No doubt you are perfectly correct."

Oliver smiled. "No, there is credit to you, as well. You are a remarkably easy man to like, as you well know. You have played on that fact since you were in leading strings." Oliver took another swig of his drink and looked away from his brother. "But what if one married for love, and the love died? Where would you be then? Take Jerome Carlyle and his wife. They married with stars in their eyes, and now Lady Vivian says they spend their days fighting tooth and nail."

"It happens. But I am speaking of real love, not lust or some fleeting infatuation. Love lasts."

"As it did with our parents?" Oliver turned a sardonic eye on his half brother. "They were madly in love till the day they died, but their life was a storm. Jealousy, vases thrown, then tearful reconciliations and wild protestations of devotion."

"Mother and Father were . . . colorful." The faint smile dropped from Fitz's mobile mouth, and he directed a concerned gaze at his brother. "But not all love is the sort they had. Look at their children. Royce and Mary are as content as lovebirds." Mary, the eldest Bascombe sister, had married Fitz's half brother shortly after returning to England. "And Eve and I have no storms. You can make better choices than other people do."

"I intend to make an excellent choice. But I don't imagine that love will figure into it."

"No? What then?" Fitz looked at Oliver with interest.

"Well, clearly the woman I marry must be able to carry the weight of being a countess, which would mean that she grew up with the responsibility of title and family."

"I see. At least an earl's daughter, do you think? Or could a lowly baron's child suit?"

Oliver raised one brow at Fitz. "You know what I mean. I have to consider whether she has been raised to be the lady of the manor or merely a pleasant decoration on a man's arm. Lineage is a factor, but that does not mean she has to be the offspring of an earl."

"So an earl's niece would meet your specifications."

"Jest all you like. I am serious."

"That is what I fear."

"I realize you think I am being pompous."

"Pompous? No. Never. Perhaps a wee bit . . . exacting."

"I intend to approach the whole matter rationally. I see no harm in that. It's all very well to say that all that matters is the beauty of her eyes or how my heart speeds up when I see her. But the fact is that the Countess of Stewkesbury will have to be witty and well-read enough to make intelligent conversation, as well as plan a ball or dinner for thirty or Harvest Day for the tenants."

"And what about this paragon's looks? Are they unimportant?" Fitz's blue eyes danced.

"Not entirely. Of course, I would wish for a wife with reasonably good looks. She must have some sense of fashion. But not one so beautiful that there are always moonstruck youths clustered at her feet. Certainly not anyone flamboyant or eccentric." Oliver scowled at the fire as he went on, "The last thing I want in a wife is the sort of woman who is always winding up in some predicament or other. Or arguing with one over every little thing."

Fitz raised his eyebrows a little at this pointed description, but said nothing.

"Marriage should be tranquil. Calm. Reasonable."

Fitz let out a little crow of laughter and raised his glass in a mocking toast. "Ah, Oliver. I cannot wait until love takes you in hand. Reason, I think, will never stand a chance."

Early the next afternoon, Lady Vivian Carlyle set out to visit her jeweler. She could have, she knew, sent for Mr. Brookman to bring his wares to her house. He would not have refused such an excellent customer as herself. However, Vivian enjoyed going to his shop. There was so much more to see, and she enjoyed traveling through London. Besides . . . today just seemed to sparkle, and she was in too high spirits to remain bottled up indoors.

It did not take much reflection to know the cause of her good mood. Oliver—the stuffy, reliable, responsible Lord Stewkesbury—had kissed her. But, no, that was far too tame a word for it. What had happened between them could hardly be described as a mere kiss. It had been far too startling, too amazing, too combustible, to use the same word one might for a simple buss on the cheek. When his lips had fastened on hers, Vivian had felt the shock all through her, down to her very toes. Who could have imagined that Oliver could feel such passion? Or, even more astonishing, that he had felt that sort of passion for her!

She was far too much of a realist to imagine that it meant anything lasting or deep. It had been a spur-of-the-moment act, one doubtless engendered by a roiling mix of fury and resentment as much as by any feeling of passion. By the time Stewkesbury had reached home, Vivian felt sure, Oliver would have been appalled and thoroughly regretting the impulse that had brought him to kiss her. Nothing would ever come of it. She would not even wish for anything to come of it. The thought of her and Oliver together was absurd. Laughable. Impossible. No doubt the earl would soon apologize to her, stiff and proper, and assure her that it would never happen again. He would have recovered his customary calm, and after that, things would return to normal between them.

Still, for the moment—for the brief, bizarre, amazing thrill of the moment—it had been nothing short of exhilarating. Vivian believed in enjoying the moment.

Vivian dressed with her usual eye to fashion. She did not believe in leaving the house looking anything but her best, even if she was going only to the jeweler's. Today she wore a deep blue wool round gown and over it a matching pelisse in a military cut with black frogged fastenings marching down the front and black braid around the cuffs and collar.

Her hat was a cunning little black one she had bought last summer, shaped like an upside-down boat, coming to a point on her forehead. Black kid gloves and half boots completed the ensemble.

Just as she stepped out of her house and started down the steps toward her carriage, she spied Lord Stewkesbury crossing the street toward her. He pulled up short at the sight of her, then continued, his face set in a look of iron determination. Vivian had to smother a smile; clearly Oliver was steeling himself to face her with an apology.

"Lord Stewkesbury," she said pleasantly, not giving him a chance to get started. "How fortunate I met you; I was just about to leave."

"My lady." He bowed somewhat woodenly. "Please, do not let me detain you. I shall call on you another time."

"Nonsense." Vivian's amusement increased at the clear sound of relief in his voice. "I am going to the jeweler's. It can wait for a moment."

"What?" He scowled. "Why? The devil. Don't tell me you are snooping about. I told you—"

"Yes, no doubt you did. But I have something to pick up at the jeweler's. Why don't you escort me, and we can talk on the way?"

He looked at her for a long moment, then said somewhat sourly, "My pleasure."

Vivian ignored his tone, smiling at him sunnily and accepting his hand to step up into the carriage.

"Here we are again," she said. "Odd, isn't it, two days in a row when it has been months since we have seen each other?"

He ignored her attempt at light conversation, settling into the seat across from her and straightening his shoulders with the air of one facing a firing squad.

"I came today to apologize, my lady, for the way I behaved last night. I deeply regret my actions."

Vivian raised her brows. "You regret kissing me? I must say, Stewkesbury, that's rather an ungentlemanly thing to say. Was it so terrible?"

"What?" He stared at her. "No, of course not. It wasn't terrible at all."

"I am relieved to hear that." A smile hovered at the corners of Vivian's mouth. "I found it quite pleasant myself."

"Vivian!" He closed his eyes.

"What? Would you rather I had found it unpleasant?"

"No! Of course not. Oh, the devil! It is more than a man's life is worth trying to talk to you. I came to apologize!"

"So you said. What I can't understand is why you should want to, since it seems that both of us enjoyed the experience." Vivian's eyes twinkled.

"Well, you shouldn't have," Oliver retorted crossly. "Or, at least, you should pretend that you didn't."

"Really, Oliver—I feel I may call you by your given name, don't you, now that we are, well, better acquainted?" He stifled a groan, and Vivian paused, one eyebrow raised, then went on, "I cannot understand why I should pretend something I don't feel and which surely would not make you feel any better."

"I did not behave like a gentleman," he replied, goaded. "And you should not be so blithe about the whole matter. You should be shocked. Upset."

Vivian laughed. "I am twenty-eight years old, Oliver, and, though I know you will think me vain, I am aware that I am pleasing to look at. I have been kissed before. It seems absurd for me to be upset."

He scowled. "You routinely go about letting fellows kiss you?"

"No, not routinely. Truthfully, there have not been many men I wanted to kiss me. And some I have even slapped because they were quite presumptuous. But I could see that you wanted to kiss me, and I did not discourage you." She looked down, casting her eyes back up at him flirtatiously. "So you see, I can hardly fault your behavior, now, can I?"

Oliver simply stared at her as though stunned. He pulled his eyes away, shifting a little in his seat. "Good Lord, Vivian, it's no wonder that men kiss you if you go about talking in that manner."

"Oh, I wouldn't speak to most men that way. But with you, it's entirely different. We have known each other this age. Why, you are practically like a cousin to me."

"A cousin! I trust you don't go about kissing your cousins so!"

Another merry trill of laughter burst from her. "Goodness, no. My cousins are generally horrid. And I never had a *tendre* for any of them when I was a schoolgirl."

She had apparently rendered him speechless again. A line of red crept along the ridge of his cheekbone, and he turned his head abruptly away, gazing out the carriage window.

"There, I have embarrassed you. I shall say I'm sorry, too, and we'll call the account settled. Let us speak of something else." Taking his silence for assent, Vivian went on, "Would you like to hear why I'm going to see Mr. Brookman?"

"Who?" He turned back to her, apparently willing to drop the matter of their kiss the night before. "I thought you were going to Rundell and Bridge."

"Oh, no. Papa always used them, of course, but several years ago I saw a magnificent brooch on Lady Sedgefield, and she told me that she purchased it at Brookman and Son. So I visited his shop, and I've gone back ever since. The man is a genius at design and just as splendid at resetting old pieces. A number of the things I buy are old, you see, and magnificent as they are, I can't wear them. They are much too ornate for today's fashion. Some are too wonderful to break up, of course, and those I simply put in my collection, but, well, what's the point of buying jewels if one cannot wear them? So Brookman resets most of them in simpler pieces. That is what he's done with the Scots Green, which I'm picking up today."

"The what? An emerald?"

"No, a green diamond. They are one of the rarest of diamonds, you know; only red ones are rarer. And ones the size of the Scots Green are most unusual. They're difficult to cut because the color can be splotchy or only on the surface."

Stewkesbury's brows lifted in surprise. "You seem to know a great deal about this."

She nodded. "I've always loved jewels, you know. Papa was wont to give them to me."

Vivian's mother had died not long after Vivian was born, and her father, freed of an unhappy marriage, had spent most of his time in London during Vivian's youth, leaving her to the care of nurses and governesses. Intermittently touched by guilt, he would send her gifts or bring them home with him when he returned for one of his infrequent visits.

"His gifts, of course, were largely unsuitable for a child," Vivian went on lightly. "Little glass figures or a pigeon's blood ruby set in a filigreed brooch. My governess would cluck over the thought of sending such breakables to a child and set them up high out of my reach. It will come as no surprise to you that I climbed up to take them down and examine them. I loved the gems—the glitter, the deep, rich tones, the glow of the gold settings." She shrugged. "So when I was older, I started buying them myself. There's something fascinating about them—not just the beauty, but the stories behind the gems."

She glanced over at Oliver and found him watching her

intently. She felt suddenly self-conscious. "Why are you staring at me so?"

"Was I? I've never heard you speak so . . . seriously about something."

"I'm not *entirely* frivolous. Though I suppose some would say that jewelry is a frivolous matter to begin with."

"Mm. I think to many, it's been a matter of life and death."

This time, Vivian raised her eyebrows in surprise. "Precisely. The diamond that I am going to pick up today once belonged to Mary, Queen of Scots. No one knows exactly how it left her possession. She had an extensive number of jewels, many of them ones she brought back with her from France. And when she fled Scotland, she had to leave much of her collection behind. Others she gave as bribes, they say, to her captors. She sent Queen Elizabeth a diamond brooch, hoping, no doubt, to keep her from sending Mary to the block. She gave some to her supporters to keep for her or to use to free her. The Scots Green was one that disappeared. It was originally part of a brooch, along with a number of smaller, colorless diamonds, but fifty years later, when it turned up again, it was set as a pendant in a necklace belonging to the Countess of Berkhamstead."

"And how did it get there?"

Vivian shrugged. "You see? That is what is so fascinating about jewels. No one knows how it came into Lady Berkhamstead's hands. But it was clearly the Scots Green; there was no mistaking it. After a few more generations, it disappeared again. This summer Mr. Brookman sent me a note saying that it had turned up in Antwerp. The necklace had been broken up, and the Scots Green was for sale. So I told him yes; I cannot resist either green gems or a tragic history. He has reset it in a necklace, but this is the first chance I have had to see it."

"And you are eagerly anticipating it." Oliver smiled as he watched her.

"You will come in and see it, won't you?"

"Of course," he replied, and was rewarded by a dazzling smile.

The carriage pulled up in front of the narrow shop on Sackville Street, not far from the more famous Gray's. By the time Oliver handed Vivian down from the carriage, a clerk had opened the door of the shop. Mr. Brookman himself met them just inside the door. A slight man with thinning blond hair and pale blue eyes, he had a grave air and a stoop-shouldered posture that made him appear years older than he was. In fact, he was no older than Stewkesbury, having come into ownership of the store at the death of his grandfather. He glanced with some surprise at Stewkesbury, but he quickly recovered, bowing, and whisked them through the outer shop and into the privacy of his office.

Vivian introduced Lord Stewkesbury to the jeweler, and Brookman offered them tea, as he always did whenever Vivian came into the store. The social ritual was part of the impeccable service that Brookman & Son offered, but from the way his grave manner lightened as they sipped their tea from delicate china cups and conversed about the weather and their health, Vivian suspected that Mr. Brookman enjoyed the convention as much as he considered it good business.

Today, however, they did not linger long over their tea, for both of them were eager to get to the Scots Green. With a touch of dramatic flair, the jeweler laid out a pad covered in rich black velvet, then took the necklace from his safe and laid it out gently on the pad.

"Oh, my . . ." Vivian breathed out a sigh of admiration. "Mr. Brookman, I believe you have outdone yourself."

Elegant links of gold formed the necklace, separated

every few links by a cluster of small diamonds surrounding a small green diamond, and in the very center of the piece was a grander cluster of white diamonds around a large green diamond. It was clear and light green, not the deep green of emeralds, but a delicate, pale color of great depth and clarity. The short necklace was designed to lie at the base of Vivian's throat, the center nestling at the delicate hollow. The goldwork was beautifully done, but subtle, almost muted, the design drawing the eye to the centerpiece of the large green diamond.

"I am glad your ladyship approves," Brookman murmured, and though Vivian knew that he tried to restrain his smile, pride shone in his eyes.

She leaned closer to examine the green diamond, and the jeweler quickly offered her his loupe. The jeweler's eyepiece was, she knew, one of his most prized possessions, adorned with a thin silver band on which were engraved his initials, GDB. He seemed to take great pleasure in handing it to her to use. Quiet though he was, a streak of artistic pride ran through him.

Putting the loupe to her eye, she bent over the jewel. "It's beautiful. So large to have so few inclusions."

"It's a stunning gem. And rare. It was a very lucky find."

"Your design is the perfect setting for it." She glanced up and found Oliver watching her. Her heart did an odd little lurch in her chest, and she turned quickly back. "I must try it on."

Brookman started to rise from his seat behind the desk, but Vivian was already turning to Oliver, holding out the necklace. He took it from her and came around behind her, lowering it over her head so that it settled on her throat. His fingers brushed against her nape as he fastened the clasp, and his touch sent a shiver of sensation down through her.

She looked down, feeling suddenly a trifle breathless, even flustered.

"How does it look?" she asked, standing up and turning.

"Beautiful." Oliver was looking at her, and something was in his gray eyes, something dark and heated, that both warmed her and disturbed her composure even more.

For a moment his eyes held hers, then Vivian turned away, going to the small mirror on the opposite wall of the office. She gazed at her image, studying the necklace long enough to let the faint flush subside from her cheeks.

"I love it," she said, looking back with a smile at Brookman. "You have outdone yourself."

"Her ladyship is too kind." He inclined his head toward her in a courtly nod.

Vivian paused, then added lightly, "I am almost afraid to wear it, however. There have been so many thefts."

Out of the corner of her eye, she saw Stewkesbury stiffen, but she kept her gaze turned determinedly away from him as she walked back to her chair.

The jeweler's mouth tightened, and he frowned. "I have heard. It's outrageous."

"Then you and other jewelers have talked about it?"

"Perhaps Mr. Brookman would prefer not to discuss the matter," Oliver began, but the jeweler was already speaking.

"It is most alarming, my lady. We cannot help but worry."

"What I wonder is what they do with the jewels they steal," Vivian went on. Oliver was staring holes through her, but she ignored him. "Do they bring them to jewelers to sell?"

Such was, she knew, a common practice among the aristocracy who'd found themselves too deeply in debt. The discreet sale of a bauble or two to one's jeweler had carried more than one of her peers through a tight spot.

"Pawn them, I suppose," Brookman replied, looking troubled. "The odd thing is—no one I have spoken with has bought jewels from anyone who seemed suspicious."

"No one?" Oliver blurted out, his curiosity apparently overcoming even his control.

The other man shook his head. "Not anyone I know. All the people who have brought them jewelry to sell have been, if not known to the jeweler, at least someone who seems to be the sort of person who would have jewelry to sell."

"I see." Vivian nodded, her eyes lighting with interest. "That would indicate that the thief is a gentleman."

Chapter 4

"Or someone who appears to be a gentleman," Oliver added.

Brookman gravely nodded to the earl. "Yes, of course you are right. Indeed, 'tis no doubt more likely that it is a man who merely pretends to be of higher station."

"I don't know," Vivian put in lightly. "I've known a few gentlemen who I would not be surprised to learn were thieves." She smiled as she reached up to unclasp her necklace. "But that is quite enough of such lowering thoughts." She carefully laid the necklace back in its case. "I suggest we look to something more pleasant—would you care to show me some of your newer stock, Mr. Brookman? It has been some time since I have been here."

"Yes, indeed, my lady." The jeweler seized on the change of subject and rose to show Vivian out the door of his office.

Stewkesbury trailed after them as they went back into the sales area of the shop. While they had been talking, the clerk had obviously closed the store to customers, for the room was empty of everyone now except for the clerk, who stood unobtrusively behind the farthest counter.

The shop was small but elegantly furnished, with fine mahogany and glass cases in which pieces of jewelry rested, as well as elegantly carved mahogany chairs placed strategically here and there for customers who wished to rest or contemplate the pieces at greater length. Like most jewelry stores, Brookman & Son sold gold and silver plate, as well, and these were displayed in a pair of tall, glass-fronted cabinets.

Vivian and the jeweler examined several bracelets and earrings while Oliver waited patiently. In the end, she needed one of the bracelets and two pairs of earrings, as well as an exquisite onyx-and-ivory cameo brooch.

A few minutes later, they were back in Vivian's carriage, her bag of purchases resting on the seat beside her. She cast a smile at Oliver, saying, "There, that wasn't so terrible, was it?"

"It was . . . enlightening. You said that you were interested in jewelry, but I did not realize the extent of your knowledge until I heard you talking to Brookman."

"You mean I am not so empty-headed as you thought?"

Oliver looked pained. "I have never thought you empty-headed. In fact, I have always believed your head is full of more ideas than is quite safe."

Vivian chuckled. "You are always a clever opponent."

He raised his brows. "Is that how you view me—as an enemy?"

She tilted her head a little, considering. "No, not an enemy. A worthy member of the opposition, let's say."

"I suppose that is better than being a tyrant—as I recall you once called me."

"No! Did I? That sounds excessively rude."

"Mm. In your defense, I believe I had told you to leave the house and not show your face again."

"That does sound a bit autocratic."

"At the time you had just switched my tooth powder for some sort of soap."

"Oh, no." Vivian had to laugh. "I was a complete handful

then, wasn't I? It's a wonder your grandfather did not bar me from the house, as well."

"I had the good sense not to tell him."

She raised her eyes. "Why? Surely you weren't trying to protect me?"

"Don't give me credit for such nobility. No, it was to save myself from a proper tongue-lashing for being unable to handle a fourteen-year-old chit." He paused. "He would have been right. I hadn't the first idea what to do about you."

"You were too much of a gentleman, no doubt, to give me a taste of my own medicine. Seyre was apt to give me a dunk in the pond when I drove him to distraction."

"Too full of my own dignity, more like. I would have liked to chase you down the stairs, but I felt it beneath a university man." He smiled deprecatingly. "God knows why I felt it necessary to retain my dignity with you."

"It does seem peculiar, given that I seemed to have so little of it myself."

He did not look at her, instead concentrating on smoothing out the supple leather of his gloves as he said, "Did you mean what you said earlier? About you having a, being, um . . ."

"Infatuated with you?" Vivian gave an expressive shrug of her shoulders. "I would scarcely admit to such an embarrassing thing if it were not true, now would I?"

He looked up at her then, his gray eyes dark in the confines of the carriage. "I never had the slightest idea."

"Not surprising. I did my utmost to hide it. But to someone who knows adolescent girls, it was probably quite obvious. Why else torment you so?"

"An odd choice of actions, I would think."

She laughed. "I might not have had any dignity, but I did have my pride. I knew you wouldn't notice a skinny, orange-headed girl otherwise—and better by far to be reviled than ignored."

He studied her for a long moment, and this time Vivian turned her head away.

Silence stretched between them, broken finally by Vivian's saying, "Ah, we are at your house. I'm sorry—I hope you did not wish to go somewhere else. I did not think to ask you."

"This is perfect. In fact, you should come inside. Fitz and Eve and the girls arrived yesterday evening. I am sure they would all love to see you."

A smile lit Vivian's face. "As I would love to see them."

Eve, the earl's new sister-in-law, was Vivian's oldest and dearest friend. Widowed and penniless, Eve had been the perfect choice for a companion for the Bascombe sisters, the Earl of Stewkesbury's American cousins. She had, like Vivian, been charmed by the forthright, engaging young women. In turn, Fitzhugh Talbot, the earl's handsome half brother, had been even more charmed by Eve, and they had been married three months ago. The couple had spent six weeks on their honeymoon on the Continent before they returned to the Talbot family estate, Willowmere, and Vivian had not seen her friend since the wedding. It had been an equally long time since she had seen Lily and Camellia Bascombe.

Apparently someone had been watching out one of the front windows, for Vivian and Oliver had hardly stepped into the foyer when the sound of running feet came from upstairs.

"Vivian! Vivian!"

As usual, the first one down the stairs was the ragged black-and-white dog. Pirate whirled and jumped around them in ecstasy until Stewkesbury made a quick gesture with his hand, upon which the animal let out one last yap and dropped into a sitting position, watching the earl with bright eyes, tongue lolling from his mouth in a way that made him look even more absurd.

An instant later two young women hurried down the stairs toward them. Lily, slightly in front, was the prettier of the two, at least in the most conventional sense. Her light brown hair was arranged in an attractive cluster of bouncing curls, adorned with a blue ribbon, and her blue eyes sparkled. She had a rosebud mouth and a strawberries-and-cream complexion, and her lively personality shone in her face. She wore a blue spencer that matched the color of the pattern in her sprig muslin dress.

Her sister Camellia was obviously as disinterested in style as Lily was attentive to it. Her dress lacked frills and furbelows, and she wore no ribbons or other ornamentation. Her dark blond hair was braided into a single long plait and wrapped around her head in a simple, easy-to-manage style. Her gray gaze was level and without artifice, and though her features were even and attractive, some said that a firmness about her mouth and chin detracted from her feminine beauty.

"Vivian!" Lily cried again as they rounded the staircase, throwing out her arms as she trotted down the last few steps. Vivian rushed forward to hug her, then turned to hug Camellia, as well. All the while Lily chattered away happily, "It's so wonderful to see you! It's been deadly dull since you went home. Aren't you happy to be in London? I love it here; I don't think I shall ever want to leave."

"You might give poor Vivian a chance to get a word in," suggested an amused voice from the top of the stairs, and Vivian looked up to see her friend Eve coming down the stairs.

"Eve!" Vivian went up to greet the woman, hugging her, then standing back to examine Eve's stylish dress. "You bought that in Paris, didn't you? It's so utterly au courant!"

"See?" Lily said in a triumphant aside to her sister Camellia. "I told you Vivian would be able to tell the difference." Turning to Vivian, Lily explained, "Cam said she couldn't see why Eve's Parisian gowns are any better than the ones we have."

Vivian laughed, linking arms with Eve as they came down the last few steps to join the other two women. "When it's a matter of guns, I will rely on Camellia, but when it comes to frocks . . ."

"If you rely on me, you'll come to ruin," Camellia finished for Vivian, grinning.

"Exactly."

"Come, let's go into the drawing room and catch up on everything. I'll ring Hooper for tea and cakes." Eve turned toward Stewkesbury, who had picked up the dog in one hand and was idly scratching him behind the ears with the other. "Would you care to join us, Oliver?"

With a look that bordered comically on horror, the earl refused the invitation and retired to his study with Pirate. The ladies crossed the entryway and went into the drawing room.

While Eve rang for the butler and ordered tea, the others clustered together on a sofa and nearby chairs. Lily immediately held out her left hand to Vivian, wiggling her fingers to make the diamond ring on her third finger flash in the sun.

"Ooh, how lovely!" Vivian took Eve's hand and drew it closer, bending over the ring.

"Neville gave it to me last month when he came to visit."

"Visit!" Cam snorted. "The man has scarce been away from Willowmere!"

Lily grimaced at her sister. "Just wait until you become engaged. You'll see how long it seems when he's away. It's been a month now since I've seen Neville. And don't tell me he writes me letters. They aren't the same, and, besides, his hen-scratching is the very devil to read."

"I doubt I'll ever get engaged," Cam retorted.

"Of course you will. That's why we're here for the Season—or you are, at least." Lily grinned. "I am here to get married."

"When is that happy event?" Vivian asked.

"The end of June. I told Cousin Oliver I didn't care about a big wedding; I'd rather have a simple ceremony right now. But he's most insistent on my waiting. He thinks I'm too young, but I ask you—how can you be too young when you know your own heart?"

Vivian smiled at the rush of words, spoken with Lily's usual drama. "How indeed?"

Lily nodded. "I knew you'd understand." Then she gave a light shrug. "But it won't be so bad as long as Neville is here, too, and it will be rather fun to have a grand wedding. Besides, Eve said I must order a proper trousseau, and it will be wonderful to have a lovely wedding gown. And Lady Carr is insistent that she throw a grand ball to announce our engagement. She already has it planned."

"I suspect she has had the plans for years," Eve added with a grin. "I've gotten reams of paper from her about the event. I'm sorry, Vivian, but I am afraid Lady Carr is most insistent on having the engagement party soon—before you even have a ball to introduce Lily and Camellia."

Vivian shrugged. "I will defer to the groom's mother. I can hardly deny the poor woman the pleasure. She has been waiting years for Neville to settle down. But it is clear that we must get to the business of buying clothes immediately."

"Yes!" Lily cried with delight.

"I don't understand why we need more clothes," Camellia said, holding out her skirt to the sides and looking at it. "We just bought these a few months ago, and we have so many of them."

"But they will never do for the Season," Vivian told her. "Those were fine in the country—and they will do as day dresses here. But you must have many more gowns for all the parties—evening gowns, ball gowns, not to mention more walking dresses and day dresses and spencers and pelisses. Gloves for day and evening wear, fans, handkerchiefs, hats—and I really think a muff would be in order; it's still cold enough."

Camellia stared at Vivian, slack-jawed. "That could take days."

"My, yes," Vivian agreed, and glanced over at Eve. "That's why we should start tomorrow."

Eve nodded. "I was just about to write you a note, Vivian, saying we had arrived and suggesting that very thing. But then you came in with Oliver—and I must say it could not have surprised me more if he had walked into the house with the Prince himself as his companion!"

"Oh, no," Vivian protested. "Prinny and Stewkesbury would be a much greater oddity—you know that Prinny calls Oliver the Earl of Strictsbury?"

"Does he really?" Camellia laughed, and Vivian nodded, dimpling mischievously.

"Yes, but that is not the point." Eve would not be diverted. "Why were you with Oliver?"

"'Twas nothing, really." Vivian shrugged. "I met Stewkesbury as I was leaving to go to Brookman and Son, and he decided to escort me. You know Oliver; he is such a stickler about appearances." Though she might have told Eve the whole story if they had been alone, Vivian was not about to divulge Oliver's apology and the reasons for it in front of his young cousins. "And he told me you had arrived yesterday, so of course I had to come see you."

"And we're very glad you did." Eve turned as the butler entered the room, carrying a large silver tray, and for the next few minutes they were all occupied in the ritual of serving and partaking in tea and cakes.

After the butler had departed and the first pangs of their hunger had been sated, the talk turned once again to the upcoming engagement ball and the other parties that awaited them this Season. Vivian, glancing over at Camellia, could not help but notice that she seemed unaccustomedly quiet. Though she was not the effervescent sort that her sister Lily was, Camellia was usually quick to speak her mind on almost any subject. It was not like her to say so little—nor to have that hint of sadness in her eyes.

"How is Rose?" Vivian asked, thinking that the root of Camellia's mood might lie in missing her older sisters. Both Rose and Mary had gotten married only two months after they arrived in England. "Have you had a letter from her recently? And Mary—when will she and Sir Royce be coming for the Season?"

"We got a letter from Rose just the other day," Lily replied. "She's very happy. And so is Mary." Her expression changed, her eyes turning brighter and a smile hovering at the corners of her mouth. "But she and Royce aren't coming to London."

Vivian looked from Lily to Eve. "What? Why?"

"It seems she is in an interesting condition," Eve said, the same sort of smile growing on her face.

"Really? Are you serious? Do you mean—"

"She's going to have a baby," Camellia put in with her usual bluntness. "Why is everyone so reluctant to say it?"

Vivian chuckled. "Because we are all very silly, no doubt. But what wonderful news!"

"We stopped by Iverley on our way here to see her and Royce," Camellia went on, smiling now. "They are absolutely up in the boughs over the news."

"I am sure they must be."

"But she isn't feeling up to traveling," Eve put in. "Mary was sorry not to be here to help Camellia and Lily."

"Yes, but she won't mind missing the Season," Camellia added. "I offered to stay. I thought she could use some help, perhaps." She sighed. "But she wouldn't let me."

"She would not want you to miss your first Season."

"It will all still be here next year," Camellia pointed out.

"Ah, but it's different every time," Vivian told her.

They fell once again to talking of the Season and parties and their shopping expedition tomorrow, but after a while the butler announced the arrival of Lady Carr. This news sent Lily into an unaccustomed silence, and she straightened her dress and patted anxiously at her hair.

"I am sure that you and Lady Carr must have much to discuss," Vivian said, standing. "And I should be on my way."

Next to her, Camellia popped to her feet. "I'll walk you out."

Lady Carr, a small woman with a die-away air, came into the room, and Vivian had to linger for a few moments to greet her and express her felicitations on the news of the upcoming marriage. But she made her escape as quickly as she could, with Camellia right on her heels.

"I see you are well acquainted with Lady Carr," Vivian murmured to the American as they walked toward the front door.

"Well enough," Camellia replied drily. "It's best to leave before she gets to her illnesses."

Vivian glanced back toward the room they had left, then impulsively took Camellia's hand and pulled her down the hall on the other side of the staircase. "Come, I want to talk with you."

"All right." Camellia glanced at her, surprised, but went along readily.

They moved quietly along the corridor, glancing into the empty rooms as they passed. The last was a cozy sitting room looking out over the small garden in the rear of the house. It was a pleasant place, open to the light and furnished in comfortable sofas and chairs. Vivian sat on a sofa, tugging Camellia down beside her.

"How are you?" Vivian asked, her gaze serious.

"Me?" Camellia eyed her somewhat warily. "I'm fine."

"Really?"

"Of course." Camellia looked down, picking at an invisible piece of lint on her skirt. "I'm always healthy as an ox. Everyone knows that."

"I wasn't really speaking of your health. I mean the way you feel in here." Vivian tapped her own chest. "You seemed a bit unhappy this afternoon."

Camellia smiled in a determined way. "I'm very happy for Lily. She is ecstatic about marrying Neville. He isn't the sort of man I would choose, but he seems right for Lily." She shrugged.

"That's all very well for Lily. But what about you? Are you happy?"

Camellia glanced at her. "I'd rather be back at Willowmere. I—the idea of a Season doesn't appeal to me. All those parties and talking to people I don't know. Trying to remember all the things I'm supposed to do and not do. I'm sure to make a mull of it one way or another. I don't really care whether the people here like me, but I'm afraid I'll do or say something that will make it harder for Lily. And it has been very kind of Cousin Oliver to do so much for us. I'm afraid I'll be a disappointment to him."

"Camellia . . ." Vivian reached out, laying her hand on the girl's arm. "It's not like you to be lacking in confidence."

Camellia flashed her a grin. "You mean I tend to be full of myself?"

"No, not conceited. But you are not one to doubt yourself, either."

The girl sighed. "I don't doubt myself with things I'm used to. I know I can shoot well and ride well—Fitz will tell you that. It takes a lot to scare me. It's just that I don't know what to do here, and I don't know why the things I say and do are wrong. I don't want to hurt Lily in any way."

"I think Lily will be just fine. She is already engaged, so she has two families standing behind her. And she, I think, will enjoy this life. You mustn't worry unduly. You may make some stumbles along the way, but Eve and I will be there. We will help you out of your missteps."

"I know. I suppose I'm being foolish. But I miss Willowmere. I miss my horse, and I wish I could ride. I don't want to seem ungrateful, for I know that you are doing a lot for Lily and me, but I don't enjoy shopping the way Lily does. It's nice, at least for a little while, to look at the fashions and materials, but . . ." Camellia shrugged. "It doesn't seem enough to keep one occupied."

"You can ride in the park. It's not the same, of course, but a number of people ride along Rotten Row."

"Rotten Row?" Camellia let out a laugh. "It doesn't sound very pleasant."

"No, but it is the fashionable place to ride. I drive a phaeton in the park now and then. Why don't I take you up with me one day? I think you would enjoy that."

"Really?" Camellia's interest sparked. "You drive it yourself?"

"Yes. Nor am I the only woman to do so."

"I would enjoy that very much, I think." Camellia smiled.

"Is that all that is troubling you?" Vivian asked carefully. "Boredom and missing Willowmere?"

"No," Camellia admitted with a sigh. "Of course not. I can always find some way to alleviate boredom." She cast a laughing little glance at Vivian. "That is, perhaps, why I so often find myself in trouble." She got up and moved restlessly across the room, stopping at the window to look out at the garden.

Vivian followed her. "Is it Lily's engagement?"

Camellia glanced at her, astonished. "How did you know? Am I so obvious?" She frowned, her teeth worrying at her lower lip. "I have tried very hard not to let it show."

"I doubt anyone else has seen it," Vivian reassured her. "Or connected it to the engagement."

"Am I a terrible person?" Camellia turned, and to Vivian's surprise and distress, tears started in Camellia's light gray eyes. "I love Lily, and I am happy for her. I truly am."

"I know you are. But you cannot help but worry a little about yourself, can you?"

"That's it." Camellia sagged a little in relief. "You do understand, don't you? I don't know what I am going to do when Lily marries. I already miss Rose and Mary so much. All my life I've had my sisters around me. We've done everything together. I never had to worry about being lonely; there was never any chance. If I wanted to be by myself, I could go off for a few hours, but if I wanted company, there was always someone around. When Mama died and we came here, I still had my sisters. But now Rose and Mary are gone. I don't know if I'll ever see Rose again. Mary is not that far; we will visit, I know. But it's not the same as living with someone."

"I know. It's not."

"Mary won't even be here this Season. In a few months Lily will be gone. She's already half-gone, always writing to Neville and thinking about him or the wedding, and when she's not doing that, she's talking about her clothes for the wedding or the arrangements for the engagement party. We hardly ever just have fun together like we used to. And after this engagement party, she's going to leave with the Carrs. They want to show her to his grandmother, who lives in Bath, and then they are going to the Carrs' estate. She'll be gone a whole month! And that is what it's going to be like forever after she and Neville are married." Camellia let out another sigh. "I'm sorry. I know I am being selfish and horrid."

"No, you're not." Vivian reached out and took Camellia's hand. "There is nothing wrong with you. Anyone would feel the same in your position. You love Lily; the two of you are extremely close. How could you not miss her when she leaves—or not feel sad knowing she is about to leave?"

Camellia gave Vivian a somewhat watery smile. "It seems silly, given the way we squabble, but there's nobody I love more."

Vivian nodded. "I can't pretend to know exactly what it's like with sisters. I love my brothers, and Gregory and I are very close, but it isn't the same as with sisters. Still, I know some of what you feel. I had close friends—Eve and Charlotte and one or two others. But after our debut, the others began to marry, one by one, and though we remained friends, it was never quite the same. They moved into a different world from me—a world of husbands and children and nurses and such. We did not stop being friends, but I didn't see them as often, didn't have those long talks anymore, sitting up late at night in our night rails, discussing everything under the sun."

"Yes! That's it exactly." Camellia nodded. "That is what I will miss."

"Yes, I'm afraid you will." Vivian smiled and gave Camellia's hand an extra squeeze. "But you will find, as I have, that your world is not empty just because they marry. You will still see them. When Mary has her baby, you will have a new person to love and dote on—for I am quite sure that Mary's baby will be perfect and not at all like my own niece and nephews, who are absolute imps."

Camellia laughed. "I don't know. That might very well be an apt description of any child Mary and Royce have."

Vivian smiled. "And you will meet many people this Season; you'll make new friends."

"Will I?" Camellia regarded Vivian skeptically.

"Of course. You'll find friends. Perhaps even a husband." Vivian's eyes twinkled as she added, "After all, you Bascombes seem to be quite accomplished at that."

"I fear I am not like my sisters. I have little interest in marrying. It seems a lot of bother and sorrow to me. I can scarcely count the number of times I found Lily crying over Neville."

"But surely that was a special circumstance."

"Perhaps, but love was not a tranquil thing for Mary or Rose, either. Being in love seems to make everyone act peculiarly." Camellia shrugged. "I have never met a man who made me feel giddy. Which is probably just as well, since I have never seen that men take to me."

"What do you mean? You had many partners at the dance at my uncle's house."

"Yes, but not the number Lily did. Anyway, we were a curiosity there; everyone wanted to see if we could actually speak, I think. They may do the same thing here, so perhaps at first I shall have a number of dance partners, but not once they get to know me. I am too blunt and outspoken for most American men. I can imagine what British aristocrats will think of me." Camellia shook her head. "Aunt Euphronia and the other relatives certainly don't approve of me." She paused, then frowned. "Will I have to spend much time with them?"

"I sincerely hope not, given that I will be with you. Unfortunately, however, Lady Euphronia is nigh inescapable during the Season. I heard she was at the party I attended last night, but I fled before I had to see her. 'Tis true you will not 'take' with Lady Euphronia and the others like her. But there are many who *will* like you, just as I do—as Eve and Charlotte do. So you must not despair. Look at me; there are a number of people who regard me askance. But I have managed to survive their disapproval, and I found a number of people with whom I have a very pleasant time."

"But you are a duke's daughter." Camellia gave her a skeptical look. "I cannot imagine that anyone would dare to ostracize you."

Vivian shrugged. "I'm not entirely sure about that. But even if that is true, I can tell you that there are quite a few who are happy to gibble-gabble about me—I am shocking; I have no decorum. There are those who call me Marchester's Hoyden."

"Really?" Camellia grinned.

"Oh, yes. And worse, no doubt, but fortunately I have not been made privy to those appellations." Vivian smiled. "Do not worry. If you hate your Season, you do not have to come back every year. I doubt Stewkesbury will insist; he dislikes the Season, too. And even though Lily gets married, you will still be her sister. You will spend time with her and Mary and Eve. And with me." Vivian's eyes twinkled mischievously. "I have no plans to marry, either. It is, as you said, a great deal of bother. You and I can become spinsters together. You must come live with me, and we'll raise a number of cats."

Camellia laughed. "I accept. But not cats. I like dogs much better."

"Dogs it is, then."

"Thank you." Camellia hugged her impulsively. "You have made me feel much better. I promise I shall not continue in this weepy manner. I am not the sort who feels sorry for myself."

"Everyone is entitled to a bit of it now and then."

"Now I must go back or else Lily will ring a peal over me later for leaving her alone so long with Lady Carr."

"Eve is with them."

"But that is not the same. Lily needs someone whom Lady Carr will disapprove of more than she does Lily."

Vivian smiled and bade the girl farewell. She watched as Camellia walked out the door; then, with a sigh, Vivian turned back to the window. She felt an unaccustomed touch of melancholy. No doubt it came from remembering her own loss as her friends had one by one gotten married and moved into other lives. As she had told Camellia, she had adjusted to a different relationship with her friends, but Vivian had not added that she was still now and then swept by loneliness.

She was aware that anyone who heard that statement would find it hard to believe, for Vivian was a social creature with a large circle of friends and acquaintances. She could nearly always be found at a rout or the opera or having dinner with friends. Seldom did she spend an evening alone, at least during the Season. But Vivian knew how easy it was to feel alone even when surrounded by people. Though she was not the sort to dwell on it, at times she wished for a closer relationship.

She had seen the looks that passed between Mary and Royce or Eve and Fitz, even the smile of quiet affection on Charlotte's face when she gazed at her husband. But then Vivian would cast her eyes around at the men of the *ton* and realize all over again that she had no interest in entrusting her heart and life to any of them. While some women did have marriages of real and lasting love, they were in her experience the exceptions, not the rule. And the women were not *her*.

She had never been like everyone else she knew. Though

she suspected that Camellia had not really believed her when Vivian told her that she had not fit in with the *ton,* it was the truth. She had managed to get by better than Camellia would, but that was largely because of an upbringing that had instilled in her how she should behave. She had learned what to say, how to act, but she had always been aware that she had not *felt* as she should. Even in her family or among her friends, she had often felt different and alone.

Something inside her was restless. Conventions bored and even angered her. She regarded much of the conversation and many of the people of the *ton* as insipid. She knew that such statements would astonish those who knew her—and sometimes, even she herself wondered why she went to so many parties when she so often found them lacking. But she knew, deep down, that she was searching—for what, she was not entirely sure.

When she had once expressed such doubts to her sister-in-law, Elizabeth had assured her that what she needed was a husband and family. But looking at Elizabeth's life, Vivian could only recoil at the thought. A faithless husband, love dissolved into quarrels . . . no, that seemed a far worse fate than the occasional touch of loneliness.

As Vivian gazed out the window without really noticing anything that lay in front of her, a dash of movement to the left caught her eye. She turned her head to see Pirate bound into the yard. She had to smile, watching his antics as he whirled and ran and jumped and barked. Then he came tearing back, and the Earl of Stewkesbury walked into Vivian's view. He, too, was grinning at the dog's gyrations. Pirate reached the earl and jumped straight up, wiggling his rear end ecstatically, then fell back down to the ground and crouched on his front legs, his hindquarters raised and the stub of his tail still wagging at full speed. He jumped forward, then jumped back and let out a sharp bark.

To Vivian's surprise, Stewkesbury mimicked the dog, jumping toward the animal, then back, and Pirate exploded into barks, leaping forward and back, then side to side. As Vivian watched, the man and the dog darted about the small yard—advancing, retreating, dashing one way, then another, and Vivian could not help but laugh at the sight of the staid earl completely abandoning all dignity as he romped with his dog. Pirate was clearly in heaven, whirling and yapping and zipping back and forth wildly. And the man—Vivian studied the earl's face, usually sober but now laughing and light, without care or pretense—yes, the man clearly loved the game as much as his pet.

Vivian leaned forward, resting her forehead against the windowpane. Something in Stewkesbury still brought up a yearning in her. Such a handsome man, she thought, and her mind turned to the kiss they had shared last night. Her lips curved in a sensual smile.

No, a husband was not what she was looking for. But a man, now, at least for a while, was an entirely different thing.

Chapter 5

The next two days were spent in a whirl of shopping. First the four women looked at the little dolls known as fashion babies that wore miniatures of the latest dresses from Paris and pored over fashion books until the different styles began to blur. They examined fabrics and laces and ribbons and trims. Camellia and Lily made decision after decision with the guidance of the older two women, and finally even Lily declared that she could not bear to think of another gown.

So the following day they turned their attention to shoes and accessories. Camellia and Lily were fitted for new kid half boots, suitable for both walking and riding, as well as slippers for daily and evening wear in a variety of colors and materials. When Camellia protested that they had already bought several pairs of shoes when they first arrived in London, Vivian pointed out that those had been only a temporary measure.

"How could we buy the shoes you would need when we had not purchased the gowns?" she asked reasonably.

Next came the millinery shops, three in a row, followed by a visit to the glovers. Camellia, who considered the three pairs of gloves she already had perfectly adequate, was quickly informed that so few gloves would never do. A lady must have long white kid gloves for evening wear and short gloves in both kid and a variety of white and colored silks. Eve and Vivian did at least allow that the undergarments and nightgowns the younger two had purchased six months earlier would be enough, although, of course, new stockings were a must, as well as new and much finer handkerchiefs—and one should really purchase a *few* new petticoats or chemises. Lily would need a number of such things for her trousseau, naturally, but that was an entirely different matter and could be taken care of much later in the Season. This subject was enough to make Lily giggle and blush, at which Camellia rolled her eyes.

They finished up their day with a visit to Gunter's, and though all but Lily deemed the day too cool for an ice, they were well satisfied with the pastries they chose. Loaded down with boxes and bags, they made their way to Stewkesbury House. After reminding Camellia of their plans to go out driving in Hyde Park the next afternoon, Vivian directed the carriage to Carlyle Hall.

A few minutes later, the coach rumbled to a halt, and Vivian heard her coachman call out to someone. Curious, she pulled aside the edge of the leather curtain. They had come to a stop outside her home, but the spot at the curb directly in front of the door was already occupied. Frowning, she peered at the large, mud-splashed coach and in the next instant recognized it as her father's comfortable, lumbering traveling coach.

The front door opened, and a footman hurried out to help her down, but Vivian was already out of the carriage and onto the sidewalk before he reached her.

"Is that my father's carriage? Is he here?"

"Yes, my lady. His Grace arrived a few minutes ago. Lord Seyre is with him as well."

"Gregory!" Now Vivian was truly astonished.

It was odd for her father to travel to London when she had left him only a week before carousing in the country with his cronies, but he was well-known to be impulsive. He could have taken it into his head to move the party to London. But for her shy, even reclusive, brother to come with the duke, especially in the midst of the Season, was almost unheard of.

Vivian hurried into the house, divesting herself of her outerwear as she went and handing it to the trailing footman. "Where is he?" She turned, glancing around for Grigsby, the butler, then lifted her voice. "Father? Gregory?"

"His Grace is in his bedchamber, my lady. I believe Lord Seyre is with him."

Vivian started up the stairs, but she had not reached halfway when her brother appeared at the top of the stairs. "Gregory! What is going on? Why are you and Papa here?"

"Don't worry. He's all right," Gregory said quickly, and started down the stairs toward her.

Vivian stopped abruptly, the blood draining from her face. "All right? Gregory! What do you mean? Why wouldn't he be all right?"

"Oh, blazes, I'm telling it all wrong." He came to the landing and stopped.

A tall man with a thin build kept lean by his devotion to riding, Gregory was quiet and scholarly. He possessed the large, dramatic green eyes and sculpted features that were considered a hallmark of the Carlyle family, but his good looks often went unnoticed by those who saw only his reticent, even self-effacing manner. His hair was dark brown with a hint of the red that flamed in his sister's hair. His eyesight was poor enough that he wore spectacles to read, and when, as now, he did not have them on, it gave his gaze a soft, almost dreamy look, an appearance that was reinforced by his boyish, endearing smile. Though dressed in clothes of the finest materials, he managed to look rumpled and thrown together.

Reaching out to take his sister by the arms, he said, "Papa fell—"

"Fell? From what? What foolish thing was he doing?"

"Nothing. Truly. It wasn't exactly a fall, more a faint—though Papa bumped his head when he went down so he has a knot on it. One moment he was standing there, and the next he crumpled to the floor. I wasn't with him. That old fool Tarrington was there, and he just stood like a stunned ox, then started bellowing for the butler."

"Was Papa in his cups?" Vivian wrinkled her brow. "I don't understand why he came to London."

"I was the one who insisted. He would have let old Smithers poke and prod at him and harrumph for a while, then recommend he cup him or leech him. You know how I feel about such antiquated methods. The French are making far greater strides in—"

"Yes, yes, I know, dear, but what about Papa?" Vivian, used to her brother's ways, gently pushed him back to the subject.

"I insisted that he come to London to see one of the physicians from the Royal Academy."

"But why? I mean, why do you think it is so serious? If he was drinking—"

"He wasn't. That is the thing—I mean, of course, he had been drinking. They all were. You know how it is when he and Tarrington and the Blakeneys and all that lot get together. But this happened in the morning before he'd even begun to drink. Papa was in a mood. I heard him yelling at Blevins." Gregory named the duke's long-suffering valet. "I think he threw a boot at him. Then he went downstairs to breakfast, and suddenly he just went down. I think—I think it may have been an apoplexy."

"Gregory, no!" Vivian's hands flew up to her heart, which felt suddenly cold in her chest.

"When he came to, he was—his speech was garbled. And he's—well, you will see him. His condition hasn't gotten worse, and I think he has improved somewhat. His speech is clearer. But still, I think he should see a good physician."

"Of course. Gregory, I must see him. Is he awake?"

"He was a few minutes ago." Vivian started up the stairs again, and Seyre fell in beside her. "When we got here, old Grigsby hustled him upstairs and into bed. He and Blevins, of course, are jockeying for position as the most indispensable to His Grace. Grigsby had the bed made and warmed just as the duke likes it, and Blevins had to point out that he would fix Marchester a nostrum, as the duke trusts no one else to do so. There were enough dagger glares and nose twitchings and sniffs for a Drury Lane farce."

"I can imagine."

"I could tell Papa was enjoying it."

"He always did like to be fussed over."

Though Gregory's words had frightened Vivian, she was glad that he had warned her of her father's condition before she entered the room. Otherwise, she would have let out a cry of alarm.

Her father had always been a robust man, even after he had gotten older. His hair, though almost entirely white now, was still thick, and his square-jawed face was handsome, his green eyes bright and arresting. His tall frame had thickened around the middle, but his shoulders were broad, with no sign of a stoop. Most of all, vitality always shone from him.

Now, however, lying there in the high-testered bed, his face and hair pale against the white sheets, Marchester looked somehow shrunken. His eyes did not sparkle, and the smile he gave her lifted only one corner of his mouth.

He held out his left hand to her, and she noted that his right hand was curled against his side, unmoving.

"Viv! My girl." His voice sounded thick, and she could see that it was an effort for him to speak. Her heart twisted inside her chest.

"Papa!" Vivian smiled brilliantly and came forward, taking his hand in both her own and bending over the bed to place a kiss on his cheek. "What lengths you will go to in order to drag Gregory to London!"

"That's it." He mustered up another faint smile. "Fool peacock Mullard . . ."

"Dr. Mullard is one of the best physicians in the country," Gregory told him firmly. "And you'd best pay heed to him this time."

"This time?" Vivian's brows lifted. "You've seen him before?"

Her father's mouth twitched. "Saw him . . . end of Season . . . told me go home. Rest. I did."

Gregory snorted. "If you call burning the candle at both ends with all your friends 'resting.'"

"Papa! You should have told us!" Vivian scolded, but she could not bear to say anything else with the duke looking so ill.

The physician had already been sent for, and after a few minutes, he came into the room with such a majestic gliding gait that it would have done it an injustice to term it walking. A large, well-fed man dressed in the finest of suits, with a brightly patterned waistcoat of embroidered silk, he came over to the side of the bed and stood gazing down at the duke.

"Well, well, Your Grace, back again?"

"Come to gloat?" Marchester asked.

The doctor allowed himself a benign smile. "I can see

that you are not done in yet, Your Grace." He turned toward Gregory and Vivian and rather majestically informed them that he must see his patient alone.

Vivian and her brother meekly left the room and waited outside in the hall until finally the doctor opened the door and came out. He looked so grave that Vivian's heart began to thump wildly.

"How is he?" Gregory asked, and Vivian heard the same nerves in his voice as danced in her stomach. "Will he be all right?"

"I will not lie to you. Your father has suffered a serious episode. I warned him how it could be if he did not moderate his . . . um, excesses. Gout was the most likely ailment, I thought, but as it turns out, it was apoplexy that struck him first. He survived the initial attack, which is good. Many pass on immediately. He appears to have regained some of the movement which he lost, and that is also hopeful."

"He is going to recover, isn't he?" Vivian asked. "I mean, since he has survived the initial attack."

The doctor looked even more grave. "I cannot promise that. There may or may not be another episode. It is imperative that he remain here for a time so that I can monitor his condition. He should rest. No strenuous exercise, and I would not advise visitors. I have written down my recommendations regarding the foods he should eat. The duke must begin to practice some moderation. He is no longer a young man, a fact I cannot seem to impress upon him."

The doctor handed a piece of paper to Vivian, and her heart sank as she read the list of foods the doctor recommended. The bland food was hardly the sort of fine cuisine her father was accustomed to.

"Thank you for coming," Gregory told the physician now. "I know my father is not the easiest of patients."

The other man smiled tolerantly. "It is difficult for a man of the duke's vigor to accept a decline in health."

Gregory saw Dr. Mullard out and returned to his father's bedroom. Vivian was just leaving the room as he came up.

"I looked in on him, and Papa was sleeping," she told her brother. "Blevins is sitting watch over him, so I did not try to dislodge him. Later, I'll relieve him for a bit and make him go down to eat supper and take a rest."

"He will sleep on a cot in Papa's room, I'm sure."

"I know." Vivian smiled a little. "One can only wonder what Papa has done to inspire such loyalty in his valet, especially given the way he's wont to roar at him."

Gregory shrugged. "Somehow the man manages to make everyone overlook his faults. Haven't you always done so?"

"I suppose I have." Vivian linked her arm through her brother's as they strolled down the hall toward the upstairs sitting room. "Do you think he will be all right?"

"It's hard to imagine him being anything less than he's always been." Gregory frowned. "It scared the devil out of me when I saw him stretched out on the floor like that."

"I'm sure it did. Poor Gregory. I'm sorry you were left to deal with all this."

He smiled faintly. "Actually, it gave me an excuse to toss out Tarrington and the others, which I rather enjoyed. It's impossible to get any useful work done when they are about. You'd think fifty- and sixty-year-old men would have given up singing drinking songs and 'view hallooing' at all hours of the day and night."

"They were probably even worse after I left."

"Oh, yes. I woke up the other morning to see one of the wenches from the tavern scampering down the hall in her shift. I think next time I will arrange to go to one of the other houses when he invites them. Though I would hate to have to abandon my experiments in the greenhouse."

Vivian could not help but chuckle. "Ah, Gregory, sometimes I wonder how you came to be in this frivolous family."

He smiled faintly. "Yes. I would be somewhat dubious about our mother's fidelity if I did not look so much a Carlyle. But I would be embarrassed to say I took after our mother's side, given what dunderheads our cousins are."

"That's true. Better by far to claim the Carlyle blood." She sank down on a sofa in the sitting room, and Gregory sat down beside her, letting out a sigh.

"Did it used to be this bad?" he asked. "I don't remember his carousing with his friends when we were younger."

"No doubt we saw less of it stuck up in the nursery. But I think he probably kept it confined to London more then. I always thought he lived in London so much because he thought we were too much of a nuisance, but perhaps it was actually to protect our childish eyes and ears. When he brought friends to the Hall, the party usually included women. I think they were more sedate."

"If one can call Lady Kitty sedate," Gregory said with a fond smile.

"Well, no, she was not that. But, while she was Papa's mistress, at least there weren't tavern wenches running up and down the halls."

"True. You know, I used to wish he would marry Lady Kitty."

"Did you?" Vivian smiled. "I did, too. I had no idea she was married already."

"Me, either, at least until after I'd gone off to school. Though I do remember our grandmother once ringing a peal over Papa about bringing Kitty to Marchester."

"Oh, Lord, the dowager duchess!" Vivian gave a theatrical shudder. "How I hated her visits."

"You think *you* did!" her brother said feelingly. "She didn't lecture you about the duties of a duke."

"No, only about all the things the ducal daughter owed her family. Fortunately, at the time I understood only half of what she was saying. 'Keeping our bloodlines strong'—I mean, really. One would think the woman had never talked to a child."

"Mm. I think perhaps she never spoke to her own four," Gregory suggested.

"Or perhaps she did, and that is why our aunts are all so odd."

"And live so far away."

"Ah, Gregory." Vivian sighed and leaned her head against his shoulder. "I am so glad that you are my brother. Please promise me you will never marry someone horrid."

"I shall do my utmost not to. Given how I've felt about most of the young women I've met, I rather imagine that I shall remain a bachelor."

"And leave the estate to one of Jerome's sons?" Vivian asked with some horror.

Gregory laughed. "I fear so. However obnoxious they are, I cannot bring myself to marry just to keep them from the title. Perhaps they will not be as bad when they are grown. Jerome is all right."

"But Jerome was all right when he was a child, too." Vivian glanced over at her brother. "You look tired. You should lie down before supper. It cannot have been easy for you the last few days."

"I think I can bear up under it. However, I do think I will freshen up a bit. And I need to write a letter or two. I suspect we'll have our hands full for a while."

"No doubt." Vivian looked over at him. She wanted to ask him again if he thought their father would be all right, but she firmly repressed the urge. Gregory knew no better than she whether the duke would live, and it was scarcely fair to put the burden of reassurance on him.

After Gregory left, however, she could not ignore the tendrils of fear slithering through her. She let out a shaky breath and got up, searching for something that would distract her. She thought of Camellia and their plans to drive in the phaeton through the park tomorrow, so she sat down at the small secretary beside the window and wrote to her friend, explaining the circumstances and postponing the drive. Then she dug several invitations out of the desk drawer and dashed off notes canceling her attendance at parties over the next week. She was sure Gregory was right in saying that they would have plenty to occupy them for a while. Their father was not the most tractable of patients, and she could imagine how he would react to being laid up in bed and fed the bland, thin soups and gruels and such that his doctor had advised.

But such activities could not keep her fear at bay, and after supper, when she shooed the duke's valet off to eat and rest while she sat with the duke, her fear returned even more strongly. Instead of raging about the doctor's prognosis and plans for him, Marchester was unusually passive, simply nodding in acquiescence to her suggestion that she read to him. She was not sure he was listening, for at times he closed his eyes or stared out into space, as though his mind were elsewhere, but she plowed through the volume of Swift, knowing that it was, at least, one of her father's favorites.

After a couple of hours, Gregory came in to relieve her. "I'll read to him for an hour or two," he said, holding up a large leatherbound volume.

"If it's one of the sort you usually read, it'll put him to sleep in five minutes." Vivian was pleased to hear a low grunt from her father that she took for assent or a laugh—or perhaps both. She turned to the bed and leaned over to kiss her father on the cheek. "You'll be feeling more lively tomorrow. Good night. Sleep well."

With a final pat on his shoulder, she left the room. Once she was outside in the hallway, she let herself sag back against the wall. She could only pray that her encouraging words would prove true. At the moment she could not quite believe them herself.

As she stood there, she heard a knock at the door, and a moment later the footman opened it. She was about to turn away, not wanting any visitors tonight, when she heard a familiar voice downstairs asking for her.

"I'm sorry, my lord," the footman began, "but her ladyship is indispo—"

Vivian whirled and hurried down the steps. "Oliver! It's all right, Jenks, I am here."

She reached the foot of the staircase and turned toward the door, where the footman was taking Lord Stewkesbury's hat and caped coat from him. He looked so solid, so calm and assured, that the little knot inside her chest eased and tears suddenly sprang to her eyes.

"Oh, Oliver! I am so glad you came." She walked toward him, holding out her hands, and he moved forward to take both her hands in his.

"Vivian. I came as soon as Camellia told me. Are you all right? How is your father?"

She smiled, blinking away the moisture in her eyes. She felt much better, she realized, with Oliver's hands wrapped warmly around hers. "I am fine. And Papa is . . . well, I cannot truthfully say that he is fine, but he is here and, Gregory says, better than he was. Please, come in and sit." She turned toward the drawing room, and he went with her, taking her hand and pulling it through his arm, keeping his other hand on hers as they walked. "Would you like something to drink. Shall I ring for some port?"

"No, I'm fine. Don't worry about me. Come, sit down and tell me about it." He led her over to a couch and sat down beside her. Vivian made no move to withdraw her hand from his. "Camellia knew nothing other than you said your father had come to London, ill."

"Yes, Gregory brought him, thinking that he would be better served by a London physician. It seems he had a fit of apoplexy. Gregory explained it a bit to me. He, of course, had done a little reading on it. He said it is when a blood vessel in your brain bleeds."

Stewkesbury nodded. "Yes, it happened to my grandfather. But your father did not—"

She shook her head. "He lost consciousness and fell, but he is still with us. At least for the time being. The doctor said he could have another one." Her hand gripped his more tightly.

"Do not think of that. I am sure it is a good sign that he has not had a recurrence already."

She nodded. "Yes. No doubt. And Gregory said that he is already able to"—her voice hitched a little—"to speak a little better and to move his arm some. But, oh, Oliver!" Vivian turned her face up to his, her eyes bright with unshed tears. "If you had but seen him. You know how he is, how strong, how alive! To see him lying there in his bed, so pale and weak, listless. There is no glitter in his eyes, no warmth or laughter. It sounds foolish, I know, but for the first time I realized that he is growing old. I realized that he might die!"

Vivian jumped to her feet, beginning to pace. "I can hardly bear to see him so. I know how it must gall him to be unable to get out of bed and do what he wants, to lie there while others take care of him, read to him. To be unable to make a quip or a compliment." She stopped, pressing her hand to her lips, fighting the tears that threatened to wash over her.

"Vivian . . ." Oliver rose and went to her.

"You were right in what you said about him the other night."

"Do not think about that. I had no right to speak about your father in that way."

Vivian shook her head. "It made me angry, but I knew you were right. No doubt he did not raise us as he should have. He was never an . . . attentive father. Nor has his life been exemplary. He is a man who indulged his vices. Gambling and drinking and . . . well, others you would be shocked for me to know about. But I love him. And if he dies . . ." Tears began to spill out and run down over her cheeks. "I don't know how I would bear it!"

She began to cry, and Oliver wrapped his arms around her, gently pulling her to him. "Of course you love him." He smoothed his hand up and down her back, murmuring low words of comfort. "It will be all right."

Vivian clung to him as she wept. It felt so good, so warm in his arms, and the anxiety of the past few hours poured out of her. She did not think of what she was doing or how odd it was that Oliver should be the one to comfort her or even of how they stood in her drawing room where any servant might look in and see them. All she could do was luxuriate in the peace and security of being held by him.

Gradually her tears slowed, then stopped, and for a moment longer she remained in his arms, tired by her crying bout but more at peace. His heart beat steadily beneath her ear, and his warmth enfolded her. She felt the rise and fall of his breath against her face. She breathed in the scent of him, a mingling of man and cologne, tinged with the merest whiff of tobacco and port. He must have been indulging in a postsupper cigar and glass of port when he heard Camellia's news. It surprised and warmed her to think that he had come over immediately, abandoning his evening's relaxation. Vivian let out a little sigh, nestling closer to him.

His arms tightened for an instant, and his body seemed even warmer suddenly, but then his arms fell away from her. He reached into the pocket of his jacket, pulling out the perfectly folded handkerchief, and he reached down to smooth away her tears. Vivian gazed up at him. His face was only inches from hers, and she could see into the depths of his pewter-colored eyes, fringed by silky black lashes. His eyes were not cold, she realized, but warm, and at the moment they were gazing at her with an expression that made her heart quiver in her chest. The soft silk of his handkerchief moved gently across her skin. She was suddenly breathless, tingling with awareness of how close they stood.

The flesh of his forefinger and thumb where he grasped her chin surged with heat, and his eyes darkened. The hand that held the handkerchief dropped away, the square of silk sliding unnoticed to the floor.

"Vivian." His voice was lower than usual, her name gliding across his tongue.

Vivian felt soft and pliant, and she sagged a little toward him, her hands going up to catch herself on his chest. Then his hands were on her sides, his fingers pressing into her, holding and lifting her to meet him as he lowered his face to hers.

Their lips met and clung. His mouth was sweet and tender upon hers, opening her lips to him. Vivian's fingers curled around his lapels, holding on as he filled her senses. For the moment everything beyond her seemed to stop, and she knew only the soft velvet of his lips, the texture of the cloth against her fingertips, the heat that snaked through her body.

His arms went around her, and he bent to bury his face

in the juncture of her neck and shoulders, softly murmuring her name. He kissed her neck, sending shivers of pleasure through her, slowly working his way up the side of her throat. Featherlight, his mouth caressed the line of her jaw, and he nuzzled into her hair. Vivian leaned into him, loving the warmth, the sweetness, the peace that lay in his arms.

Finally he raised his head and pressed his lips softly against her forehead. "Vivian . . ."

She shook her head. "No. Don't say it."

He smiled, his arms falling away as he stepped back. "How do you know what I was going to say?"

"I don't." She took his hands in hers, smiling back at him. "But I know you."

"All right. I'll say nothing." He squeezed her hands and released them, and they moved apart.

There was the sound of footsteps on the stairs, and a moment later Gregory walked in. "Stewkesbury. Jenks told me you were here." He strode over to shake Oliver's hand. "Good of you to come."

"I heard about your father."

"Yes. He'll be better soon, I'm sure." Gregory glanced over at his sister, humor lighting his eyes. "I left Father with his valet. He fell asleep as I read to him. I'll warrant you'll find that no surprise."

"No. I do not," Vivian replied with a wry grin. "Now, if you gentlemen will excuse me, I think that I, too, shall retire."

"Of course. Exhausting day." Gregory turned to Oliver. "Come with me, Stewkesbury, and we'll have a glass of brandy to warm you up before you go back out into the cold."

"Thank you. That sounds delightful." Oliver turned back to Vivian and sketched a bow. "Good evening, Lady Vivian."

"Good night. And thank you."

He nodded to her, his gaze lingering for an instant, then turned to walk with her brother out of the room. Vivian stood, listening to the sound of their footsteps retreating down the corridor. Then she bent down and picked up the handkerchief that Oliver had dropped earlier. She lifted the snowy white silk to her face and rubbed it gently against her cheek.

With a little smile, she stuck the square of cloth into her pocket and started up to her room.

Chapter 6

The Duke of Marchester was not an easy patient, which was borne home to his two children in the days that followed. He disliked spending his time in bed, but he found sitting in a chair overlooking the garden little better. He was not accustomed to inactivity, as he was quick to tell them, and though he could not deny that his right side was weak, making him unsteady on his feet, that only irritated him further. He did not like being read to. He hated the food his valet was bringing to him. Most of all, he hated the doctor's visits.

Dr. Mullard was a fool, he declared, and his visit every afternoon invariably left the duke growling or pouting, sometimes both. Though the duke grew better with each passing day, he refused to believe that his doctor had anything to do with it, declaring that he would have gotten better just the same without the man and his starvation diet. Privately, Vivian could not help but wonder if that was true. Mullard's prescribed diet of soups, oatmeal, biscuits, and tea was poor fare indeed for a man who was accustomed to dining on pheasant and turtle soup followed by fish, pork, and beef in the richest of sauces. Even worse was the banning of all port and brandy, with only a glass or two of light sherry allowed.

Vivian pointed out to her father that the doctor warned him that he could die if he did not follow the diet, but she could not help but silently agree when the duke snapped back, "Eating this, I might as well be dead already!"

Blevins, Marchester's valet, had taken to sneaking his employer small dishes of food from the cook, whose opinion of the doctor's diet matched the duke's, and Vivian decided to turn a blind eye to it. After all, she reasoned, her father was improving, and that meant that before long he would be up and in command once more, well able to order his food prepared however he liked it.

The duke preferred to while away his time playing cards or listening to the latest gossip, but Vivian soon ran out of gossip to tell him, and after playing a few games of whist and faro with Vivian and Gregory, the duke declared that both his children were utter flats and there was no fun in fleecing them. Therefore, most of his days were spent with Vivian reading to him.

Gregory took as much of the burden as he could. He stayed with his father during and after each of the doctor's visits, a task that no one else, even the faithful Blevins, was willing to take on. Gregory read the *Times* to the duke in the mornings, but after a session or two of listening to the sorts of books Gregory read, Marchester refused to allow Gregory to read him anything but the newspaper.

So Vivian spent most of the afternoon and evening every day reading and talking with her father. The activity was not strenuous, but as someone who was accustomed to getting out of the house frequently, she was left feeling locked in and often bored. She wound up being both restless and exhausted, as well as somewhat irritated with herself for feeling that way.

It was not what she did that tired her, she knew, so much as the emotional turmoil she went through trying to deal with her father. Sadness and sympathy would almost overwhelm her sometimes as she watched Marchester struggle to speak and walk with his former ease. A few moments later, she would find herself having to struggle not to quarrel with the man when he complained at length about his food or his inactivity or one of the hundreds of other things he could find to carp about.

Finally one afternoon, after the duke had fussed about the sun being in his eyes, then complained that the room was too dark after Blevins drew the curtain, then opined that his pillows were abominably flat and that Blevins could not correctly place them behind his back, Vivian jumped to her feet, slamming shut the book she had been attempting to read to him.

"For pity's sake, Papa, try to have a little patience!" she snapped. "Poor Blevins has been dancing attendance on you for six straight days, as has everyone else in this house, and you haven't a kind word for anyone!"

Her father's brows, thick and straight and still liberally sprinkled with the black his hair had once been, drew together. "Easy words for you! You aren't laid up in bed!"

"No, I'm not, but I sincerely hope that if I were, I wouldn't be some petty tyrant who took out his misfortunes on everyone around him! I'd hope I might have the grace to thank God I was alive and not six feet in the ground—as you very well could have been!"

The duke drew himself up in his bed, his eyes lighting with temper. Then, suddenly, astonishing Vivian, he relaxed and began to laugh.

"Ah, Viv, Viv, thank God. Someone finally has some spine around here!"

"What?" She gaped at him.

"Everyone's so damned careful I feel like I've got one foot in the grave already."

"Is that why you've been such an absolute bear? You were trying to goad someone into answering you back?"

"Lord, no. I'm a bear 'cause I'm bored and I drag my foot and I talk like Denny Summers in the village!"

Vivian burst out laughing. "You don't talk like Denny. You are much improved in your speech."

He shrugged a little and sighed. "I know. But I feel like someone stuck a cow's tongue in my mouth. And I have to *think* about everything I do."

"It's dreadfully hard." Vivian went over to his bed and sat down, reaching out to take his hand. "But you are getting better. You see? The first day you were here, you could not make your hand take hold like that."

"I still haven't got a grip worth anything. I couldn't control the reins."

"If I were you, I'd worry about walking before I fretted about riding."

He chuckled. "Now you're getting cruel. Ah, Vivvy . . ." He leaned his head back against the headboard. "I used to be a handsome man, you know."

"You are still a handsome man." She grinned and struck a pose, declaring haughtily, "We are a handsome family."

His green eyes sparkled at her in their former roguish way. "We are, aren't we? Even that brother of yours, despite his best efforts to grow stoop-shouldered hunched over those damnable books."

It was a long speech for him, and she knew it required effort, so she squeezed his hand supportively. "No, he won't do that. He enjoys riding too much."

"Yes. He does take after me that way, for all the rest of it." The duke turned his head, regarding her. "I haven't been a good father, I know."

"Now, Papa . . ."

"Don't worry. I'm not about to turn Friday-faced. Just speaking the truth."

"I wouldn't want any other father than you."

"Is it—" He paused and glanced away, plucking at the cover, as he went on, "My mother tells me I'm the reason you've never married."

"What? Oh, Papa, how foolish!"

"She says"—he turned to her as though determined to face something—"it's because I set such a bad example. Of a husband. Of a man."

"How could that be true?" Vivian asked, shaking her head. "I never even saw you be a husband. Grandmother cannot resign herself to the fact that I refuse to marry just to please her. I am happy as I am. It's more likely that I haven't married because no other man can measure up to you."

He shot her a speaking look, his mouth twisting into a little smile. "Now, that's doing it much too brown."

Vivian laughed, then leaned over to hug her father, whispering, "I love you, Papa. Please don't scare me like that again."

"Don't be a fool, girl. I'm not about to die yet." He patted her back. "Now, get over there and read me some more from that blasted book. Blevins, come turn this pillow. It's gotten devilish hot."

Vivian rolled her eyes and sat down in the chair by the bed, picking up her book to read again.

Gregory, the fifth Marquess of Seyre, strolled out of the door of Hatchard's bookshop and paused, undecided about which way to go. He had left Carlyle Hall for the first time this afternoon, unable to stand being cooped up inside any longer. A ride was what he would really have liked, but a walk, he had thought, would help. His steps had naturally turned toward the bookstore.

Other young men were drawn to the city for the entertainments it offered—the clubs, the gambling and drinking, the evenings flirting with a young lady at a party, and the nights spent pursuing women of lesser virtue. When Gregory came to London, he visited the bookstores. He enjoyed other places, of course—meetings now and then of various scientific and historical societies where papers were read and discussed, ideas bandied about. Such gatherings could almost make a visit to London worth the rest of it.

Gregory glanced around him and let out a small sigh. *Or perhaps they could not.* He disliked London—he hated the noise, the bustle, the cry of the cartmen in the mornings, the rumble of carriages and wagons in the street, the way houses were set all one upon the other. There was no room to walk in peaceful solitude, no place to ruminate on one's thoughts or to look about at the scenery. Indeed, there was no scenery. Everywhere one looked, there were buildings and streets and people.

He liked people—in moderation—but he was uncomfortable around people he did not know and even more ill at ease when those people were in large numbers, such as at a soiree or a dinner or, worst of all, a ball. He knew he was intelligent, well regarded by men of learning. He could quite happily discourse on many matters for hours. But put him among strangers and expect him to chat about polite nothings, and he was hopelessly lost. His tongue froze. His lively brain failed him. He would stammer or gaze blankly and answer in monosyllables.

He was at his worst when the person to whom he was speaking was a young lady. He did not dislike women. After all, he had been closest to his sister, Vivian, his whole life. And he found females as pretty and alluring as the next man. But the time he spent with young women, aside from his sister and some of her friends, was generally excruciating.

He could manage an invitation to dance, for there, at least, he was armed with the knowledge that few girls would turn down the opportunity to dance with the future Duke of Marchester. But off the dance floor the conversation would limp through the usual exchanges of opinions on the weather or one's health or the enjoyment of the party, and then he would be left searching his brain for something to say.

In general, the young ladies were little help. They tended to giggle or blush or ply their fans flirtatiously, none of which gambits he had any idea how to respond to. On the occasions when he tried to discuss with them something he was interested in, he was met by blank stares or murmurs of vague acquiescence. He knew that few people, male or female, were interested in scientific matters or history, but he was able to discuss other things, such as philosophy or music or books, but the young women rarely expressed an opinion on those topics, either, simply gazing at him with wide, limpid eyes and nodding occasionally. Some had been inspired to say breathlessly that he was so deep or learned or profound, and such statements had immediately filled him with such embarrassment that he had stopped talking.

If he pressed a girl for her opinion of some matter, she would invariably say she did not know or would ask him what he thought. Since he had usually just said what he thought, this seemed nonsensical, and in any case, he *knew* what he thought. It was the woman's thoughts he wanted to learn. He was not sure whether he talked only of such boring things that none of the young ladies wanted to discuss them or if it was simply, alarmingly, that young women truly did not have any thoughts of their own to express.

If he could simply have avoided speaking to most women in London, he would have been all right. But to what he considered his great misfortune, Gregory was deemed the most eligible bachelor in England. He was a marquess and the heir to a dukedom; any woman who married him would have one of the highest titles in the land. This, coupled with his family's wealth, would have made him a great catch. But that he was young, sane, and attractive (if one looked past his retiring manner and the spectacles he wore for reading and often forgot to remove) turned him into the most hunted man in England for young ladies and their mothers.

Not a hostess in London did not dream of his presence at one of her parties nor a mother not impress on her marriageable daughter the importance of catching Seyre's eye. When he came to town, he was besieged by invitations, which he universally ignored. He wouldn't have minded attending a party or two, he would tell Vivian, but whenever he did, he was invariably surrounded by mothers swooping in and carrying him off to meet their daughters, and he could hardly take a step, it seemed, without some girl dropping her fan or handkerchief in his way to force him to stop and politely pick it up. He felt foolish, harassed, and often appalled, and so he simply avoided all parties.

Even walking down the street, there was always the danger of someone's stopping him to chat. He could not get away without being impolite, and so he was introduced to the woman's daughter or niece or cousin or at least pressed to come to some party. For that reason, he had taken to walking on the street without looking around, keeping his focus on the sidewalk in front of him.

Thus in this manner he left the bookstore and turned toward Hyde Park. There, he thought, he could feel almost as if he were in the country again. He would have to avoid the members of the *ton* who might be walking there or riding along Rotten Row, but—he pulled out his watch to check it—it was earlier than the fashionable hour of presenting oneself in the park. He could slip past the popular paths and go deeper into the park.

Still, when he reached Rotten Row, he could not keep from stopping to look at the riders. He wished he had thought to bring a horse with him, but the departure from Marchester had been rushed. He could hire a horse, but he was sure that he would not find any mount satisfactory after the prime animal he was accustomed to riding. Besides, walking or trotting along Rotten Row, where the riders' main purpose was to see and be seen, could not compare to riding across his own land, sailing over fences and walls, splashing through streams, the sun on his back and the sweet scent of the country all around him.

With a sigh, he realized that he was simply standing there, daydreaming. He started to move forward, and that was when he saw her. She rode a bay mare, an unimpressive mount, but a confidence, an enjoyment, a *presence,* about the woman who rode drew Gregory's eye. She wore a dark blue riding habit of military cut, decorated with black frogging, and the fitted jacket showed off a trim figure. She rode beside a handsome man whom Gregory vaguely felt he should recognize, and the two of them were talking and laughing.

As he watched, she suddenly spurred her horse forward, and the mare took off. In defiance of all the rules of the *ton,* the woman galloped down Rotten Row. She rode as one with her mount, leaning forward over the mare's neck as she urged the horse on. Her hat flew off, and her hair came loose, tumbling down and flowing out behind her like a dark-gold banner. Gregory had thought her attractive the moment he saw her, but her face was beautiful now, bright with joy. His heart rose up inside him as she flew along, swelling with an answering joy. He knew that thrill, understood in a deep and visceral way the emotion that must be coursing through her now.

Then she thundered past and was gone. Behind him, he heard a shocked exclamation: "Who *was* that girl!"

A goddess, he thought, looking after the figure disappearing around a bend in the path. *A Valkyrie.* And he could not help but echo the woman's words—who was she?

He started forward again, striding away from the other people who stood about chattering over the girl's gallop. He felt suddenly energetic, excited. He could find out who she was, he thought. Within a day's time, the gossip about her gallop down Rotten Row would be all over the *ton.* Vivian knew everyone, so he had only to tell Vivian about it, and before long he would know her name and everything there was to know about her.

Father was improving; they could take the time to go to a party or pay an afternoon call. Why, there was that ball that Lady Carr was giving the following weekend to announce her son's engagement to the Bascombe girl; he knew Vivian would be attending it unless the duke took a decided turn for the worse. She would be happy for the escort. He might not have to tell Vivian about the girl at all. If he went to the ball, he might see her; from what Vivian had told him, the ball would be one of the events of the Season, and everyone who could do so would be there.

Oddly, he realized that he was a trifle reluctant to bring up the subject of the girl to Vivian. He rather liked the idea of keeping his Valkyrie to himself. Besides, much as he loved Vivian, if he expressed interest in any young lady, his sister would be on it like a hound catching the fox's scent. Vivian would not only have him meeting the girl, but dancing with her, seated beside her at some dinner, escorting her to the opera . . .

Gregory slowed his steps, his thoughts beginning to order themselves in his usual rational way. What did he know about the girl he had just seen, other than that she rode well? She was high-spirited; she was beautiful. Did he really want Vivian matchmaking for him just because he had responded for a moment to the way a girl sat a horse? If he met the young woman, how likely was it that she would be any different from any other lady he had met? He thought of being introduced to the girl and having her bat her lashes at him over her fan. He imagined her gazing at him vapidly or saying, "What do you think, Lord Seyre?" or perhaps chattering about her dress or her gloves.

It occurred to him that it might be better not to meet his Valkyrie at all. Perhaps it was better to let the girl remain a perfect memory in his mind.

Vivian had just left her father sleeping in his room when Jenks appeared to tell her that she had a visitor downstairs. She started to tell him to make her excuses, but then she saw the card he held out on the silver tray to her, and instead she said, "Show Lord Stewkesbury into the blue drawing room. I shall be down directly. I'll ring if we require refreshments."

Quickly she slipped down the hall to her bedchamber and went to her vanity table. Her dress would do, she thought, but she shrugged off the old shawl she had thrown around her shoulders and slipped on a spencer of forest green that deepened the color of her eyes. She smoothed a strand or two of hair into place and pinned them, then pinched a little color into her too pale cheeks. She had looked better, certainly, but she could do nothing right now about the shadows under her eyes or the weariness in them.

Putting on a smile, Vivian went downstairs and into the smaller drawing room, which was her favorite for daily use. Oliver was standing by the fire, warming his hands, and he turned at her entrance.

"Lady Vivian."

"Stewkesbury." She came forward, extending her hand, and he bowed over it. "How kind of you to call about my father's health."

He smiled faintly. "How kind of *you* to attribute such sterling motives to me. Actually, I came to see how you were doing, though I hope, of course, that the duke is better."

"He is, I think, and his doctor seems to agree."

"But I can see that his illness has taken its toll on you." His brows pinched together. "You look tired and pale."

Vivian raised a brow. "Indeed? How like you to manage to find a disagreeable remark to make about me."

"Ah, but you always make that so easy," he tossed back with a grin, and Vivian could not help but smile. "You know I did not mean it as a criticism. I am concerned that you are wearing yourself out taking care of your father."

"I do little enough other than worry."

"Worry can be more tiring than physical activity."

"Well, hopefully I shall not have so much of it now that he seems to be improving."

She had not taken a seat, so they still stood facing one another. Vivian could see Oliver gathering himself, and she was certain what he was about to say before he opened his mouth.

"I should apologize about the other night."

"No, please, Oliver, do not ruin it."

"Ruin it?" He looked astonished. "I don't know what you mean. I ruined the other night, acting as I did. I came here because I was concerned, and yet I wound up acting on my basest instincts."

"I never thought you were a saint." A faint smile played at the corners of Vivian's mouth. "Or even a parson, for that matter."

"I hope I am a gentleman. I took advantage of your emotions. I don't know why I did so. I never act in that manner."

Vivian chuckled, and a flirtatious dimple winked in her cheek. "You did it because you wanted to. If you will remember, you did the same thing the night of Lady Wilbourne's ball."

Stewkesbury drew himself up even more stiffly. "It was an aberration."

"Twice?" Vivian's eyes danced. "Really, my lord. Once may be an aberration. Twice is more of a habit."

Oliver set his jaw, glaring at her. "This is scarcely a laughing matter."

"Is it not?" Vivian moved closer to him, a wicked smile playing on her lips. "What you did was not so terrible. I, for one, quite enjoyed it. Didn't you?"

Looking harassed, he took a step backward, coming up against the mantel. "Blast it, Vivian, of course I enjoyed it. That is not the issue."

"Oh, but I think it is. Perhaps you ought to try giving into your 'basest instincts' more often. You might find it rewarding."

"Vivian . . ." His voice was a low growl, warning her.

"No?" She stopped only inches from him, one eyebrow arching up. "Well, then, I suppose that I will just have to."

With that she went up on tiptoe, her arms curling around his neck, and kissed him.

Chapter 7

For an instant, his mouth remained unmoving beneath hers, frozen in shock. Then, as if a floodgate had opened, his body surged with heat, his arms wrapping around her hard and fast, and his mouth opened to hers.

The sudden fire of his passion startled Vivian, but she responded to it eagerly. She pressed her body up into his, her arms tightening around his neck as their lips clung and parted and came together again. Her skin had become supremely sensitive, so that she was aware of the touch of the fabric of her dress upon her skin as she stretched up against his body. Her nipples prickled and grew taut, and she could not refrain from rubbing her body experimentally against him, causing her nipples to tighten even more with pleasure.

At her movement, he let out a low noise and tore his mouth from hers, kissing his way across her cheek and over the line of her jaw down to her throat. Vivian shivered at the feel of his lips on her sensitive skin, fire springing up in her wherever his mouth touched. She had started out kissing him teasingly, but now he filled her senses, delighting and confusing her. She was at once weak and filled with power, aching and happy. She knew a fierce yearning, a need to melt into Oliver, to fill herself with his scent, his taste, his very breath.

He seemed driven by the same forces as his arms crushed her against him and his mouth returned to consume hers. Vivian felt his hardness, his strength, his muscle and bone pressing into her. She knew she wanted to feel him more and deeper, wanted him with a hunger that made her tremble. His mouth left hers only to change the angle of their kiss as his hands slid down her back and over her buttocks in an intimate caress. The hard length of his desire pushed against her, and heat blossomed between her legs, setting up a low, throbbing ache.

Vivian had never known anything like this—had never expected to know anything like this. It was primitive and urgent, without thought or temperance. She thrilled to the sensations, amazed by them almost as much as she was by the fierceness of Oliver's passion. She would not have imagined that this kind of desperate, hungry desire could live in him, and it aroused her to know that she had evoked it.

Even as she yearned to know more of his touch, to feel his hands all over her body, he broke away with a groan, turning and grasping the edge of the mantel. He stood there, head lowered, his back rising and falling with his hard, rapid breaths. Vivian could not move, could only watch him, feeling her body throbbing with need and knowing that he would not return to her arms.

"Bloody hell, Vivian," he said at last, his voice taut and rasping. "Do not play with me. I am not one of your fools to dance attendance on you, begging for your notice."

"I did not think you were," Vivian retorted, stung.

He swung around. His face still carried the stamp of desire on it, a certain softness and malleability, but his voice was flat and hard as he said, "You know we would never suit."

"No, of course not." Vivian was surprised by the small, vivid slash of hurt that pierced her chest at his words.

He paused for a moment, and Vivian thought he was about to say more, but then his lips tightened and he took a step away. "I should leave."

Vivian simply nodded and watched as he walked away. After she heard the front door close behind him, she turned and walked over to sink down in a chair, her knees suddenly weak.

Two days later, Eve came to call. "I hope I am not intruding," she said, rising as Vivian came into the drawing room where the footman had seated her.

"You could never intrude," Vivian replied, coming forward to take her friend's hands. "And I am happy for the respite."

"Stewkesbury told us that your father was improving," Eve said as the two women sat down. "I am so glad."

"Yes, he is. He's able to get about with a cane, though he has not tackled the stairs yet. I think the doctor is beginning to believe that Papa is not about to have another attack just yet."

"That is excellent news."

"How are you?" Vivian asked. "Have you found a house?"

Eve shook her head. "No. It seems as if each one has some sort of drawback. But it's just as well. I have been so busy with Lady Carr's engagement party and Lily's trip to meet Neville's grandmother that I would not have time to move now, anyway. I have already fallen down on my duties chaperoning Camellia."

Vivian's brows rose. "Really? What happened?"

"Camellia has been fretting about missing her horse, so the earl hired her a mount and Fitz took her riding on Rotten

Row." Eve sighed. "I should have gone with them. It didn't occur to me to tell Fitz to keep Camellia from galloping."

"Oh, no."

"Oh, yes. She took off, and of course then it was too late. Fitz could hardly go tearing after her and ride her down. Her hat came off, and her hair came down."

"And it's the talk of the *ton,*" Vivian guessed.

"Naturally. At least it was not the most popular hour to ride, but there were still a number of people who saw her. And they were more than happy to tell everyone what had happened."

Vivian nodded. "It's early enough in the Season that there are few scandals to discuss."

"Precisely. If it had been May or June, it would probably be over in two or three days, but now . . . and with the engagement party only a week away . . . it's bound to be in everyone's mind at Lady Carr's party. Camellia's contrite, of course. Poor thing, she did not mean to create a firestorm. It's just that the rules seem like sheer nonsense to her." Eve shook her head, her expressive blue eyes full of sympathy.

"Sometimes they are sheer nonsense."

"True. But it does not make the gossip less damaging."

"How did Lily receive the news?"

"She stood up for Camellia, as she always does. However anxious she is for Lady Carr to like her, she would not blame Camellia. Lady Carr, needless to say, was not best pleased, but I did all I could to soothe her."

"It's nothing that Camellia can't live down. There may be a few whispers at the ball, but as soon as something more interesting comes along, it will be forgotten." Vivian paused, thinking. "Now that Papa is doing better, I should take her up in my phaeton, as I promised her. It won't stop the whispers, but it should alleviate some of their effect."

Eve nodded. Though Vivian was not considered a paragon of propriety, her position as a duke's daughter was lofty enough that being her friend could provide one with some degree of protection. No one would dare snub Camellia in Vivian's company. Besides, it would give the gossips something more positive to say about Camellia.

"That would be just the thing," Eve agreed. "Are you sure you can spare the time?"

"Oh, yes. It's probably long past time for me to get out of the house. Besides, it will enable me to bring home some bits of gossip for Papa. He has been growing quite bored."

Two days later, Vivian drove to Stewkesbury House in her high-perch phaeton. A bright yellow in color, with the high seat hung precariously forward over the smaller front wheels, it was the height of style, and the small groom in his crisp blue-and-silver livery standing on the "box" behind the carriage added to its look of luxurious elegance. Camellia, coming out of the house, was immediately wide-eyed with wonder.

"Oh, Vivian!" she cried as she climbed up lithely onto the high seat. "This is all the crack! How long have you been driving it?"

"Just got it last Season." Vivian deftly maneuvered into traffic.

Camellia grinned broadly. "I'd love to drive one of these! Benjamin Dawkins let me drive his father's wagon once, but that was nothing compared to this. Could I learn, do you think?" She turned to Vivian, her eyes sparkling.

"Of course. I'd be happy to teach you. You'd have to start on something easier, though. The balance on a high-perch phaeton is much more delicate."

Camellia nodded, then added somewhat uncertainly, "It won't be something I'll get into trouble over, will it?"

"No. There are other women who drive their own phaetons. Not so many drive a high perch. But it's acceptable—unless, of course, one makes a mull of it. But I'm sure you will be good."

"Good. Because I have sworn to act like a proper lady. I have apparently committed a terrible sin."

Vivian laughed. "Galloping on Rotten Row. I heard. Fitz should have thought to warn you. So should Eve. For that matter, so should I."

"Eve did tell me earlier, when she was trying to mold us into proper young ladies back at Willowmere. I remembered as soon as I stopped and saw all the shocked faces. It was just so wonderful to be back on a horse, and when I looked down that path, I could not resist. I thought Fitz would race me, as he used to back home, so I dug in my heels, wanting to get the start on him." She sighed. "I doubt I'll ever remember all the things I'm not supposed to do."

"It will pass, I promise you. It isn't scandalous enough to really damage your reputation. There will be some chatter, but we shall calm that down a bit today. I intend to stop to chat with everyone we see. They'll have to meet you and be polite or risk being rude to me—not that there aren't a number of people who would love to be rude to me, but they aren't because they're too eager to say to their friends, 'The other day when I was chatting with the Duke of Marchester's daughter . . . ,'" Vivian said in an exaggeratedly upper-class voice.

Camellia giggled. "You sound like Aunt Euphronia."

"Heaven help me. Did she ring a peal over your head?"

"Yes. But she doesn't bother me. I was afraid Lily would be angry because of Neville's family and all, but she wasn't. And Cousin Oliver didn't even lecture me."

"You're jesting."

"No, truly. I was most surprised. He told Fitz he was a fool, but even that was only halfhearted. He has been . . . a trifle odd recently."

"Stewkesbury?" Vivian turned to look at the girl. "What do you mean, odd?"

Camellia shrugged. "I'm not sure. He seems . . . distracted, I guess, as if he's thinking about something else. Not always, of course, but now and then. Someone will say something to him, and he won't have been listening. Or I'll come into a room and find him staring out the window at nothing. And the other evening when he came in and we told him about my ride in the park—you know Cousin Oliver, he never yells or anything, but he gets that look in his eyes, and his tone turns to ice."

"Yes, I know."

"Well, after I told him how I'd galloped along Rotten Row, I expected him to look at me that way and tell me how terrible that was, but do you know what he said? He said, 'I'd never have thought that animal could gallop.' Then he told Fitz he was a fool, and he went off to his study."

"Well." Vivian considered. "What do you think is wrong with him?"

"I haven't the faintest idea."

"What does Fitz say?"

"You know Cousin Fitz; he made some jest about it. But I think he found it peculiar."

Vivian was silent for a moment, seemingly concentrating on executing a right turn. Then she said mildly, "I suppose one must expect even Stewkesbury to be odd on occasion."

"I suppose so. Lily thinks that he has a new *chère amie*."

"What?" Vivian turned to her, eyes wide. "Camellia . . ."

"I know. We aren't supposed to know what a *chère amie* is, let alone talk about one. But that's awfully silly, don't you think?"

"Yes, but please don't talk so with anyone besides me or Eve."

"We know better than that."

"Um, why does Lily think . . . ?"

"You know Lily. She always thinks the reason for everything is love. She claims that he's distracted because he's thinking about a woman. And she says it can't be someone acceptable because he hasn't been attending any parties or going to the theater or anything like that where he would have been seeing a respectable woman."

"Stewkesbury is not a very social sort."

"No, but he'd obviously been somewhere the other evening after my galloping fiasco. Lily thought he had the look of a man who'd been 'up to something.' I didn't notice, but then, as Lily said, I would not."

"Mm. I'm not sure it's enough evidence to prove that Stewkesbury has found a light o' love. It might as easily be that he was thinking of some business problem."

"Probably. But it's more exciting Lily's way."

Vivian chuckled. "It usually is."

They turned into the park, and Vivian cast a glance at Camellia. "Here we are. Now we have to get down to work. Ah, there is Mrs. Harroway. She's a complete rattle." Vivian lifted her hand in greeting and pulled her team to a stop so that she could chat with the other woman, which gratified Mrs. Harroway to no end.

After that, they drove no more than a minute or two before Vivian spotted a stylish barouche. Despite the nip in the air, the carriage's occupants had the soft top pushed back—what was the use of a ride through the park if one was not seen?—and the two women inside compensated with a lap robe, fur muffs for their hands, and ermine-trimmed cloaks.

It was, Vivian had to admit, a perfect setting for the younger of the women. Her delicate heart-shaped face with its cluster of dark curls falling on either side was perfectly framed by the white fur of the cloak's hood, and the cold had brought a rosy color to her cheeks, giving her the perfect strawberries-and-cream complexion that was the hallmark of the English beauty. A rosy cupid's bow of a mouth and bright blue eyes completed the pretty picture. The woman beside her was obviously her mother, though time had put its stamp on the other woman, adding gray to the dark hair and marking her eyes and mouth with small lines.

"Lady Parkington." Vivian smiled with more pleasure than she felt.

She had never particularly liked Lady Parkington, whose primary goal in life had been to marry her four daughters off to the most wealthy and important men she could find. Since her daughters were pretty, she had managed that feat with the first three, the oldest of whom was of an age with Vivian. Each of the daughters had pursued Vivian's friendship with almost as much zeal as they had chased husbands, but Vivian had been well aware that it was not she whom they liked but her connection to her eminently marriageable and rather reclusive brother. None of them had succeeded with either Gregory or Vivian. Vivian had enjoyed the lack of the family's attentions for the last three years, but unfortunately, she saw now, the youngest of the sisters must have made her way up to marriageable age and would be setting out on her own husband hunt this Season.

"It's so wonderful to see you," Lady Parkington cried. "My, it's been an age since we have had a chance to chat, hasn't it? Allow me to introduce you to my daughter Dora. Dora, dear, say hello to Lady Vivian Carlyle. You know, the one of whom Jane is so fond."

Vivian suspected that the aforesaid Jane would have walked over Vivian with jackboots if it meant catching the eye of a wealthy suitor, but she merely smiled pleasantly and greeted the girl. "This is my friend Miss Bascombe. She is Lord Stewkesbury's cousin."

"My goodness, is this your first Season, too, child?" Despite the warmth in her voice, the eye Lady Parkington ran over Camellia was coolly assessing. "You and Dora will doubtless be great friends. I'm afraid our Dora is a bit shy, so perhaps you will help her along."

The girl, on cue, cast her lovely, long-lashed eyes down, the very portrait of demure young womanhood. Camellia gazed back at the other girl with curiosity. "Help her along where?"

Lady Parkington chuckled as if Camellia had made a joke. "You young girls, always so clever. You know, introduce her to people, stand her friend."

Camellia frowned a little. "I'm afraid I'd be no help there. I don't know anyone in London except for my family."

Lady Parkington let out another appreciative chuckle. "Ah, Lord Stewkesbury—one of the most elegant and refined gentlemen in this country. So admired. Of course, your other cousin has long been one of the most popular bachelors in London, but I understand that he has been taken off the marriage mart."

"Yes, he married my good friend Mrs. Hawthorne," Vivian said.

"A number of hearts were broken at that news, I can assure you," Lady Parkington replied with a roguish smile.

Vivian mustered up a smile at the woman's witticism. She could see from the corner of her eye that Camellia was regarding both Lady Parkington and her daughter with her usual direct gaze, and Vivian wondered what Camellia would think of them. She had the suspicion that Camellia would not readily be deceived.

Dora looked up at Vivian with her large, limpid blue eyes. "My lady, I vow I am in awe of your skills with the reins."

"Thank you," Vivian responded politely. "Are you interested in driving?"

"Oh, my, no." The girl let out a little laugh, as tinkling and light as bells in the crisp air. "I should never have the courage to do that." She cast her eyes over at Camellia. "Would you, Miss Bascombe?"

Camellia grinned. "Yes, indeed. I'm hoping Viv—that is, Lady Vivian—will teach me how to drive a team."

Dora's eyes widened. "You must be very brave indeed. But, then, you are an excellent rider, I have heard." A quick glint of something steely was in her eyes before they were once again great blue pools of innocence.

Vivian felt Camellia stiffen beside her, but Camellia said only, "Have you?"

"Oh, dear." Dora looked chagrined. "I should not have brought that up, should I?" She cast down her eyes in embarrassment. "I am so sorry. Mother tells me I am quite scatterbrained."

Vivian smiled. "You were only telling the truth. Miss Bascombe is an excellent rider, indeed. However, I fear she is finding that one's every movement is scrutinized when one's cousin is the Earl of Stewkesbury. And there is nothing the *ton* enjoys as much as gossiping about each other."

"Indeed," Lady Parkington agreed solemnly. "I always tell my girls that their reputations are their most precious asset."

"Really? I have always ranked heart and courage most highly myself."

Lady Parkington's smile grew a trifle forced, but it did not waver.

"Will we see you at Lady Carr's ball next week?" Vivian went on pleasantly. "It will be Miss Bascombe's and her sister's first London ball. Lady Carr is so happy to be presenting her future daughter-in-law to the *ton*. Of course, alas, there is another eligible bachelor who has been taken off the market," she added with a wicked sparkle in her eyes.

"Yes, all of London has been talking of the Misses

Bascombes and their great success." Lady Parkington's voice was merry. "You naughty girls." She shook her finger at Camellia playfully. "You must leave some of the young men of England to the rest of the girls."

"Oh, Mama." Dora smiled sweetly. "It's not at all surprising to me now that I have seen Miss Bascombe. Her sisters are doubtless equally beautiful."

"Lily and Mary are far prettier than I," Camellia said with her usual candor.

"You are being modest," Dora murmured.

Camellia grinned. "No. I am rarely accused of that. For instance, I'm a better shot than either of them."

Vivian stifled a smile at the startled expressions on the other two women's faces. "Yes. Camellia has been giving me lessons this last summer."

"My," Lady Parkington said inadequately.

"It is great fun. Mr. Talbot joined us, as did the earl at times," Vivian went on blithely. "I am convinced that target shooting will become all the rage."

"Indeed."

A few moments later, after Vivian and Camellia had said their good-byes to the Parkingtons and driven on their way, Camellia turned to Vivian, laughing. "You told such a plumper—saying Cousin Oliver joined us shooting."

Vivian smiled. "Well, he did come out to watch sometimes. I didn't say he participated."

"I made another mistake, didn't I—saying I was a better shot? So you had to rescue me by saying you were learning how to shoot, too."

"No, I did that because I find the Parkingtons profoundly irritating. I just wanted to see Lady Parkington's face when I said it. I am a wicked creature, I know, but it was most satisfying."

"I thought so, too." Camellia grinned back at Vivian.

"I didn't like them. I'm not sure why, for Miss Parkington seemed to be trying to be nice. She can't help it if she's scared of driving a phaeton, I suppose, but I couldn't help but feel . . ."

Vivian looked at her. "Feel what?"

"I'm not sure. Just that there was a false note there. She meant what she said about my riding as a barb, didn't she?"

"No doubt. I don't think sweet Dora does much that is not calculated. Not if she's anything like her sisters, and she certainly acted it today. Your instincts were quite correct." Vivian glanced ahead of her and sighed. "Ah, dear, there's Mrs. Farthingham and Lady Medwell. Well, there's nothing for it but to stop. I do wish I had picked a day when more interesting people were taking the air."

So stop they did, not just for Mrs. Farthingham and Lady Medwell, but for at least five more carriages. Camellia tried her best to mind her tongue and smile and be polite, but she found it slow going. So it was with real pleasure that she recognized the horseman approaching them.

"Cousin Oliver!" she exclaimed, smiling.

"Stewkesbury." Lady Vivian watched the earl closely as he pulled his horse to a stop beside their carriage and doffed his hat to them.

It had been several days since she had last seen Oliver, and she was well aware of his conflicting emotions regarding her. She herself was given to a number of differing feelings regarding the earl. The difference, of course, between the two of them was that she did not mind a bit of uncertainty; it added spice to one's life. Oliver, on the other hand, liked to know what he was doing and why. She wondered what course he had decided to take with her. She suspected that he intended to put her firmly back into her role as casual family friend. Vivian had to smile to herself. Stewkesbury's world, she thought, could use a little shaking up.

She offered him a dazzling smile and had the satisfaction of seeing him look unsettled for an instant. She was glad she had worn her new bonnet with the ruched emerald green lining.

"Lady Vivian." He nodded to her a trifle stiffly, and his gaze went to his cousin. "Cousin Camellia." His eyes then swept across the vehicle, and he released a little sigh. "So you are driving a high-perch phaeton now."

"Yes. Isn't it a beauty? I got it last summer before I left London, and this is only the second chance I've had to drive it."

"Vivian says she will teach me how to drive," Camellia put in, her voice charged with excitement.

"Did she now?" Oliver raised one brow at Vivian. "A high-perch phaeton? I think not."

"Not at first," Camellia agreed reasonably. "But eventually."

"It is not an appropriate vehicle for a young lady."

"Vivian drives one!"

"Yes, Stewkesbury, are you saying that I am inappropriate?" Vivian shot him an amused look. "Or perhaps you are intimating that I am no longer young?"

"Blast it, Vivian, don't try to turn this around on me. You know good and well what I mean."

"I'm not sure," Vivian said thoughtfully. "I've noticed that lately your words don't always match your actions." Her eyes danced at the light that sparked in his eyes at her comment. It was almost too easy to get a response out of Oliver, and yet, she thought, she never tired of doing it. Just something about the way his eyes silvered and his mouth tightened was most agreeable.

He looked as if he would like to say more to her, but with a visible effort, he pulled his gaze away and focused on Camellia. "I mean that there is a deal of difference in age between you and Lady Vivian."

"Oliver! You wound me."

He cast Vivian a quelling glance. "Do stop teasing. I am serious. Camellia, you are making your come-out, and, more than that, you are unknown to anyone in London society. Vivian, on the other hand, has been out for a number of years and everyone is well acquainted with her fits and starts."

"Fits and starts! Really, driving is scarcely some capricious thing I've taken up. I've done it since before I even came out."

"Exactly." He gave her a satisfied nod. "And I'll wager your father taught you."

"Actually it was my brothers."

He shrugged. "The point is, you were taught by experienced drivers, and you learned in the safety of your estate." He looked at Camellia. "Which is precisely the way that you shall learn it. I shall teach you—or Fitz or Royce—and it will be done at Willowmere, where it won't matter if you take a turn too late or haven't complete control of your team. It's far too difficult to learn in the city. I shall teach you this summer, after the Season." He paused, then added, "And it won't be a high-perch phaeton. If Lady Vivian had a regard for her safety, she wouldn't drive one either."

Vivian chuckled and said in a low, teasing voice, "Really, Oliver, when have you ever known me to be cautious?"

He looked at her, and for an instant, a flicker of heated frustration was in his eyes. "Never," he said. "God help us."

Chapter 8

Lady Carr's ball the next week was the first truly noteworthy party of the young Season. Ecstatic that at long last her son was taking a bride and eager to overshadow any shortcomings of that prospective bride, she had not spared any expense for the party. No string quartet would suffice; instead a small orchestra sat at the end of the ballroom, and the midnight supper would feature a number of delicacies and exotic foods as well as providing a full repast for even the heartiest of appetites. One location would not contain all that she offered: there was the grand ballroom for dancing and a separate game room for cardplayers, as well as the public room downstairs for the midnight supper buffet and numerous tables and chairs for diners and weary dancers. Flowers twined around balustrades and banisters and stood in massive arrangements. Candles glittered in chandeliers, and sconces glowed around the edges of the room.

The duke had recovered enough that the doctor was allowing him to return to his estate the next day, so Vivian approached the party in good spirits. She wore her newest ball gown, a froth of palest sea green gauze and silver lace floating around her in layers of sheerness that hinted at much and revealed nothing. Her hair was done up in an intricate arrangement of curls in which diamonds winked here and there, and around her neck she wore the Scots Green, showcased by the expanse of her soft, white shoulders that the scooped neckline of her dress laid bare. Silver satin slippers completed the picture of ephemeral, luxurious beauty.

Gregory was to drive with their father back to Marchester the following day, but Vivian had cajoled him into escorting her to the party before he left. It was a rare treat for her to have her brother with her in London, and she wanted to introduce him to the Bascombe sisters. That was easy enough to do with Lily, for she stood in the receiving line with Lord and Lady Carr and their son Neville. Stewkesbury was there, as well, determinedly performing his social duty, but there was no sight of Camellia. Her presence was not required, and Vivian felt sure she had fled to the opposite end of the room.

Shortly after they arrived, Lady Parkington descended upon Vivian and Gregory, flanked by her daughter Dora, all coy smiles and alluring glances. Lady Parkington froze Gregory in his tracks as she spewed out effusive greetings.

"La, it's so rare to see you at these gatherings, Lord Seyre. We must thank your sister for bringing you to London again. Please allow me to introduce my daughter Dora. She's the youngest of all my girls and my pride and joy. 'Twill be hard for me to let her go. But, of course, when a girl is as lovely as Dora, one cannot expect her to remain unmarried for long."

"I am pleased to meet you." Dora looked at him with doelike eyes, then dropped her gaze modestly, blushing, and raised her fan to cover the lower half of her face.

"Um, uh, yes. Pleased to, um . . . lovely party . . ."

"I'm sure you must enjoy a chance to be around other

young people after spending so much time at Marchester, Lord Seyre," Lady Parkington plowed ahead.

"I, ah . . ."

"No doubt you young people would enjoy a promenade while your sister and I catch up on all the gossip," Lady Parkington told Gregory, beaming benignly.

Vivian smothered a smile at the incipient panic on Gregory's face.

"Well, that is . . ." Gregory cast a pleading glance at Vivian.

Vivian took pity on him, saying, "How kind of you to think of him, but my brother has promised this dance to me, Lady Parkington. I am afraid I must steal him away. It was so nice to see you."

Linking her arm through her brother's, Vivian gave a bright smile and a nod to the other two women and whisked Gregory off to the dance floor.

"Thank you," Gregory murmured. "I thought I was doomed."

Vivian chuckled. "You must learn how to slip out of such situations. You are not obligated to walk with every young lady whose mother asks."

"I *have* learned how to avoid it. I don't come to London."

"I meant something a bit less extreme. What will you do for the rest of this ball? You can't dance every dance with me."

"Simple. I shall take refuge in the Carrs' library."

Vivian could not help but laugh. "What am I going to do with you?"

He smiled and shrugged, pulling her into place at the end of a set. "Dance with me."

The Earl of Stewkesbury slipped away from the latest well-wisher with an inward sigh. Lady Carr must have invited everyone she knew—and every last one of them must have attended. They were driven by curiosity, he knew. Not only was it news that Neville, the perennial bachelor and rake, had finally taken the fateful step of becoming engaged. Even more titillating was that instead of the long-expected engagement between Neville and Lady Priscilla Symington, Lady Priscilla had wed a French balloonist, of all things, and Neville had pledged to marry the American cousin of Lord Stewkesbury's. When one added in the additional gossip generated by the sudden appearance of the American cousins and the long-ago scandal of their mother's elopement and subsequent banishment by her father, few in the city could resist the opportunity to glimpse the couple.

They doubtless would have liked to see Lily's sister as well, of course, but Oliver noted that Camellia had had the good sense to flee to the opposite end of the room with Fitz and Eve when they first arrived. It had not taken Oliver long to fervently wish he could have left the receiving line, too.

Not, of course, that he would have done so. Little as he liked meeting people and trying to avoid their often impertinent questions, he was expected to do this sort of thing, and Oliver was accustomed to doing what was expected. It was all very well to pass through life simply enjoying the many gifts he had been given, as his half brother Fitz did, but when one was the earl and had been raised from childhood to understand the weight and solemnity of one's duties, as Oliver had, such a haphazard approach to life was not even thought of. One did the small things as well as the large ones, and life ran smoothly for everyone concerned, not only himself, but his family and everyone else dependent upon him.

Still, Oliver turned away with relief when the receiving line broke up. He walked to the ballroom and paused just inside the doors, his eyes sweeping over the crowd, looking for a certain flash of bright red hair.

"Lord Stewkesbury!" a merry voice sounded to the right of him. "How nice to run into you again."

With a sigh, Oliver turned, expecting to face another curiosity seeker. Even worse, he realized when he saw the woman and the pretty dark-haired girl she had in tow, he was facing a mother pushing her daughter onto the marriage mart.

He bowed, searching for a name. She was someone he had met before, but his lack of interest in social affairs—coupled with the fact that the main thing he recalled about the woman was that he had spent several years avoiding her pursuit of him for her other, older daughters—had left him blank when it came to her name.

"My lady," he finally said, relatively certain that she was titled rather than a plain *Mrs.*

"It's such wonderful news about Mr. Carr and your cousin. And how happy you must be to have your cousins living with you now. Such stories they must have to tell about life across the seas."

"No doubt."

"Pray allow me to introduce my daughter Miss Dora Parkington."

"Miss Parkington." He nodded to the girl, grateful that the woman had at least slipped him her last name. "I believe I have met some of your sisters."

The girl smiled and cast her eyes down modestly. "I fear I shall have difficulty living up to my sisters, my lord."

"Such a sweet girl." Her mother beamed. "She's my youngest and, the truth is, the greatest beauty." Lady Parkington tittered, hiding her laugh behind her fan. "Though do not let any of my other girls hear that!"

"Mama, you shouldn't say such things. You know it isn't true." Dora smiled sweetly at her mother and cast her eyes up at the earl, making the most of her thick, long lashes.

This, he knew, was where he was supposed to deny her modest statement and assure her that none could be more beautiful than she. But Oliver felt the move too practiced, and despite the girl's undeniable attractiveness, he found himself reluctant to engage in the expected flattery. Perhaps, he thought, he had become too accustomed to the blunt ways of his American cousins, but he could not help but think that Miss Parkington would be more appealing if she looked at a person directly and spoke straightforwardly.

"Mothers must be forgiven for their prejudices," he told the girl, and saw the flash of quickly concealed surprise, then resentment, in Dora's eyes.

The mother, however, was undeterred by the setback, and she forged ahead, saying, "We met one of your cousins the other day in the park. Not Miss Lily, but Miss Camellia Bascombe. Such lovely names these girls have."

"I believe their mother was fond of flowers." He wondered how much longer he would have to make conversation before he could take his leave without seeming impolite. Fitz, he knew, would probably already have charmed both women and managed to slip away without either of them noticing what short shrift he had given them. But, then, he had never had Fitz's ease of manner.

"Such an attractive young girl, Miss Bascombe. She and Dora quite enjoyed meeting; I feel sure that they will become great friends this Season."

Oliver gave a fleeting thought to Camellia being friends with the girl in front of him, and he had to hide a smile. He found himself wishing that he had witnessed the meeting between the two of them.

"No doubt," he replied noncommittally. Then, glancing

over Lady Parkington's shoulder, he caught a glimpse of bright red hair that was quickly concealed again as one of the young men standing around her shifted his position. He flashed what he hoped was an avuncular smile at Miss Parkington. "I am sure you will have a delightful Season, Miss Parkington. Now, if you will excuse me, I must speak with my brother. Good evening, Lady Parkington. Miss Parkington."

With a nod, he set off toward the spot where he had seen the momentary flash of red. He would just stop by to say hello to Vivian before he made his way over to Fitz. It was only polite, after all, to inquire about her father. And if Seyre was still with his sister, he could chat a bit with him. As he approached, he cast a rather jaundiced eye at the cluster of men around Lady Vivian. One would think that after all this time, some of these fellows would have given up pursuing her. It was clear none of them were going to win her hand, and he could not help but wonder if it was a lack of intelligence or a lack of pride that impelled them to flock to her.

Before he reached the group, one of the men bowed and left, and for a moment Oliver had an unimpeded line of sight to Vivian. There was another reason for the way men sought her out—a simple inability to resist her. He was honest enough to admit that he felt the same visceral tug when he looked at her. The pale green dress she wore seemed to be made of gossamer, as light and insubstantial as mist, yet clinging to the enticing curves of her body. She was laughing at something one of her admirers had said, and her face was lit from within, the pale skin glowing, her cheeks delicately pink and her lush mouth a deeper rose. Her green eyes sparkled, and when she turned and caught sight of Oliver, a deeper warmth flashed in her gaze, calling forth a respondent warmth in him.

"Lord Stewkesbury." She smiled, slipping through the circle of men toward him.

"Lady Vivian." Oliver could not keep from smiling back at her as he bent over her hand in an elegant bow.

"I am so glad to see you," Vivian told him. "I feared you might have forgotten."

"Forgotten?" He hadn't the slightest idea what she was talking about, but gamely he went on, "No, how could I forget?"

She turned back toward the other men, slipping her hand into the crook of his arm as she did so. "If you gentlemen will excuse me, I am afraid that I have promised this next dance to Lord Stewkesbury."

Oliver was far too carefully controlled to let any surprise at this blatant lie touch his features. Instead, he nodded toward the men and turned, strolling with Vivian toward the dance floor. Her perfume drifted up, entangling his senses, and he was very aware of the warmth of her hand upon his arm.

He pulled his mind back from the dangerous paths it was racing down and said, "I fear it must be advancing age, my lady, but I cannot recall you promising this dance to me."

She cast a laughing glance up at him. "Well, I would have if you had had the good sense to ask me."

He chuckled. "Then I must be thankful that your good sense is greater than mine."

"You should be. If I had not asked you to dance, you might have continued avoiding me for several more days."

"I have not been avoiding—"

"No, do not waste your breath trying to deny that it scared you silly when you kissed me the other day, and you have been hiding from me ever since."

It never failed, Oliver thought, irritation rising in him. No matter how charming and beautiful or, yes, utterly desirable

Vivian Carlyle might be, in the next instant she would say something so irksome that he had to clench his teeth to keep from shooting back a most ungentlemanly retort.

"I was not *hiding,* as you so colorfully put it. I was exercising restraint."

"Ah. I see."

"One of us had to."

"And you knew, of course, that it would not be me."

He raised one brow, saying drily, "Restraint is not known as one of your virtues."

"But honesty is."

They took their places on the dance floor among the other couples, the earl frowning down at her. He raised his hand to take hers and set his other hand at her waist. He could feel her pliant body beneath the layers of thin cloth, and the sudden fierce desire that stabbed him made his scowl even fiercer.

"Are you implying that I am not honest?" he asked.

"In all other regards, you are the most honest man I know," Vivian replied calmly. "Regarding your own feelings, however, I am not even sure you know what they are."

Oliver ground his teeth together and regretted that he had asked her to dance. Of course, he amended to himself, he *hadn't* asked her to dance. *She* had asked *him,* which was exactly the bold, even brazen, sort of thing that Vivian did. He should have known better than to have approached her. If it would not create a storm of gossip, he would just lead her off the floor and back to her gaggle of suitors right now.

The music started up, and they stepped automatically into the movements of the waltz. Oliver hoped that Vivian would let the subject drop while they were dancing, but of course she did not.

"I think we should talk about what happened between us," she told him.

"Nothing happened."

"Nothing?" Vivian raised a mocking eyebrow.

"You know what I mean. Nothing irrevocable. Nothing that will damage your reputation."

"Oliver . . ." She looked at him with some exasperation. "You do not need to run from this. Or deny it. There was nothing wrong in what we did. You were not taking advantage of me. I am not some girl of eighteen, and you are not the first man who has found me attractive."

A fierce light leaped into his eyes, surprising her. "I sincerely hope that you don't go about kissing every man who admires your looks."

Vivian let out a throaty chuckle that had the same effect on him as her running her fingers up his spine. "No. But you see, I find you attractive, too."

Oliver swallowed hard and struggled to bring his suddenly scattered thoughts back together. "Vivian, have a care. You should not say such things."

"Not even to you?"

"No! Bloody hell, I am not made of stone, no matter what you have always thought."

She smiled at him in a way that he could only deem provocative. "No, I know that you are not."

"Surely you must realize that there can be nothing between us!" He spoke in a fierce whisper, leaning toward her.

"I know nothing of the kind. Why can't there be?"

"Because you are a woman of genteel birth, a lady."

"That does not make me any less a woman."

"It makes you a woman to whom it is offering a grievous insult to kiss as I have kissed you and not marry. And surely it must be obvious that we could not marry."

Vivian began to chuckle. "You think that I would not be a proper wife for you?"

"Good Gad, no. I cannot think of anyone less suitable for my wife. You are irreverent; you do not give the slightest thought to what sort of scandal you may cause. You are outspoken and light-minded. Independent. Willful. And stubborn."

"Am I?" The light of battle came to Vivian's eyes. "It may shock you to learn that you are not what I would seek in a husband. You are arrogant and overbearing, always certain that you are right. No doubt any wife of yours would spend her life under your thumb. You sermonize; you lecture. You seem to think it is a sin to laugh or enjoy yourself."

"I have nothing against enjoying myself. I simply do not regard it as the only thing in life."

"No, the only thing in your life is duty!" she shot back.

"There are some who might be better served to think more about their duty. And their family."

"You think that I care any less for my family because I do not spend my life doing what others think I should? That is not loving your family. It is living in fear."

Throughout their conversation, Oliver had been growing progressively stiffer and his steps more forceful, so that they were now whirling about the floor with such energy that other couples moved out of their way. Catching sight of one couple doing so, Vivian's ready sense of humor bubbled up, and she let out a little laugh.

"Oliver! Are we in a race?"

"What? Blast." He realized suddenly what he was doing, and chagrined, he forced himself to slow his steps. At least the music was approaching its end. He drew in a long breath and released it. "Well . . . I suppose we can agree that you and I are wrong for each other."

Vivian looked up at him, and he was struck all over again by her breathtaking beauty. "You are right, of course. We could never be husband and wife." She smiled, her eyes lighting with mischief. "But there are other relationships besides marriage, you know."

Oliver stumbled to a halt, staring at her in shock. Fortunately the music ended so that his abrupt and awkward movement went unnoticed. Vivian smiled and walked away.

Oliver remained immobilized for an instant, then whirled and hurried after her. He grabbed her by the arm and, ignoring her protest, swept her through the nearest door into the hallway outside the ballroom. Several people were standing in the corridor, and laughter rolled out of a room where a number of the guests were playing cards. Oliver turned away from them and whisked Vivian down the hall in the opposite direction.

"Oliver! Really, what are you doing?" Vivian hissed as he ducked into the last room on the right, pulling her with him.

As they stepped inside, he reached out to take a small candelabra from the hallway table and bring it with him, setting it down on a sideboard. He closed the door and turned to face Vivian, his arms crossed. Vivian glanced pointedly around the small room, lit only by the shifting, shadowed light of the single candelabra, then turned back to Oliver, her eyes wide in an exaggeratedly innocent look.

"My lord, whatever are you doing? Dragging me into this cozy, dimly lit room? One could almost think that you were intent on seducing me."

He ground out an oath. "Don't joke about such things, Vivian! I am accustomed to your bizarre sense of humor, but others are not."

"I was not joking. At least, not about the possibility of our having some other relationship than marriage."

"You can't—Viv—don't be absurd." Oliver could feel the flush mounting in his face, and he felt ten times a fool.

Vivian was making a jest of him; he was sure of it. Yet, he could not stop the heat that rushed through him at her words. He could hardly think with her standing so close to him, her eyes huge and dark in the dim light, her lips curving up in a provocative smile. Her perfume wrapped around him, sweet and seductive.

"For all the things that don't suit about us," Vivian said, moving closer to him, "there is one thing that seems to . . ." She was only inches from him now, her face turned up to his.

His brain whirled. All he could think of was the taste of her mouth, the softness of her lips beneath his. His breath rasped in his throat, and he leaned forward. Abruptly he stopped and turned away.

"Bloody hell! Blast it, Vivian, you may be mad, but I am not." The anger that burst out of him offered some release. "We cannot have an affair. Surely you are not seriously suggesting that."

"With most men, I would not have to be the one suggesting it," Vivian retorted. "Is your blood really so cool?"

He gaped at her. "Now I am at fault because I have some concern for your reputation?"

"My reputation does not have to suffer. I presume you know how to be discreet."

"Yes, of course, but—"

"We are both mature adults, free to do as we please, well aware of the ways of the world. Why should we not act on what we feel?"

"Think about what you are saying! Someday you will marry, and you would not want . . ." He fumbled to a halt. "I mean to say, there must not be any question—it's not the same as if you were a widow. You would not want there to be any doubt that you . . ." Oliver could feel the blush spreading across his cheeks, and he felt even more a fool, something that was becoming a common occurrence where Vivian was concerned.

She raised an eyebrow coolly at him. "Exactly why do you presume I am so innocent?"

Oliver stared, shock mingling with an upswell of lust, followed by a sudden, vicious stab of jealousy. His hands tightened into fists at his side. What man had seduced her? Who had lain beside her, stroked her smooth white body, opened her legs and moved between them? Fury rolled through him, red and hot, and he had to struggle to retain control of himself.

"Anyway," Vivian went on lightly, turning and strolling away, "I have no intention of marrying." She stopped, putting one hand on the back of a chair and turning to face him. "There is no need for me to marry. And I see no advantage to a woman in the married state. So why marry?"

"Surely protection, security, children, love, a home and family . . ." He managed to keep his voice as even and unconcerned as hers despite the emotions roiling inside him.

"I have a home. I have a family. My father's name and my brother's provide me ample protection and position. As for children . . ." She shrugged. "Jerome has children, and someday Gregory may marry and have children. I can dote on them if I feel the urge. That leaves nothing but love, and I do not think that love is for me."

"Don't be nonsensical."

"I'm not. Tell me, Oliver, do you plan to marry for love?" She folded her arms, watching him.

He started to speak, then stopped, knowing that to say anything other than no would be a lie. He glared at her for a long moment, then turned on his heel and left the room.

Camellia was bored. The evening had begun well enough. It had been fun to get dressed with Lily in their elegant new gowns from Madame Arceneaux, Lady Vivian's favorite modiste. Much to their surprise, Stewkesbury had presented each of them with a pearl necklace, appropriate for a young girl making her come-out, in honor of the occasion. The necklaces were lovely, but more than that, Camellia had been warmed by the thought behind the gift. Perhaps the earl was coming to see them as more than just an obligation.

The pleasant feeling had lasted until they arrived at the party. Lily, of course, had been compelled to stand in the line to receive guests along with the Carrs, and Stewkesbury had stayed with them. Camellia had escaped with Fitz and Eve. It was easy and fun talking to them, but before long Eve was introducing her to this lady and that young man, and Camellia was faced with remembering names, as well as all the things she should not say or do. She simply could not commit some social sin at this party, which was so important to Lily. As a result, Camellia said as little as possible and smiled until her face ached.

She saw Vivian a time or two during the evening, usually dancing or talking to a group of people, but she had always been at a distance, and so Camellia had not even spoken with her. Camellia was now standing with a group of young people to whom Eve had introduced her. Her feet hurt from her new slippers; her head ached from the mass of hair piled and twisted and pinned on her head; and even her back was tired from standing all evening. Worst of all, she was utterly, incredibly bored.

No, that was not the worst, she corrected herself a moment later, for she saw Dora Parkington strolling toward them, accompanied by two young men who were falling all over themselves to vie for her attention. Dora and the young men paused to chat with some of the people in Camellia's group, and Camellia was grateful that she was standing at the farthest point from Dora. Camellia saw Dora's eyes flicker toward her, then quickly away.

"Such a lovely ball, don't you agree, Miss Parkington?" one of the girls closest to Dora said. It was, Camellia reflected, a variation on the same remark she had heard at least fifty times this evening. She had even, God help her, said it herself.

Dora smiled as if it were a new and interesting question and nodded her head in agreement. "Yes, Lady Carr is such an elegant hostess." There was a murmur of agreement. "You would never realize, from looking at her, what a disappointment this must be for her. I mean, everyone knows Neville was supposed to marry Lady Priscilla, but now, of course, she will have an *American* as a daughter-in-law. One cannot help but feel sorry for her."

Camellia stiffened, anger surging up in her. One of the other girls glanced over at Camellia, and Dora followed her gaze. Dora let out a little gasp of surprise, her hand flying up to her mouth.

"Oh!" she cried in a sweet little voice, suddenly all blushes and stammers. "I'm sorry. I did not see you there, Miss Bascombe."

That, Camellia knew, was a lie. She had seen the girl look at her, and she was certain that Dora had insulted Lily on purpose to get a rise out of Camellia. But Camellia kept a firm grip on her temper. She wasn't about to let this girl draw her into a fight, in which Camellia, would naturally, come out looking like an uncouth American.

"I didn't mean anything bad," Dora went on appealingly. "I would never say anything to hurt anyone."

One of the suitors and another girl immediately began to murmur assurances that of course she would not. Camellia simply gave her a long, even look.

"It's quite all right, Miss Parkington," Camellia said. "I am sure that no one gave any weight to your words."

Beside Camellia, another young lady snickered, quickly smothering it. Dora's eyes widened in dramatic hurt, then filled with great crystal tears.

"Oh, p-please, Miss Bascombe, do not be so unkind. I don't know what I shall do if you don't forgive me."

Dora looked, Camellia thought, like a doll, perfect and porcelain, tears trembling on her dark lashes, and if Camellia had not been certain that Dora had arranged the entire scene, she would probably have felt sorry for her. One of the young men whipped out his handkerchief for Dora to dry her eyes, and one of the girls patted Dora's hand, shooting Camellia an accusing glare. Camellia's hands curled into fists, and she was aware of a strong desire to jab Dora right in her adorably pouting mouth.

That would be a social sin that would never be forgiven. But shouting at Dora would be only slightly less unpardonable, and even a sharp, angry exchange would be looked upon askance, especially after the faux pas Camellia had already committed by galloping in the park. There was nothing for it, she knew, but to get out of this situation as quickly and quietly as she could.

So with a supreme effort, she forced a smile onto her face. "Why, Miss Parkington, I wouldn't dream of being unkind to you, any more than you would be unkind to me. Now, if you will excuse me . . ."

Without waiting for an answer, Camellia slipped away from the group. Fury was shooting through her, making her almost tremble with the effort of suppressing it. She could not bear to stay in this room, among these people, a moment longer. Camellia headed for the door, skirting around groups of people in conversation. Within moments, she was in the corridor, walking as fast as she could away from the sounds of people. She passed a couple of closed doors and slipped around a corner into a back hall. Paintings graced one wall of the hallway, and the other was lined with tall windows that Camellia guessed looked over the garden when there was light enough to see. The corridor continued the length of the house, but it was soon intersected by another hall leading back toward the front. She turned up it and saw a door, half-opened, that led into a library.

Eager to escape anyone who might come looking for her, Camellia slipped through the door and closed it behind her. She sagged against the door, breathing a sigh of relief. The walls of the room were filled with books, and in the center of it was a conversational grouping of wingback chairs with small tables and lamps beside them. Camellia started toward the chairs.

Much to her surprise, there was a noise, and a man leaned out from one of the tall chairs, peering warily at her.

Chapter 9

"Oh." Camellia stopped, startled.

The man blinked, staring at her for a moment, then unfolded himself from the chair and stood to face her. He had a book in his hand, a finger holding his place.

"Hello." Camellia gazed back at him with more interest than she had felt all evening. This man looked . . . well, different. His dark reddish brown hair was mussed and flopping down over his forehead, and his neckcloth was askew, as though he had tugged at it. Round glass spectacles perched on his nose, somewhat obscuring his eyes and making it difficult to read his expression.

"Hello," he answered.

"I'm sorry. Am I intruding? I thought the room was empty."

"No. I mean—well, it's just me. That is . . ." He trailed off, a line of red creeping into his cheeks. "I'm sorry. I'm blathering."

Camellia smiled, liking him immediately. He had none of the stiffness or arrogance that she had seen in so many of the young men tonight. She strode forward, holding out her hand and saying, "I am Camellia Bascombe."

"Oh." He started to reach out his hand, then seemed to

remember his glasses and reached up to whip them off and stuff them into his jacket pocket before he shook her hand.

"What's your name?" Camellia asked, then hesitated, looking uncertain. "Or is that one of those things I shouldn't ask?"

"No. I'm the one who should apologize for not introducing myself. I'm, uh, Seyre."

"It's nice to meet you, Mr. Seyre." Camellia shook his hand.

"Yes. That is—" He stopped, then smiled, and his face lit up boyishly. "It's a pleasure to meet you, Miss Bascombe. Would you care to join me?" He gestured toward the chair across from his.

"I'd love it. I have been dying to escape for hours."

He laughed. "I'm afraid I never do well at this sort of thing—parties and talking and such." He lifted the book, looking rueful. "I'm more at ease with books."

"What are you reading?"

"Actually, I was reading a treatise on Newton's laws of motion." He looked a trifle sheepish.

"What are they?"

He raised his eyebrows a little. "Are you sure you want to hear?"

Camellia nodded. "Why not?"

"Well, the first is that a body in motion stays at the same rate of motion unless acted upon by an external force."

Camellia thought for a moment, then nodded. "That makes sense."

"The second is that a body is accelerated when a force acts on the mass, and the greater the mass, the greater the force would have to be. The formula is F equals ma."

"I don't know anything about formulas. But that means that you would have to push something to make it move."

"Exactly. Or if you hit a croquet ball with a mallet."

"And you have to push harder or hit it harder if it's heavier."

He smiled, nodding. "Exactly."

"That makes sense, too."

"The third, and last, is that for every action there's an equal and opposite reaction. Take the croquet mallet. When you hit the ball, the mallet moves back."

"That's like a gun." Camellia sat forward, intrigued. "When you fire, the gun recoils."

"Yes!" He, too, leaned forward.

"But surely it's not an equal thing. I mean, the bullet shoots out a lot farther than the gun comes back."

"Ah, but you see, that's the matter of the mass. The gun is much heavier than the bullet, so the force is the same, but the mass of the two objects is different, so their acceleration is not the same."

"I see." Camellia nodded. "That's interesting. I never learned anything like that. My mother and father taught us, but they weren't very interested in science and such. We read a lot of Shakespeare. And poetry."

"Science is fascinating." He paused. "Well, at least I think so. I'm afraid I tend to run on a bit about it. I hope I haven't bored you."

"No. It was interesting. I like things that are real. And practical. I'm not so fond of philosophy. And I'm not much of a reader. At least, not like my sister. Lily loves books—well, stories, not anything real." She grinned. "We're not very alike."

"I'm not very like my siblings, either."

"I'd rather ride than sit around reading."

"Given the way you ride, that's perfectly understandable."

Camellia looked at him blankly, then blushed. "Oh! Oh, no, did you see my infamous ride?"

Seyre laughed, showing even white teeth, and it occurred

to Camellia that she had never seen a smile more winning. She felt warmer somehow, just looking at him, and it surprised her how relieved she felt that he was smiling and laughing, not frowning in disapproval over her escapade.

"I did indeed see it, and I was awestruck."

"Now you are teasing me."

"No. Truly. I was impressed by your skill on a horse."

"Well, you are the only one," Camellia retorted wryly. "Everyone else seems to think it was scandalous." She shook her head. "I don't understand people here. They are concerned over such odd things. I understand why you wouldn't want someone galloping through the streets, but the path was virtually empty, so I can't see why it was a sin. And I can't fathom why it's right to wear a certain dress in the morning, but you'd never wear it to supper. Or why men have to have so many fobs upon their watch chain."

"That indeed is one of life's imponderables."

Camellia chuckled. "You're making fun of me."

"Only a little. I, too, see little reason for piling fobs onto a chain. But, then, I am often taken to task because I forget even to wear the watch."

"And why is everyone so enamored of titles? I overheard a girl earlier confiding to her friend that she intended to marry at least a baron. She wants a title, not a person. How does it make one a better person to be an earl instead of a plain mister?"

"I cannot see how it does."

"I'm so glad. I mean, you would not be any different if you were an earl, would you?"

"Indeed not."

"I would be the same person if someone called me *lady* instead of *miss*. It means nothing about you except that you were born into a certain family; it's nothing you've earned, nothing you've accomplished."

"A trick of fate," he agreed with a smile. "Being born first."

"Exactly."

He was silent for a moment, then said, "I take it you are not, ah, fond of our country? Do you wish you were back in America?"

Camellia shook her head. "No. I don't mind England, just some of the people I've met. I love Willowmere. And I love riding. I never had a horse back home."

"You've become this good a rider in the time you've been here?" he asked, surprise making his brows shoot up.

"Anyone at Willowmere will tell you, I've ridden nearly every day since we arrived. I'm not that good at jumping yet." She flashed a grin. "But I will be one day."

"I'm sure you will. You should try riding at Richmond Park. You'd enjoy it far more than trotting down Rotten Row." He described to her the large open park just outside the city, a frequent day trip for Londoners, with plenty of room to roam and to let mounts run.

The talk soon turned to the horse Camellia had left behind at Willowmere and then to Seyre's own steed. Her companion, Camellia realized, loved horses and riding as much as she, and so they chatted quite happily, moving on after a time from horses to Seyre's interest in farming and the experiments he was performing on his own land and then to America and in particular to Camellia's home there. He listened with fascination to her description of her father's peripatetic ways and of the various places in which they had lived as Miles Bascombe drifted, searching for a profession that suited him.

"He wasn't trained to be anything but a gentleman, you see," Camellia told her companion. "But that isn't very useful in a new country."

"No, I can see it wouldn't be. No doubt I would be in the same predicament."

Camellia smiled. "No, you, I think, would be a teacher—probably at a college."

He grinned back. "You are probably right. A bit dull, I'm afraid."

"No. Why?" Camellia frowned. "You can talk about almost anything."

"Would it were that easy," he murmured. He looked at her, uncertainty in his eyes, and started to speak.

At just that moment, a woman's voice said, "There you are! I knew I'd find you—" She stopped abruptly. "Camellia!"

Camellia and her companion turned to see Lady Vivian standing in the doorway. To Camellia's surprise, Seyre's cheeks reddened, and he stood up, tugging at his jacket.

"Er, hallo. I . . . um . . ."

"So both of you have been hiding in here!" Vivian continued merrily, smiling and walking toward them. "I'm glad you met my brother, Cam; I wanted to introduce you, but I couldn't find you anywhere."

"Your brother!" Camellia stared at her, stricken. "You mean the one who's a . . . a duke?" Her voice rose almost to a squeak at the end.

"Gregory! Do you mean you didn't introduce yourself?" Vivian scolded. "Really, if that isn't just like you. Camellia, this is my brother Gregory, Lord Seyre. And he's not a duke, not yet anyway. Gregory, this is Miss Camellia Bascombe—"

"Yes, no, I mean, I did introduce myself," Seyre said in a rush.

"Not entirely," Camellia murmured.

"Lily has been looking for you," Vivian told Camellia, her brows knitting at the dark expression on the girl's face. "I had come to tell you, Gregory, that I think I am ready to go home. I have developed a bit of a headache."

"Oh! Well, yes, of course." He cast a sideways glance at Camellia. "We'll, um, leave right away."

"Thank you. I'll go make our good-byes to Lady Carr." Vivian smiled and nodded to Camellia. "Good night, Camellia. I'll see you soon."

As soon as Vivian left the room, Camellia whipped around to face Seyre, fury and embarrassment surging up to replace the astonishment that Vivian's words had caused. "You lied to me!" she hissed.

"No! I didn't." He shoved a hand back into his hair, his eyes troubled. "I did tell you my name."

"But not who you were!" Camellia retorted. "You let me go rattling on about—about snobs and titles and everything! And all the while you were *laughing* at me!"

"No! No, please, Miss Bascombe. I wasn't laughing . . . I didn't mean . . . that is, I just wanted . . ." He trailed off, looking frustrated.

"What? You just wanted to see me make a fool of myself? Thank you, I have been managing that quite well on my own. I don't need any help from you!"

Camellia swung away. When he started after her, reaching out toward her arm, she whirled and glared at him. "Don't! I don't want to talk to you. I don't want to see you. Just leave me alone."

She turned and hurried from the room, striding down the hallway in the swift way she had been told a thousand times not to. She didn't care if she looked unfeminine. It was clear she was not a lady, so why bother trying to act like one?

Camellia was furious with herself as much as with Lord Seyre. She should have known better than to speak so openly and freely. She had been warned time and again about how dangerous it was to navigate the waters of the *ton*. *And to think that I had worried about Lily being too naïve and trusting!* Just because she had liked the man, because his smile had been so open and warm and he'd seemed, yes, even a bit shy and stammering, she had talked to him without restraint. She had revealed her dislike of the *ton*; she'd gone on and on about how silly titles were and how meaningless. And he had just let her! He hadn't had the common courtesy to tell her that he was a—well, whatever it was; she could not remember all these titles. But whatever his title was, he was next to being a duke, which he would someday become when his father died, and a duke, she knew, was as high as one could get without being a prince.

She had no doubt that inside he had been laughing at her the whole time. She remembered how she had asked him if he would be any better if he were an earl instead of what he was. There had been a little spark of amusement in his eyes as he had assured her he would not—having his own private little jest, of course, because an earl would be a step down for him. Camellia thought of all the social errors she must have committed while they were talking, starting with her having walked right up to him and introduced herself, something that no lady would ever do. She wondered if he would tell Vivian how badly she had misbehaved—or would he save the story to tell his friends over port and cigars?

When she reached the ballroom, Camellia found Eve and Fitz looking for her. They whisked her away to the midnight supper, and fortunately even Lily was exhausted enough from the excitement of the ball to want to go home soon after the supper.

Back home at Stewkesbury House, Lily linked her arm through Camellia's as they trudged upstairs. "I am so very tired. Aren't you, Cam? But it was a splendid evening, wasn't it?"

"Yes, and you were the most beautiful girl there."

Lily giggled. "Since Vivian was there, I can hardly claim that. And that Parkington girl is lovely, isn't she?" At Camellia's unladylike snort, Lily laughed. "I know. I felt the same way about her. She's just like Lady Sabrina back at Willowmere, only younger."

"And not as skillful," Eve commented from in front of them. "But give her time. I think she has the potential."

"Who are you talking about? That pretty little black-haired girl?" Fitz asked. "I thought she seemed rather sweet."

"That is because you are a man," his wife retorted, smiling. "She is very sweet toward men, I'm sure, especially handsome ones."

Fitz flashed a sideways grin at Eve. "Handsome, eh?"

"Yes, but don't get too full of yourself." Eve gazed back up at him, her tender smile at odds with her tart words.

Lily glanced at Camellia and giggled. "Come on, Cam, let's leave these two lovebirds alone. Come into my room, and we'll gossip about everything that happened tonight."

Camellia sighed inwardly. She wanted only to go to bed and nurse her wounded pride, but she followed her sister into her bedroom. Lily's maid was there to help them, but Lily sent the girl to bed, saying that she and Camellia would manage by themselves. As soon as the girl had left, Lily turned to Camellia.

"All right. What's the matter?" Lily came around behind her and began to unhook Camellia's gown.

"What?" Camellia looked at Lily blankly.

"With you. There's something bothering you. I could tell it as soon as I sat down at the table with you at supper. What happened?" Lily turned her back to Camellia so that Camellia could do the same service for her.

Camellia shrugged. "It doesn't matter. It was your big night, and we should talk about that."

Lily made a *pfft* noise and waved her hand, as if tossing aside the engagement party that had so occupied her thoughts for the past two weeks. "We can talk about that all day tomorrow. In fact, I'll insist on it. But right now, I want to know why you were looking like thunder at the supper table."

Camellia couldn't keep from frowning in memory, and soon the whole story came tumbling out, beginning with Dora Parkington's snide comments at the dance and ending with Vivian's coming into the library.

"What a horrid man!" Lily exclaimed, her eyes flashing. "I hope you gave him a good setdown."

The girls had slipped out of their dresses as they talked, and Lily handed Camellia her dressing gown, grabbing up a shawl to wrap around her own shoulders. She pulled Camellia over to the chair and stool in front of the fireplace. Firmly, she pushed her sister into the chair and plopped down on the stool herself, facing Camellia.

"I don't think I know how to give someone a setdown." Camellia smiled, relief sweeping through her at her sister's reaction to her news.

"You should learn. Or better yet, give him a 'bear-garden jaw.' "

"A what?" Camellia's smile turned into a laugh. "Where did you hear that?"

"Cousin Gordon. He was there tonight. Didn't you see him?"

"No, thank God. At least I was spared that. I'm not sure I could have borne to talk to him as well as Dora Parkington and Lord High Whatever Seyre, all in one evening."

"The Marquess of Seyre," Lily corrected, laughing. "That's right below a duke. Eve's been drilling the ranks into me."

"I don't care what his title is. He's a thoroughly detestable man. I know he was laughing at me the whole time."

"He has a most peculiar sense of humor, then. He ought to be thoroughly ashamed of himself."

Camellia laughed. Lily's typically emotional, unguarded response to Camellia's story had made her feel a great deal better.

"It was most vexatious, but it doesn't matter now. I shall make it a point to avoid him in the future." Camellia shrugged. She was not going to admit, even to her sister, that what made her feel the worst was that she had *liked* the man. It had been such fun to laugh with him, and she had felt a delicious little flutter in her stomach whenever he smiled at her. "I'm just glad that you—well, I was afraid that you might be unhappy with me."

"Me?" Lily looked amazed. "Why would I be upset with you?"

"For getting myself into the predicament. I shouldn't have done any of the things I did." Camellia began to tick her wrongs off on her fingers. "I talked too freely, not stopping to inquire or even to think about whether he had a title. I was alone with a man for a long time. I spoke to him without being introduced. In fact, I introduced myself to him. And then, when I found out who he was, I told him what I thought of him, so I was quite rude to a marquess, which I imagine does not stand one in good stead with the *ton*. What else—oh, yes, I was rude to Dora Parkington, too. I'm sure she will be spreading it about."

Lily grimaced. "What do I care what Dora Parkington thinks? Or her friends? And why would I get mad at you because that beastly man let you think he wasn't titled? It served him right for you to say rude things about titles and noblemen. It's exactly what he deserved. Less than he deserved, I'd say."

"It's just that—well, lately, you've been so, so caught up in all this—your wedding and the Carrs and the *ton* and all that. Sometimes I think—I feel as though things aren't the same anymore. That you and I aren't—"

Lily stared. "Aren't what? Sisters?"

"Of course we're sisters. But maybe not in the same way we used to be. That we've grown . . . apart a little, I guess. That you're different."

"I'm not!" Lily cried, reaching out and taking Camellia's hands. "How can you say that? I haven't changed. I mean, not in any way that's important. I have been trying to please

Neville's mother because I love him so much, and it would be dreadful if she hated me, and I feared she might, you know, because of his being supposed to marry Priscilla. So I have been trying to learn all the titles and their precedence and all that sort of thing. But that doesn't mean I've changed. You know I've always been romantic, and I like parties and clothes and all those things you don't. But I'm the same old Lily—only in marvelous gowns!"

Camellia laughed and hugged her sister. "Of course you are. I'm the one who's being silly. I'm just an old grump at the prospect of being left to live out my days with only Cousin Oliver for company."

"But I'm not going anywhere!" Lily protested. "I mean, well, of course I am, because I have to go visit Neville's dragon of a grandmother—which is absolutely terrifying. But I'll only be gone a month or so, and then I'll be back. And after Neville and I are married, why, you can come live with us. I'll be an old married lady and all the chaperone you need!"

"Silly! As if I would shove myself into your lives with you just married!" Camellia retorted. "It's all right. I have become resigned to being a spinster and growing old at Willowmere. I daresay Cousin Oliver and I will manage to stay out of one another's way. We have well enough so far." She looked into Lily's eyes. "Are you really scared of meeting his grandmother?"

"Heavens, yes! She sounds like an utter tyrant. I'm scared of all of them. I'll be all by myself with them, and I've never gone anywhere without you. Neville will be there, but it won't be the same. I mean, he's accustomed to them, and he doesn't think they're that fearsome—except for his grandmother. They all live in dread of her. But he doesn't understand how I feel so . . . so oppressed by the thought of them. I'm so scared I'll do or say something wrong. That they'll think I'm a horrible American nobody and not good enough for Neville."

"You're good enough for anyone," Camellia assured her stoutly. "Don't forget that. Neville is lucky to have you. The whole family is lucky that you came along, or they'd still be trying to get Neville to marry. Only Priscilla would have run off with her fellow, and there wouldn't even be someone he was obliged to ask."

Lily laughed. "So I did them all a favor, didn't I? It's a good thing I came to England so that Neville could fall in love."

"Absolutely right."

"Then I guess we are both wonderful people, and this whole silly *ton* better realize that!"

"That's right."

They smiled at each other, their moods considerably improved.

"Now," Lily said in a confidential tone, "tell me all about the horrid Dora . . ."

When Vivian came down to breakfast the next morning, she found her father and brother both there before her, dressed for their journey and almost finished with their meal.

"You really are determined to go today?" she asked, looking from one to the other.

"Yes." The duke nodded his head decisively. "That doctor gave me leave to go, and I'm not staying around to let him change his mind. I can walk with a cane, and I can work up to walking without one just as well at home as here. Better, in fact. I've got more space to roam about in."

"I will worry about you."

"No need. I'm going to be a good patient." He gave her

a wry smile. "I promise. I won't invite any of my friends. I shall be abstemious in eating and drinking. And Gregory will be there to be a mother hen. One of you is ample."

"But what will I do for company?" Vivian responded. "Now I shall have to invite Cousin Katherine to come be my chaperone."

"I didn't notice her here when we arrived," her father shot back. "Besides, Katherine's no bother. One hardly knows she's around. I'll return later. Once I've gotten to where I can walk without looking like a child in leading strings tottering about. I've never missed an entire Season yet."

He pushed back his plate and rose to his feet, a lengthier process than it used to be. When Gregory started to rise, he waved him back to his seat. "No, don't get up yet. Stay and talk to your sister. It takes me a while to get ready these days."

Gregory sank back down, and both he and his sister watched as their father picked up his cane and thumped his way out the door.

Vivian frowned. "He'll be all right, won't he?"

"The doctor seems to think he's doing all right. He hasn't had another apoplexy, and I gather that's encouraging. Of course, who knows how long he will stay with his new way of living."

"I suspect that fully adhering to it would be too much to ask of him," Vivian said.

"No doubt you're right. Still, I do think he's scared enough that he will adjust his habits."

"Hopefully." Vivian picked up a piece of toast and took a bite, her eyes twinkling as she looked across the table at her brother. "What about you? Wouldn't you like to linger in London a little longer? You seemed rather taken with my friend Camellia."

A dull red color crept up Gregory's neck. "No. I mean,

yes, she was quite, um, nice. But I'm no good with women. You know that. Besides, she'll doubtless have scores of suitors hanging about her. It stands to reason; she's so pretty."

Vivian stared at her brother. "Gregory! Do you really like her? I was just teasing . . ."

He shook his head, not looking at her. "Don't be silly. I barely know the girl. She was, um, easy to talk to. Anyway, it doesn't matter. She dislikes me thoroughly."

"What?" Vivian's brows shot up. "I doubt that. The two of you were chatting away when I came into the library."

"Yes, well . . ." He shrugged. "Things change rather quickly sometimes. Don't worry about it." He straightened, looking alarmed. "And *don't* say anything to her about me. I am not about to have my sister trying to matchmake for me, too."

"No, I won't. Not if you don't want me to." Vivian regarded Seyre thoughtfully.

The more he said, the more Vivian wondered if her brother was interested in Camellia. It certainly gave her something to think about. Vivian would enjoy having Camellia for a sister-in-law. She certainly was not above a bit of subtle matchmaking. Still . . . it was hard for her to picture her shy brother with someone as blunt and high-spirited as Cam. It would be awful to encourage him to pursue Camellia if Camellia did not return his affection. It was nonsense, of course, for Gregory to think that Camellia disliked him. It was typical of her brother to be unaware of the appeal of his good looks and kind disposition.

But Camellia might only like him as a friend. Vivian had never noticed the girl seeming particularly interested in any man. She might regard Gregory in the same way she did her male cousins. No, it would be much better to wait and see on this matter. After all, there was plenty of time. It wasn't as if either of them was likely to jump into marriage anytime soon.

Before long, the duke and Seyre departed. Vivian bade them a fond farewell, then turned back to the suddenly empty-seeming house. What, she wondered, was she to do now? She could pay calls, of course. The Season was well under way, and most people she knew had returned. Or she could go to Stewkesbury House and spend the afternoon discussing the party of the night before with Eve and Lily and Camellia. But then she might run into Oliver, and it was better, she thought, to let him spend a few days away from her.

Vivian smiled to herself. She wasn't sure what she expected to come of this little dance she and Oliver were performing. Not anything permanent, of course. She had meant it when she told Oliver that she did not intend to marry. She might have intimated to him that she had a good deal more knowledge and sophistication about men than she actually did, but her firm opinion was that marriage was an institution that did not favor women and that a woman should be just as able as a man to engage in affairs without having to shackle herself for life. That Vivian had never actually done so did not matter. She had simply never found a man who interested her enough . . . until now.

The height of absurdity was that it should be the steady, responsible Earl of Stewkesbury who should catch her eye. There were men more handsome—his brother Fitz, for one. And certainly there were men more charming; she could rattle off the names of a handful. But just something about the way his mouth curved up on one side and his pewter-gray eyes lit in shared amusement melted her inside. Even when he was at his most annoying, she did not wish him somewhere else; oddly, arguing with him was entertaining. Invigorating. Pitting her determination against his resistance offered a challenge she could not resist.

Best of all, with Oliver there would be no question of

either of them falling in love. Vivian was certain by now that she was not a woman who was apt to tumble into love. And Oliver was the sort of practical, unemotional man whose head ruled him, not his heart. Only his sense of propriety held him back, and once she had breached that wall, they could have an affair that would be mutually satisfactory. There would be no need to worry about fallen expectations or bruised feelings. When it was all over, they would go their separate ways, with no hearts broken.

However, pleasant as it was to think about, Vivian knew that she must step back for the moment. Stewkesbury was not a man to be pushed, and Vivian was certainly not the sort to dangle after a man. No, Oliver would have to come to her, she thought, not the other way around.

That left her with nothing to do that particularly interested her. Even the prospect of planning the ball she would have in a month or two for the Bascombe sisters did not appeal. She supposed she could simply wait to receive afternoon callers, but that seemed an even more lackluster way to spend the day.

So it was with real pleasure that she received a note an hour later from Lady Mainwaring. Kitty could be counted on to keep life interesting. Vivian broke the seal and unfolded the letter. Her eyebrows floated upward as she read:

> *Dearest Vivian,*
> *I am in the most dreadful straits! I must see you on a matter of the most VITAL importance. Please, please, call on me this afternoon. I would not ask you were I not on the Edge of Despair!*
>
> *Yr Loving Godmother,*
> *Kitty, Lady Mainwaring*

Chapter 10

Vivian was not alarmed. She was familiar enough with Lady Kitty Mainwaring's ways to know that the woman's proclamations of disaster usually contained as little truth as her claim to be Vivian's godmother. Lady Kitty had been her father's friend and longtime mistress, and she had lavished Vivian with a careless but heartfelt affection throughout the often lonely years of Vivian's childhood. Vivian doubted that the situation was anywhere near as dire as Lady Kitty claimed, but she welcomed the prospect of visiting her.

She sat down to dash off a reply to Kitty to expect her that afternoon, then went upstairs to dress. Shortly after luncheon, Vivian set off in her carriage for the Mainwaring mansion, a great gray-stone pile of a house, built after the Great Fire and in an area that was no longer the most fashionable part of London. Its location had vexed Lady Kitty, but on that point her much older husband had refused to budge, and she had become resigned to the place over the years, opining that at least it was closer to the gambling clubs she favored.

Vivian was accustomed to visiting her friend there; Kitty never called on her. Kitty had married young to a man poles apart from her not only in years, but also in temperament and interests. Her marriage had been for duty and prestige, and like a number of others of her generation and class, she had looked outside her marriage for love and affection. Kitty, however, had been less discreet than many, and because of her scandal-marked past, she was no longer received in the very best households. She did not mind, she told Vivian, for she cared more about enjoying her life than she did about pleasing the ladies of the *ton*. Vivian knew that Kitty's behavior had been no worse than her own father's—better, really, for Kitty did not drink to excess and carouse with her friends—and Vivian found it unfair that her father was not exiled from society, but Kitty was, simply because she was a woman. Vivian had told Kitty so and had assured her many times that Kitty was always welcome at her house, but Kitty would not call on her, not wanting to bring any question to bear on Vivian's behavior.

When Vivian arrived, she was shown into the drawing room, where her old friend sat with Wesley Kilbothan, the "poet" who was currently her "protégé." Lady Kitty rose with a cry of pleasure and held out her hands to Vivian. Though in her fifties, Kitty was still an attractive woman with golden blond hair miraculously untouched by gray and cornflower blue eyes. If her figure had thickened a little over the years and her complexion faded, those were kept hidden with stays and a subtle application of lip rouge, and her blue silk round dress was in the latest fashion. Diamonds winked at her ears and fingers, and a sapphire necklace graced her throat.

"Vivian, my love, how entrancing you look! Doesn't she, Mr. Kilbothan?" Kitty half turned toward the man, who had politely arisen at Vivian's entrance and now stood waiting to greet her.

"Indeed—but then, Lady Vivian always looks enchanting." Kilbothan came closer and made an impeccable bow.

He was a slender man of medium height, whose age Vivian would have guessed to be around forty. His face was attractive in a sharp way, with a narrow nose and lean cheeks, his brows flying slashes of black. He was well dressed, wearing a jacket of bottle green kerseymere, with a shirt of white cambric and a waistcoat of a green-and-blue floral pattern. And if his collar points were higher and his clothing more colorful than, say, Lord Stewkesbury's, he was no dandy, either. He was, as always, polite and well-spoken, yet Vivian could not find it in herself to like the man. She was aware that her distrust, even dislike, of the man stemmed from the fear that he was taking advantage of the generous and loving Kitty, but that knowledge did not make her feelings any kindlier toward him.

The look he sent toward Vivian was knowing as he went on, "I fear I must leave you ladies. The Muse is calling, and one must not ignore her."

"Of course, dear." Lady Kitty smiled and watched him walk out of the room. She heaved a little sigh of satisfaction. "Such a lovely man. And so thoughtful. Dear Wesley knew I wanted to speak with you alone."

"And I am eager to speak to you." Vivian led her friend over to the sofa. "Now tell me, what has brought you to such a pass?"

"Oh, it is the most idiotic thing!" Something more like exasperation than despair flashed across the older woman's face. "But that can wait. First, you must tell me about your father. I heard he had been carried to London, all but on death's door. Tell me it isn't so!"

"It certainly is not. I would have written to tell you if it were so serious." Vivian smiled. Kitty was not fond of bad news, so Vivian kept the story light. "He had a bit of a turn, that is all, and Gregory wanted to make sure he was fine. He does not trust the doctor at home—Gregory, I mean; Papa, as you know, quite likes the man, for the doctor allows Papa to bully him."

Kitty chuckled, her fondness for the duke evident in her eyes. "Of course. Then Marchester is not ill?"

Vivian knew how little her father would like her telling his former lover about his physical ailments, and she knew how equally little Lady Kitty wanted to learn that her former lover was vulnerable to the effects of age. It was better all around not to delve too deeply into the details of her father's condition. "The doctor says he must reform the way he lives."

"Well! *That* will make Marchester ill."

"I have no idea how long Papa's good intentions will last. But for the moment, at least, he is willing to change in order not to have to see the doctor again. He and Gregory have returned to the Hall already."

"Without even gambling or going to parties?" Kitty looked alarmed.

Vivian shrugged. "I believe he felt the need to recover in the peace of the country."

Lady Kitty looked vaguely puzzled. "I suppose . . . if it makes him feel better. Although, my dear, I never could understand why everyone says the country is peaceful. All those birds set up such a clatter at dawn, and the dogs bark at just everything, and that dreadful peacock of Mainwaring's! I nearly fainted the first time I heard it screech. It's a wonder to me that anyone can have any rest there. Although at Marchester, Buttons was always careful to have them put me on the side away from the stables and the kennels, and he wasn't foolish enough to have a peacock, thank God."

"'Buttons'?" Vivian repeated, gaping at her. "Are you talking about my father?"

Kitty let out a trill of tinkling laughter. "Oh, my, yes, that was my nickname for him. And the way he got it was so amus—" She cut a sideways glance at Vivian and stopped, clearing her throat. "Perhaps that's a story best left untold."

Vivian suppressed a smile. "Dear Kitty, why don't you tell me why you wrote me?"

Kitty sighed. "Oh, Viv, I have made a dreadful mistake. I cannot think what your papa would say." She paused, considering. "Actually, Marchester would doubtless tell me not to worry my head about it—that is always what he would say when I'd done something foolish. He would think nothing of it, for he is not a man who cares about possessions."

It seemed an odd thing to say about a man who owned seven homes, at least that many vehicles, several stables of horses, and baubles, paintings, and statues too numerous to detail, but Vivian understood what her friend meant. The duke had never been unduly attached to anything he owned. He had no interest in possessing things simply to have them.

"I don't understand, Kitty. What are you talking about?"

"The brooch your father gave me. Do you remember it? It was diamond and shaped like a heart in a circle."

Vivian nodded. She had spent much of her time with Lady Kitty exploring that woman's jewelry box, and she remembered the diamond brooch well. It was beautiful, a large center diamond cut in the shape of a heart, blazing with that special fire of diamonds, surrounded by a circle of smaller stones.

"He gave me other things, of course. Your father was nothing if not generous. I treasure them all. But that brooch was my particular favorite. I remember he told me I was his heart when he gave it to me." Kitty smiled mistily.

"Did something happen to the brooch?" Vivian asked, bringing the conversation back to the point. "Did you lose it—oh! Do not tell me! Was it stolen from you?"

"Stolen! Lud, girl, no. Though one could say it was, for

I was certain that I would win. I cannot imagine how Sir Rufus could have managed to win all three tricks—it was most absurd. I was wearing my lucky turban—the dark blue velvet one with the feather that curls round. Well, I hardly ever lose when I wear it—or at least not a great deal of money, which is, you will allow, as much as one can ask for some evenings."

Vivian reached out and took the older woman's hand. "Dearest ma'am, pray tell me—are you saying that you lost the brooch in a card game?"

"Yes, of course. I would not have given it up for the world, but I was certain I would win, so it seemed only a small risk. I had run out of all my money, and Sir Rufus said he would not take a vowel. Can you imagine? The man is most rude; I think the rumors must be right that his grandfather was in trade."

"Are you unable to buy it back from him?"

"I have tried!" Kitty's eyes flashed with indignation. "The truth is, I contracted a case of catarrh right after that, and I was laid up for a week or two, and I quite forgot it. But when I was feeling better, I went to get it from my box to wear, and I remembered that Sir Rufus had it. So I sent a note round to the man. I had a new month's allowance then, you see, so I was quite able to buy it back—which Sir Rufus knew I wanted to do. I had told him so that very evening I lost it, and he said, of course, he would rather have the money. But when I tried to pay him, he sent me back a note telling me it was too late! I had forfeited it!" Kitty's eyes filled with tears, and her mouth crumpled. "He is the meanest thing! I know he did it just to punish me, for he told me once that I am unreliable. Unreliable! I always pay my gambling debts; you know I do. Sometimes I may forget for a while or I have to sell a bit of silver or some such thing, but I never default."

"Of course not," Vivian replied soothingly, patting her

hand. "It's most unreasonable of Sir Rufus not to let you redeem it. I take it you hope that I might be able to retrieve the brooch for you?"

"Would you?" Kitty, her face lighting up, gripped Vivian's hand tightly. "I hated to ask, but I didn't know where to turn. I did not tell dear Wesley, for he quite dislikes my gambling. But then I thought of you. You are so good at getting things accomplished."

"I shall certainly do my best. I shall write Sir Rufus immediately. I do not know him well, but I have met him once or twice when Papa had one of his card parties."

"There, I knew you would rescue me." Kitty beamed at Vivian and reached up to pat her cheek. "You are such a dear girl." Kitty relaxed, apparently putting the matter out of her mind with ease. "Now, let us talk of something more interesting. What are you doing these days? Does the Season promise to be exciting? You are in such good looks—you are always beautiful, of course, but there is such a glow about you today—" She stopped, her eyes narrowing shrewdly. "There is a man, isn't there?"

Startled, Vivian could not help but laugh. "No, no. I mean, well, perhaps there is a man. But nothing serious."

"But why? Who is it? Is he not an eligible *parti*?"

"He is most eligible. But I am quite on the shelf and intend to remain there. You know I do not believe in marriage."

"It *is* so often a drudgery," Lady Kitty agreed. "But, my dear, you could have any man you want. You needn't marry for wealth or family or anything but your own heart. I wonder now and then how my life would have been if I had married your father instead of Mainwaring." The corner of her mouth turned down, but then she smiled, her eyes twinkling. "Not, of course, that I had the chance, for I did not even meet your father until after both of us were married."

"Nevertheless . . . I do not intend to take the risk."

"Well, a flirtation is always fun." Kitty cut her eyes at Vivian. "Or perhaps more than a flirtation?"

Vivian could not keep the smile from her lips. "Perhaps . . . I am not sure."

"Who is this man? Do I know him?"

"The Earl of Stewkesbury."

Kitty's eyebrows lifted. "Eligible indeed! A veritable pattern card. But, surely . . . a trifle dull?"

Vivian laughed. "Not necessarily."

"I knew his father—a handsome man; those Talbots generally are. Lawrence Talbot was one who knew how to live for the moment; I always liked that in a man."

"Kitty! Do not tell me you and Oliver's father—"

"No, no, my goodness. He was madly in love with his wife, though God knows they fought as heartily as they loved one another. Not Oliver's mother, of course—she died rather young, and I never knew her—but Barbara, Fitz's mother. Now Fitz Talbot—there is a man worth setting one's cap for. Married now, I hear." Kitty sighed.

"Yes, to my friend Eve—you remember her."

"Indeed. A pretty little thing—parson's daughter, wasn't she? But I always heard that Oliver was more like the old earl than his father. Lord Reginald was a terrible sobersides."

"Mm. He was rather . . . rigid, as I recall. But Oliver was close to him; he reveres him. Perhaps too much so, for there is more than that in his nature; he does not let it out often enough."

"That is what you intend to do?" Kitty chuckled. "Let it out?"

"Maybe. I—oh, Kitty, I feel differently about him than any other man."

"Goodness." Kitty blinked. "In what way?"

"I'm not sure. When he is about, I feel . . . excited . . . on edge, but in a good way. Do you know what I mean?"

"Indeed I do. But I have never heard you say so before."

"I have not felt so. I have flirted with other men. One or two have made my pulse quicken. But Oliver—" Vivian paused, looking a little surprised. "I had not thought of it before, but I trust Oliver. I feel safe with him. That must sound silly, for what could be less exciting than feeling safe? But I know I can do or say what I please, and he will not use it to seek an advantage. I know he does not want anything from me."

Kitty's brows soared again. "Does not want you? No, Lawrence's son could not be so poor-spirited, even with his grandfather raising him."

Vivian laughed. "No, I do not mean that. He wants me, but he does not *want* to want me. What I mean is, he has no need for my money or influence. He has no interest in marrying me. Indeed, he told me quite plainly that I would not suit as his countess." Her eyes brimmed with laughter. "It would have been quite lowering if it had not been so freeing. It isn't only fortune hunters whose eyes turn greedy at the sight of a duke's daughter." She tilted her head to one side, thinking. "On the other hand, sometimes Stewkesbury is utterly maddening, and I cannot understand why I like him at all."

"He is a man, dear. One must expect that. But if he makes you happy, that is the important thing. There is nothing like the feeling that rushes up in you when that special man walks into the room." Kitty smiled reminiscently. "I know that there are a number of people who think I have led a wicked life. But I can tell you this: I would not trade my life for theirs. When I look back on it, I have no regrets. When happiness offers itself, even for the moment, one must seize it. Else, you will never know what you might have had, will you?"

"No. You're right."

"Now then, tell me." Kitty scooted closer, her eyes sparkling with eagerness. "How did this come about? I want to know all the details."

Smiling, Vivian began to tell her.

Vivian found it harder to keep her promise to Kitty than she had expected. She sent a note to Sir Rufus, requesting that he call upon her as soon as possible. She expected a reply or a visit, but she was surprised when her footman returned with the news that Sir Rufus was not in the city, having retired to his country home for an indefinite stay.

What a bother, she thought. Letters were never as effective as visiting in person, particularly when one wanted something. She wondered where the man's country estate was. If it wasn't far from one of her father's houses, perhaps she could make a trip to that house and, while she was there, pay a call on Sir Rufus. As she sat, pondering the notion, the butler entered, announcing the arrival of the Earl of Stewkesbury.

"Oliver!" she exclaimed, bouncing to her feet and going toward him, beaming. "Just the man I wanted to see."

He raised his brows slightly in surprise. "Indeed? I am fortunate. I think."

"You always know this sort of thing. Where does Sir Rufus Dunwoody live?"

"Sir Rufus?" His expression registered even more astonishment. "What in the world do you want with that old bag of wind?"

Vivian laughed. "Why, Oliver, what a tactless thing to say."

"Tact is a useless commodity with you," he retorted. "I believe he lives near Grosvenor Square."

"No, not here. His estate in the country."

"Oh, that's in Kent, I believe. Why?"

Vivian shrugged. "I just wondered."

He gave her a narrowed look. "What are you up to?"

"Up to?" She widened her eyes innocently. "Why should I be up to anything?"

"No doubt you should not. But you have that certain look in your eye. Why do you want to know about Sir Rufus's estate?"

"Well . . ." Vivian gestured toward the sofa in an invitation to sit and took a seat herself on the chair at right angles to it. "I went to see Lady Mainwaring yesterday."

Oliver sighed. "I know you did."

"You did? How? It was only yesterday afternoon."

"Gossip travels quickly in the *ton*. You know that. Even when the person in question is no longer accepted. I should say, especially when the person involved is no longer accepted."

"Is that why you came here?" Vivian's voice took on a dangerous coolness. "To lecture me about Lady Mainwaring?"

"No. I have no desire to lecture you."

"And yet, remarkably, you do it so often."

"Vivian . . . you know as well as I do how everyone talks. How it looks for you to visit someone with the sort of . . . of past that Lady Mainwaring possesses."

Vivian's eyes flashed. "Lady Kitty is my friend. She has been my father's friend for years and—"

"It is precisely her relationship with your father that is the problem. Your father and a number of other men, including the chap who is living in her house now—her protégé, indeed. The day Lady Mainwaring ever cared about poetry . . ."

Vivian jumped to her feet. "I will not listen to you speak against Lady Kitty. I know what censorious people like you say about her, but she has never been anything but kindness itself to me. And I am not the sort of person to desert my friends because other people hold them in poor regard."

Oliver rose, too, saying rather ruefully, "Pray, do not ring a peal over my head. I do not dislike Lady Mainwaring. She is a charming and lovely woman. But she is not an appropriate companion for a young, unmarried lady."

Vivian shot him a disgusted look. "Well, neither am I appropriate, according to you."

"It is scarcely the same. The things you do are the result of your liveliness, your high spirits and disregard for others' opinions."

Vivian's brows rose. "Careful, Stewkesbury, you will find yourself saying something nice about me."

"I could say any number of nice things about you, and you know it. You must be aware of the way I—but that is neither here nor there. The point is that these small indiscretions all accumulate, Vivian."

"Indiscretions?" If her voice had been cool before, it was iced now. "Pray, what, exactly, are you referring to?"

"Calling on a lady no longer accepted in the best circles. It might not be commented upon if it were done by a woman, even an unmarried one, whose own actions were unremarkable. But you—you call attention to yourself. You flout convention."

"I do not call attention to myself. I do as I choose, and I cannot help it if other people feel it necessary to talk about what I do."

"That is exactly what I mean." His tone roughened with irritation. "You drive a high-perch phaeton."

"There are other ladies who do it."

"Not many, and I cannot think of another who is not married."

"It is scarcely a crime to be unmarried. You are not."

"There is a certain standard expected of a young unmarried

woman of good breeding. And it does not include arriving at parties with a monkey upon your shoulder."

Vivian stared at him for an instant in astonishment, then let out a laugh. "That was four years ago! And it did not cost me my place in the beau monde, if you will notice."

"No, but it caused a great deal of talk. As, no doubt, you driving a high-perch phaeton does. Not to mention the fact that you are living here alone without a chaperone in sight."

"I am surprised you are willing to tarnish your reputation by calling on me, then."

"I am serious, Vivian. Now you are talking about purchasing a house, moving out of your father's house and living alone. You visit Lady Mainwaring. You are happy to tell anyone your unorthodox views on marriage and women and affairs."

Vivian crossed her arms. "And you think such things put me beyond the pale?"

"They create talk. And, given the fact that you are sponsoring two young girls through their first Season, one would think that you might be more careful in your behavior."

"If you are so concerned about your cousins being seen in the company of someone as scandalous as I, then perhaps you should remove them from my influence. As for what I do and say, it is none of your business. Nor do I plan to drop one of my dearest friends because of the opinions of some sanctimonious, stiff-necked prigs. Lady Kitty asked for my help, and I intend to give it to her."

"I am not talking about removing Lily and Camellia from your company. Nor am I trying to dictate to you whom you should see. But I wish you would have a care for your reputation! Once it is lost, it is not easily recovered. And—wait." He paused, his brows swooping together. "What do you mean, you are going to help Lady Mainwaring? Help her how? What are you thinking of doing?"

"Nothing scandalous, I assure you. I am merely trying to recover a piece of jewelry she lost in a card game to Sir Rufus. He refused to sell it back to her, and she is exceedingly distraught over the whole matter. It is something my father gave her and quite dear to her."

"Is that why you asked me where he lived? Are you planning to write him about the matter?"

"If he is as close as Kent, I think I shall ask him in person. I find it works much better."

"Alone? You are planning on going to Kent and confronting him on your own?"

"It's Kent. Scarcely the ends of the earth. If he is close enough, I could go and return in one day."

"Vivian! An unmarried young lady driving out to visit some old roué? No."

Vivian pursed her mouth thoughtfully. "While Sir Rufus is much given to gambling and drink, I do not think he can be said to be a libertine."

Oliver's color rose at her lighthearted answer. "That scarcely makes it acceptable. You cannot go to his estate alone."

Vivian faced him, planting her hands on her hips. "Just how do you plan to stop me?"

"I don't. I am going with you."

Chapter 11

Oliver arrived the next morning while Vivian was still at the breakfast table. She looked up in surprise, and amusement sparkled in her eyes.

"Stewkesbury! I had not realized you intended to join me for breakfast."

He cast a look at her plate. "I ate breakfast over an hour ago, thank you."

Vivian sighed. "Ah, I see, you are one of those depressing sorts who find it a virtue to rise and eat at the crack of dawn."

"Hardly the crack of dawn, my lady. It is nine o'clock. I am here to escort you to Sir Rufus's house. Surely you cannot have forgotten."

"I have not forgotten." She smiled and waved a hand toward the chair across the table from her. "Sit down and have a cup of tea, at least. It will be a while; I am not yet dressed."

He raised his brow as he turned a pointed look at her. "You appear dressed to me."

She chuckled. "This is a simple round dress, Oliver. I have to put on a carriage dress and half boots for traveling. And my hair is not even up." She gestured toward the fat braid of bright red hair that hung over her shoulder and trailed across her breast.

His eyes lingered for a moment on the rope of hair before he pulled them away and concentrated on the cup of tea the footman was pouring.

"Clearly you are not accustomed to traveling with women," Vivian went on lightly.

"I am not accustomed to traveling with you."

Vivian smiled. "Now, Oliver, don't be surly. We have all day, you know, and you said it was not far."

"It is not, but one does have to start. If we hope to get there and back in one day, we must leave in the morning."

"Yes, yes, I know." Vivian sighed and stood up. "I shall go up immediately and dress."

Only thirty minutes later, not the hour Oliver had expected, Vivian returned in a rust-colored carriage dress with a high-collared, snug-fitting bodice. Supple black leather gloves and a jaunty little tipped-forward hat matched the black braid that decorated the bodice and hem of the dress.

"There," she said as she strolled toward Oliver, who was seated on a bench in the entryway. "I am ready—though I shall blame it on you that I look all thrown together."

Oliver grinned, rising and extending his arm for her. "Stop fishing for compliments. You look stunning, as always, and you know it. You wouldn't leave the house otherwise."

Vivian cast him a sidelong laughing glance. " 'Tis nice to hear it, nevertheless."

The earl's carriage waited outside, and Oliver handed her up into it, then climbed in after her, taking the seat across from her. Vivian settled back into the luxurious leather seat, noting the hot, wrapped brick in case her feet grew cold and the folded lap robe on the seat. She smiled across the carriage at Oliver.

"You have provided all the comforts, I see."

"I could hardly have you arriving at Sir Rufus's house

frozen like an icicle. My butler would have put it in anyway; he was highly offended that I suggested he do so."

Vivian felt sure that Oliver's butler would indeed have thought of all the creature comforts for the earl and his guest, but Vivian could not keep from feeling a warm little tickle of pleasure that Oliver had obviously thought of her comfort, as well.

"You needn't have made the trip," Oliver went on, spoiling her mood a trifle. "I wish you would have let me go to retrieve the blasted brooch for you."

"Mm. I can hear how happy such an errand would make you. Anyway, I could not ask it of you. It is *my* duty, not yours. You don't even like Kitty."

He looked affronted. "I don't dislike Lady Mainwaring. She is a charming woman."

Vivian rolled her eyes. "Just not one I should visit."

Oliver sighed. "I know you are going to visit her. Just as you're going to run this errand for her. It's not in you to value your reputation over a friendship."

Vivian looked at him quizzically. "Would you value me more highly if I did?"

He smiled ruefully. "No. You know I would not. I just wish you would have a care, Vivian. People are eager to talk, and you have so few qualms about giving them something to talk about."

Vivian shrugged. "It's not my concern if people like to wag their tongues about me." She fell silent for a moment, then said in a quiet voice, "The Hall was such a huge, lonely, dark place—just me and my brothers, and, of course, they were older and could do all number of things that I could not because I was a girl. I enjoyed it when my aunt Millicent came to visit." Vivian cast a sparkling glance his way. "You know, the radical one who taught me about those dangerous things like Mary Wollstonecraft and the rights of women."

He gave her a dry look in return, the corner of his mouth twitching with amusement.

"But when Lady Kitty came to visit," Vivian went on, "it was as if the house came to life. She lit up the rooms. The Hall would suddenly be full of people and talk and laughter. Papa would trot me out to greet them all, but only Lady Kitty wanted to do more than see me. She would come up to the nursery and sit and talk to Gregory and Jerome and me. It was wonderful. Gregory said he remembered our mother doing so, but of course I could not. Kitty wore such beautiful dresses and jewels. She glittered. I could not help but love her."

"It must have been hard for you," Oliver said. "After Father married Barbara, they were usually gone to London, but I had Royce and then Fitz. And there was my grandfather."

"Your parents preferred London?"

"Yes. Willowmere was very far away from it. They were home for only a couple of months each winter—except when Barbara was carrying Fitz and for a little while after that. They loved the excitement of the city, the Season." He paused, "I understand your fondness for Lady Mainwaring. I'm glad that she was there when you were young."

Vivian smiled. "She is to blame for my love of jewels. She was never without her jewelry case—a huge wooden thing with drawers and doors and even hidden compartments. Only Kitty's personal maid was allowed to carry it. In the evening, as her maid was dressing her and doing her hair up for dinner, Kitty would let me sit on the floor and go through the jewelry box and try them all on. I remember that I would put her sapphire necklace on my head like a tiara." Vivian chuckled softly.

"I am sure you looked like a princess."

Her laughter increased. "I looked like a skinny little thing with a necklace on her mop of orange hair. But I *felt* wonderful."

They continued to talk as the carriage rolled along, their conversation ranging freely from Vivian's childhood to their memories of summers at Willowmere to the latest scandals of the London *ton*. In this manner the first two hours of their drive passed far more quickly than either of them would have imagined.

Oliver, checking his watch, announced in a self-satisfied voice that they would be back in London by the time evening fell. Just as he tucked his watch away, they rounded the corner and came upon a carriage with a broken wheel sitting by the side of the road. Two women sat on a trunk just beyond the carriage, parasols raised, looking on glumly as a man struggled with the broken wheel.

There was nothing for it but to stop and offer assistance. While Oliver's coachman assisted the other driver in removing the wheel, Vivian and Oliver helped the two women into Oliver's carriage and listened to their tale of travel woes. It took over an hour to get the wheel off and secured to the back of Stewkesbury's carriage, then take the travelers into the next village. Afterward, the pair of women—a mother and a daughter returning from a visit to an ailing aunt—insisted that Vivian and Oliver partake of luncheon with them.

Therefore, Oliver's carriage rolled up in front of Ashmont, Sir Rufus's country house, closer to midafternoon than noon. There they discovered that Sir Rufus was out and was not expected back until tea.

The butler escorted them to the drawing room, assuring them that he would return with tea to refresh them after the journey. Oliver turned to Vivian, one eyebrow elegantly raised.

Vivian shrugged in reply, saying somewhat crossly, "How was I to know he would choose this afternoon to go out? I wouldn't have thought there was any place for him to *go*."

"Did you not write him to tell him you were coming?"

"Of course not. I would get here as soon as the message. Besides, Kitty told me that he was quite obstructive about returning the brooch. I was afraid that if I told Sir Rufus I was coming, he might absent himself from the house."

Oliver cast her a speaking look. He strode to the window to look out, his arms crossed over his chest. "God only knows when he might return. We could be stranded here for hours."

"I am sure they will feed us if it grows too late."

He swung back to her. "It could be midnight before we get back to London."

"If it bothers you to travel after midnight, I'm sure Sir Rufus would put us up—or there must be some sort of inn nearby."

Oliver grimaced. "We are *not* spending the night here."

Vivian shrugged. "Very well, then, we'll travel late. I have done it before."

Oliver did not favor this remark with an answer, and they settled down in silence to wait, the earlier bonhomie of the carriage ride vanished. When the butler returned some minutes later with the tea, he offered each of them a bedchamber in which to refresh themselves from their journey. Vivian quickly took advantage of the offer, glad of the opportunity to wash the dust of the road from her face and hands. Besides, she thought, it would get her away from the chill of Oliver's company. Really, one would think that she was personally responsible for Sir Rufus's being out when they arrived.

She couldn't help but smile to herself, though—she was perfectly aware of why the prospect of spending the night here or on the road irritated Oliver. He was scared of having to sleep in proximity to Vivian, a fear that could only arise from knowing how tempting that prospect would be.

When she returned downstairs sometime later, Oliver was not there, and after a few minutes of sitting, she went to the piano and began to play the sheet of music that lay atop it. It was an unfamiliar piece, and she was so focused on following the notes that she did not notice that Oliver had entered the room until she finished and he clapped.

She looked up, startled, to see him standing in the doorway, smiling. He came over to her, saying, "I didn't know you played."

"A well-brought-up English lady?" she responded in a teasing tone. "How could I not? And do not say that I don't act in any other way like a well-brought-up English lady."

"I would never make so slanderous a statement." He paused. "I have never heard you play."

She shrugged. "I do it for my own amusement. Fortunately, my grandmother believed that my name was all that was necessary to attract a bachelor, so she did not make me demonstrate my talents at the piano every time an eligible bachelor was around. And, I must say, I never saw how playing the piano would make a man want to propose."

"I think it is more the opportunity to have everyone look at you. But you, of course, have that just by walking into a room."

"My, my, aren't you the silver-tongued fellow? A bit of rest seems to have lightened your spirits."

He smiled. "Not to mention the brandy that Sir Rufus's butler brought to revive my spirits."

"Oliver! Are you bosky?"

"My dear Vivian, please . . . one brandy would not make me bosky. I am, however, more resigned to the wait. After all, we shall be able to get back to London this evening, and that is all that really matters. Please, go on playing."

They passed the rest of the afternoon in easy amity at the

piano, Vivian playing and Oliver standing beside her to turn the pages. Vivian began to sing one song and was surprised to find Oliver joining in with an agreeable tenor voice. And if a certain vibration was in the air, a hum of excitement, at having Oliver standing so close, his body only inches from hers, Vivian enjoyed that tension. She couldn't help but wonder if it had any effect on Oliver, as well.

As Vivian finished the song, she twisted her body to look up at Oliver. He was gazing down at her, and something in his eyes took her breath away. She rose slowly, turning to face him, almost as if his gaze were pulling her up. They stood there, eyes locked, unmoving. Vivian's senses were suddenly sharper, more aware, so that she heard the ticking of the clock on the mantel across the room, the click of footsteps along some distant hall, the rasp of Oliver's breath in his throat. She could feel the heat from his body, the cool cotton of her dress where her hands hung at her sides. The scent of him—a blend of brandy and wool and the warm male smell that was uniquely his—filled her nostrils. His eyes darkened as he looked at her, and he seemed to lean toward her—or was it her moving toward him?

A hearty voice boomed from the doorway, "Lord Stewkesbury! 'Pon my soul! Never thought I'd see you here!"

Oliver stepped back quickly, turning to face Sir Rufus Dunwoody as he strode into the room. Sir Rufus was a large, square man with a ruddy complexion, today made even redder by the same wind that had obviously blown his hair into wings beside his face.

"Sir Rufus." Oliver bowed politely. "Please accept my apologies for intruding on you."

"Nonsense! Nonsense." The man shook Oliver's hand forcefully. "Can't tell you how glad I am to see you. It's the devil of a thing being stuck here in the country, I can tell you." He turned toward Vivian. "My lady, welcome to my home. I've known your father forever. How is Marchester? Hale as ever, I trust."

"He is doing well," Vivian replied, having no desire to get into the specifics of her father's recent illness. "He and Seyre are at the Hall now."

"Egad. Don't know how he bears it." Dunwoody gave an expressive shudder. He reached up and swept his hands back through his graying hair, bringing some degree of order to it. "There's nothing to do. Went riding all the way over to Middle Gorton today out of sheer boredom. Course, if I'd known you were coming, I wouldn't have bothered."

"Sir Rufus . . . ," Vivian began.

The man waved them over toward the chairs. "Come. Sit down. Sit down. Tell me all about London. What are the latest on-dits? Haven't heard a decent bit of news since I've been here."

"London is as it always is," Vivian said with a smile. "Full of rumors."

Dunwoody nodded eagerly. "Tell me all. I've been in exile here almost two weeks. Last I heard, Thorpe and Lord Denbar were racing their curricles to Tottenham."

"They never got that far, as I understand it," Oliver told him. "Thorpe nicked a mail coach as he was passing it and wound up in the ditch. Broke his collarbone, I believe."

"Thorpe never could handle his horses as well as he likes to think," Sir Rufus said. "Ah, here's Cummings." He beamed as the butler brought in a tray with glasses and bottles. "Have some wine before supper? Ratafia, my lady?"

"We really should not," Oliver said. "We need to get back on the road soon."

"Nonsense! You must stay for supper. Keep early hours here, I'm afraid—nothing much to do but eat and sleep."

"We must return to London this evening . . . ," Vivian

began, but Sir Rufus was already energetically shaking his head.

"No. No. No need to do that. None at all. Cummings has gotten rooms ready for you, haven't you, Cummings?"

"Naturally, sir," the butler replied. "And Cook is preparing a very pleasant repast."

"There. You see? Have to stay to eat now, or you'll throw Cook all out of temper." Sir Rufus laughed heartily. "Cummings knew I'd welcome the company, you see. Very downy one, Cummings."

Sir Rufus thrust a glass of ratafia into Vivian's hand, and she could do little but take it, sending Oliver an apologetic glance. He was taking the wineglass, too, she saw, looking resigned to spending a few minutes talking with Sir Rufus. The poor man had clearly been pining away for company.

"I am surprised you did not remain in London," she said to their host.

"Oh, would that I could have . . ." Dunwoody fetched up a lugubrious sigh. "I'm in dun territory. Had to repair to the country, you see. Could have gone to the gullgropers, but . . . after I saw poor old St. Cyr run off his legs that way, I knew it wasn't for me. No. I'll just have to put up with the country for a few months. It'll come around."

"We might be of some help in that regard. Lady—," Oliver began.

The older man held up a hand. "My lord, there's a lady present. Can't talk of business. There will be plenty of time for that after supper."

"But, Sir Rufus, I am the one who came here to speak to you about it," Vivian put in. "Lord Stewkesbury merely accompanied me."

"Quite right, too." Sir Rufus nodded his head and reached out to refill Oliver's glass as well as his own. "Can't allow a beautiful young lady to be jaunting about the countryside by herself. Never would have been done in my day. Women have become too independent."

And so the conversation went. Oliver and Vivian tried time and again to steer the talk back to the purpose of their business, but Sir Rufus sidestepped it each time. He was clearly delighted with having visitors and just as clearly intended not to let them go without a lengthy conversation. After a while, Vivian gave up trying to bring the man to talk of Lady Kitty's brooch. They were obviously going to have to stay for supper.

She settled down to entertain him with as much London gossip as she could recall. Oliver, apparently reaching the same conclusion Vivian had, chatted with Sir Rufus about his club and also indulged the man with an account of a boxing match he and Fitz had attended the week before.

By the time supper was served, Sir Rufus and Oliver had made their way through the bottle of wine. They went straight to the meal, Sir Rufus declaring that there was no need to dress for dinner since it was the country, and as they had no clothes to change into, neither would he. Another bottle was broken out and consumed as the dinner progressed. Sir Rufus's color grew more florid and his gestures more expansive as the meal went on, accompanied by yet another bottle of wine. Even Oliver's eyes, Vivian thought, had taken on an unaccustomed glitter.

When at last the dishes were cleared away, Vivian knew that it was time for her to excuse herself so that the gentlemen could have their port, but she was not about to leave without broaching the subject of Lady Kitty's jewelry. By the time Sir Rufus had had his port, she was not sure he would be in any condition to discuss the gambling debt.

"Sir Rufus," she said firmly. "We must talk about Lady Kitty."

He looked at her with rounded eyes. "But, my lady, it's time for the port."

"Have the port. I don't care. But I must talk to you."

Dunwoody, shocked, turned toward Oliver for help. "Stewkesbury . . ."

Oliver shook his head solemnly. "She won't stop. You might as well give in. Everyone else does."

"Oliver! I believe you're in your cups." Vivian stared at him.

He looked at her, offended. "Don't be absurd. I am not in my cups, if you must use that vulgar expression. I am merely . . . truthful."

"Mm." She turned back to Sir Rufus. "Sir, do you remember the game where Lady Mainwaring put up a diamond brooch as surety?"

He nodded. "Course I remember. Wasn't surety, though. She lost it." His head bobbed again. "Lost it."

"Yes, well, what matters is that the brooch was a particularly favorite piece of hers, and she would very much like to have it back. Surely, if she pays you what the jewel is worth, you could resell it to her. You can have little use for a woman's brooch, after all, and it is most important to Lady Kitty."

"I told her it was gone." Sir Rufus scowled. "Don't know why the woman keeps bo—"—he hiccupped, then went on—"bothering me. Debt of honor. Tell her, Shtewksbry."

"Debt of honor." Oliver lowered his head in acknowledgment.

The butler brought in the port and glasses for the gentlemen and placed them on the table, casting a scandalized glance at Vivian. Sir Rufus rather sloppily poured the bottle into two glasses. He tried to put the cork back in, but it wouldn't go in properly, and after gazing at the unruly cork for a moment, Sir Rufus let it lie on the table where it had fallen and picked up his glass to take a healthy gulp.

"But surely, Sir Rufus, you could use the money more than the brooch right now. It would make sense to sell it back to Lady Kitty. I brought money with me. I could buy it right now and take it back to London with me."

"Love to. Love to." Dunwoody polished off his glass and poured another, sloshing another serving into Oliver's glass as well.

"Wonderful." Vivian brightened. "Just tell me what you want for it . . ."

"Can't. I can't." Sir Rufus sighed, gazing down into his glass as though it held some sort of secret.

Vivian cast a pleading look across the table. "Oliver . . ."

"Yes, my dear?" Oliver gave her a questioning look.

"Help me!" Vivian nodded her head sharply toward Dunwoody.

"Oh! Yes, right." Oliver cleared his throat. "Better sell it to her. No peace till you do. She's very pre . . . per . . . persistent. Loveliest woman in London, of course," he added with a thoughtful air, "but bloody pershis—" He paused, looking faintly puzzled, then finished, "Well, you know what I mean."

Vivian grimaced and turned back to Sir Rufus, wondering if she had left the matter till too late. The man was making no sense. "Why can't you, Sir Rufus? Why can't you sell it back to me?"

"I don't have it."

Vivian blinked in surprise. "You mean, you pawned it? Or sold it to a jeweler? Please, sir, just tell me where, and I can go buy it."

He shook his head morosely, finishing off his second glass of port. His voice was slurred as he said, "Went to another game after, you know . . ."

"After you won the brooch from Lady Kitty," Vivian

finished for him. When he did not continue, she prodded, "You went to another game. And what happened?"

He raised his hands and his eyebrows in an almost childish look of astonishment. "I don't know. It's lost."

"You lost it in a card game?" Vivian asked, her heart sinking. "Or you just lost it . . . somewhere?"

He nodded his head. "Exactly."

Vivian frowned. "I beg your pardon. Which was it—lost or stolen?"

Sir Rufus spread his arms out in an extravagant gesture. "Thass the thing. Don't know. Iss just gone."

Vivian looked at Oliver, who simply shrugged.

"Where was this gambling club?" Vivian said after a moment. "Did it have a name?"

Sir Rufus held a finger up to his lips. "Not the sort of thing for a lady's ears."

"Well, why don't you tell Lord Stewkesbury then?" Vivian gestured across the table. "That would be all right, I imagine."

"Course." Sir Rufus leaned forward, bracing his elbows on the table, and said in a stage whisper, "Cleveland Row. Number five."

"Ah. Excellent." Oliver nodded.

"I'll leave you gentlemen to your port," Vivian said, standing up.

Both men made an attempt to rise. Rufus made it barely a few inches out of his chair before sitting back down with a plop. Oliver, apparently more in control of himself, stood all the way up and made a sweeping bow. The gesture was somewhat spoiled when he wobbled at the bottom of the bow and had to grasp the chairback to stay balanced.

"I assume we shall stay the night here now," Vivian remarked.

"Nonsense. I am fine." Oliver tugged his waistcoat straight as he spoke and adopted a serious air.

"And after you finish the bottle of port with Sir Rufus?"

Oliver turned a contemplative gaze to his glass on the table. "Perhaps it would be better to remain."

A faint smile touched Vivian's lips as she walked out of the room. She started to go upstairs, but it occurred to her that it would be a while before she grew sleepy. Instead she turned her steps down the hall, looking for a library. What she found was less a library than a study with a wall of bookshelves, and she had some difficulty finding a book that wasn't deadly dull. As she searched, she heard the sound of Sir Rufus's voice raised in song, and she could not help but giggle. What a night this was turning out to be for Oliver! She could not remember ever seeing him even a trifle inebriated, but tonight he looked well on his way to becoming foxed. She wondered how Oliver would regard this night's venture tomorrow.

Finally settling on a clergyman's diary that looked, if not exactly exciting, at least dry and witty enough to entertain her, Vivian left the library and started toward the stairs. She noticed that the voices in the dining room had died out. She paused, then slipped quietly down the corridor to peek in.

Sir Rufus lay with his head on the table, snoring away. Oliver sat regarding him, his jacket off and one leg hooked negligently over the arm of his chair, one hand curved around his glass.

Vivian walked over to him. "Oliver?"

Oliver turned and smiled at her without a touch of his usual reticence. "Ah. 'She walks in beauty . . . ' "

Vivian's eyebrows lifted. "You are quoting Lord Byron? I change my mind—you are not just bosky, you are drunk as a wheelbarrow."

"Don't be vulgar. I am merely"—he made a sweeping gesture—"relaxed."

"I see." She came to stand beside him, her eyes dancing in amusement. "Are you so relaxed that you need help getting up to bed?"

"Never." He swung his leg to the floor and stood up, then hastily grabbed the table. "The thing is . . . would you happen to know where that bed might be?"

"Come, I'll show you," she told him, holding out her hand.

He started toward her, weaving a little, and she quickly looped her arm around his waist. Oliver's arm settled on her shoulders, and they started out of the room.

"Sorry you didn't get your brooch," he said, bending his head closer to hers. "Poor Viv."

She chuckled. "You'll think 'poor Oliver' tomorrow, the way your head will feel."

"Nonsense. I never drink to excess."

"Of course not. " She hid a smile. "I am sorry that you wound up having to spend the night here."

He gave an airy wave. "My pleasure."

They started up the stairs, Oliver taking a firm grip of the banister and hauling himself up.

"I must say, you are most agreeable when you've been drinking," Vivian told him.

"Am I? I must appear a veritri—veritab—well, an ogre the rest of the time."

"No, not an ogre. Just not the sort of man who ever kicks over the traces."

"I kick over the traces," he protested. "I kick them over all the time. Indeed, I *love* to kick over those blasted traces."

Vivian laughed. "I apologize. No doubt I am mistaken."

He gave an emphatic nod. They had reached the top of the stairs, and he stopped, blinking owlishly in either direction.

"This way." Vivian guided him into a left turn and led him down the hall to the chamber just past hers. "I believe this is it."

She guided him through the door and across the room to the bench at the foot of his bed. His arm grew heavier across her shoulders and he leaned against her, but Vivian had had some experience with helping her father up to bed more than once or twice, and she swiveled neatly when she reached the bench, depositing him on it.

He blinked up at her. "Lovely Vivian." He grinned. "Vivacious Vivian."

"Yes, very clever. I think we'd best get you out of those boots. It wouldn't do to muddy the sheets."

"No, indeed." Oliver leaned back against the footboard of the bed, draping his arms across it, and stuck out his booted foot.

Vivian bent, grasping the boot firmly, and wiggled it, then pulled with a firm twist, and the boot came off. She set it aside and started on the other one.

"You make a devilishly handsome valet."

Vivian set the other boot aside and straightened. "You, sir, are far too drunk to believe a word you say."

"I am the soul of honesty," he protested. "You know that. Your hair is—it's like the sun."

"My hair is *red,*" she told him drily.

"The setting sun," he amended, and she couldn't help but laugh.

"Well, the port hasn't slowed you down too much. Here." She reached out and began to unbutton his waistcoat.

Oliver made no move to help, simply watched her, his eyes growing darker and more slumberous with each movement of her fingers. When she finished, she tugged on the waistcoat, and he rose, letting her slide the garment back and off his shoulders. Tossing it onto the foot of his bed, Vivian reached up to start on the folds of his neckcloth.

He watched her with that steady gaze, heat growing in his eyes. Vivian's fingers trembled on the starched muslin. The ends of the neckcloth slid out of their intricate arrangement with a soft whisper of sound, the material gliding over her fingertips. She pulled it off and laid it atop the waistcoat. Her fingers went to the top tie of his shirt, and he covered her hand with his.

"I think I can do it from here." His voice was low, with just the breath of a hitch in it.

"All right." Vivian started to pull her hand away, but his fingers tightened on it, keeping her palm pressed to his chest.

"Though it feels much better the way you do it." His fingers curled around her hand, lifting it, and he pressed his lips into her palm.

His breath was hot upon her skin, igniting a spark low in her abdomen. He raised his mouth from her palm only to lay another tender kiss in another spot . . . and then another, moving onto the delicate skin of her inner wrist. She knew the vein there must throb with the accelerated beat of her heart, and she wondered if he could feel it. Did he know how his kiss stirred her? How hot tendrils twisted deep inside her, turning her breathless and shaken?

"Have a care, Oliver," she murmured. "I do not want your regrets."

He looked up at her, and a stark hunger was in his face, a blunt expression of need with no courtesy to cover it. She felt suddenly as if she had never really known him before.

"How could I regret wanting you?" he asked. "Kissing you?"

He leaned forward, his hand releasing hers as he grasped her waist. He pulled her into his body, and a soft moaning sigh escaped Vivian's lips as his mouth met hers.

Chapter 12

He kissed her tenderly, leisurely, his lips rocking against hers and opening her mouth to the sweet exploration of his tongue. Vivian leaned against him, her fingers curling into the front of his shirt as if hanging on to the one solid thing in a suddenly unstable world. She felt crazily as if she might begin to tremble all over, so exquisite and slow was his mouth on hers, pulling from her deep, delicious sensations.

As he kissed her, Oliver's hands began to move over her body, gliding over her hips and buttocks and back up to her sides, sliding in between their bodies and upward to cup her breasts. Vivian's body seemed to blossom under his touch, warming and opening, and a low, aching throb started deep in her belly. She pressed herself up into him, her fingers sliding up his neck and sinking into his hair. He wrapped his arms around her, pressing her even more tightly against his hard body.

She could taste the heavy sweetness of the port he had drunk, smell its heady scent, but it was his mouth, his touch, that intoxicated her. Her skin was supremely alive to every sensation. Every movement of his lips, each stroke of his tongue or brush of his fingers—firm, then gentle, then teasingly light—sent pleasure rippling out through her body.

Her body ached to feel his fingers without the frustration of cloth between them, to have the heat of his hands upon her naked flesh. Instinctively, she moved against him, wordlessly seeking what she longed for.

He let out a groan as he broke the kiss, and he buried his face in her hair. "Vivian, Vivian . . . are you sure? Do you truly want this?"

"I do," she whispered. "You know I do."

"You are so beautiful." He kissed her ear, taking the lobe between his lips and toying with it, gently scraping his teeth across the sensitive flesh, then soothing it with his tongue.

Vivian made a sound, a wispy susurration of breath as desire flamed into hot, urgent life all through her. "Show me," she murmured. "Show me how beautiful I am to you."

A long shudder ran down him, and his arms tightened convulsively around her. His mouth came back to cover hers, and he kissed her deeply, thoroughly. She answered with all the passion inside her, and they clung together as if they sought to meld into one. It seemed to Vivian that she could feel the thud of his heart right through their clothes and flesh—or was that simply the pounding of her own heart, so loud and hard that it must surely burst out of her?

Oliver wrapped his arms around her tightly, picking her up and turning, tumbling back onto the bed. She sank into the feather mattress, his weight pressing her deeper into the softness. He rolled onto his side, continuing to kiss her as his hand roamed down over her front, caressing her breasts through the cloth of her dress. His lips trailed down her throat, and his fingers went to the double row of buttons fastening her bodice. Quickly he unfastened them and laid open the bodice, revealing the thin, beribboned chemise beneath.

He raised up on one elbow and smiled down at her a little wolfishly. His lips were full and reddened from their kisses, his eyes heavy-lidded with desire. Vivian's heart seemed to roll in her chest at the sight of him. She reached up to smooth her forefinger across his lower lip, and he nipped at her playfully. His forefinger slipped beneath her chemise and glided across her breasts, stretching the top of the garment. He watched the movement of his finger, his face growing heavier and slacker with desire. Taking the dainty bow that fastened her chemise, he pulled it apart. The chemise loosened and sagged, and he slid his hand beneath it, pushing it down below her breasts.

Vivian's breath stuttered in her throat as he curved his hand around her breast, taking its weight in the cup of his hand and stroking his thumb across the nipple. Her nipples tightened in response, and everything deep inside her turned hot and liquid. He continued to caress and explore her breasts, and Vivian moved restlessly against the bed. She was aware of an ache growing between her legs, of moisture pooling there.

His hand left her breasts, and she wanted to protest the loss of his touch on the sensitive skin, but he bent and kissed the soft top of her breast, and she felt herself sliding down into an even more potent pleasure. His mouth roved over the lush orbs, teasing her with lips and tongue and teeth while his hand slid down her body, exploring and caressing. He reached down to grasp Vivian's skirts and petticoats and pull them up to her waist. She jerked a little in surprise at the touch of his fingers on her leg, separated from her skin only by her thin lawn pantaloons.

But then his mouth fastened upon her nipple, his tongue stroking it into a hard point, and Vivian forgot all modesty as he aroused her with his mouth and hands. His hand slid down the outside of her thigh and then ever so slowly back up the inside, then repeated the movement on the other leg. He halted each time just before his fingers reached the juncture of her legs, and Vivian was left breathlessly waiting, wanting, aching to feel his touch there. His fingers brushed over the flat plain of her abdomen, circling ever lower, closer. Finally, his hand slipped between her legs, pressing gently against her. Teasingly his fingers stroked along the cloth, creating even more of the spiraling blend of yearning and pleasure. Her breath came in pants, and unconsciously she moved her hips up against his hand.

Oliver let out a low noise, almost a growl, and sat up, startling her. Disappointment flooded Vivian, and her eyes flew open, her lips parting to protest. But she saw the desire that flooded Oliver's face as he gazed down upon her, and her words died in her mouth. He slid off the bed and pulled the half boots from her feet in quick, efficient movements. Leaning forward over the bed, he grasped the sides of her pantaloons, and in one swift motion he yanked them down and off her legs.

He stood for a moment, his eyes glittering as he gazed at her. Then he lifted her leg, bracing her foot against his chest, and reached down to hook his fingers in her garter. Slowly, inexorably, he peeled the stocking from her leg, his hands smoothing over her flesh as he pulled the silken material up and off over her foot. Oliver looked back up at her then, his gaze a mixture of question and raw, blatant intention. Vivian's lips curved up slowly, her eyes sparking with a flame that left little doubt as to her wishes.

With a final caress back up her leg, Oliver guided it back down to the mattress and started on her other leg. In exactly the same way, he lifted it and slid his hand beneath her stocking, working it down her leg, his fingertips caressing her skin as he went. Vivian's breath caught in her throat, fire sliding over her skin in the wake of his touch. With both hands, he rolled the stocking down and off her foot. Then he turned his attention to her bare skin. His hand drifted upward from her ankle, fingertips barely touching her flesh, but that faint brush of his skin upon hers ignited a fire. He trailed his fingers up to her knee and down again, teasing her with his caresses. His hand slid up above her knee, and Vivian sucked in her breath sharply.

Oliver smiled as he lowered her leg and crawled onto the bed beside her. He leaned down to kiss the side of her knee. His mouth slid an inch or two higher and kissed her again, then moved still higher. Vivian twitched, shocked and titillated all at once. He sent a roguish glance up at her.

"No? Perhaps later." He moved to her other leg, laying his kisses upon her skin, moving gradually up her leg.

Heat surged in Vivian's throat, and she quivered beneath his touch. Nudging her legs apart with his knee, Oliver moved between her legs, stretching up to cover her with his body. Bracing himself on his forearms, he lowered himself upon her, pressing her back into the soft mattress.

Vivian welcomed the weight of him, the hard press of his bone and muscle as he sank into her softer flesh. The fabric of his shirt and breeches was faintly rough against her bare skin, and somehow that, too, aroused her. She slid her hands up his arms, gazing up into his eyes. She could lose herself in him, she thought, and she knew that right now she wanted nothing more than to do exactly that.

"Make love to me, Oliver," she whispered. "I don't want it to be anyone but you."

Confusion flashed for an instant in his eyes and was gone, burned away by the passion surging through his body. She felt him harden against her, and he lowered his head and kissed her again. His mouth was no longer gentle, but fierce and demanding, pouring his need into her and drinking in hers in return. He kissed her until she could scarcely breathe, then he trailed his lips down her throat, tasting and teasing each inch of that tender flesh along the way.

Vivian ran her hand over his back and shoulders, her touch impeded by his shirt. With a low growl of frustration, he rose, whipping the shirt off over his head, then divesting himself of the rest of his clothes as quickly as he could. As he did so, Vivian unfastened the remainder of her buttons and pulled off her dress and petticoats.

He came back to her, sliding once more between her legs. Vivian wrapped her arms around him, luxuriating in the feel of his warm flesh pressed against hers. She could feel him throbbing against her, hungry and insistent, and she instinctively moved with him. Her body was aflame, aching for him, but still he did not take her, instead lowering his mouth to her soft white body. Kissing, teasing, caressing, he stoked the passion in Vivian and in himself until it burned as hot as the center of a flame.

She dug her fingers into his back, moaning in the depths of her need, and at last he came into her, thrusting deep and sure. Vivian tightened, arching up and back as pain slashed her. Oliver froze, his head lifting and his eyes widening in surprise.

"Vivian?"

She shook her head. "No, don't stop. Oliver, please . . ."

He bent, kissing her long and hard, and slowly, as gently as he could, he began to move in her once more. His thrusts were long and deep, and desire built in Vivian again, sweeping aside the twinge of pain. She wrapped her legs around him as he stroked in and out, filling and satisfying her in a way she had never imagined. Yet the satisfaction was not completion, for desire knotted ever tighter in her, hunger ratcheting up with every movement he made.

Vivian clung to him, her mouth pressed against his shoulder as he moved harder and faster. The tight coil of passion burst within her, and she dug her teeth into his flesh as the tide of feeling rippled through her. With a hoarse cry,

Oliver plunged deep within her, shuddering. For an instant, everything seemed to stop, every pain, every trouble, vanished, and for that moment there was nothing but joy.

Oliver collapsed against her and lay still, his breath rasping harshly in his throat. He rolled to the side, his arms going around Vivian and pulling her to him. She nestled naturally into him, her head on his shoulder, floating in a dreamy haze of pleasure.

"Vivian, why?" he murmured, his voice replete with satisfaction but tinged with a vague confusion, as well. "Why didn't you tell me . . ."

"Shh." Vivian snuggled closer, brushing her lips against his chest. "Don't spoil it. Don't talk."

He kissed the top of her head, his arm tightening around her. Gently they drifted into sleep.

Vivian hummed to herself as she walked down the stairs the following morning. She had wound her hair into a simple knot atop her head, and her clothes were a bit bedraggled, but she scarcely cared about such trifles—not when she held such happiness inside her that the glow must be visible to everyone.

She had lain in Oliver's arms last night for as long as she dared, basking in a warm, satiated, utterly relaxed state. Finally, stretching and sliding out from beneath the thick cover, she had pulled on her clothes, leaned over to give the sleeping Oliver a last kiss on the cheek, and slipped out the door and down the hall to the bedchamber the butler had assigned to her. She had fallen into a quick, deep sleep, and this morning she had awakened happy, smiling almost as soon as she opened her eyes.

What had happened last night had been magical, more than she had ever imagined it would be. Was it always like that . . . or was it simply because it was Oliver? Vivian smiled to herself, remembering, and the half smile was still on her face when she walked into the dining room.

Oliver was sitting at the table, a plate half-full of food shoved to the side. He sipped at a cup of tea, his face paler than normal and a frown pinching his forehead. He glanced up as Vivian walked in, and his face flooded with color and as immediately drained of it, leaving him ashy.

"Vivian!" He jumped to his feet, then winced slightly. He glanced over at the footman by the sideboard, then back at Vivian. "I—um, good morning." His retied cravat might look a little crumpled, but ample starch was in his expression.

Vivian released a small sigh, the smile falling from her lips. She might have known that it would not be easy with Oliver. He stood there for a moment, unmoving and stiff, his napkin clenched in his hand. Vivian sauntered into the room, keeping her voice light. "Headache, Stewkesbury?"

"What? Oh, um, yes, I mean, nothing to speak of."

Vivian sent him an amused glance as the footman came forward to pull out her chair. "And what of our host? Is he not here?"

"He is, I believe, ah, not feeling well."

The footman poured tea into Vivian's cup. Oliver cast a constrained glance at the servant, and when the footman stepped back from the table, Oliver gave him a short nod. "That will be all."

The man bowed and left the room. Vivian could see Oliver gathering himself to speak, so she forestalled him by getting up and strolling over to the sideboard to fill her plate. "I notice you scarcely touched your food." She glanced back at him, laughter in her eyes. "Not a comment on the taste, I hope?"

His mouth tightened. "I was not much in the mood for food this morning."

Vivian returned with her plate, and this time Oliver pulled back her chair. She tucked into her food with an appetite, gaily making idle chitchat about the food, the weather, and their return trip to London. Oliver waited, his body tensely upright, now and then glancing at Vivian and away.

"We appear to be at a dead end," Vivian opined. "Poor Kitty. I don't know how I'll get her brooch back. Of course, there is the gambling den where Sir Rufus lost her pin . . ."

Oliver made an odd noise deep in his throat, as though holding back a groan. "Please. Vivian. Do not pursue it. The matter is over."

"Perhaps." Vivian popped a last piece of bacon in her mouth. Her eyes met Oliver's. It was unavoidable now, she thought with an inward sigh. Oliver straightened and rose to his feet. He looked, she thought, like a man approaching the scaffold.

"Lady Vivian, I must apologize for my unwarranted behavior last night."

Vivian slapped her napkin down on the table and stood up to face him. "No. I refuse to listen to another apology from you."

"What would you have me say? Would you rather I was the sort to ignore my—"

"If you say *mistakes,* I swear I shall slap you." Her eyes flashed. "What I would *rather* is that you give me some credit for having something to do with the matter."

"I think you have already said altogether too much, don't you?" he shot back. "You misled me. You implied that you were . . . were . . . well, not an innocent. That you had experience in such matters."

"I never *said* I was not a virgin."

"Good Gad, Vivian." He glanced toward the open doorway. "Must you be quite so—"

"Honest? I thought you just accused me of being deceptive."

"I don't mind honesty." Red slashes of anger flared on his cheeks. "In fact, I would welcome it. However, I would prefer that you did not express yourself quite so openly or loudly where Sir Rufus's servants can hear you."

Vivian rolled her eyes. "Of course. Appearances."

"Don't think that you can distract me this way. I am talking about your deliberately leading me to believe that you were a woman of the world, so to speak. That there had been other men . . . that I was not, in short . . ."

"The first?" Vivian crossed her arms. "You are angry because you *are* the first? While that is certainly an unusual reaction, I cannot see why it matters."

"Are you being deliberately obtuse? Of course it matters. I would like to think that even inebriated as I was last night, I would not have acted as I did if I had been aware of the true nature of your—that is to say, that I would have had enough restraint not to besmirch a young lady's virtue."

"God give me strength!" Vivian flung her arms out. "You sound as if I had nothing to do with it! *I* made the decision. You did not force me. You did not ply me with strong drink and seduce me. Indeed, you were the one who was not in full possession of his faculties. If anything, you should be accusing me of seducing you."

"Blast it, Vivian! Don't you see that the responsib—"

"No." She held up one hand sharply, cutting him off. Her face was set in obdurate lines. "I won't hear it. I think it's best if we stop talking now. I refuse to continue to quarrel with you about . . . about . . ." She stopped and swallowed hard, fighting back the silly, treacherous tears that rose in her. "The best thing for both of us is to forget about it. Pretend last night didn't happen. Because clearly we cannot get along long enough to even have an affair."

He glared at her for a long moment. "Fine." His voice was clipped, and he reached up, pinching the bridge of his nose between his fingers. "If that is what you wish. We will ignore last night."

"Yes. That is what I wish." Vivian's back was straight as a board, her gaze cool and hard; she looked every inch the descendant of dukes. "Now, if you will be so good as to have the carriage brought round? I believe it's time we returned to London."

"I'll be glad to." Oliver bit off the words, his gaze every bit as fiery as hers was cold. He swung around and stalked out of the room.

Vivian watched him go, fists clenched. She would have liked to pick up something and hurl it after him, but whatever Oliver might think of her behavior, she was not indiscreet enough to do something like that in someone else's home. Instead, she stood stiffly, waiting until she heard the front door slam after Oliver. Then she rushed out of the room and up the stairs to her bedchamber, where she threw herself on the bed and indulged in a hearty fit of tears.

Finally, she rose and splashed water on her face to erase some of the evidence of her tears. Grimly she stalked out of the room and down the stairs to join Oliver. It was, she thought, going to be a long, silent drive back to London.

Camellia stared discontentedly out the window. Lily had been gone for only two days and already Camellia was at loose ends. She had industriously sat down to write letters to Rose and Mary, but she had never been much of a correspondent, and it had not taken long to finish those duties. Mending and such was done by the servant, and Camellia had never been much good at fine work with a needle. She could hardly go out and practice target shooting, as she had done at Willowmere, nor could she ride in London without a companion. Indeed, she found riding along Rotten Row so boring as to almost not be worthwhile. What did young women *do* in London?

A sharp bark made her whirl around. "Pirate!"

The scruffy-looking dog stood in the doorway, a well-chewed red ball in his mouth and his stumpy tail wagging furiously. He trotted forward and stopped in front of her, dropping the ball at her feet.

"Ah. You want to play catch, I see." Camellia grinned. "Well, that might be just the thing."

The garden behind the house was small, but with enough grassy area for the small dog to chase a ball. While the weather was by no means warm yet, it was at least no longer freezing cold outside. Camellia ran lightly up the stairs to put on a pelisse and gloves, choosing a woolen pair that she did not mind ruining, then returned to the sitting room. There she discovered that Pirate had set a small rag doll and a well-chewed bone next to the ball.

"Been raiding your cache, I see," Camellia said with a chuckle.

One of the dog's quirks was to take his treasures and hide them under the backstairs, an area that he had adopted as his den. Then, at his leisure, he would pull them out and carry them about to chew on or play with or offer as a gift to one of the residents of the house. (He seemed to be especially fond of presenting one of his trophies to ladies who came to call, perhaps because his offerings were so often met with gratifyingly shrill exclamations of disgust and horror.) The members of the household had grown accustomed to searching Pirate's hiding place whenever some small possession of theirs went missing.

Camellia scooped up all three objects, dropping the bone in the trash on their way out to the rear garden. She threw the ball, then the rag doll, and Pirate chased them merrily, bringing them back to her—though in the case of the doll, he was apt to first spend a few moments shaking it to make sure it was thoroughly subdued. He was trotting back to Camellia after one of her throws, the red ball in his mouth, when he came to an abrupt halt, dropped the ball, and began to bark ferociously at something behind Camellia. Camellia whirled around to see a slender man in rough clothes pushing open the outside gate.

Her stomach dropped. "Cosmo!" Frozen for the moment with a swift and instinctive fear, Camellia stared at the man as he strolled forward and doffed his hat to her in a jaunty manner. At his insouciant gesture, however, a saving anger spurted up inside her, shoving aside all else, and she snapped, "What the devil are you doing here?"

Pirate charged up to stand next to Camellia, letting out a piercing series of barks.

"Now, is that any way to greet your dear old father?" Cosmo asked, eyeing the little dog uneasily.

"Stepfather," Camellia corrected coldly, and crossed her arms in front of her, scowling.

Cosmo Glass had married Flora Bascombe a year after her beloved husband, Miles, died. Cosmo had been Miles's partner in the tavern, and the girls' mother, desperate to provide for her daughters, had married him. It had not taken long for her to discover the awful mistake she had made. At best lazy, at worst given to criminal enterprises, Cosmo Glass had been more a millstone around their necks than a provider. Even after their mother died, he had tried to use the girls for his own benefit, following them to England in an attempt to steal their property.

All the Bascombes despised him, but Camellia's feelings were the strongest. Only twelve years old at the time her mother married Cosmo, Camellia had been as scared of her stepfather as she was disgusted by him. Unafraid as she was in general, she had never been able to completely eradicate her initial fear of the man. That icy little finger of panic—and the shame Camellia felt at being even vaguely afraid of such a low, insignificant creature—spurred her to loathe Cosmo even more than her sisters did.

Pirate continued to bark and jumped forward to nip at Cosmo's leg. Cosmo hopped to the side, whipping off his hat and waving it frantically at the dog. "Stop it! Get him off me! Get him off!"

Camellia was tempted to let the dog do what he pleased, but she gestured to Pirate, saying, "Stop! Sit!"

It was never a certainty that Pirate would do as ordered, but this time he plopped down into a sitting position between Camellia and Cosmo and stared at the man, growling softly.

Camellia turned a hard gaze on Cosmo. "Why are you still in England?" Her way of fighting any sort of fear was to attack the object of it head-on. "Fitz told you to leave. If he finds out you're still here—"

Cosmo snorted. "That fancy bit of work? He don't scare me."

"That proves how foolish you are. He's the best shot in England."

"The likes of him ain't going to soil his hands on somebody like me. I know what those swell coves are like. Too scared of what somebody'd say about them."

"I wouldn't try to test that theory if I were you," Camellia remarked drily. "Why did you come here? I'm not giving you a handout, if that's what you're thinking. Neither will anyone else here."

"Not a handout I'm looking for. Just a little bit of help." Cosmo smiled in what he must have thought was an ingratiating way. "Won't you do one little thing for your old papa?"

"Stop saying that!"

At the rise in Camellia's voice, Pirate jumped to his feet, his growl deepening.

Cosmo cast a wary look down at the dog, but went on, "All I'm asking for is a little information. You don't have to do nothing."

Camellia frowned. "What do you mean? What kind of information?"

"Just tell me where this Stewkesbury fella keeps his jewels."

Camellia was so stunned that for a moment she could not speak. Then fury flamed up in her. "What! Do you seriously think that I would tell you that? That I would let you steal my cousin's things? Have you gone completely mad?"

"Now, Cammy . . ."

"Don't even say my name." Camellia clenched her fists. "You needn't bother being afraid of Fitz. You better be afraid of me. If you come around here again, saying things like that, I'll get out my pistol and remind you what a good shot *I* am! Now get out of here!" She took a step forward, raising her fist.

Cosmo took a quick step backward. "Now don't be hasty, Cammy girl. Just wait and listen to what I have to say."

"You couldn't possibly say anything that would make me tell you where Oliver keeps his valuables."

"Yeah? Well, you might think about what I could tell this precious Oliver." He raised his chin pugnaciously. "What do you think about that? Huh? You got a sweet little life here, don't ya? Wouldn't want to risk losing that."

"I don't have the slightest idea what you're talking about."

"What if someone was to tell this earl fella that you wasn't really related to him?"

"What?" Camellia gazed at Cosmo blankly. "Have you taken leave of your senses? Oliver knows that I'm his cousin."

"He may know them others are his cousins. But I

remember my Flora talking about how your birth record got burned up. Hard to prove who you are 'thout any records."

A prickle ran down Camellia's spine, but she said only, "Don't be ridiculous. The other girls all know I'm their sister."

"They could be lying. It'd look pretty suspicious if I was to tell that Stewkesbury fella that you was my daughter, that Flora was only your stepma, not your real one. Anybody what knows those Bascombe girls knows they stick together. They'd be happy to lie if it meant keeping the lot of you together."

"Oliver knows better than that." Camellia firmly pushed down the insidious little leap of doubt. "He wouldn't believe you over us."

"No? What man goes around laying claim to a child that ain't his? Tell me that. Pretty powerful proof, I'd say. And look at you. You don't look like the rest of them. Not a single one of them is yaller-headed except you. That earl'd be bound to wonder. Even if he was stupid enough not to, I bet he wouldn't like anybody else hearing that story—how he's been taken in by a bunch of girls. How that girl he's telling everyone is his cousin really ain't."

"So you want me to help you steal from Oliver so that he won't be *embarrassed*?"

Cosmo nodded happily. "Men like that don't like to be thought a fool."

"Obviously it doesn't worry you."

Cosmo's brows drew together, clearly aware that she'd insulted him, but unsure how.

"I am not helping you." Camellia's voice was flat, and the look in her eyes would have frightened a wiser man than Cosmo Glass. "Tell the earl whatever you want to. I'm sure he would like to have a nice laugh. Now get out of here."

"All right. All right. You always were a prickly one. But

you think over what I said. I'll give you a little time. You'll see it's best for you."

"Get. Out. Now." Camellia advanced on him with each word, and Pirate, encouraged by her actions, began to bark again, running around them in circles and jumping forward every now and then to take a nip at Cosmo's ankles.

Cosmo backed up quickly as Camellia marched toward him, and after Pirate managed to nose beneath the bottom of his trouser leg and sink his sharp little teeth into the man's flesh, Cosmo let out a yelp and ran from the yard.

Even in her anger, Camellia could not help but grin at the picture he presented—rushing out of the garden, the little dog on his heels, yapping and lunging at his ankles. But the grin quickly fell from her face as she turned away. She stalked to the wrought-iron bench that sat at the edge of the garden and threw herself down into it.

Blast Cosmo! Was she never to be free of the man?

She thought for a moment of going to Fitz and telling him what had just happened. But it did not take her long to discard that idea. Camellia hated the idea of being beholden to anyone, even someone as pleasant and easygoing as her cousin Fitz. She took care of her own problems, thank you very much, without running to a man to solve them for her. That she felt a bit of unease at having to deal with her stepfather only served perversely to make her more determined to handle it on her own. She had no desire to let anyone, even Fitz—and especially not that slimy scoundrel Cosmo Glass!—think that she did not have the courage to deal with him herself. Besides, talking about her stepfather, especially to her proper English relatives, no matter how agreeable they might be, was too embarrassing. Even though he was no real relation to her, she could not help but feel a stab of shame at the thought of revealing his plan, as though his low, greedy actions tarred her with the same brush. No, she was determined to take care of Cosmo alone.

There was no question of her doing what he had asked. She had made that clear, and if he approached her again, she would reiterate her refusal. That was easy enough. The problem was to keep Cosmo from making good on his threat. It would not help Cosmo to spread his story about, but if she refused to help him, she knew that he was small-minded enough to tell his lies just for spite.

She remembered the suspicion with which Oliver had looked at her and her sisters when they first arrived. What if Cosmo's tale reawakened Oliver's suspicions, at least where she was concerned? The problem was that Cosmo's story was all too plausible. He was right in believing that his claiming her as his daughter would work to his advantage. Men were much more likely to try to avoid the claim of paternity than to announce it—especially when saying that he was her father would appear to gain him nothing. Also, she did not resemble the other three sisters, and she didn't have any proof of her birth.

Of course, Mary and Lily would swear that she was their sister, and surely Cousin Oliver would believe them. Still, she hated the thought of his looking at her with even the least bit of suspicion. Camellia was well aware that her blunt American ways had never sat well with the earl. Though he had never given any overt indication that he did not like her as well as the other girls, Camellia felt rather certain that he did not.

As Cosmo had pointed out, it did not matter whether his claim was the truth. That he had raised the issue would be enough to create a scandal. Camellia's gallop in the park had proved to her just how little it took to cause gossip, as well as how quickly that gossip could get around the city. She had no illusions that news she might not be a true Talbot would not spread like wildfire through the *ton*. Dora Parkington and her mother, Camellia thought, grinding her teeth, would be all too happy to help.

Stewkesbury despised scandal. He would be furious . . . even if he would only show it in that tight-lipped British way of his. Camellia hated for him to be put in such a position after all the kindness he had shown them. Not to mention that a scandal would be dreadful for Lily. The Carrs would be appalled, and the wedding would be buried in the avalanche of gossip.

No. She simply could not allow Cosmo to go about telling his story. Somehow, she was going to have to stop him.

Chapter 13

The drive home from Sir Rufus's estate was as chilly and silent as Vivian had imagined it would be. Vivian's anger had faded by the following morning, however, and she hoped that Oliver, too, would regret the way they had parted. When that happened, he would doubtless seek her out at some social function and they would be able to apologize to each other and reestablish their rather bumpy relationship. But it was imperative that *he* seek her out, so there was frustratingly little that Vivian could do except turn up at as many events as she could.

Vivian was resigned to this course, buoyed by her confidence that it would not take Stewkesbury too long to come around, but it presented her with a ticklish situation in regards to her friendship with Eve and Camellia. If she called on them at Stewkesbury House, she might run into Oliver, and he might think she had arranged the visit precisely to run into him. That would never do. However, she needed to take Camellia with her on calls to the various leading ladies of the *ton* if Vivian was to establish the girl properly. Even more important, Vivian felt sure that Camellia was feeling rather downhearted now that her sister had left on her tour of the Carrs' various relatives, and it would cheer Cam up to have a little company.

Finally Vivian sat down to pen a note to Eve suggesting that the three of them pay a few visits together the following day. Fortunately, as she was struggling over how to express the idea that Eve and Cam should come to her home to begin their calls without arousing their curiosity as to why she was reluctant to call at Stewkesbury House, the butler entered the room to announce that Miss Bascombe was here and he had put her in the smaller drawing room.

"Oh, dear." Vivian stood up quickly. Had Camellia walked over here by herself? It would be another black mark against her if anyone found out.

But Grigsby, perspicacious as always, added, "Miss Bascombe was accompanied by her maid."

Vivian smiled. "Thank you, Grigsby."

She went lightly down the stairs and into the small drawing room, holding out her hands to Camellia. "Cam! How kind of you to visit me."

Camellia, who looked, Vivian thought with approval, quite stylish in her sprig muslin dress and green spencer, rose and came forward. "Hello, Vivian. It occurred to me after I got here that I had probably committed some horrid error by coming to see you without an invitation, but at least I remembered to make my maid walk over with me."

"You are always welcome in my home. You needn't an invitation. But I am pleased you remembered your maid. And your dress is lovely. Which bonnet did you wear with it?"

"It has a green velvet ribbon."

"The one we saw in Turlington's window?"

"Exactly." Camellia laughed. "How can you remember such things?"

"Oh, my dear, I rarely forget a fetching bonnet." Vivian

led Camellia to the couch and sat down beside her. "You look complete to a shade. I am sure the young men are lining up to dance with you."

"I always have partners," Camellia admitted, sounding a little surprised. "Although I can't imagine why. No matter how hard I try, I always seem to say something that makes some girl gasp and start fanning herself."

Vivian chuckled. "Many young ladies love to ply their fans; they think it makes them interesting."

Camellia cast her a doubtful look. "I suppose. All I can see is that it makes people look at them."

"Then their goal is accomplished."

"But do men really fall in love with someone because she's always astonished by everything?"

Vivian shrugged. "Some men do seem to be strangely drawn by a lack of intellect. But clearly not all. It sounds as though you have your fair share of admirers." Vivian paused, studying her friend. She remembered her brother's words to her before he left, and she could not help but wonder if Camellia had any liking for Seyre. Camellia and Seyre had not talked long, of course, but surely Camellia must have had some feelings about him, one way or the other.

"What about you?" Vivian went on carefully. "Are there any young men who have caught your eye?"

The surprise on Cam's face was answer enough. "No. I mean, well, Lord Breckwell seems nice enough, but . . . I don't know, he's rather dull."

Vivian heaved a little internal sigh. Much as she loved her brother, she was well aware that his conversation was termed dull by everyone except his loving family or learned friends, so Vivian could not hold out much hope that Camellia had found Gregory interesting. Still, the two of them had seemed engrossed in their conversation when Vivian walked into the library, hadn't they? Vivian wished she could remember

Camellia's expression when she had interrupted them. It would be much easier if she could just ask Camellia outright how she felt about Gregory, but in this instance Vivian was reluctant to speak in her usual forthright manner. She was all too aware that she was in a delicate position between her good friend and her beloved brother. She would not want to raise hope—or apply pressure—with either of them.

"Although," Camellia went on, "Dora Parkington seems to find Lord Breckwell extremely interesting." Her gray eyes took on a mischievous twinkle as she went on, "I have to admit that has made me dance with him two or three times."

Vivian chuckled, abandoning her attempt to discover Camellia's opinion of her brother. "My dear, I do believe you are beginning to fit into the *ton* admirably. Has Dora been dreadful?"

"Oh, she's never *unkind* to me." Camellia grimaced. "I wish she *would* say what she really thinks sometime. Her manner absolutely drips with honey. You would think it was her dearest wish to be my friend. But somehow whatever she says about me makes me seem as if I'd been a coldhearted wretch."

"She is quite skillful. I think she will probably surpass all her sisters. She's only slightly prettier than they, but far more treacherous."

Camellia sighed. "When is it that the Season begins to be fun?"

"Oh, Cam . . ." Vivian laid her hand on her friend's arm. "Has it been so very bad? Is Dora making you so unhappy? I can undermine her, you know."

"No, I wouldn't wish you to resort to anything underhanded. Dora Parkington isn't worth it. She irritates me whenever I am around her, but that is all. No. I'm just . . . bored. And I miss the country."

"And Lily?"

Camellia nodded. "Yes. She hasn't been away long enough to even write me a letter, and she's not very good about that sort of thing anyway." Camellia paused, then added candidly, "Well, neither am I. It's not too bad when Eve and Fitz are here. But they've been so busy with their house plans while Lily is gone. And Cousin Oliver was gone for a couple of days, and since he came back, he's been in the most dreadful mood."

"Really? Imagine."

"Yes." Camellia nodded. "It is most odd, for he usually is so civil and correct that you cannot even tell when he is upset. But yesterday I heard him tell Fitz to go to the devil. And he didn't say a word at breakfast this morning. Even Fitz didn't tease him; he just cast a look at him and then raised his eyebrows at Eve, and she shrugged."

"So no one knows the reason for his black mood?"

"No. Nor where he went. Eve asked him at dinner after he returned, just in a courteous way, you know, and he was polite, but he never answered really, just turned it aside."

"Probably better not to ask, then."

Camellia nodded. "No doubt Lily would say that his love affair is going badly."

"Mm. Indeed."

"Do you think she could be right—I mean, that he's actually having an affair of the heart? He seems too staid. Too logical and . . . and, you know, even-tempered."

"It sounds unlikely." Vivian paused. "I shall have to pay more attention next time I see him. Perhaps he will be at the Moretons' rout tomorrow."

"Perhaps, but I heard his valet telling the butler that he—Cousin Oliver, that is—had told his valet to toss out all his invitations."

"You seem to have heard a great deal," Vivian said with a smile.

"I told you, I've been deadly bored."

"Well, we shall have to do something about that. I had planned to take you out with me today to pay calls." Camellia let out a sigh, and Vivian chuckled. "But now I think that perhaps we ought to spend the afternoon somewhere else. What do you say to a visit to Bullock's Museum?"

"The Egyptian Hall?" Camellia's eyes lit up. "Vivian! I've been wanting to go there since we first arrived in London. Fitz told me it had all sorts of weapons—"

"And costumes."

"And preserved animals like giraffes and elephants and such!"

"Then it's done." Vivian stood up. "I'll just ring for the carriage."

"Right now? Oh, Vivian, you are the best of friends to do this for me."

Vivian laughed. "Don't be nonsensical. I love the museum. You're the first friend I've had who's been willing to accompany me!"

Smiling, she strode over to the bellpull and tugged. Vivian was not at all averse to going to the museum, though she had thought of it more to lighten her friend's spirits than from any desire to visit it herself. Still, it would occupy a few hours. From the way it sounded Stewkesbury was acting, she might well have some long and lonely hours to pass before she saw him again.

As it turned out, in only two more days Vivian ran across the earl. She was at Lady Fenwick's ball, a deadly dull affair she would normally have avoided, but as it was also the largest party being given that night, she thought it the one Stewkesbury would be most likely to attend. She had not seen him there, so she had contented herself with quizzing Vincent Mounthaven, an inveterate gambler, about the club where Sir Rufus had lost Lady Kitty's brooch. Vivian soon regretted her choice, for after Mounthaven had told her all he knew about that club, he started in on the attributes of nearly every other club he frequented, apparently intending to regale her with his vast knowledge of the gambling world.

Vivian raised her fan to the lower half of her face to hide her boredom and plotted how best to ease herself out of this conversation. Glancing over, she saw Stewkesbury wending his way through the crowd toward them. She was glad that she had the fan up, thus hiding the involuntary smile that flashed across her face, though she suspected that her eyes had probably given away her pleasure.

"Stewkesbury!" she said, not caring that she cut into Mounthaven's monologue. "I was beginning to think that you had given up social life altogether."

Oliver bowed to her. "Lady Vivian. Mounthaven." Oliver nodded to Mounthaven, his look as cool as his tone. "I am surprised you noticed. You seem well occupied." His mouth turned down in a grimace of distaste as again his glance flickered to Mounthaven.

Vivian struggled to suppress a smile. Unless she was mistaken—and she rarely was about such things—Oliver sounded jealous.

"I have been searching for you recently," Vivian told Oliver. "There are a few things I need to discuss with you . . . concerning my party for your cousins." She turned a sweet smile on Mounthaven. "You will excuse us, won't you, sir?"

Mounthaven could say little after her request, so he nodded, murmuring a polite "Of course."

Vivian took Oliver's arm, steering him away from Mounthaven and toward a less occupied part of the room. "Thank you for rescuing me," she murmured when they were out of earshot of the other man. "I was about to drown under an absolute ocean of information about gambling dens."

"Gambling dens! What a thing to bring up with a lady. Good Gad, Vivian. The man's a roué, not to mention a complete slave to the roll of the dice. I can't imagine why you were talking to him."

"Can't you?"

He stopped and looked at her. "No. Do not tell me—you were not asking him about the place Sir Rufus lost Lady Mainwaring's brooch?"

Vivian shrugged. "All right. I won't tell you."

"Vivian . . . what the devil have you got in your head now?"

"I don't know what you mean," Vivian told Oliver airily.

He snorted. "I'm no Johnny Raw, my dear. I know that look. You are planning something, and I am sure it is not at all advisable."

"There is so much that you think is not advisable that it would be bound to be."

"I am well aware that you consider me an old fussbudget," he began gravely.

"No, indeed—you are not *old.*" Vivian's eyes twinkled up at him.

Though he obviously struggled not to, Oliver gave in and smiled. "Do you win every argument?"

"Hardly any with you. 'Tis fortunate that I enjoy the struggle almost as much as winning."

"Vivian . . ." He sighed. "I cannot help but think that you want to go to this gambling den yourself and find out what happened to that blasted brooch."

"You know me well."

"Can you not this once consider your reputation?" he asked in a weary voice.

"Women go to gambling clubs."

"Not unmarried young ladies. Yes, sometimes women do frequent the better sort of places, but it is always married women and never without an escort. It would put paid to your reputation to show up there, especially since you haven't any idea what kind of place it is. It could be the worst sort of gambling hell."

"That is what I asked Mr. Mounthaven. He said it is a perfectly respectable club, although he characterized it as being the sort of place old men favor, ones who are not as full of pluck and daring as he."

"Meaning ones who are not as intent on running themselves into the basket as he is. The man's a fool."

"I'm sure he is, but not the kind of fool who would not realize a place was a gambling hell."

"I will admit that," Stewkesbury allowed somewhat grudgingly. "Still, for *you* to go there . . ."

"I am not entirely unmindful of the proprieties," Vivian told him loftily. "I would wear a mask, of course."

He let out a crack of laughter. "Hah! That would do it, no doubt. I am sure no one would look at your hair and know immediately who it was."

"That is easily enough taken care of. I can wear a turban. They are quite fashionable, and I saw a rather splendid one the other day in the window of a millinery shop. It was deep blue, with the most dashing peacock feather curling over it."

Oliver let out a groan. "That does it. Now you will *have* to go, if only to wear that hat."

"It does make the excursion even more appealing."

"You cannot go without an escort, and this time I refuse to let you talk me into it."

Vivian shrugged. "I would prefer your escort, of course, but if you won't, you won't. I shall have to ask Mr. Mounthaven."

She could hear Oliver's teeth grinding, and the look he sent her was lethal. "Bloody hell, Vivian . . . you never play fair, do you?"

"I find it is more useful not to." She smiled up at him. "Come, Oliver, would it really be so terrible? I shall be disguised. I'll even wear a domino if you want. It will be an adventure—and one that is without risk, really. What could be better?"

He let out a hefty sigh. "I am sure I will regret this . . . but, yes, I will escort you."

"Tomorrow evening then?"

"Doubtless I will get no peace until we go, so, yes, tomorrow evening." He turned to face her, a faint smile on his lips. "You will be the death of me."

"No, do not say that!" Vivian's brows drew together. "Do I really make you so unhappy?"

He looked faintly surprised. "No. By God, sometimes I wish you did. You make me . . . *afraid* is too strong a word. *Apprehensive,* let's say. *Unsettled.*"

Vivian smiled in that way that made men weak, her lips curving upward seductively, her eyes lighting with promise. "*Unsettled.* I like *unsettled.*"

"You would. Vivian . . . about what I said to you at Sir Rufus's house."

"Nay." She raised her hand as though to cover his mouth, but stopped and let her hand fall. "I do not wish to talk about that here. Not in the midst of a party."

"I was not angry at you; that is all I wish to say. Only at myself. And I was wrong to . . . to be so churlish."

"I have been around men who have drunk too deep before. I have seen them the morning after, as well."

"But I am not that sort."

"I know you are not." Her voice was quiet. "And, in truth, however much I tease you about your staidness, that quality is something I find I like about you. Not," she added with a teasing smile, "that you were not most amusing when you were in your cups."

He rolled his eyes. "Sir Rufus is a wily old rascal. He was determined to keep us there for company."

Vivian chuckled. "Yes. But I, for one, cannot regret it." She cast him a challenging look.

He held her gaze for a long moment, then said ruefully, "Bloody hell, woman, neither can I."

The following evening Lord Stewkesbury was admitted to Carlyle Hall just as Vivian descended the staircase. He looked up at her and barely managed to keep his jaw from dropping open. She was dressed in a gown of rich deep blue velvet that lay like a midnight sky against the creamy white tops of her breasts. Her colorful hair was piled atop her head and covered by a turban of blue silk, with a peacock feather curving over it, catching the light in its gleaming colors. Sapphire drops hung from her ears. A half mask covered the upper part of her face.

She was, he had to admit, in disguise, but she was in no way likely to go unnoticed. He could only hope that with the mask and the turban she would not be recognized—though he was certain that he would instantly have known her. How could anyone mistake those vivid green eyes, more highlighted than hidden by the black satin mask around them? And the full mouth and stubborn, pointed chin could belong to no one else. Her figure was recognizable as well, and he decided reluctantly that she had to wear a domino, as she had offered. It was a shame to cover the glory of that white bosom swelling over the top of the blue gown, but he imagined few men of the *ton* would not find her form familiar after years of seeing her at parties.

He stood still until he managed to push down the swift and forceful desire that had surged in him the moment he saw her. It was, he knew, the height of folly to continue to put himself in Vivian's presence. She tested his vaunted control much too often. Much too deeply. Yet, he could not seem to keep from placing himself in temptation's way. It hadn't been necessary for him to agree to accompany her to this club tonight. A dozen men, including ones far more honorable than Mounthaven, would have been happy to escort her. But he could not think of her being escorted by any other man without his blood beginning to boil.

He did not want Vivian going there—or, indeed, anywhere—with another man, even with a man whom he could trust not to dishonor her or encourage her in one of her mad, willful schemes. He wanted to be the man beside her, the one who heard her laugh and saw her smile, the one who brought a glint of temper or challenge or amusement to her eyes. Most of all, he did not want her to find some other man good company. Or desirable. Or a suitable husband.

Even the thought of it brought a sharp stab to his chest. That, he knew, was the most dangerous thing of all. It was absurd to think of marrying her himself—she was entirely unsuitable, whatever her fine bloodlines. They would be at each other's throat before they walked out of the church. Yet . . . yet it cast him into a black mood to think of her marrying anyone else.

None of this was like him—the dog-in-the-manger attitude, the inability to control himself, the deadly boredom that fell on him when Vivian was not around. This morning he had missed at least ten minutes of his businessman's report while staring out the window, daydreaming about seeing Vivian this evening. He frowned now, thinking about it. The woman was a menace.

"What? Already scowling?" Vivian asked, laughter brimming in her voice. "We haven't even set forth."

"You said you were going to wear a domino." Oliver knew that he sounded like some grumbling old man, disapproving of every little thing. Vivian did that to him, too—she reduced him to the worst possible aspects of his character.

Vivian sighed. "I know. Still, I hate to hide this dress." She turned around, the skirt swirling a little, caressing her hips, so that he could see the low-cut back, as well.

His mouth went dry, and he fumbled for something to say. How was it possible for her to rob him of speech so often and so thoroughly?

"Are you certain that someone will recognize me?" she asked.

"No. But it's safest not to take the chance. You are . . . well known."

"At least you did not say *notorious.*" Vivian smiled and turned toward the stairs, down which a maid was hurrying, a black garment in hand.

"You intended to wear it all along," he said accusingly as he watched her maid help Vivian into the garment and tie the two strings in the front. "I might have known—you just wanted to make me tell you not to."

Vivian chuckled. "Ah, Oliver, you take the darkest view of things. Why should I do that?"

He scowled at her. "Because you seem to enjoy making me appear a villain."

She tucked her hand into the crook of his arm, leaning in toward him to murmur, "Perhaps it was that I wanted *you* to see me without disguise."

Once again, he thought ruefully, she had rendered him speechless.

Oliver escorted Vivian out to the carriage he had hired for the evening. He had not wished to depend on catching a hackney when they left the club that evening, but neither had he wanted to leave Vivian's participation in this excursion open to servants' gossip. While he considered his servants quite loyal and did not think that the coachman would tell anyone that he had driven Lady Vivian with the earl to a gambling club, Oliver was not willing to chance any smudge on Vivian's reputation on his belief. Therefore, he had wound up hiring a carriage to take them and wait for them.

The club was not in a disreputable area, and when they entered, Oliver saw that it was indeed one of the more elegant gambling clubs. He relaxed a little, though he was aware of the way half the heads in the place immediately turned to stare at Vivian. Even with the domino and mask, one could see enough to indicate a woman of elegance and beauty.

"Lord, Oliver, there is old Aspindale." Vivian brought up her fan and whispered her words to him behind it. "I thought he died five years ago."

"He looks as though he might have," Oliver responded, "and someone simply forgot to ship him home."

Vivian chuckled. "And there is Lord Harewood's son, is it not? He looks as though he is in the grip of gambling fever."

Oliver glanced over at the roulette table where the young man was standing. His eyes were bright, and sweat dotted his forehead as he gazed intently at the wheel going round and round. Vivian was right; Harewood's son looked to have already fallen into the snare of many a young aristocrat. One could only hope that he would get free of it before he inherited his estate.

They continued to stroll through the club, glancing at the tables, taking in the games and the patrons. Oliver nodded at several men whom he knew, and he noticed that more than one glanced at him in surprise. His presence at a gambling club was rare; for him to have a mysterious beauty at his side was even more astounding. He smiled to himself, thinking what sort of gossip would be flying around the *ton* tomorrow. He suspected that tongues would be clacking, giving him a new mistress who was judged to be a diamond of the first water. He could not say that he minded giving everyone a little jolt . . . so long as no one guessed the identity of the woman at his side.

Vivian kept up a running commentary on the people they saw, and Oliver could not help but laugh at her wry observations. He would not have admitted it to her for the world, but he was enjoying being here with her more than he would have imagined possible. They paused at one table to roll the dice a few times. Oliver went down in defeat each time, but Vivian won on nearly every roll.

"Fulhams," Oliver commented tartly as they left the table.

Vivian laughed. "Just because you lost doesn't make the dice false. If you'll notice, *I* did very well."

"They were hoping to pull you in. If you had stayed, you'd have found your luck going very sour soon."

Vivian linked her arm through his, leaning into him, and reached over to pluck a piece of lint from his jacket. "Well, if it makes you happy to think so . . ."

The gesture was more intimate than she would usually have made in a public situation, and Oliver knew it was because she was in masquerade. The situation created an enticing atmosphere of mystery and secrecy. He felt the lure of it himself, as if they were in private while in the midst of a crowd. Unknown even though they were the center of attention.

Oliver could not deny the frisson of excitement that ran through him at the feel of her side pressed against his arm, the sound of her voice pitched low just for his ears. Her eyes gleamed, huge and mysterious behind the mask, and her mouth, exposed by the lower edge of the black satin mask, looked even more kissable than usual. Perhaps, he thought, he had underestimated just how dangerous this evening might prove for his own equilibrium.

He cleared his throat, trying to pull himself back to a more businesslike mood. "What exactly do we hope to do here?"

Vivian glanced around thoughtfully. "I wanted to see what it was like. Whether it was the sort of place frequented by thieves."

"No more than normal, I would say. It seems respectable enough. Still, the patronage is not restricted, by any means."

"No. Easy enough for someone to pick Sir Rufus's pocket—especially if he was in the state he was the other evening." Vivian paused, thinking. "It would be nice if we could talk to someone who was here that night, who might have played cards with him."

"I would say that chap making his way toward us"—Oliver lifted his chin toward a slender, well-groomed man winding through the players and tables—"is in all likelihood the owner or manager of this establishment, so perhaps we should ask him."

"My Lord Stewkesbury," the man said, making a courteous bow as he reached them. His voice was cultured, his tone hitting just the right note of deference. His gaze went assessingly to Vivian, and he added, "Madam. I am honored that you have chosen to visit us tonight. My name is O'Neal. If there is any way that I can serve you . . ."

"Pleasant little place," Oliver commented, adopting his most aristocratic attitude as he glanced around the room. "Someone told me about it, so I thought I'd give it a look. No sharps here, then?" He ended on a faintly inquisitive note.

"No, indeed!" The man looked shocked. "I run an honest place, my lord. I trust you have not heard anything to the contrary."

"No." Oliver turned his gaze back to the man. "But then, one can never be too certain, can one?"

"Of course not. Is there any game you would particularly like to try tonight? Faro? Whist?"

"Actually," Oliver went on, "we are here on a matter concerning Sir Rufus Dunwoody."

O'Neal's eyebrows rose. His dark brown eyes were shrewd as he studied Oliver. "Sir Rufus? I fear that I am not at liberty to discuss the patrons of this establishment. You understand, I'm sure. Discretion is one of the benefits we offer the discerning player."

"We are not asking you to break any confidences, sir." Vivian leaned forward, turning the full wattage of her eyes on the man. "Sir Rufus confided in us that he was in your establishment when he lost a certain piece of jewelry."

"Lost?" The man glanced from her to Oliver, his face growing even more guarded. "I am not sure what you are saying."

"The truth is that Sir Rufus had indulged a bit that evening, and he cannot remember what happened to the brooch," Oliver told O'Neal. "He was here, but he is unsure whether he might have lost it at play or dropped it or perhaps . . . even had it stolen from him."

Now O'Neal look truly alarmed, and Vivian noticed that a tinge of an Irish accent crept into his voice as he said, "I assure you, my lord, that nothing was stolen from Sir Rufus or anyone else that night. This is a very respectable club; you can ask anyone here. There is no thievery, no fuzzed cards, no uphill or downhill dice."

Vivian reached out to place a hand on the man's sleeve. "Mr. O'Neal, Lord Stewkesbury does not mean to imply that you or your establishment had anything to do with Sir Rufus losing the brooch. 'Tis likely, you see, that he lost it in a game of cards, and if we could find the people with whom he was playing that night . . . You see, we are trying to locate that bit of jewelry. Sir Rufus won it earlier that evening, and it has great sentimental attachment to a very dear friend. She would like to have a chance to buy back the jewel."

Oliver added, "I was hoping that we could sit and play a bit of faro while you asked around the club—discreetly, of course—to see if anyone remembered seeing Sir Rufus here one night, carrying a diamond brooch of particular beauty."

It took some doing, but between the two of them, they managed to soothe O'Neal's ruffled feathers and convince him to do a bit of discreet investigation for them.

"What do you think?" Vivian asked Oliver in a low voice after O'Neal left. "Is he as honest as he claims?"

Oliver bent his head to hers to answer, "Doubtful. Few gambling establishments are as pure as they would have you think." This close to her, the scent of Vivian's perfume teased at his nostrils, reminding him forcefully of the smell of it on her skin the other night as he had kissed his way down her body. He straightened, gritting his teeth and willing the surge of heat to dissipate. "But we didn't accuse him of any wrongdoing, and he has to weigh the advantages of doing an earl a favor against the possible affront to his patrons. I imagine he will make some attempt to help us."

True to his promise to the club's owner to cast some business his way, Oliver sat down at one of the faro tables. Vivian declined the offer of joining in the game.

"I shall just sit here and bring you luck," she told him, hovering at his shoulder.

He cast her a dry look. "Then I hope it's better than the luck you brought me at dice."

A middle-aged man on the other side of Vivian gave her a roguish look and said, "You can bring me luck anytime you wish, miss."

Oliver kept his lips firmly together so that he would

not tell the man to address her ladyship with more respect. Such a display would scarcely aid Vivian's disguise. He did, however, allow himself a long, cool warning glance at the man, who immediately subsided.

It was several minutes before O'Neal made his way back to them, but fortunately Oliver found the card game more engaging than tossing dice, as well as something he was more apt to win, at least now and then, so he did not mind the wait. He would not have admitted for the world that much of what made the wait pleasant was that Vivian was standing close beside him, bending down now and then to peruse his cards or whisper advice in his ear. Of course, whenever she whispered in his ear, all thought flew immediately out of his head, so that he usually lost that hand—but Oliver could not bring himself to regret it.

Finally, however, O'Neal returned, with another man in tow. "My lord, this is Jackson," he told Oliver in a quiet tone, indicating the young man behind him. "He was working here a few weeks ago, the last night anyone remembers Sir Rufus coming in. But I fear he does not remember anything particular about him that night."

"I'm sorry, my lord." Jackson, too, bowed. "I fear it was a night much like any other. Sir Rufus was as *he* usually is. I don't remember anything about a brooch."

"He did not offer it as payment or collateral?" Oliver asked.

"No, my lord. He had money that night. Said he'd been lucky that week."

"Not so lucky here, I'll warrant."

"No, sir."

"Well, thank you." Oliver nodded to the man and handed him a coin for his troubles. As Oliver turned back toward Vivian, he saw the man on the other side of her watching him, eyes bright.

"Sir Rufus?" the man asked. "You talking about Dunwoody?"

"Why, yes. Do you know him?" Vivian turned and smiled encouragingly at the man.

"Course I do. Know that brooch, too. Leastways, I guess it's the same one."

"Really? You saw him with it?" Vivian's smile widened.

"Sure. Well, I saw him flashing around a brooch one night. Might not have been the same. A pretty thing, diamond in the middle, looked like a heart. Big as a baby's fist, it was."

Oliver glanced at Vivian, and she nodded. "That's it."

"Did he wager it?" Oliver asked the man.

"No, he was full of the ready that night. I remember. Kept talking about how much he'd won. Taking that jewelry out and flashing it around." The man shook his head in disgust. "In his cups, that was the problem. Hadn't a bit of sense, had he?" He looked shrewdly at Oliver. "Why are you so interested in that brooch?"

"It belongs to a friend," Oliver said smoothly. "Lost it to Sir Rufus, and he can't sell it back to her because he cannot remember what happened to the thing."

The man let out snort. "He wouldn't. He lost plenty of money that night, right enough. But I never saw him wager the brooch. My guess—the way he was flashing it around, I'd say somebody slipped it out of his pocket."

"Not in here!" the owner of the club protested indignantly. "We run a clean place, I assure you, gentlemen. My employees and I keep an eye on everything that is going on. No one is going about nabbing things from the players."

"I am certain that no one holds you or your club to blame," Oliver said soothingly. He did not add that if the employees were as watchful as O'Neal claimed, then Jackson would surely have seen the diamond brooch that Dunwoody had apparently been showing off to everyone. "But someone might have seen it and followed him out. It'd be easy enough to pick the pocket of an inebriated man."

The man beside Vivian snorted again. "Hell, the state Dunwoody was in, he was probably lucky no one knocked him over the head to take the thing." He paused, tilting his head to the side. "Course, could be someone did and Dunwoody can't remember it. Not to speak ill of the man, but when he's in his cups . . ."

Oliver felt Vivian sag a little in disappointment against his arm, an impression that was verified a few minutes later when they left the club and climbed into the hired carriage.

"Well!" Vivian exclaimed, sinking back into the seat and turning to Oliver, her expression downcast. "I fear poor Kitty is doomed to be disappointed. I did so want to find that brooch for her, but I am sure that man is right and Sir Rufus had it picked right out of his pocket."

Oliver nodded. "Yes, or he dropped it on his way home."

"Or was held up at gunpoint, for all he can remember," Vivian added in disgust. With a sigh, she leaned back her head against the seat. She was silent for a moment, then said, "Another person robbed of jewels."

"What?" Oliver looked at her. "Yes, but what—oh. You think Sir Rufus was a target of the same man who stole Lady Holland's necklace?"

"You said there had been others. So did Mr. Brookman."

Oliver nodded. "At least two that I have heard of. Lord Denmore and—" He straightened slowly. "Lord Denmore was robbed after he left a gambling club one night."

"Do you think it's someone in the gambling world? One of the workers at a club, say, like that Jackson who saw nothing despite what the customer said Sir Rufus was doing?"

"Yes, like Jackson. Or Mr. O'Neal."

Vivian nodded. "He was terribly eager to deny that

anything untoward ever happened in his club. The sign of a guilty person?"

Oliver shrugged. "Or of a business owner who does not wish to have any taint attached to his enterprise. A not unreasonable way for even an honest man to act."

"Mm." Vivian fell into a thoughtful silence.

Oliver's eyes narrowed. "Vivian . . . what are you thinking?"

Vivian glanced at him. "Why, whatever do you mean? Why should I be thinking anything in particular?"

"Because you have that look about you. The one that says you are contemplating mischief."

Vivian laughed lightly. "Really . . . ah, here we are."

She glanced out the window. Oliver followed her gaze and saw that they had, indeed, almost reached Carlyle Hall. The carriage pulled to a stop, and Oliver got out to hand Vivian down from the carriage. He sent the carriage on its way and turned to escort Vivian into her house.

"Are you not keeping the carriage?" Her eyes sparkled with laughter. "Why, Oliver, one might almost think you were planning to stay here."

He glanced at her, startled. "What? No! Blast it, Vivian, you know I have no intention of . . . of . . ."

She smiled up at him, moving closer. Her perfume teased at his nostrils. He could not pull his gaze away from her mouth, full and luscious, sensually beckoning below the stark black of her mask.

"Of what?" she murmured. "Spending the night with me?"

"Yes. I mean, no."

She let out a low, throaty laugh that shivered all through him. "You don't have to stay *all* night, you know." She turned and ran lightly up the steps to the door.

Oliver followed her.

Chapter 14

Vivian stepped inside and nodded to the footman who had opened the door. "Thank you, Thomas. That will be all for tonight."

The footman bowed, not betraying his curiosity by so much as a glance at Oliver, and walked away. Oliver grimaced as he swept off his hat and tossed it onto the hall table.

"There was no need to send him off. I shall be leaving in a few moments."

"Do you really need him to show you out?" Vivian asked. "Would you care for a drink?" She took off her mask and domino as she led him toward the smaller drawing room.

He followed, grumbling, "Of course I can find my own way out. But it doesn't look right. The footman will gossip."

"You must be joking. He has been here through years of Papa's being in residence. I suspect he has seen things that would make you blush. He would not still be here were he not discreet."

"I know what you are trying to do with this show of—of having an assignation with me."

"Hardly an assignation. That would have to be planned, wouldn't it? You didn't plan to come in, did you? I thought you were quite spontaneous." She looked thoughtful. "Or did you arrange this entire evening in order to be alone with me? Oliver, I must say, I am surprised."

"Don't be absurd. I did not arrange this evening for any purpose. It was entirely your idea."

Vivian chuckled as she sat down on the sofa and patted the seat beside her. "You are so dreadfully easy to tease. Come, sit down. I promise I shall not make any untoward advances."

Pointedly, he sat down in the chair across from her. "Do not think you can use these tactics to distract me." When Vivian raised a questioning eyebrow, he went on, "From the subject of what you were thinking about in the carriage. I've known you too long. You had something in your head that you know I wouldn't approve of."

"Dear Oliver, I could have a hundred things in my head that you wouldn't approve of."

"Vivian . . ." The word was almost a growl.

"Oh, very well. It was not much of an idea, anyway. I was just thinking about Mr. O'Neal and wondering whether Lord Holland might have gambled at that very same club before Lady Holland's necklace was stolen. Wondering if that was the same club Lord Denmore had just left when he was robbed."

Oliver let out a soft groan. "I knew it. As soon as I saw that look in your eyes. There is no reason for you to keep after this. It is none of your concern."

"Perhaps not, but it is an interesting puzzle, don't you think?"

"Yes, but you won't stop at an interesting mental puzzle. The next thing I know you'll be off on some start or other, trying to solve it."

"I cannot think of any start I could go on to solve it, do you?"

"No, but I haven't a mind as given to mischief as you,"

he retorted, surging to his feet and beginning to pace in agitation. "I wish you would drop it, Vivian. It's enough to drive a person mad, wondering what you are going to get up to next. It isn't as if I didn't already have enough to worry about with wondering whether Camellia will offer to show Princess Esterhazy how to shoot a rifle or some such thing. Now here you are wanting to track down a jewel thief."

"I would be doing everyone a service, don't you think?"

"The devil take it, must you joke about everything?" He stopped and glared at her in exasperation. "One of these days, you are going to get hurt following one of your mad schemes."

Vivian rose and went to him. "Would that matter to you?"

"How can you ask that? Of course it would matter to me. Do you honestly think I do not care?"

She was so lovely that Oliver wondered how he could have thought the mask had hidden her beauty. Her green eyes were luminous and soft, her skin so smooth it was all he could do not to stroke his hand across her cheek.

"I think you find me attractive. Men seem to." She gave a little shrug. "But giving in to a seduction when you are in an inebriated state is not the same as caring."

He drew a shaky breath. "You were seducing me?"

"Of course I was. I have been trying to seduce you for some time now. Have you not noticed?" Unfettered by the concerns that bound him, she lifted her hand and laid it against his cheek.

"I am never sure with you, Vivian. You have the devil's own sense of humor."

"I am not laughing. I am not teasing. I want to be with you."

Oliver let out a soft groan. He curled his hand over hers and brought it to his mouth, pressing a kiss into her palm.

"Dear God, Vivian, do you think I don't want to be with you? Do you know how often I think of you? How little attention I pay to anything else these days? There is no lack of *wanting* . . ." He took a half step closer, bending to rest his head against hers. "No matter how much I desire you, you know how ill we would suit."

"I am not asking for your hand, my very dear earl. I am not even asking for your heart. I am not a woman suited for either." Vivian put her hands on his chest and slid them beneath his jacket.

He sucked in his breath at the feel of her fingers gliding warmly across his chest and down his sides. "Would you have me forgo all honor? How can I in good conscience ruin your good name?"

"Whatever happens to my name, it is mine to ruin, not yours." Vivian tilted back her head to look at him. "I am responsible for myself. Surely 'tis not dishonorable for you to take what is freely given." She smiled faintly and went up on tiptoe, so that her lips were barely a breath away from his. "I do not intend to marry for love or money or family duty. And I have never met another man I wanted except you."

"Vivian . . . oh, God, Vivian. Vivian." Her name was an incantation as he kissed her lips, her cheeks, her throat, interspersing her name with his kisses. "This is madness."

She giggled girlishly and, pulling away from him, reached up to pull off the stylish turban she had worn to conceal her hair. Pins came popping loose, and her hair tumbled down over her shoulders in a glory of orange-red flame. Vivian shook her head, running a hand back through her hair to dislodge the remaining pins. She was a vision, he thought, wild and free and beautiful, and it occurred to him that no man could ever truly possess her. She was, as she said, her own, and however much he might curse himself for it, Oliver knew he could not resist her lure.

Vivian smiled and held out her hand to him. Throwing aside his doubts, Oliver reached out and took it.

She led him up the stairs to her bedchamber.

There was no haste in their lovemaking this night. The fevered rush to fulfillment was set aside in favor of long, honeyed kisses and slow caresses. The desire that thrummed in his loins was no less insistent, but Oliver held back, exercising all his control to delay and stoke his pleasure. Slowly he undressed her, as he had been doing in his imagination for the past few days, unfastening, then peeling each garment from her body, revealing with agonizing slowness the pale, satiny skin beneath. Then he stood, skin trembling beneath her fingers, as she did the same to him. It was agonizing and glorious to feel her fingertips feather across him, the little scratch of her nails as they slipped inside his waistband, the damp heat of her lips as she pressed them against the hard centerline of his chest.

With a low growl, he picked her up and turned, spilling them both across her bed, but even then he did not hurry, but took his time, exploring all the soft dips and curves of her body and luxuriating in the pleasure of her hands and mouth exploring him with the same avid curiosity. When at last he slipped inside her, surging with hunger and need, he moved with deep, long thrusts, letting the passion build inside them both until they were almost desperate for release. Then, with a low cry, the tide of desire broke and washed over them, sending them shuddering over the brink and into the mindless abyss of pleasure.

They lay warm and boneless in the aftermath of their passion, talking desultorily. Vivian snuggled against him, her head on his shoulder. He idly toyed with the long, fiery strands of her hair.

"Your hair is like sunset," he murmured.

Vivian giggled. “So you say now. I remember when you called me carrot-headed.”

“Would you hold the follies of my youth against me?”

“It was last summer. I believe the exact words were ‘that carrot-haired hoyden who used to hang about our house.’”

He chuckled. “Perhaps I did. But I am sure I never intended for you to hear it.”

“No, you have always had excellent manners.”

“Which is more than I can say for you,” he retorted. “You used to drive me mad with your tricks. I don’t know what I ever did to you to deserve such treatment. Frogs between my sheets, salt in the sugar bowl, shaving soap that smelled like lilacs.”

She laughed. “You didn’t have to do anything. All you had to do was be there, so terribly handsome and so terribly unnoticing of me. You called me a child, as I remember, that summer when I was fourteen and you were just up from Oxford. I had to make you aware I was alive.”

“I was aware, all right!” He laughed, burying his face in the shiny fall of her hair. “I was aware I would have liked to strangle you.”

“But you cannot deny that I was unforgettable.” She rolled onto her back to smile at him.

Oliver propped himself up on his elbow and looked down at her, bringing his forefinger up to trace the curve of her cheek and jaw. “You are still unforgettable.” He smiled. “In a much nicer way.” He bent and brushed his lips against her forehead, then her cheek and chin, settling finally on her mouth for a long, deep kiss.

“Much nicer,” Vivian murmured in agreement.

Suddenly she stiffened and turned her head, listening. Oliver, too, went still, watching her.

“What was that? Did you hear something?” she whispered. “It sounded like . . . voices. Outside.”

There was a knock on the front door, the large brass ring of the knocker rapping sharply upon its plate, echoing through the house like a shot. It was followed a moment later by the indistinct sound of a man's voice.

"Gregory!" Vivian shot straight up in bed.

"What? Here?" Oliver, too, sat up in alarm.

"Oh, my God! What is he doing here? He's supposed to be at Marchester!"

Vivian jumped out of bed and ran to throw on a nightgown. Behind her she heard Oliver let out a low oath and start scrambling for his clothes. Downstairs came the clatter of footsteps as one of the servants ran to open the front door. Vivian went to her door, pulling on her dressing gown and belting it, and opened the door a crack.

"My lord!" came a voice from below. "Forgive me. I did not realize . . ."

"Don't worry, Thomas. It is I who should apologize for waking everyone up. I should have thought to bring my key."

Vivian closed the door softly and turned around. Oliver was dressed, though his neckcloth was wadded up and stuck in a pocket of his jacket and his waistcoat was unbuttoned. He set his jaw and started forward, buttoning his waistcoat, but Vivian stopped him with a raised hand.

"What are you doing?" she hissed.

"I'm going down to face Seyre." He raised a brow. "Did you think I would skulk about up here?"

"Are you mad?" Vivian planted her hands on her hips. "Of all the idiotic notions—what is Gregory supposed to do then, call you out? What would that accomplish, other than make the two of you look extremely foolish? And put my name on everyone's lips?"

The mulish look on Oliver's face eased somewhat reluctantly, and he whispered back, "What would you have me do—climb out the window?"

"Don't be absurd. It's a straight drop. I shall go down and distract Gregory, and you will leave by the front door."

"And you called me mad."

Vivian held up a finger for silence and opened the door again. Downstairs she heard the front door open again, and she slipped out into the hallway, tiptoeing over to the stairs to peer down. She came scurrying back an instant later.

"All right. Thomas is bringing up Gregory's things, and Gregory is still downstairs. I heard him tell Thomas to go on to bed, so as soon as you hear Thomas leave Gregory's room and go up the servants' stairs, you go down the stairs and out the front door. I shall take my brother straight back to the study and keep him occupied." She looked a question at him, and Oliver nodded.

"You're enjoying this, aren't you?" he asked with some bitterness.

Vivian couldn't keep from smiling. "A little." She cocked her head, listening to Thomas's heavy footsteps coming up the stairs. She turned back to Oliver and went up on her tiptoes to give him a quick, hard kiss. Then she slipped out the door, closing it firmly behind her.

Thomas was entering Gregory's room as she left hers, and she took the time to stop at the mirror in the hallway and check herself. She could see nothing that would give herself away other than the glow of happiness that suffused her face, but she trusted that her brother was unlikely to notice that—or, if he did, to attribute it to the correct cause.

She ran lightly down the stairs. "Gregory!"

He pivoted and smiled at her ruefully. "Viv. I do apologize. I hadn't thought that the servants would be in bed yet—well, really, I didn't think about it at all. I didn't mean to awaken you." He frowned. "Though, come to think of it, it's a bit early for you, isn't it? It's scarcely after one."

Vivian chuckled and came forward to hug him. "I do

occasionally go to bed before then. I didn't attend a party tonight."

"Are you ill?"

She made a face. "I do not go out every night."

At that moment, her eyes fell on Oliver's hat, sitting where he had placed it on the hall table. She slipped over and stood in front of the table, shielding the hat with her body.

"There wasn't anything terribly exciting happening tonight," she went on. "But that isn't important. I want to know what brought you back to London. I didn't expect to see you again. Come, let's go to the study where we can sit and be comfortable, and you can tell me why you're here." She moved forward, taking his arm and propelling him with her down the hallway.

He went along easily, not even glancing toward the table behind her, and they strolled down the hall and into the study. He walked across the room to the liquor cabinet to pour himself a drink and offered her a glass of ratafia. She agreed, strolling over to sit down in one of the comfortable armchairs.

"Now tell me. What are you doing here?" A sudden thought occurred to her, and she said in some alarm, "Is there something wrong with Papa?"

"No! Oh, no. I'm sorry. You mustn't think that. I wouldn't have left if he hadn't been doing well. He has recovered almost all the use of his arm and leg. He walks with a bit of a limp, but his speech is fine. He has a little trouble reading . . . but then Papa was never much of a reader. No, I left because . . . well, I have been meaning to talk to Townshend." He named one of his scholarly friends.

Vivian's eyebrows rose. "You just saw him when you were here before."

"Yes, but the experiments he's been doing on the

properties of—" He broke off, looking at her, and sighed. "I was bored."

"Bored?" Vivian stared at him, stunned. "With your books and your experiments and your horses, you were bored?"

"Even I get bored now and then," he said somewhat defensively, running a hand back through his hair. "There's no one about except Papa and the servants. No one to talk to, really, if you aren't there."

"So you came back to London for my company?" Much as she and her brother liked one another, she had never known him to visit London because he missed her conversation.

"Well, and, you know, activities. People. I'm not entirely unsociable." He glanced at her, then quickly away.

"Of course not." Vivian's suspicions were aroused even more, but she kept her voice free of any disbelief. "Then perhaps you'll escort me to another ball or two."

"Of course. Whenever you'd like." He smiled. "Or the theater. Maybe, um, maybe you could make up a party to ride out to Richmond Park one day."

Vivian struggled not to show her astonishment. "Yes, if you'd like. Who shall we invite?"

"I don't know. Stewkesbury, maybe, he's a good fellow."

For an instance, she froze, wondering if somehow her brother could possibly know about Oliver. But, no, that was ridiculous; no one knew about her and Oliver. No one could.

Her brother's next words relieved her momentary fear. "He could bring his cousins, perhaps. Miss Bascombe and her sister."

"Camellia!" Vivian leaned forward, grinning. "Gregory! You *are* interested in Camellia Bascombe!"

The bright red blush spreading along his cheekbones was confirmation enough.

"You are! You want me to set up a trip to Richmond so you can spend time with Camellia!"

"No! I mean—I heard she's an excellent rider, and I'm sure she would enjoy—oh, Viv, I'm being an utter fool, aren't I?"

"Of course not." Vivian reached out to lay her hand on her brother's. "There's nothing foolish about it. I was just surprised—after the party, you sounded as if you weren't going to pursue her. But Camellia's a wonderful girl."

"She's beautiful, isn't she?" Seyre smiled, his eyes lighting up as they did when he was on one of his favorite subjects. "I saw her riding in the park before I met her at the Carrs' party. She rode like she was born to it. And her face!" He jumped to his feet and began to pace, his hands jammed into his pockets. "I enjoyed talking to her. I was *able* to talk to her without feeling like a fool. She wasn't empty-headed like most of the girls I've met. After I went home, I thought everything would be like always. But nothing appealed. I was bored—if you think that surprises you, just imagine how I felt. I didn't want to read or write letters or check my experiments. I kept thinking about Miss Bascombe and wondering what she was doing. Imagining her at parties and the theater, talking to other men. And the thought of it made my blood boil."

He turned to his sister, astonishment stamped on his features. Vivian had to laugh. "Oh, dear. Have you never felt the pangs of jealousy?"

"No, I suppose not. Sometimes I've envied another man's ease of address with a woman. But not something like this—wanting to draw some chap's cork because a lady was dancing with him instead of me. It's not a comfortable feeling—and I didn't even see her dancing with anyone. I only thought about it."

"Poor Gregory. You do have it badly." Vivian stood up

and went over to him. "But don't worry. I shall certainly do something to help. I'll send a note round to Eve tomorrow, asking all of them to join our party to Richmond Park. It will make it less obvious if we ask them all. Let's see, when shall we go? Thursday, do you think?"

"I defer to your judgment in all things social. But perhaps you oughtn't to tell her I am accompanying you. She may refuse if she knows I am to be there. I made a proper mull of it when I met her."

Vivian looked at him oddly. "How? Whyever would Camellia dislike you?"

He frowned. "I think, well, this sounds most peculiar, but I think it's because I'm a marquess."

Vivian began to laugh. "Oh, my. That does sound like Cam. Do not worry. Once she has been around you longer, she will lose her distrust of marquesses." Smitten as her brother appeared to be, Vivian could only hope that Camellia would also see the wonderful person beneath Gregory's shy demeanor.

They talked a while longer about the expedition to Richmond Park and whether it was warm enough yet for a picnic. Smothering a yawn, Gregory confessed to being tired.

"It will doubtless take me a while to become accustomed to the sort of hours you keep," he told Vivian with a smile.

They left the study and started toward the stairs. As they emerged into the foyer, Vivian cast a secret glance over at the hall table and was pleased to see that Oliver's hat was now gone. Trust Oliver, she thought, not to foolishly leave something behind.

At the top of the stairs, they parted, and Vivian went into her room, closing the door behind her. The lamp on her dresser cast a dim glow across the room, showing the rumpled bed and her clothes, carelessly thrown across bed and chair and floor. Vivian crossed the room and began to pick up the garments to lay them more neatly across the chair. Her maid would never expect her to hang up her clothes, but she might wonder why they were scattered about so carelessly.

Vivian reached out and touched the crumpled sheets, aware of a faint bittersweet pang as she thought of lying there with Oliver. How different, how sweet it would be, if they were able to lie there talking as they pleased, not having to hide or to part.

Something glinted on the floor, and she bent to pick it up. Oliver's gold-and-onyx tiepin. Her fingers curled around the stickpin, and she smiled to herself. Blowing out the lamp, she climbed into bed and curled up on her side. With the pin clutched in her hand, she fell asleep.

Chapter 15

The first thing Vivian did after breakfast the next morning was to pen a note to Eve, inviting her and Camellia, as well as the men of the family, on an expedition to Richmond Park on Thursday. She got dressed and was about to leave the house, but when she went downstairs, she found her brother cornered in the entryway by Dora Parkington and her mother. The two ladies had obviously come to call and had run into Gregory, much to his misfortune and their delight.

"Vivian!" Her brother's eyes lit up when he saw her descending the stairs. "There you are. Lady, um, Parkington and Miss Parkington came to call on you. Now, if you'll excuse me, I'll leave you ladies to chat."

"Oh, now, Lord Seyre, there's no need to leave!" Lady Parkington said gaily, sending him an arch look.

"Yes, Seyre," Vivian echoed with a wicked smile. "Why don't you join us?"

His eyes widened in alarm. "Um, ah, thank you, but I'm, um—"

"Off to your club?" Vivian asked helpfully, unable to hold out against Gregory's wild-eyed look of panic.

"Yes. Exactly." Seyre relaxed with relief. "I have to meet a colleague at the club." He turned toward the hovering footman. "Thomas, my hat?"

"Yes, my lord."

"Lord Seyre was just telling us about Thursday," Dora Parkington said, smiling sweetly at Vivian.

"Thursday?" Vivian raised her brows slightly.

"Yes, the riding party to Richmond," Lady Parkington explained, her smile broader and more wolfish than her daughter's. "It sounds delightful. Just the sort of thing you young people will enjoy. It was so kind of your brother to invite us."

"Yes, Gregory is so good that way." Vivian kept the brittle smile on her face. "Thomas, why don't you show Lady Parkington and Miss Parkington into the library." She turned to the women. "If you'll excuse me, I have to ask my brother a question before he leaves."

"Of course. I am sure you must depend on his advice."

"Indeed." Vivian nodded. "Gregory always tells me just what I need to hear."

She watched the two women follow the footman down the hall, and when they were gone, she swung back to Gregory, who was standing by the front door, turning his hat around and around in his hands, his face a mixture of guilt and frustration.

"I did *not* invite those women," he whispered. "I didn't even intend to tell Lady Parkington about the riding party, but she was pressing me to come to some musicale or some such thing on Thursday, and I said I couldn't, and somehow it came out that we were going riding. I didn't ask her to come, truly, much less her daughter. But then she was talking as if I had and thanking me for being so gracious. And I couldn't *dis*invite her. I didn't know what to say. Then she told you I had asked them, which is utterly untrue." He stopped, looking miserable. "Now I've ruined it, haven't I? I should have a keeper, like mad Lord Devers."

Vivian could not help but chuckle. "I don't think you are in need of a keeper yet. I suspect few men could have held out against Lady Parkington. She is an absolute artist at getting her way. How else could she have married off all her daughters so well even though the men know that they are acquiring her as a mother-in-law?" She sighed, then reached over to pat his arm. "The situation is less than ideal, I'll admit. But I shall do what I can. You go ahead and make your escape."

Gregory smiled ruefully and left the house. Vivian stood for a moment, thinking, before she joined the other women in the drawing room. She rang for tea, then, smiling, she settled down for a cozy chat.

"I am so glad you are able to join us Thursday," Vivian said. "Lord Stewkesbury and his brother Fitzhugh Talbot will be joining us, as well as Mrs. Talbot, and, of course, their cousin Miss Bascombe. Miss Bascombe is quite the horse enthusiast. Such an athletic girl." She strung out the last words in a careful tone, stopping just short of a note of disapproval.

"Yes, so I've heard." Dora Parkington barely covered a smirk.

"You, of course, are such a sweet, feminine girl." Vivian's voice warmed now, and she smiled at Dora. "I usually find that men prefer a softer, more genteel woman. Don't you, Lady Parkington?"

"You are exactly right. That is always what I have told my daughters. Men prefer a sweet, submissive female."

"Yes. Gentlemen enjoy a quiet home life," Vivian went on. "My brother, for instance, enjoys reading and thinking, writing letters to his colleagues. He's more a man of thought than of action."

"A quiet gentleman, yes." Lady Parkington nodded emphatically. "I could tell that about him. Not at all the loud, sporting-minded man."

"Indeed. He never wants to watch pugilists, as some men do," Vivian added truthfully. "Or wagers on races." That much was true, too, Vivian thought—Gregory never cared about the betting part of a horse race.

"A scholar—that's Lord Seyre," Lady Parkington summarized.

Vivian nodded. "Yes. I hope he does not find the ride to Richmond too dull."

"I am sure we shall manage to keep him engaged in conversation, shan't we, Dora dear?"

"There will be a number of other young gentlemen there, not just Seyre," Vivian told them. "I vow, I don't know how a young lady as pretty as you will keep them all from buzzing about you. Showing off their riding skills to impress you. Clamoring to ride beside you."

"Oh, I don't care for that," Dora said with a wide-eyed, guileless look at Vivian. "I much prefer conversation to riding. I am a trifle quiet myself."

"Of course you are." Vivian smiled. "Perhaps, then, we should take the barouche, as well. You would look such a picture in it. Wouldn't she?" Vivian turned toward Dora's mother for agreement. "The barouche will be perfect for those who like to sit and talk—while the ones who are wild to ride can race on ahead."

"That sounds like just the thing," Lady Parkington agreed.

"And dresses are so much more attractive than riding habits, don't you agree?" Vivian hoped she was not over-doing it.

Apparently she was not, for Dora smiled and said, "Oh, yes, riding habits can be so mannish-looking, can they not?"

"Indeed." Vivian smiled. "Not at all the style for a lovely creature such as yourself."

It took a cup of tea and fifteen more minutes of vapid conversation with the Parkington women to end their call. Vivian graciously walked to the door with them, more from a determination to see them gone than from politeness, then turned away, sagging with relief and letting the smile drop from her face. Her cheeks were going to ache for an hour, she thought, from smiling so constantly and so determinedly.

Vivian went to the sitting room upstairs and seated herself at the small secretary. She thought for a moment. She had not planned to invite anyone else, intending a small, intimate group of family and friends. Dora's presence would change all that. What she needed now was several young men. There was Oliver's cousin Gordon, Lady Euphronia's son. He was an irredeemably foolish young man, but he was exactly the sort to attach himself to Dora, spouting romantic nonsense. And, of course, Viscount Cranston; his title would appeal to the Parkingtons, and his ample girth would ensure that he would opt to ride in the barouche. It took only another few minutes to come up with three more young men of the kind who were always dogging Vivian's own footsteps, declaring themselves hopelessly in love with her. She added the sister of one of the young men and another young girl, neither of whom would outshine Dora but who would make the party look more normal. Then she dashed off invitations to all of them and sent them off with one of the footmen.

Finally, she was able to leave the house, though somewhat later than she had intended. She ordered the carriage brought round and set forth for Lady Mainwaring's. She found that lady in her drawing room, a charming cap on her hair and a shawl around her shoulders, scribbling away at a piece of paper on the narrow table before her. When the butler announced Lady Vivian, Kitty looked up in surprise, and delight spread over her features.

"Vivian! Isn't that wonderful? I was just writing to you, and now here you are. It is something—what is that word?"

"Serendipitous?" Vivian suggested, coming into the room and going over to kiss her friend on the cheek.

"Surely not. That sounds much too foolish. But it scarcely matters. I wanted to talk to you, and here you are."

"I wanted to talk to you, as well. I fear I have bad news, ma'am. I could not recover your brooch. Sir Rufus—"

"But that is why I was writing you!" the older woman exclaimed happily. "To tell you that you do not need to look any further."

"I don't?"

"No, indeed. I have it back!"

Vivian stared. "You what?"

"I have it again. See?" Kitty pulled back one side of her shawl, revealing the familiar heart of diamonds pinned to the bosom of her dress.

"But how . . . where . . . ?"

Kitty laughed merrily. "There! I have put you at a loss for words! Isn't it wonderful? My darling Wesley found it for me."

"Wesley?" Vivian looked puzzled. "What do you mean, he found it? Was it here in the house? Was it not the one you lost to Sir Rufus, after all?"

"Oh, yes, it is the one I lost. I am never mistaken about my jewels. I hadn't told Wesley about my little mishap, you see." Kitty lowered her voice conspiratorially. "He doesn't much like my gambling. He worries I shall lose too much and find myself at *point non plus*."

"I'm sure he does."

"He could tell something was upsetting me, and finally

he coaxed it out of me. He is so very knowing that way. When I told him, he grew quite angry—at Sir Rufus, not at me. He said that the man had taken advantage of me, which was very sweet of him, don't you think? Not that Sir Rufus really had, you know, for in general Sir Rufus is more apt to lose than I. He is not a very good player. But that is neither here nor there. The thing is, Wesley said I should have told him about it, not bothered you with it. He was sure, you see, that Sir Rufus no longer had the brooch or he would have sold it back to me, which, of course, does make sense, and, truly, it did seem terribly unfeeling of the man to refuse to let me redeem it."

"So what did Mr. Kilbothan think happened to the brooch?"

"He said that Sir Rufus must have pawned it. I knew he was likely right; Sir Rufus is always short of money because, as I told you, he is such a poor player. So Wesley said the thing to do was to go around to the pawnshops and the jewelers to see if he had sold it. Of course, that was the sort of thing that neither you nor I could do, but Wesley offered to do it for me. And last night, he came home with my brooch! He'd found it in a pawnshop and bought it for me—at only half of what it's worth. So it was really quite a savings."

"Obviously." Vivian couldn't help but grin at her friend's reasoning. Still, she found the tale somewhat worrisome. "How lucky that he was able to find it so quickly."

"Yes, wasn't it?" Kitty beamed. She glanced past Vivian, and her smile grew even brighter. "Wesley! Look who has come to visit! I was just telling Vivian about your finding my brooch."

Wesley advanced into the room to bow over Vivian's hand and offer a polite greeting. Vivian watched him carefully as she said, "Yes, finding it was quite remarkable, I must say."

He shrugged, smiling faintly. "Not that remarkable, I'm afraid. I have myself been purse-pinched before, so I knew the most likely places for Sir Rufus to have taken it. I had to try several shops before I came across it, but"—he turned toward Kitty, his handsome, rather sharp features softening—" 'twas little trouble, really, since I did it for Lady Kitty."

As she always did, Vivian wondered how much, if any, of the man's purported love for her friend was real. It was easy to love Kitty, and she was still a handsome woman for her age. Still, it seemed very convenient for a penniless poet to fall in love with a wealthy older woman. As convenient as it was for him to "find" Kitty's brooch.

"Sir Rufus told us that he lost the brooch at another game," Vivian remarked.

"Indeed?" Wesley raised his brows, his face pleasant but unreadable. "Well, a man might hesitate to admit he had to pawn the jewel. Or perhaps it was whoever he lost it to who pawned it."

"Or the person who stole it."

"Stole it!" Kitty exclaimed.

"Yes. I had come to think that someone picked Sir Rufus's pocket. He would have been easy prey, considering his state."

"Foxed, you mean?" Kitty asked with a sigh. "Yes, he so often is; that is one reason his game is so poor."

"Yes, I suppose that could be how it happened. It could just as easily have been a thief who pawned the brooch," Wesley agreed.

"It scarcely matters now," Kitty said happily. "I have it back, and that is what's important. Vivian, darling, will you stay for tea?"

"Thank you, but, no, I fear I have other errands to run." Vivian stood up, and Kitty rose with her.

"I'll walk you to the door," Kitty said, linking her arm through Vivian's. As they strolled into the hall, leaving Wesley behind them, Kitty leaned toward Vivian and murmured, "And what about that other matter we discussed?"

Vivian turned to her, momentarily puzzled, but when she saw Kitty's bright eyes and knowing smile, she remembered that she had confided in the older woman about her feelings for Oliver.

"Oh!" Vivian colored slightly. "That."

"Yes, that." Kitty chuckled. "The little matter of the Earl of Stewkesbury. Are you still . . . entertaining thoughts about him?"

Vivian smiled secretively. "Yes."

"And more than entertaining?"

Her smile grew as she admitted, "Perhaps I am."

"Ah." Kitty drew out a satisfied sigh. "Well, he isn't who I would have chosen for you." She stopped and took both Vivian's hands, looking earnestly into her eyes. "But are you happy?"

Vivian looked back at her just as seriously. "Yes." Her voice contained a note of wonder. "I really am."

Kitty gave a decisive nod. "Then I approve of him."

They turned and walked on to the door.

The footman opened the front door and stepped back. Kitty stepped out onto the stoop with Vivian and kissed her lightly on both cheeks. Vivian started to turn away, then stopped and turned back to her. Her eyes searched the older woman's face earnestly as she asked, "Kitty . . . did you ever regret your time with my father?"

"Regret?" Kitty smiled and shook her head. "My, no. I have regretted many things, but I've never regretted anything I did for love."

As Vivian climbed into her carriage, her first thought was to tell Oliver about the reappearance of Kitty's brooch, and she was aware of a distinct sense of disappointment when she realized that she could not. It would never do to pay a call on a man. She could, of course, go to Stewkesbury House on the pretext of making a call on Camellia and Eve and hope that Oliver would be there and would join them. But this was not really a subject for a group conversation, and besides, what if Oliver suspected that she was doing exactly that, using the pretext of the call to be with him? Vivian had too much pride for that, even with Oliver. On the spur of the moment, Vivian directed her coachman to drive to Brookman & Son.

Even though he was not expecting her, Mr. Brookman came from the back of the shop to greet Vivian with all his usual deference. "My lady. I am so honored. May I show you something in particular? I shall be happy to bring it to you." He gestured toward the inner sanctum of his office, at the same time subtly signaling to one of his employees to take care of the customer whom he had just left.

"I'm sorry. I only meant to talk to you. Although"—Vivian smiled—"I might be tempted to look if you had something you thought I would like."

As it turned out, he had several things, one of which was a necklace of opals, milky white and rippling with hints of blues and pinks, that caught Vivian's eye. She tried on the opal necklace, turning this way and that to see herself in the small mirror atop his desk.

"One of your own designs, Mr. Brookman?" she asked, glancing over at him.

He smiled. "You always know, my lady. Yes, I made it. But there is also a necklace of cabochon rubies which I bought from another jeweler in France. He claims it belonged to a French nobleman who had to flee the Revolution." He gave a half shrug. "These things are always said to come from French aristocrats who fled or were beheaded, if not from the tragic queen herself. But whatever the truth of the matter, it is an old setting, and the jewels are of the best quality. Still, I think it is probably a little heavy and . . . obvious . . . for you."

Vivian examined the necklace and agreed that it was rather ornate for both her personal style and the current fashion, but she agreed that the opal necklace was exactly what she had been wanting even though she had not known it until she saw it.

"Now." Mr. Brookman sent the jewelry off with an employee to be boxed, and he turned back to sit at his desk. "How else may I help you? You said that you wished to talk to me?"

"I did. I was wondering if you had heard anything further about the matter we discussed the last time I was here." At his blank look, she went on, "The jewelry that had been stolen recently."

"Yes, of course. I remember. I am sorry, but I'm afraid I won't be much help. I have kept my eyes open for anyone trying to sell me jewelry, but, frankly, there have been only one or two, and they were both customers well-known to me, and the jewelry, I am positive, was their own."

"So no one has offered to sell you a piece other than those few?"

"No. I am very sorry." He looked regretful. "I have asked some of my fellow jewelers, as well, and I'm afraid no one remembered buying any pieces that seemed suspicious to them. I am sure that most thieves would know that I buy only from reputable dealers or sometimes from a customer who is in dire straits. I would not purchase a piece brought in by someone who roused my suspicions. I feel sure that most of my colleagues are the same way."

"Would the thief more likely go to a pawnshop, you mean?"

"Perhaps. Or to a store where the owner is not so particular. Sad to say, there are some jewelers who have little concern about where a piece of jewelry is acquired."

"Do you know what places those might be?"

Mr. Brookman looked slightly startled, but after only a moment's hesitation he drew out a piece of paper and began to scribble down a few names with a pencil. "This is not a complete list by any means; they are only stores or pawnbrokers about whom I have gotten a certain sense . . . if you know what I mean."

"Yes, I think so." Vivian reached out and took the piece of paper he extended toward her.

"But, my lady . . . ," he began somewhat nervously. "These are not the sort of places where a lady would go. Certainly not alone."

"Don't worry. I won't be going alone."

Thursday morning dawned bright and clear, a little cool perhaps, but still a perfect day for a ride outside the city. Servants would follow with a cold collation of meat pies, rolls, and other treats to stave off the appetite worked up by a good ride. But for now, only a stylish barouche stood in front of Carlyle Hall, along with several elegant horses, stamping and whickering in eagerness to get started. Gregory, stepping out of the house after Vivian, turned to her with a questioning look.

"Why is the barouche here?"

Vivian's eyes danced. "You shall see."

He shrugged as he went over to run a hand over his own horse. "As long as you don't expect me to ride in it."

"Never," Vivian responded with a chuckle.

At that moment the Talbot party arrived, already mounted, followed shortly by several of the other guests, and the next few moments were taken up by greetings.

Camellia, Vivian took note, looked as dashing and vital as Vivian had expected her to. Her new military-styled, dark blue riding habit fitted her form perfectly, and the saucy little hat perched atop her neatly braided and wound blond hair was just the right accent to draw attention to her face, now glowing with happy eagerness. From the expression on her brother's face, Vivian was sure that Gregory agreed with her assessment.

The rest of the guests were soon there. Dora and her mother were the last to arrive, as Vivian had suspected they would be. It made more of an impression to arrive alone rather than in the midst of the crowd. The Parkingtons' arrival created exactly the stir Dora wanted among the young men of the party . . . except for the one whom Vivian was sure Dora hoped most to impress. Only Gregory stood apart as the other bachelors jockeyed for position to help Dora from the Parkingtons' carriage and escort her the few feet to the sidewalk.

Dora, however, made sure to come over to greet Vivian and her brother personally. "Lady Vivian. And Lord Seyre." Dora offered a modest little curtsey. "I cannot tell you how much I appreciate your invitation."

Vivian, casting a quick glance over at Camellia, caught the curl of distaste that touched her lips, and Vivian had to suppress a smile as she assured Miss Parkington that she was welcome. Gregory, beside Vivian, stared in some amazement at Dora's dress, a floating, fluttering thing of white dimity that enhanced Dora's delicate good looks. Vivian was sure that at least one young gentleman—probably Cousin Gordon—would feel moved before the day was through to tell Dora that she looked exactly like an angel.

It would not be Gregory, however, for he blurted out, "Surely you cannot ride in that."

"Oh, no," Dora told him, smiling and regarding him with her limpid blue eyes. "I do not care to ride. Lady Vivian said there would be a barouche, and I find that much more conducive to conversation. Don't you, my lord?"

"Uh. Why, yes, I suppose it would be." Gregory's smile was quick and sincere. "Please allow me to help you into the barouche."

Dora smiled and lowered her eyes modestly, stretching out her hand to Gregory. He handed her up into the carriage and proffered the same service to her beaming mother. Then, with a bow, he walked away as Cousin Gordon hastened forward to get into the barouche, followed by the portly Viscount Cranston. Dora's jaw dropped in surprise.

Vivian, keeping her head carefully turned away from the carriage, waited for Gregory to give her a leg up onto her mount. As he leaned down to cup her foot, Gregory murmured, "Thank you."

"Think nothing of it," she retorted as she sprang up onto the mare's back. Reaching down to take the reins, she added, "And good luck to you."

Gregory grinned and swung into his saddle, and the party started off.

Chapter 16

There was little conversation as the group made its way through the crowded streets of London, but once outside the city, the riders began to form small groups. Vivian watched her brother fall in beside Camellia, but the Overbrooks came up to join them, Percy on Camellia's left and his sister Felicity on Seyre's right. It was a clever bit of maneuvering by the pair, Vivian had to admit, especially when she saw Felicity slow down, apparently having a bit of trouble with her stirrup. For courtesy's sake, Gregory was forced to stop alongside the young woman and bend down to slip the stirrup more securely under her foot. Miss Overbrook was all smiles and thanks, but her pace was slow, and Gregory could scarcely ride off and leave her by herself. Vivian was about to speed up and take Felicity off Seyre's hands when Oliver drew up alongside Vivian. She smiled at him, the familiar tingle of anticipation running through her.

"Whatever possessed you to invite my addlepated cousin Gordon?" Oliver asked, the laughter in his voice erasing any harshness from the words.

"He was, I thought, the perfect gentleman to entertain Miss Parkington."

"I noticed that clever arrangement. Was the barouche your idea or hers?"

"I may have mentioned how her delicate beauty would be shown off to perfection in an open-topped barouche. But the decision to ride in it was hers alone."

"Of course it was. One can only wonder why she was invited in the first place." Oliver slanted a curious glance at Vivian.

"Not through any doing of mine, I assure you. Lady Parkington managed to wedge her way into it. She's quite skillful in that regard."

"Mm. They could use her in the Foreign Office."

"Only if her daughter's marriage prospects were at stake," Vivian retorted, and Oliver chuckled.

They rode in silence for a time. Vivian breathed in the air, untainted by the city's smells and smoke. The temperature was a bit crisp, not yet the soft warmth of spring, but just right for riding. A breeze touched her cheeks, bringing pink to them and stirring the delicate curls around her face. She savored the perfection of the moment—the smell, the air, Oliver's presence beside her. All it lacked was a bird singing out its heart. At that instant, a bird began to twitter in a nearby tree, and Vivian could not help but chuckle.

She glanced at Oliver and found him watching her, a faint smile on his face. Her heart seemed to swell in her chest, and Vivian looked hastily away, almost frightened by the sudden burst of emotion.

"I went to see Lady Mainwaring yesterday," she said, snatching at the first thing that came into her head.

"Did you? To tell her we could not locate her jewelry?"

"Yes, but the odd thing was that she already had it back in her possession."

"What?" Oliver's eyebrows soared and he edged his horse closer to her. "How?"

Vivian related the tale of Mr. Kilbothan's involvement. Oliver listened, a faint frown forming between his brows.

"Very convenient," he said when Vivian finished.

"Yes, isn't it?" Vivian nodded. She turned her head to regard Oliver seriously. "Do you think that he could be our thief?"

"'Our' thief? I disclaim all ownership of either Mr. Kilbothan or the thief. However, I suppose it is possible. Being around Lady Mainwaring, he would certainly encounter a number of wealthy gamblers. Of course, one could wonder why he would go to the trouble of thievery when he has the lady's patronage."

"I would think that it would be preferable to have money of one's own. It would be rather galling to have to depend on another for allowance. Generous as my father was, I was happy to reach twenty-one and come into my inheritance."

"But supposing Kilbothan did seek financial independence in that manner, why not take the brooch directly from Lady Mainwaring? Why steal it after she had lost it? In fact, why steal from any of the other people? There must be any number of things that could be taken from her house, probably without her even noticing."

"No doubt. Kitty is not terribly observant—except, I would say, about her jewelry. She would not notice the gold plate going missing, but I daresay her butler would notify her of it. He might even tell Lord Mainwaring."

"That could be a delicate situation," Oliver mused. "And Kilbothan would be the most logical suspect for those disappearances, aside from one of the servants. So he might have chosen other people whom he met through Lady Mainwaring but staged the thefts away from her house so there would be no reason to suspect him. But then why steal one of her ladyship's own jewels? Especially one that had great meaning for her."

"He might not have known about the meaning. I doubt she discusses her past lovers with her present one. Would you do so?"

"I? My dear, you malign me. You make it sound as if I had had a string of mistresses."

Vivian raised her brows. "However proper you may be, you are still a man."

"Yes. But not, I hope, a fickle one. I am generally known to be wise in my choices and steadfast in my ways." His eyes were warm on her.

Vivian looked away to conceal the little leap of delight inside her. "Kitty is not steadfast, perhaps, but she is not lacking in courtesy, either. I think it quite likely that she did not tell him that my father gave her that item. I think it is also possible that he did not even realize that it was Kitty's. She told me that he does not like her gambling and she did not tell him about losing the brooch to Sir Rufus until recently."

"A little censorious for a jewel thief, don't you think?"

Vivian grimaced. "The point is that he did not know she lost it to Sir Rufus. And he might not be familiar enough with her jewelry to recognize it when Sir Rufus was flashing it about."

"Even if Kilbothan did recognize it, he would feel safe since he was taking it from Sir Rufus, not Lady Mainwaring. He couldn't have known that she would call you into the matter . . . or that you would pursue it so doggedly. Once that happened, he could have decided to remove you by returning the brooch."

"Then you think he *is* the thief?"

Oliver shook his head. "I have no idea. I think it could be a possibility. On the other hand, his story could be true. I have no way of judging the man or his tale. " He glanced at her. "Perhaps you simply dislike him."

"I do dislike him," Vivian agreed without hesitation. "But that doesn't mean I'm not right to be suspicious of him."

"True."

"Mr. Brookman thinks it is likely that the thief is pawning the jewels."

"What? Who?"

"My jeweler. You remember."

"Yes. You mean you were questioning him again about these thefts?"

"Of course." Vivian nodded. "After I talked to Kitty, I drove over to his shop to see if he had learned anything about the thefts."

"And had he?"

"No. He thinks that the thief is not likely to try to sell to him and other reputable places. He thinks he would go to moneylenders and such. No doubt he's right." Vivian sighed. "It makes it much more difficult to find out anything."

Oliver's sigh was a gusty echo of her own. "But you intend to continue to try, don't you?"

"If I can think what to do next."

"I am sure you'll come up with something . . . though I dread to think what."

"Would you let go of a puzzle so easily? Don't you want to find out the answer? To stop the thief?"

"I would prefer that it stopped, yes. I'm not sure I want to go chasing about trying to find the answer myself. That is why I hired a Bow Street Runner to look into the matter."

Vivian glanced at him, surprised. "You did?"

He nodded. "I knew you would not stop, so I thought I had better do something to resolve it before you dragged me into another gaming hell."

Vivian laughed. "O'Neal's club wasn't a *hell*."

"Yes, but who knows what the next one will be like."

"Dearest Oliver, you always look on the bright side of

things." Vivian was not sure exactly why, but Oliver's hiring a Runner made her happy. It said something that neither of them could have—or perhaps would have—put into words. She cast him a flashing grin. "Now, I suppose we'd better rescue my poor brother from his unrelenting courtesy."

She nodded toward where Seyre was plodding along with Felicity Overbrook, glancing wistfully now and then toward Camellia and the others ranging ahead. Oliver followed her gaze and chuckled, and the two of them turned their mounts to join Gregory and his companion.

Seyre let out a sigh of relief when his sister and Stewkesbury trotted over to join them. It had been irritating enough when Overbrook and his sister joined him and Camellia just when he was hoping to start a conversation with her. But somehow he and Felicity had been separated from them, and she had had the trouble with her stirrup, and they had fallen behind. Then, instead of hurrying to catch up with the others, Miss Overbrook had grown slower and slower, so that now Camellia was far ahead of them and Gregory knew that he was doomed to finish the ride out to Richmond listening to Felicity Overbrook's inane chatter about an appallingly boring book she was reading.

This sort of thing happened so often to him with young ladies. Vivian accused him of being unbelievably naïve, but it wasn't so much naiveté as that though he could see he was being manipulated, he could not get out of the situation without being rude. He had seen far too many noblemen being arrogantly rude for him to indulge in such tactics himself.

Vivian, however, was a master at politely extricating one from any situation, so when she appeared, the earl in tow, she slipped in between Gregory and Miss Overbrook, then engaged the young lady in a deep conversation about the new, lowered waists on the most recent fashion plates in Ackermann's. Gregory gratefully gave a nod and murmured a polite farewell to the three of them, then was off before Miss Overbrook could say a word.

It did not take him long catch up to Camellia's group. His gelding might not have quite the speed of the bay stallion he had stabled at Marchester, but he was swift enough and like Gregory had been chafing at the slow pace of Miss Overbrook. But even when Seyre joined the group, he found it difficult to talk to Camellia. Percy Overbrook and Charles Whitten had taken up positions on either side of Miss Bascombe, and they clearly had no intentions of giving way to anyone else.

They continued in this way until they drew close to the park, and then Gregory had the inspired idea of suggesting a race to its entrance. Knowing Whitten's inferior riding skills and Overbrook's preference for horses that were more showy than swift, it didn't surprise Gregory that by the time they reached the park, Gregory and Camellia were far out in front, riding almost neck and neck. He considered for a moment reining in his gelding a bit to let Camellia win, but he suspected that not only would the American girl realize what he had done, she would dislike it. So he gave his horse its head, and he surged in front of Camellia's mare.

Gregory eased up as they passed through the gates, but neither of them stopped. Instead they continued to gallop along the lane, putting more and more distance between them and the others. Finally, when they had pulled out of sight of the rest of the party, Gregory slowed down, and Camellia, after a moment, did, too, falling back to join him.

"Oh, that was wonderful!" Camellia turned toward him. "I can't tell you how much I've missed that."

Delight shone in her face, making her beautiful, and just looking at her made Gregory's heart stutter in his chest.

She was without artifice, without reserve—unlike any other woman he had ever met.

Gregory smiled at her. "Yes, I miss it, too."

She started to speak, then stopped, and the unabashed joy on her face cooled a little, her expression turning cautious. Gregory felt certain that she had just remembered that she disliked him, and he sighed inwardly.

"Well," she said. "I suppose we ought to turn back."

He nodded, even though rejoining the others was the last thing he desired. They turned their mounts and started back at a walk. Gregory glanced at Camellia and found her watching him, but as soon as their gazes met, she looked away. His fingers tightened around his reins.

"Miss Bascombe . . . I hope you will forgive me. I should have told you who I was as soon as we met. I—it was wrong of me, I know, but it was so pleasant to talk to someone who didn't know I'm Marchester's heir. To just chat, you see, without being judged."

"Judged?" Camellia shot him a startled glance. "You? But you're a duke's son. That's the top of the list, isn't it?"

He let out a short laugh. "I suppose you could put it that way. But that's exactly why everyone judges one. Are you acting the way a duke's son should act? Do you do what everyone thinks you should? If you do aught wrong, it reflects badly on your family, your title, your father and grandfather and who knows who else. If you're reserved or quiet, they'll say you are stuffy or too proud, and if you're friendly, they say that you don't show the proper respect for your position. That you are too egalitarian or you don't know how to act or your dear departed grandmother would be horrified to hear you speak so familiarly. People watch everything you do because you are the marquess."

Camellia stared at him in astonishment, and after a moment, she began to chuckle. "But that's how they treat me! They watch me, waiting for me to take a misstep, and they talk about it. But it's because I'm an outsider—an American—and I don't know what I'm doing. Because I *don't* belong."

Gregory smiled. "I think that simply proves that the *ton* loves to gossip."

"And criticize," Camellia added feelingly. "I didn't think about it like that—that perhaps it was a relief for you not to have to be the future duke for a few minutes."

"Yes." Relief rushed through him. "That is exactly how I felt. As though I could be myself, not Marchester's son, and it was . . . well, it was wonderful. I couldn't bring myself to tell you who I was." He smiled a little crookedly. "Especially after you told me how you felt about the aristocracy."

"Oh." Camellia blushed. "That. My sisters can tell you that my tongue runs away with me sometimes. I don't dislike you because you are a marquess. The reason I got angry was because you hadn't told me the truth. I thought you were playing a game with me, pretending not to be a nobleman just so you could trick me."

"Why would I do that?" he asked, puzzled.

Camellia shrugged. "I don't know. But I frequently don't know why people here do the things they do. I thought you must somehow be making a jest of me, and it stung because . . ." She paused, then went on softly, "Because I liked you." She looked over at him. "It made me feel foolish that I had enjoyed talking to you."

"I enjoyed it, too." He looked at her. "I would never make a jest of you. I swear it. You have only to ask Vivian; she will tell you that I am far too serious."

Camellia smiled faintly. "I don't have to ask her. I believe you."

"Good. Then perhaps we can do that again sometime . . . enjoy talking to each other?"

"I'd like that." They exchanged a smile, and slowly they rode back to join the rest of the party.

Vivian shaded her eyes, watching her brother and Camellia returning. Gregory and Camellia were talking, she saw with satisfaction. She darted a look over at Dora. The girl had gotten down from the barouche and was almost literally surrounded by young men, all trying to get her attention. But Dora, Vivian saw, was looking past her admirers, her gaze on Gregory.

"I believe it will be some time before the wagon arrives and they are able to set up the luncheon," Oliver said from close behind Vivian. "Shall we take a stroll while we wait?"

Vivian smiled. "It sounds far more enjoyable than standing here watching Miss Parkington work her wiles on the gentlemen. Still . . . they must have chaperones."

"Let Fitz and Eve chaperone them." Oliver had no compunction about tossing his brother and sister-in-law to the wolves. "After all, they're married now, far better as chaperones than a bachelor and a spinster."

"A spinster!" Vivian raised her brows in mock indignation. "I like that!"

"My lady, it is you who are always trumpeting your single state," Oliver reminded her with a twinkle in his eye.

"It is far different if *I* say it. I ought to refuse to go with you for that insult . . . however, I fear I will be the one to suffer if I stay."

She turned, putting her hand on his arm, and they walked away from the others.

"I am an unfeeling sister to leave poor Gregory at the mercy of Miss Parkington," Vivian confessed.

"No doubt. But comfort yourself with the fact that you have rescued me from listening to Miss Willis-Houghton's giggles any longer."

Vivian laughed. "Then I have saved your sanity, in short."

"Indeed you have."

They strolled along a path that wound through a stand of graceful birches. Though they were in view of everyone, Vivian could not help but think how no one was around to hear them or see their expressions. They were as close to alone as they could be among a party of people. The thought stirred a spark of desire deep within her. She cast a sideways glance up at Oliver. He seemed to feel her gaze, for he turned his head and looked down at her. Something changed in his face, his mouth softening, his eyes turning brighter and more piercing.

"I don't know which is more difficult," he said. "To not see you and spend all my time thinking about you, as I have the last two days, or to see you, be with you, and be unable to touch you."

"We are touching now," Vivian pointed out, looking at her hand on his arm.

He followed her gaze and grimaced. " 'Tis not the touch I imagined." He made a low growling noise. "Bloody hell! I hate this—creeping out of your bedroom, hiding from the servants and your brother, hopping in and out of your bed."

"I know. It isn't your way." Vivian tilted her head a little, considering. "And I like that. Which makes it even more imperative that I purchase a house of my own. My man of business has found one or two that might do, he thinks."

Oliver glanced at her sharply. "You know what I think of your moving into a house on your own."

"Yes, but it will make things easier."

His expression was clearly that of a man torn. "Your reputation is more important."

"I got a note from my agent this morning before I left the house. He suggested I see one of the houses. I think I shall look at it tomorrow afternoon. Would you like to come?"

"I must be mad, participating in this . . ."

"Mm. No doubt." She paused. "It would be perfectly natural for me to seek the advice of a man, after all."

Oliver let out a snort. "To anyone who did not know you, perhaps it would seem natural."

"Maybe you are influencing me to become more proper."

He stopped and turned to her. "You do not need me there."

"No." Vivian gazed up steadily into his gray eyes, stormy now in his indecision. "Nor do I need a new hat. But that doesn't stop me from wanting it."

"You know I will go with you. Only send me a note to tell me the time."

He stood for a moment gazing down at her. Vivian wished he would lean down and kiss her. It would cause a perfect uproar, of course, but at the moment she thought it would be worth it. She could almost feel his lips on hers, soft yet demanding, as they had been the other night. It had sent a shiver through her to hear him say that he had been thinking about that night, too . . . wanting her. Just as she had lain in her bed last night, wanting him.

"Do you always get your way?" he murmured, his eyes glinting.

Vivian smiled up at him. "Almost always."

By the time they walked back to the group, the servants had arrived, and they were spreading out rugs for the members of the party to sit on and laying down the glasses and plates for the cold luncheon they had brought in the wagon.

Vivian noticed that Dora managed to maneuver her way over to stand near Gregory as the servants laid out the food. When everyone started toward the feast to sit down, Dora stumbled and had to grab Gregory's arm. He glanced at her, surprised, but steadied her with his other hand. Dora raised her large, lovely eyes to him, murmuring a sweet thanks, and kept her hand looped through his arm the rest of the way to the rug. When Camellia sat down beside Eve, Gregory took a step toward her, but Dora gripped his arm more firmly, declaring that she must sit down, for she was feeling a trifle faint. Though two other men sprang forward to help her, Dora kept her iron grip on Seyre's arm.

Vivian watched with some interest as her brother politely helped the girl to sit down on the rug spread out on the grass by the servants. So far Dora had completely outmaneuvered Gregory, and Vivian wondered if she ought to step in and rescue him.

"Let me get you some water," she heard Gregory say, and Dora gave him another of her grateful, gracefully weak looks.

Much to Vivian's surprised delight, her brother straightened up, grabbed a glass of water from one of the maids, and handed it to Dora, then nodded to the girl politely and excused himself. Vivian chuckled as she watched Dora gape at Gregory as he walked over to join Camellia.

"Well, well," Vivian murmured as she sat down at some distance from Dora and her admirers. "So he cares enough to fight it."

"What?" Oliver glanced at her curiously. "Who? What are you talking about?"

"Miss Parkington has been relentlessly working her wiles on Seyre for the past few minutes, but he left her to sit beside Camellia."

"I would think so." Oliver made a face. "If he sat with Miss Parkington, he would find himself so busy doing things for her that he wouldn't have time to eat."

Vivian chuckled. "Too true. But Gregory usually finds himself outmaneuvered by girls such as Miss Parkington. All

I can think is that for the first time, perhaps he cared enough not to let her do so."

"Cared enough?" Oliver asked, and Vivian answered by nodding toward where her brother sat beside Camellia.

"Camellia?" Oliver's eyebrows rose. "Seyre is interested in Camellia?"

Vivian couldn't help but laugh. "Yes, they seem quite different, I suppose."

"That is a model of understatement." Oliver studied Camellia and Gregory for a moment. "Does he realize that one of her hobbies is sharpshooting?"

Vivian shrugged. "I believe that he has nothing against firearms. And he does like to ride."

"Yes, but in every other way I would say they are ill-suited."

Vivian shrugged. "I imagine there are those who would say that you and I are ill-suited."

Oliver glanced at her. "My dear Vivian, *I* would say you and I are ill-suited."

Vivian laughed and leaned closer, saying in a low voice, "Not in *every* way, my lord."

She was rewarded by the faint line of red that spread across the earl's cheekbones, and the look he sent her held more heat than reproof. "Careful, my dear, you will make me forget myself."

"I should like to see that." Vivian's eyes danced.

The look in his eyes then took her breath away, and for once, Vivian was the one who had to look away.

Her gaze fell upon Miss Parkington. Two gentlemen were on one side of her and another man on the other, all of them trying to outdo the others, but Dora's eyes kept straying to Seyre, sitting beside Camellia. Vivian studied the young girl's face as she watched Camellia and Gregory, and she knew, without a doubt, that Camellia, without even knowing it, had acquired a fierce enemy.

Dora spent the rest of the afternoon trying in one way or another to pull Gregory into her retinue of admirers. Vivian, observing her, had to admit that the girl was skillful. First she tried to gain Seyre's attention and arouse his jealousy by laughing and flirting with her admirers. When it became clear that Vivian's brother had not even noticed what Dora was doing, she moved on, announcing with a pretty little shiver that the afternoon was too cold for her. Four young men solicitously offered her the use of their own jackets, and one of the maids went to fetch a carriage robe to lay across the girl's legs.

None of these solutions, however, seemed adequate. The only thing that would help, apparently, was to sit in a place more sheltered from the spring breeze—and that place was on Lord Seyre's left side. When confronted with Dora's large-eyed helplessness, Miss Willis-Houghton somewhat reluctantly moved over to make room. Gregory seemed happy to comply, moving closer to Camellia to give Miss Parkington space.

After starting up a conversation with Miss Willis-Houghton and Lord Cranston, Dora then began to pull Seyre into it with questions and remarks. Any answer he made was regarded with considerable attention, even awe, by Miss Parkington. She admired his knowledge, his gift of speaking, his foresight, his hindsight, and his opinion on everything.

When Dora exclaimed in her soft voice, "Oh, Lord Seyre, you are so intelligent," for the fourth time, Camellia could not hold back a laugh.

Dora turned to Camellia in astonishment. "Why, Miss Bascombe, do you not agree that the marquess is an unusually learned man? I vow, I have never before heard a man so able to discourse on almost any subject."

"No doubt he is quite smart," Camellia agreed. "But he was only answering a question about some plants in his garden."

"But I could tell you all about every plant there," Gregory assured her, grinning at Camellia.

"I wish you would not," Camellia responded with a horrified look, and the two of them laughed.

Dora glanced from Camellia to Gregory in bafflement. Had Miss Parkington been a more good-hearted young woman, Vivian would have felt sorry for her. It was clear—even to Miss Parkington, Vivian thought—that all her never-miss tactics were failing with Lord Seyre. Indeed, Vivian could have told the girl that everything Dora did—from cutting Camellia out of the conversation to regarding Seyre with girlish admiration to requiring his strong masculine help at every turn—only drove Gregory further from her. Being made the center of attention embarrassed him, as did false flattery. And since his primary interest was in conversing with Camellia, Dora's frequent interruptions and diversions only irritated him.

By the time the luncheon had ended and it was time to make the trip home, Miss Parkington seemed to have given up her campaign. She let herself be escorted by Lord Cranston and Mr. Overbrook back to her barouche, flirting madly with the two men as she went. Vivian stood watching the girl, wondering if Dora had actually surrendered her hopes of catching Seyre or if she was once again attempting at make him jealous.

"Thank God Cranston and Overbrook don't mind escorting her," Gregory said in a low voice, coming up beside his sister. "I think I'd throw myself under the carriage if I had to ride back to the city with Miss Parkington."

Vivian turned to look at Seyre, suppressing a smile. "I think some men find her quite alluring."

"Really?" Seyre studied Dora for a moment, then shrugged. "I suppose she's attractive. But . . . well . . . I don't understand how she's able to get through a day, being so unable to do anything for herself or have a thought of her own."

Vivian laughed. "Ah, Gregory, I am so glad you are you. I could not bear it if you brought home a girl like Dora Parkington as your wife."

To her further amusement, a look of sheer horror crossed her brother's face. "Good Gad, Viv, what a thing to think!"

The groom led over their horses, and they mounted. Ahead of them, Stewkesbury turned his horse aside and looked back, waiting for them, and Vivian noticed with a great deal of interest that Camellia, too, looked back and held her horse in check. Vivian smiled a little to herself. Perhaps things were going to work out well for Gregory. She clicked her tongue, urging her horse forward to join Camellia and Oliver. It was, Vivian thought, a perfectly glorious day.

When they reached London, the party rode past Stewkesbury House on the way to Carlyle Hall, so the Talbots turned off there. As the Talbot party made their good-byes, Vivian glanced at Camellia and saw that she was staring over at the narrow walkway beside the house that led toward the back garden. Vivian followed her gaze curiously and saw a short, slight man standing on the edge of the walk, watching them. He leaned against the wall, and in his dark, drab clothes, he blended into the shadow cast by the house.

Vivian looked back to Camellia and saw that she had dismounted, handing the reins of her horse to one of the grooms. Vivian's attention was then distracted by Oliver, who came over to bid Vivian good-bye. Vivian leaned down from her horse, stretching out her gloved hand, and he took it, bowing briefly.

"You will come with me tomorrow afternoon?" she asked. A peculiar little pain was in her chest, and she realized that she wished she did not have to wait until tomorrow to see Oliver. It would be different, she thought, when she had a house. She could see him frequently. It would not bother her so much then to part from him. Indeed, it seemed foolish that it should make her feel so lonely and disappointed now.

"I shall be there," Oliver assured her, and the smile that lit his eyes warmed her.

Vivian straightened, watching him stroll into the house with Eve and Fitz, and it struck her that Camellia was not with them. Vivian glanced back and saw that Camellia had walked over to the small, sandy-haired man standing in the shadows. As Vivian watched, the American girl exchanged a few short words with the man. Camellia shook her head, and the man appeared to plead with her. He pressed a piece of paper into her hand.

Vivian frowned and turned away. Her gaze fell on the barouche, and she realized that she was not the only person who had observed Camellia and her odd companion. Dora Parkington, a faint, self-satisfied smile on her lips, was watching Camellia, too.

Chapter 17

Oliver arrived at Carlyle Hall promptly at one o'clock the next afternoon, just as Vivian had expected him to. There was something to be said, she thought, for knowing that a man would be exactly on time. Indeed, she was discovering a number of things about Oliver that were quite appealing—completely aside from the heady feeling of excitement that arose in her whenever he appeared. It seemed absurd that a man as steady and reliable as Stewkesbury, a man one had known practically all one's life, could cause such a jangle of nerves and lust as soon as one saw him.

Vivian had been ready and waiting for almost fifteen minutes—another absurdity and one she was not about to reveal to him—and at the sound of Oliver's voice in the entryway below, she jumped to her feet, grabbing up her bonnet and gloves. She forced herself to pause at the door for five seconds before she started down to greet him. A quick glance in the hall mirror assured her that every hair was in place and she was looking her best. She was wearing a carriage gown from last year, something she rarely did, but the deep dull gold color and the simple, almost military lines were especially flattering. These days, she found, she was more concerned with how good an outfit looked on her than she was with being in the first stare of fashion.

Oliver was standing at the foot of the stairs, waiting for her, and she saw the slight, appreciative widening of his eyes as she walked down the steps. She smiled, drawing on her gloves as she came.

"You must be a man of great faith not to sit down in the drawing room to wait for me. Everyone will tell you I am rarely on time."

He smiled back at her, coming forward to give her his hand down the last two steps. "Ah, but we are going somewhere you are eager to visit. That makes all the difference, doesn't it?"

Vivian saw no point in telling him that the difference was that she was eager to see him. She was aware of an urge to reach out and caress his cheek, but that was unthinkable with the footman standing by the door, waiting to open it for them. Instead she turned to the mirror and put on her hat, taking an extra moment to tie the bow and let her emotions settle. Then she slipped her gloved hand into the crook of his arm, and though it was a poor substitute for caressing his face, it made her heart beat a little faster anyway.

Outside, Oliver took her hand to help her up into the carriage, and his hand lingered on hers longer than was necessary—just as it had when he'd reached out to her on the stairs earlier. He was, she thought, as eager to touch her as she had been to touch him. The desire that simmered not far below the surface turned such courtesies into a titillating taste of the full repast they wanted—and aroused that hunger more than it fed it.

Vivian settled into the carriage, and Oliver took the seat across from her. The look in his eyes was enough to take her breath away. She wondered what would happen if she moved across the carriage and sat beside him. Would he pull her into his arms and kiss her? She imagined him knocking her bonnet askew, sinking his hands into her hair, his mouth taking hers deeply, hungrily . . .

Oliver cleared his throat and turned his head to look out the window, shifting slightly in his seat. "Um . . . I received a report from the Bow Street Runner this morning."

"Indeed?" Vivian had little interest at the moment in the Runner or the jewel thief, but she tried to turn her thoughts along that path. "Has he discovered something?"

"Possibly. He told me when I hired him that he was aware of the number of thefts lately. His suspicion was that it was the work of a ring of thieves. He has been looking into it the past few days, and he's convinced that it is indeed more than one thief who is operating in the city."

"So he is looking for several men?"

"Yes, but he also believes that there is one man in charge—guiding their operations, supplying the thieves with information, targeting the victims. Unfortunately, he has not been able to come up with even a whisper of the identity of the leader, and without that, it is of little use to capture some of the thieves who are doing the legwork. The operation will continue with other people."

"What does he intend to do?"

"He thinks that the ring is operating out of a particular tavern."

"Not a gambling club?"

"No. A tavern with a much less savory reputation than the club we went to. Of course, that does not exclude the possibility of one or more of the thieves operating out of gambling dens. Or even the possibility of our friend Mr. O'Neal being the leader of the ring. He would not want to connect his business to the thefts."

"What is the name of the tavern?"

"The Dancing Bear. The Runner went there, but he was unable to learn anything of value. It seems that he has become too well-known to the criminal community to pass undetected."

"Ah." Vivian's eyes sparkled.

"No," Oliver said quickly.

"You haven't even heard what I was going to say," Vivian protested.

"I didn't need to hear it. I knew from the look in your eyes that you were about to suggest something wild and totally improper, like going to that tavern yourself."

"Why, Oliver, what a wonderful idea!"

He grimaced. "Please. Don't pretend that I was the one who came up with it."

"I would not deny that the thought occurred to me, as it did to you. I think it goes to show that our minds must run alike." Vivian let out a little laugh. "You needn't look so horrified."

"Vivian, be serious for once. You cannot go to the tavern. It's impossible. The place isn't fit for anyone, let alone a lady. It is, quite literally if Mr. Furness is correct, a den of thieves. And, I am sure, a number of other equally unsavory characters."

"I won't go there as a lady. I shall wear a disguise. I'll dress as a man."

"Don't be absurd. No one would believe you are a man."

She looked thoughtful. "Then perhaps I should dress as a lady of the evening."

"What!" He straightened, his eyes bulging so comically that Vivian burst into laughter. "Vivian! My God! You can't be serious! Have you run mad?"

"No. I'm sorry." Vivian reached out to pat his arm. "Poor Oliver. I should not tease you that way. I will not dress up like Haymarket ware." She let out a little sigh. "Though I must admit, it would be rather fun."

"It would *not* be fun," he told her firmly.

"Just dressing that way, I mean." She cast him a teasing glance. "Would you not enjoy it if I dressed that way?"

"No." But the sudden heat that flared in his eyes belied his denial.

Vivian leaned forward, a provocative smile curving up her lips. "Really? I think you're lying. What if I had come down the stairs today wearing, let's see . . . a bright red gown, taffeta, I think, because it would rustle so nicely when I walked, with the neck cut down to here." She drew a fingernail slowly in a line across the bosom of her dress, watching Oliver's eyes following the movement. "What would you have done?"

His eyes glittered, but he said only, "I'd have sent you straight back upstairs to change."

"Would you?" Her laugh was low and throaty. "I think you'd have followed me up there."

"Perhaps I would have." His mouth softened sensually. "To make sure."

"Of course." The look on his face set up a heated thrumming deep in her abdomen. She could feel her insides softening, like wax in the afternoon sun, opening, yearning. "I would want you to make sure."

"Vivian . . . you are starting something we cannot finish."

"No? But it's fun, isn't it? Just to talk?"

"It would be a great deal more fun to do more than talk."

Vivian grinned, leaning forward. "You mean here? Now?"

Flames leapt up in his eyes. His fingers curled around the edges of the seat as he stared at her. It was so quiet she could hear the rasp of his breath in his throat. It took them both another moment to realize that the silence meant that the carriage had halted.

"We're here," Vivian said weakly, and turned to look out the window. Her man of business trotted down the steps of the house and made for the carriage. Across from her, Oliver bit back an oath.

"My lady!" Mr. Barnes opened the carriage door, bowing to her. "It is an honor. So good of you to come personally to see the house."

"I could hardly expect you to bring it to me, now, could I?" Vivian gave the man her hand and stepped out of the carriage.

Oliver followed, giving a businesslike nod as Vivian introduced him to the agent. Mr. Barnes bowed and assured Stewkesbury that he was honored to meet him. Vivian could see the trace of curiosity on the man's face, much as he strove to conceal it with polite blankness. Her man of business was aware, of course, how rarely Vivian needed anyone's advice. Barnes would be bound to wonder why she suddenly needed Stewkesbury's counsel.

Of course, she didn't *need* it, she knew. It was just that . . . well, it was more enjoyable to have Oliver with her. And she could not help but feel that the house was bound up in him. She had first broached the subject to him as much as a jest as anything. Now it had become something that she wanted because of him, where she could have the freedom to be with him.

Vivian studied the narrow three-story house of white stone. Far smaller than Carlyle Hall, it had none of that manor's grandeur, but its address was excellent, and the trim, graceful lines appealed to Vivian. Most of all, the house would require few staff, and she could live alone there with only her quiet and obliging cousin as chaperone. There would be no father, no brother, no servants who had known her from childhood.

Mr. Barnes showed them through the house, though he would have skipped the cellar, kitchen, and servants' quarters had Vivian not insisted upon examining them.

Oliver followed Vivian, saying little, and though she glanced back at him now and then, she could tell nothing from his expression. She had trouble concentrating on the house and her business agent's words. She was too aware of Oliver behind her and of the low hum of arousal vibrating through her. Walking through the bedchambers on the second floor was curiously intimate. Even though there was no furniture, it was easy to imagine the beds. It was difficult, in fact, not to picture a bed dominating each room.

She could not glance around the large front bedroom, considering it for her own chamber, without thinking of Oliver there . . . kissing her, touching her, lying with her throughout the night. A shiver ran through her, and she cast a quick look back at Oliver, wondering if he had seen it. She found his gray eyes on her, and she could not help but wonder if he was thinking the same things she was.

Vivian turned toward Mr. Barnes and gave him a politely dismissive smile and nod. "Thank you, Barnes. I will let you know what I think. But right now I would like to walk through the house again by myself. Just to make sure how I feel about it."

"Of course, my lady." If her statement surprised him, he covered it well, bowing in acquiescence. His gaze did not even flicker toward Oliver. "I shall wait for you downstairs, then."

"No, please, don't bother. I'll take the key and send it round to you later."

"Of course." Barnes handed her the key, bowed, and murmured a good-bye.

Vivian wandered over to the window, gazing out at the houses along the street. Barnes's footsteps sounded on the stairs, followed by the sound of a door closing. She watched for a moment as Barnes strode off down the street. Turning to Oliver, she untied her bonnet and set it aside on the window seat.

"Well?" she asked, strolling toward him. "What do you think of it?"

"It is a pleasant house." Oliver moved forward, stopping a few feet from her. "Though it hardly seems a grand enough stage for you."

"You think I require something magnificent?"

"It matches you more nearly." He came closer. "As your jewels do." He reached out and lightly touched the gold-and-amber earring that dangled from her ear. His hand dropped down to graze the puffed upper sleeve of her dress as he went on, "Your clothes."

Vivian's pulse throbbed in her throat. She was intensely aware of his hand on her arm, the weight and warmth. "This house is practical."

"That alone should tell you it doesn't suit you." Oliver smiled. His hand remained on her arm, but curved gently around it.

"It will suit my purposes." Vivian moved in closer to him and grasped the lapels of his jacket, tilting her head back to look up at him.

He swallowed. "We should not be here like this. You should not have told Barnes to leave."

"I wanted him to leave."

"What if he gossips? He knows the two of us are in here alone together."

"He knows better than to gossip about me or my business. He wouldn't handle my money if he did."

"I should have stepped outside with him. Let you look at the house alone."

A dimple winked in Vivian's cheek as she smiled flirtatiously. "But if you had done that, how could I do this?"

She went up on tiptoe and kissed him. Stewkesbury froze for an instant, too startled by her action, too stunned by the raw lust sweeping through him, to even move. Then his arms wrapped around her, crushing her body into his, and he kissed her, his mouth hot and hungry, devouring hers. Vivian clung to him, passion rushing up in her like a wave. The kiss was intoxicating. Consuming. Addictive. She pressed against him, wanting more. Wanting it now.

It didn't matter that her businessman and the coachman knew she was in here alone. It didn't matter that Barnes could turn back to ask her something or that her servant might take it into his head to come looking for her. The front door was unlocked. She was tempting fate. But Vivian could not bring herself to care. All she could think of right now was Oliver and the desire that pulsed through her body, hot and driving.

"We shouldn't. This is madness," Oliver murmured as he kissed his way down the column of her throat.

The front of her dress was fastened in large brass buttons, and he undid them, his fingers clumsy with haste. He slipped his hand inside her dress and beneath her chemise, curling around her breast. His lips moved down over the white expanse of her chest and onto the soft tops of her breasts. Vivian sucked in her breath, her hands coming up to dig into his hair. Her fingers clenched as his mouth found the hard, pointing center of her nipple.

Her head fell back, her breath coming in short, hard pants as he teased at her nipple, using lips and teeth and tongue, arousing her in sharp, hard bursts of pleasure. One of his arms was hard around her back, holding her up, and with the other hand he grasped her skirt, clenching and unclenching to work it up her leg. At last his fingers touched the silk of her stocking. His breath shuddered out, and he raised his head to take her mouth in another deep, possessive kiss.

His fingers trailed up over her stocking, their heat searing her though the filmy material, and skimmed over the garter that held the stocking. He slid his hand higher onto her bare flesh, then stopped abruptly. Raising his head, he stared down into her face, astonishment mingling with fierce arousal.

"You're not wearing anything beneath—?" His voice rasped to a halt, as if he could get out nothing else.

Vivian shook her head, her eyes gleaming with seductive mischief. "I thought it would be easier that way."

"You planned this?" His eyes widened.

She smiled slowly. "I thought I should be open to the possibility."

His face flushed, and his hand was suddenly fiery against her skin. Slowly, deliberately, not moving his gaze from her face, he slid his hand up her leg. Curving it around her hip and onto the swell of her buttocks, he caressed her naked flesh. Moving his hand downward, he slipped it between her legs, moving them apart. Then he circled back over her hip and onto the plain of her stomach, gliding downward in slow, teasing increments.

Vivian's breath was ragged in her throat, and everything in her was afire. She could feel the dampness pooling between her legs, the throbbing ache that blossomed there. His fingers found her, and she shuddered as he separated the slick folds of flesh, exploring, teasing, sending bright cords of longing deep into her.

He watched her, his eyes bright with hunger, hard with purpose, as his fingers moved, gentle and insistent, stoking her pleasure. He saw desire flicker across her face, heightened with every movement of his hand. He watched it build and gather, pushing her ever higher onto that taut, high peak until she was poised, trembling, above the precipice. He saw her slide over that edge, shuddering with the intensity of her passion.

He bent then and took her mouth with his, drinking in

her pleasure, her need. Vivian flung her arms around his neck, straining up against him, and he lifted her, his hands digging into her buttocks. Wrapping her legs around him, she pressed herself against him, longing to feel him inside her, filling her, losing himself in her.

Oliver moved forward blindly, unwilling to release her or move his mouth from hers, and they came up hard against a wall. Bracing her against it, he unbuttoned his breeches and shifted, and Vivian could feel him, hard and prodding, against the most intimate part of her. She moved, taking him into her, and he thrust deep inside. A thin exhalation of satisfaction escaped her, and she arched back against the wall, moving with him in a deep, primal rhythm as he drove into her again and again. She could feel the storm building in her all over again. Everything about the moment was almost unbearably arousing—the low guttural noise he made as he buried his face in her neck, the heated scent of him, the touch of his lips upon her sensitive skin, the spice of recklessness, even the feel of his jacket beneath her hands, reminding her that they were both still clothed.

He plunged deep inside her, shuddering in a paroxysm of pleasure, and Vivian let out a choked cry as she, too, hurtled into that deep abyss.

They remained that way for a long moment, too stunned and depleted to move or speak. Oliver kissed her neck gently and breathed out her name. Finally he moved, letting her slide back down to put her feet on the floor, but still he stood curved around her for another long moment. Then he turned away, adjusting his clothing as he gave her time to set herself to rights. Vivian felt far too languid to move, but she made herself shake out her skirts and rebutton her bodice.

Oliver turned back to her. His face was still loose and warm with pleasure, but gravity was returning to his eyes. He shook his head. "God, just looking at you—" He looked away, setting his jaw. "You must be mad to take such risks. Someone could have walked in on us at any moment."

"I am not the only one who took the risk. I have never done such a thing before, so if I am mad, it is clearly you who has made me that way." Vivian gave him her provocative little smile and started to walk away.

He followed her, grabbing her arm and pulling her back around. He wrapped his arms around her, pulling her to him and holding her tightly.

Vivian let out a little laugh, startled. "Oliver! Surely you cannot want me again already."

"I want you all the time." His voice was thick. "Dear God, I am the one who is mad. I cannot keep from thinking about you. Remembering your smile, your laugh, the way you cast that sideways glance at me that leaves me feeling I am either a fool or a king."

Vivian chuckled again, warmed by his words, and she wrapped her arms around him, nestling into his chest. "Perhaps you are both."

"How like you to say that." Oliver smiled, rubbing his cheek against her hair. "Any other woman would have assured me that I am never a fool. And what does it make me that I would far prefer your words?"

"Ah . . . that is the thing that makes you *not* a fool."

"I worry about your reputation," he went on soberly. "I know you are cavalier about it, but I cannot help but be concerned. I know I should stop. I tell myself so time and again. Someone is bound to suspect if we keep on. And yet . . . I cannot make myself end it."

"There is no need to end it." Vivian leaned back and smiled up at him. "It will happen as it happens. Oliver, for once, why don't you let go and enjoy the moment? Forget about planning or controlling or making things fit. Just be . . . happy."

He leaned down and kissed the top of her head, then rested his cheek against her hair again. "All right. If you ask it, I shall try."

He had lost his mind, Oliver thought as he walked home half an hour later. A strong desire was inside him to smile at nothing and to nod cheerfully at people he didn't know. He could not stop the aura of goodwill and supreme satisfaction that floated within him like a cloud. Indeed, he could not even bring himself to wish it were not there. After all, nothing was wrong in feeling good, or unusual about a man's being content and satisfied after a bout of vigorous sexual union.

The problem was that it was all part of the madness that had afflicted him for the past month. The madness that was Vivian Carlyle. He realized that he was smiling just at the thought of her, desire stirring again in his loins. What the devil was he doing? What was he going to do?

He knew the correct course of action. The honorable thing. He should end the affair. End it immediately before any real harm was done. No one knew about it; there were no whispers or rumors. They could part now, and no one would be the wiser; Vivian's reputation would not suffer.

It was up to him to stop it, he knew. Vivian would never be that rational, that cool-minded. A woman of fire and impulse, she did as she pleased and let the world be damned. She would not take the steps necessary to protect herself. So he had to be the one to think instead of feel, to do what should be done instead of what he wanted to do. That was usually the case, and Oliver was long accustomed to it. It had been he who had shipped Royce off to their Scottish lodge to get him away from his disastrous love for Lord Humphrey Carlyle's wife. It had been he who had fished Fitz out of all sorts of tangles at Oxford and when he was first on the town. When Oliver's American cousins had shown up in London, he had not hesitated to take them in and establish them as English ladies.

Oliver did not mind being the responsible one. He had accepted that role long ago when his grandfather had made it clear that their family's future rested in his hands, not his feckless father's. The old earl had prepared him for it, taught him and helped him, and Oliver had been perfectly willing to be the head of the family. If pressed, he would admit that he enjoyed the role. He liked to plan; he liked to solve problems; he liked to set things right. Until Vivian.

For the first time in his life, he knew what he should do, but he could not bring himself to do it. He could not bring himself to give her up, not even for her own good. Just the thought of not seeing her again made his chest tighten and his throat close up, so that he felt as if he could not breathe.

There was another option. He could marry Vivian.

But that was unthinkable. Every time the idea popped into his head, he had shaken it off immediately. He could not marry Vivian. Aside from the very real, quite lowering probability that Vivian would not even accept his proposal, the unalterable fact was that he and Vivian would make the most dreadful match. They were fire and ice, night and day. He was rational, responsible—yes, he would admit it, he was *staid*—whereas she . . . she was all glittering beauty, impulsive and emotional, like quicksilver. His calm, his propensity to plan, his tendency to consider all the things that might go wrong with a course of action would drive her to a fury. They always had. How much more so if she had to live with him night and day?

It was all very well right now, when the things she did made him laugh even while he shook his head over her foolhardiness, when her impulsive actions were as arousing and deeply satisfying as what she had done today. But eventually, he knew, that would change. If he were tied to her, it would not be so easy to overlook her eccentricities. She would come to be infuriating rather than entrancing. Once this intense hunger she inspired in him died down, Vivian would begin to grate on his nerves. Attraction only lasted for so long; after that, a married couple needed mutual interests and agreeable personalities to get along.

Look at the way his own father and stepmother had fought. He could not count the number of their jealous accusations and bouts of temper. Of course, those had been followed by equally emotional reconciliations. They were a tempestuous couple. And they had been in love.

Oliver was anything but tempestuous. Nor was he in love with Vivian. He could not be. What he felt around her was excitement. Exhilaration. Lust. That was not enough for marriage. He was not fool enough to try to convince himself that it was. He would not salvage the situation by marrying Vivian. Which left him no choice but to leave her.

Oliver stopped. He had been so lost in thought that he hadn't realized how quickly and how far he had walked. He was standing only a few feet from his house. He looked up at the great gray stone edifice of Stewkesbury House. He thought about going inside and working on his accounts. He would have dinner with Camellia and Fitz and Eve, then go to the library and spend the evening reading. Or he could go to his club. Perhaps among all the invitations on the hall table, a party would interest him. All things that had nothing to do with Vivian.

He knew he would do none of them. He would go see Vivian. In all probability, he would get caught up in one of her mad schemes. No doubt he would regret it. But, however foolish it might be, he could not give her up. Not yet.

Chapter 18

Vivian was sitting in the drawing room when the butler announced Lord Stewkesbury. She put aside the hoop of embroidery she had halfheartedly been working on and stood to greet him.

"Stewkesbury." He looked, she thought, especially handsome in his dark driving coat, decorated at the shoulders with several capes.

"Lady Vivian." He took her hand and bowed formally, his eyes gleaming at her in a way that told Vivian he was remembering what they had done this afternoon.

"Come. Sit down, and tell me what brings you here tonight." Vivian gestured politely toward the sofa.

"Must I have an excuse to pay a call on you?" he countered, sitting down.

"No, indeed. It is just that I find you usually have a reason for whatever you do." She paused, and when he said nothing, she went on, "What are your plans for the evening?"

He shrugged. "I'm not sure. Perhaps I'll go to my club." With elaborate casualness, he added, "What party are you attending this evening?"

"I had not planned to go to any." Vivian's eyes were steady on his.

"No?" His eyes narrowed. "What exactly are you planning to do?"

Vivian chuckled. "Why, go to that tavern your Runner told you about, just as you intend to do."

He grimaced. "Devil take it! I knew you would."

"Of course. That's precisely why you came here."

He scowled at her. "Don't be nonsensical."

"Then you are not going to the Dancing Bear?"

"Yes, I'm going," he admitted gruffly. "But you are not." As she began to smile, he added quickly, "And I didn't come here to take you to it, whatever you might think. I came to make sure you don't go."

"Oliver, I'm not sure—are you lying only to me or to yourself as well?"

He frowned even more fiercely for a moment, then relaxed, letting out a soft groan. "I'm not sure. I may be lying to myself more than anyone." He leaned back, rubbing his hands across his face. "You shouldn't go. I shouldn't let you."

"What nonsense." She thought it was better, perhaps, not to remind him that he had no control over her. So she turned the conversation to another path. "I have my costume ready."

"You are *not* going as a bird of paradise." He shot upright again.

"Of course not. That was a jest. I am going as a boy."

"You will never pass as one."

"Wait right here. I will show you."

Shortly Vivian came back into the room, wearing the rough shoes, collarless shirt, and breeches of a working-class boy. Oliver stood up, his eyes going to the swell of her breasts beneath the large shirt, then to the nicely shaped calves exposed by the breeches.

"However large your shirt may be, there is no disguising that you are a woman," he told her severely.

"That is why I am wearing a jacket." Vivian held up the long jacket she carried and put it on, buttoning it up so that it covered the curving shape of her body. Then she pulled a soft cap out of the pocket of the jacket and settled it on her head, pulling it down so that it covered every bit of her hair. "There. You see?"

She faced him, plunging her hands in the pockets of the jacket and standing with her legs a little apart, adopting a look of defiance.

"If you look like a boy, then I have a problem because all I can think is that I would like to kiss you."

Vivian laughed. "Go ahead. I won't be shocked."

He reached out and gripped her shoulders, pulling her to him, and kissed her thoroughly. "Vivian . . . ," he murmured, leaning his forehead against hers. "Don't you see it won't work? You are far too beautiful to be a boy."

"I'm not finished." Vivian reached in her other pocket and took out two small bags. The first one held several small rounded objects.

"What the devil are those?" Oliver peered at them.

"Plumpers. Haven't you ever seen an old lady wearing them? They make their cheeks look fuller and therefore younger."

She carefully placed them between her cheeks and jaw, filling out the delicate lines of her jaw. Then she opened the other bag and smeared some of the dirt inside it over her forehead and cheeks. She turned to Oliver again, posing.

"Now you look like a dirty pretty woman with odd lumps."

"You are impossible." Vivian slapped at his arm playfully. "The tavern will not be well lit. No one will be able to see me well enough to tell."

"Do you need some clothes?" Vivian asked. "I got some larger things for you, as well."

He shook his head, silently unbuttoning his coat and opening it to show Vivian the rough work clothes he wore underneath.

"You came prepared. You intended to take me with you all along, didn't you?"

"Only if you were planning to go without me." He paused. "Would you have gone if I had not dropped by?"

Vivian smiled. "I knew you would come. And if you had not, I would have gone to fetch you."

"I feared you might invite Cam to go with you."

"I thought about it. But if it were discovered, it would hurt her reputation. Besides, I decided that your size was more imposing."

"Thank goodness for that." Oliver started toward the door, stepping back politely to allow her through first.

"What is Cam doing tonight?" Vivian asked as she walked past him. "At a party with Eve?"

He shook his head. "No. She was tired and decided to stay home. So thankfully she is in bed, and I don't have to worry about her."

Camellia inched her bedroom door open and peered out. The hall was empty, the house quiet. Eve and Fitz had left an hour before for a soiree and hopefully would not be back for several hours. The servants had finally gone up to their rooms.

She turned back and threw on her cloak over her white dress. It was a trifle warm, but the black cloak with its concealing hood was much better for blending into the background than her fashionable new cloak, which was lighter in both weight and color and had a distinctive edging of pale blue braid. Picking up her pistol from the dresser, she slipped it into the capacious pocket of the cloak, then bent to check that the small scabbard belted around her right calf was still in place, the knife inside it easy to slide out. She pulled a small bag from her dresser and stuck it in the other pocket. Turning, she cast a last glance over the room. The pillows looked realistic enough under the bedcovers, the nightcap stuffed with a nightgown peeking just above the cover—or at least hopefully they would look so with the room dark.

Camellia blew out the candle, plunging the room into darkness, then opened the door and stepped out into the hallway. Her heart thumping, she tiptoed to the stairway and peered over the rail to the wide expanse of the entry hall below. A footman was seated on the bench by the door, head tilted back against the wall, catching a few winks while he waited for the occupants of Stewkesbury House to return home. She would have to take the longer route by the back stairway.

Camellia started quietly down the hall, pushing aside her guilt at deceiving everyone. She hated to lie to the people she cared about, and she had felt low and guilty telling everyone at supper that she was tired and wanted to retire early. It had been doubly aggravating since she had, for once, actually wanted to attend the party Eve and Fitz were going to. She had hoped that Lord Seyre might be there. Not, of course, that she was interested in him the way all the other young women were. It was absurd to think that there could be anything romantic between her and a man who would someday be a duke. But he was nice and easy to talk to, with interesting things to say, unlike most of the men she met. And if she was honest about it, she would have to admit that he wasn't hard on the eyes, either. She liked his dark brown hair, warmed by red highlights, and she found it somehow charming that it always looked vaguely mussed. His eyes, so green and thoughtful, crinkled at the corners when he smiled. His long, lean form was pleasant to look at, as well.

But that was neither here nor there. However guilty she might feel, however much she might have liked to see the marquess, she had more pressing problems to attend to. Yesterday when they had returned from Richmond Park, she had seen Cosmo lurking about near the house. She had gone over to send him away before anyone saw him, and he had pressed a note into her hand.

"Come meet me, Cammy," he had whined. "Please, you have to. You know I don't want to do anything to hurt you. But I gotta give him something. He'll kill me. You gotta help me."

Camellia had little liking for Cosmo Glass; she had despised her stepfather almost from the moment she met him, and nothing she had seen of him since had changed her opinion. But real fear had been in Cosmo's face yesterday, which she found hard to ignore. Besides, she knew what Cosmo was like when he was scared; he might very well tell everyone Camellia was his daughter instead of his stepdaughter, simply lashing out in his desperation. That would embroil them all in a scandal, including Oliver and Lily, and she could not let that happen.

So Camellia had decided that she must meet him tonight as he had asked and do whatever she could to keep him from spreading his lies about her. This afternoon she had asked a few careful questions of one of the maids and spent some time poring over a map of the city, and she was reasonably certain that she would be able to find the address Cosmo had written on the note. But even though Camellia was not easily frightened, she did wish that the man had set the time for this afternoon instead of after dark. If nothing else, it would have made getting out of the house easier.

Camellia paused at the servants' stairwell, listening for any sound from above or below. When she heard nothing, she started down, hoping no squeak of the boards would betray her.

She made it down to the kitchen without any noise and let out a sigh of relief when she saw that the kitchen was empty. She started toward the back door, then froze. Whirling, she saw Pirate, the earl's dog, happily trotting out from his favorite spot when the earl was gone, the little space beneath the back staircase where he liked to hide his dubious treasures. He wagged his little stump of a tail vigorously and bounded forward, his mouth open and his tongue lolling out in that way that looked as if he were maniacally smiling. Perhaps he was, Camellia thought; Pirate seemed to have a nose for getting into trouble.

"No, Pirate!" Camellia hissed, and waved her hand toward his den beneath the stairs. "Go back. You can't come."

The animal ignored her words, trotting up to her and rearing up on his hind legs to plant his front paws firmly on her knee, still wagging and grinning enthusiastically. Camellia tried to shoo him away, but then he went into a little dance in which he jumped back and forth in front of her, his hindquarters going up in the air and his front legs bowing down. His eyes gleamed in the dim light. Camellia had seen this dance often enough to know what would come next—he would start to bark merrily. Hastily, she opened the door and slipped outside, but Pirate squeezed like an eel between her and the doorjamb and shot out into the back garden.

"Blast! Pirate!" Camellia hissed.

The dog sniffed the air and trotted off to mark his favorite spots. Camellia stood for a moment, assailed by indecision. If she tried to chase Pirate down and force him back inside, it might very well make enough noise to wake one of the servants. But if she left him alone here in the garden, he would doubtless become bored and start barking to get back in, which would definitely wake the servants. Still, on the whole, that seemed the wiser course. Even if someone had to get up and let the dog in, wouldn't he simply assume that someone had forgotten to let Pirate in earlier? They wouldn't go check her room to make sure she was there.

She eased over to the back gate and opened it, easing quietly out. Even though he had been a good thirty feet from her the last she looked, suddenly Pirate shot past her. He stopped and whirled around to face her, wagging.

"Pirate!" Camellia hissed, afraid to raise her voice. She did her best to shoo him back, but it didn't work, so she reached out to grab him. He darted away, and she ran after him. He stopped at the end of the walkway, regarding her expectantly, but as soon as she bent to pick him up, he scampered away. They proceeded halfway down the block in this manner before Camellia stopped with a sigh.

"All right, you little beast." She pulled up her hood to cover her head and started forward. Perhaps it wouldn't be so bad to have company on her trek, even if it was only a dog. "But I won't carry you."

As she walked, she became aware of the sound of steps behind her. Pirate, bounding ahead of her to sniff all about and pounce on shadows, did not seem aware of the sound at all. Camellia slipped her hand into her pocket, taking a grip on her pistol. She had not expected trouble to start so soon. The steps were growing nearer.

She whirled, whipping the pistol up to train on the man behind her. "Stop right there. Why are you following me?"

The figure froze, then said mildly, "I say, Miss Bascombe, it's only me." He took a half step forward out of the shadows and lifted his hat politely.

"Lord Seyre!" Camellia relaxed in relief, lowering the pistol. "Whatever are you doing here? You scared me half to death!"

"I'm sorry. Truly, I didn't want to frighten you. I would have called to you, but, well, I had the feeling you wouldn't want me trumpeting your name."

"No! Thank you. I am glad you didn't." She slipped the gun back into her pocket, but regarded him somewhat suspiciously. "Why are you here? Why were you following me?"

"Oh, well." He paused and glanced about. "I was, um, just walking by."

Camellia raised an eyebrow. "You aren't a very good liar. You expect me to believe that you just happened to be walking by right then? Were you spying on me?"

"No!" Even in the dim light, she could see the blush that spread across his cheeks. "It isn't so odd, really. We don't live far apart. I frequently walk along this street." When she continued to stare at him skeptically, Seyre went on, "And when I saw you sneaking out, I—"

"I wasn't sneaking," Camellia protested.

"Of course not. When I saw you, um, walking the dog . . ." Seyre came closer. "I thought you might enjoy some company."

Camellia's mouth tightened in frustration. She would, in fact, appreciate the company, especially his. But she had no desire for him to learn what she was doing. "Actually, I would prefer to be alone. It is just a little walk, really, and I won't be gone long."

The corner of his mouth twisted, and he looked decidedly uncomfortable. Camellia could not help but think that he also looked rather adorable, which, she knew, was excessively foolish, but there was simply no getting around it. She wondered if all the girls who sought him out in their mad pursuit of his title even realized how good-looking he was in his own sweetly shy way.

"The thing is, I just can't," he told her. "I know you

probably wish me at the devil, but I cannot in good conscience abandon you here. I realize you don't wish to tell me where you are going, but if—if you are meeting a man, I have to tell you that he isn't a gentleman or he would not ask you to meet him this way."

"I'm not meeting a man!" Camellia gasped. "I mean, well, I guess I am, but it's not what you think. And he isn't a gentleman, that's something I'm certain of."

"Must you meet him, then?" Seyre asked carefully.

Camellia sighed. "Yes. I really must. I know it isn't proper for me to be walking about the city alone at night like this."

"Well, no, I suppose not, but that's not the problem. The thing is, London is dangerous for a woman alone at night, and I don't think your dog would be much protection." He cast a doubtful glance at Pirate, who was standing and regarding them both with doggy good humor, his rear end wiggling in anticipation.

Camellia chuckled. "You haven't seen Pirate in action." She sobered and said, "And, remember, I have my pistol." She leaned down and raised her skirts enough to show him the knife in its scabbard strapped to her calf just above her ankle. "As well as this."

"My." He bent down. "What a cunning device." He straightened. "Perhaps I could walk along with you then, and you could protect me."

Camellia could not help but laugh. She turned and started on, and Lord Seyre fell in beside her.

"I think you're supposed to tell me how very unladylike my behavior is," she told him.

"Am I? But I really have no desire to."

"You are a very different sort of man, Lord Seyre."

"So I have been told. But perhaps you could call me Gregory—I mean, now that you've threatened me with a pistol, it seems that you could use my given name."

"All right. Gregory. And I am Camellia."

"Camellia. It's a beautiful name. Beautiful flower. I'm rather partial to horticulture, you know."

"The man I'm going to see is my stepfather." Camellia was surprised that she had blurted out that news. But she realized that she wanted very badly to confide in him. The story would end any chance she had with a man as aristocratic as he, of course. But did that really matter? It wasn't as if someone like him would want to be anything more than a friend to her . . . not that she had any interest in marrying him.

"Your stepfather! Your stepfather asked you to meet him at night? Alone?"

"He isn't the sort to consider what harm might come to me. He is more concerned about harm coming to him." The whole tale then tumbled out of her. She told him about Cosmo and his base nature, about the dreadful mistake her mother had made in marrying him, trying to protect her daughters. She recounted the criminal activities Cosmo had already engaged in since he came to England and finished with his visit to her a few weeks ago and the threat he had made.

"The devil!" Seyre exclaimed when she finished. "The man's a scoundrel! Trying to take advantage of you in that manner. We won't let him, that's all. We shall do something about it."

"I plan to," Camellia told him grimly.

"Do you plan to shoot him?" he asked in a tone of mild inquiry.

Camellia found herself chuckling again. "You don't sound disapproving."

"I imagine he deserves it. But it might cause a bit of a scandal."

"I don't plan to shoot him, however much I would like

to. The gun is just for protection. I'm going to offer Cosmo all my money and try to convince him to take it and leave London. He sounded as though someone was threatening him, so perhaps he might be willing to run away if I give him the money to do so."

She reached into the other pocket of her cloak and pulled out the small bag. Opening it, she showed him the contents: coins and paper money, as well as a pair of gold earrings and a cameo necklace.

"The earl has given me a generous allowance every month, and I haven't spent much of it. Unfortunately, I haven't much jewelry." She glanced up at him. "It probably doesn't seem like much to you, but I think Cosmo might find it enough. It isn't the Stewkesbury jewels, of course, but it's much easier to use."

"That's true." Gregory felt in his pockets and pulled out some bills. "I'm afraid I haven't much cash with me." He stuffed most of the bills into the bag. "I'll just hold this back as I think it might behoove us to find a carriage if this place is very far. Oh." He snapped his fingers and reached up to pull the stickpin from his neckcloth. A dark red jewel in a setting of gold gleamed at the end of the pin. He tossed that in with the money.

"Gregory!" Camellia stared at him, shocked. "No, you mustn't! I cannot ask that of you."

"Oh, no." He looked embarrassed. "It's nothing. A mere trifle, really. Thing is, I have quite a bit of blunt, actually, and I rarely buy anything but books. Papa and Vivian have quite given up on me. You'd be doing me a favor to take it."

Camellia chuckled. "I am beginning to believe that you are a complete hand."

"Do you think so?" He grinned back at her. "I don't believe anyone has ever accused me of that."

"Then they clearly have not been paying attention."

They walked on, talking agreeably. The evening, Camellia thought, was turning out to be astonishingly pleasant. She showed Gregory the address Cosmo had written down for her. His eyebrows rose, and he declared firmly that they really should take a carriage. He caught the next one that came by, and the driver agreed to take them, though his manner was reluctant and he added decisively that he would not carry them clear to the door.

"No place fer a lady," he told Gregory, nodding toward Camellia's hooded figure. "Ner fer a gennulman, either." His gaze paused on Pirate, and he fell silent, merely shaking his head.

The coach let them down a few blocks from their destination, and they started forward once again on foot. It was a narrow street, lit only infrequently with streetlamps. The buildings on either side were dark, with few and narrow windows, and they loomed over the street. Pirate, who had been napping in the carriage, seemed disinclined to walk now, so Gregory picked him up and tucked him under his arm. They did not speak as they walked; the atmosphere of the street did not encourage talk.

A man emerged from one of the buildings ahead and started toward them. His hat was pulled low over his head, and he crossed the street before he reached them and continued on the other side. Camellia kept her hand in her cloak pocket, firmly wrapped around the butt of the pistol. They walked past the door they sought the first time, only realizing a few doors down that they had missed the number. They circled back, searching for numbers, but could find none. Counting back, Gregory surmised that they had reached the door they wanted and opened it.

"I think," he told Camellia in a low voice, "that I must break the rules of courtesy and enter first."

Camellia peered past him through the doorway. A dark,

narrow hallway stretched away in front of them, and to their left was a similarly dark staircase. The air was thick with the sour smell of garbage and other, even fouler odors. Her heart quailed a little at stepping into the dank, dark place, but she shook her head firmly.

"I'm the one with a pistol," she reminded him, drawing out the weapon.

"I don't suppose you have another one?"

She shook her head but bent down and pulled her knife from its scabbard and handed it to him. They looked at each other, then, by some sort of silent agreement, they started up the staircase side by side. Gregory set down Pirate, and the little animal bounded up the steps in front of them. Halfway down the hall, one of the doors stood partly open, a low light issuing from it. Pirate stopped in front of the door and stretched his head forward, not moving his body. A long, low growl came out of him, and the short hair at the ruff of his neck stood up.

Gregory clutched the knife handle more tightly, moving on tiptoe after the dog. Camellia kept pace beside him. Gregory stretched out his hand, cautiously pushing the door open. The room inside was small and contained little in the way of furniture. A small, three-drawer chest had been knocked over so that it tilted crazily against the narrow bed, and the items that had been atop it were scattered on the floor. A chair lay on its back on the floor. A candle sputtered on the floor in a puddle of wax.

But none of these things drew their eyes. All either Camellia or Gregory could look at was the still, slight form of a man lying on the floor, the side of his face covered in blood.

"Cosmo!"

Chapter 19

Camellia's stomach rolled. She had seen blood before, and injured men. At times at their tavern customers had gotten into fights, and they had frequently wound up bloodied. But something about the way her stepfather lay on the floor, utterly still, his head a bloody mess, told her this was worse than anything else she had seen.

She pressed her hand to her stomach to try to still the queasiness there. "Is he—is he dead?"

Gregory entered the room, carefully stepping over and around the broken and spilled objects. Reaching down, he picked up one end of the candle, leaving a charred spot in the floor. Holding up the candle, he squatted beside the body and felt for a pulse in Cosmo's scrawny neck. "Yes, I fear he is dead."

Pirate followed Gregory into the room, sniffing at everything he found. Gregory scooped him up and stood for a moment, looking down at the man. Camellia walked over to join him. She felt faintly ill and more than a little strange, almost as if she were disconnected from her own body, but she made a determined effort to pull herself together and act rationally.

"I suppose that is what killed him." She pointed to a

thick, round metal candleholder that lay a couple of feet from the body, coated with gore.

Gregory nodded and turned to her. "There is nothing we can do here. We should leave and contact a magistrate. Hire a Runner if you wish to find out who did it."

"Yes, I want to. I have no love for the man, but no one should die like that." She walked back to the door, followed by Gregory. He stopped and handed Pirate to Camellia, then pinched out the candle he held and laid it on the floor, closing the door behind him.

They started down the stairs, moving carefully in the dim light. The darkness around them felt oppressive, almost as if it were a tangible thing, weighing them down. It seemed as if a weight had been lifted from them when they stepped back into the street.

"Do you think—that man we passed—he could have been the killer!" Camellia said, speaking the thought that had been churning in her brain from almost the time they spotted the body.

Gregory nodded. "I'm not sure what door he came out of."

He cast a look up and down the street. The narrow lane had looked dangerous before, but it seemed far more so now, the doorways pools of shadow, the buildings pressing in on the street. Grasping Camellia's arm, he picked up their pace, all the while glancing carefully around them.

They reached an intersection, and as they started to cross it, they saw two men walking toward them down the side street. Pirate began to struggle in Camellia's arms. Startled, she reached to wrap her other hand around his collar, but he leapt nimbly from her arms before she could do so.

"Pirate! No!"

The dog paid her no heed, just raced straight at the other men.

Vivian sighed and glanced around the room. It was dark and noisy and filled with the stench of smoke and unwashed bodies. Their adventure this evening had turned out disappointingly so far. They had been here for over an hour and had learned absolutely nothing. She was not sure how they *could* learn anything here. The dimly lit room was crammed with men, most of whom had been drinking blue ruin for some time now. They were loud, talking and periodically raising their voices in song or in argument. One such argument had ended with the two men going at it with their fists. It had ended fairly quickly when the men had stumbled over the hearth and ended up singeing their arms at the edge of the massive fireplace.

She and Oliver had just sat here, pretending to drink the vile-tasting gin. Oliver had managed to down most of his, but Vivian had surreptitiously poured hers out onto the floor, where it had dripped through the wide cracks between the wooden planks. No one had spoken to them aside from a serving wench, and though nearly all of the customers looked capable of almost any villainy, there was no way to ascertain if one of them was a jewel thief. Oliver had finally gone over to talk to the barkeep, and after a few coins crossed his palm, he had nodded his head toward a table in the corner. Oliver had then made his way to the table and sat down with the three men there. Vivian watched him curiously and wished she had gone with him. However, she knew he was right; it would not take much to see through her disguise, and it was better that she stayed here in the shadowy reaches of the tavern.

As she watched, Oliver rose and walked back to her. Dropping down on the stool beside her, he said in a low voice, "The barkeep pointed out that fellow over there as knowing all the news around this area. He was reluctant to tell me any of it, of course, but a bit of money opened his mouth finally. He says that the slender chap seated at the bar, the one at this end—"

Vivian glanced over. "Blond-haired?"

"That is he. He is rumored to be making a good bit of money for himself these days. Spending it freely, too. Was never that good as a thief, my source told me, but he's large and intimidating, and apparently he's gathered a number of followers who keep him in plenty of brass."

"You think he's the ringleader?"

Oliver shrugged. "It certainly seems a possibility."

"What are we going to do?"

Oliver tossed her an amused glance. "I assumed *you* would have a plan of action."

She smiled. "I do. He's unlikely to tell us anything freely, so it would take either force or money, and I imagine either of them would do better outside the tavern. So let's watch and follow him when he leaves."

Oliver nodded. "My thoughts exactly." He studied her for a moment, then leaned over to say, "Does it not worry you at all? The possible danger?"

Vivian smiled up at him. "I know I'm safe with you."

He looked startled, then pleased, but his face quickly turned serious. "I will do my best to keep you so. Vivian . . ."

"Oh, look." She had caught a movement out of the corner of her eye, and she straightened. "He's leaving now."

The man they sought had slid off his stool at the bar and was weaving his way through the crowd. Oliver stood up and unobtrusively followed, with Vivian on his heels. By the time the man reached the door, they were only a few steps behind, and in the empty street outside, they quickly closed the gap.

"Excuse me!" Oliver's voice was not loud, but it was sharp and loaded with authority.

The man in front of them turned around. He was a good two inches taller than Oliver and a stone heavier. His eyes flickered over the two of them assessingly. Obviously dismissing them as threats, he shrugged and started to turn away again.

"I have a few questions for you," Oliver said quickly, and again the firm tone of authority seemed to have an effect on the other man.

"Yeah? Maybe I don't want to answer them." He looked at them suspiciously, but stayed where he was.

"I doubt that a magistrate will be concerned with your wishes."

"A magistrate. I ain't seeing no magistrate." The man sneered.

"No? Then I fear you will have to talk to me."

The man grinned and swung his large fist at Oliver. It would have been a hard blow had it landed, but Oliver easily ducked beneath the swing and came up hard, popping the other man in the nose. After a sickening crunch, blood spurted from his nose. The man swung again, enraged, and Oliver lightly sidestepped him, delivering two quick jabs to his opponent's side. They continued in this fashion, with the larger man swinging his fists or trying to pull Oliver into a bear hug and Oliver darting in and out, his feet always moving as he ducked blows and delivered punches to the man's torso and face.

Finally, blinded by blood and fury, his opponent charged Oliver. Oliver jumped to the side, sweeping one leg out low in front of the man and connecting sharply with his shins. The man stumbled and crashed to the ground, and Oliver was immediately on him, one knee planted firmly in his back. He seized one of the man's arms and twisted it painfully up behind him, so that the man could not move or buck him off without causing himself excruciating pain.

"Perhaps now you'd like to answer my questions."

"Yes. Yes! All right. Just let go!"

Oliver eased up on his hold. "You've been stealing jewelry the past few weeks."

"Not me! I swear! It's others as does it. I just get it from them."

"Get it? They just give it to you?"

"No, course not. I pay 'em."

"And then what do you do with it?"

The man shrugged, and Oliver twisted his arm tighter. He let out a yelp. "All right! All right! I take it to somebody and he pays me."

"You pawn it, you mean? You sell it?"

"No, I mean, yes, I guess I sell it to him."

"Who?"

"No! I can't tell you that!" The man turned his head toward Oliver as much as he could, his eye wheeling with fear. "He'd kill me, he would."

"The leader, you mean? The one who organizes it?"

The man nodded frantically. "Yes. Yes. It's him as runs it all. I don't know nothing about the others."

"What others?"

"The others he's got stealing things. There's more'n me. I'm just one."

"More intermediaries, you mean?" At the man's blank expression, Oliver went on, "More chaps like you, with several people thieving for each of them."

"Yes!" The man nodded. "Yes. Men like that. There's the ones that creep into houses and the ones that work round Drury, then the ones round the toffs' gambling dens."

Oliver let up a little in astonishment. "How many of them are there?"

At that moment the door to the tavern burst open and two men came tumbling out, followed by a swarm of their compatriots, all of them punching, swinging, and kicking. One of the combatants knocked into Vivian, sending her tumbling, and Oliver jumped up to try to catch her. He missed, and she went down, and one of the fighters reeled into Oliver. Oliver dispatched him with a swift uppercut, then shoved another fighter out of his way. By the time he reached Vivian and dragged her to her feet and out of the melee, the man he had been questioning was gone.

Letting out a curse, Oliver whirled to see the fellow racing up the street, a good half block ahead of him and gaining speed. Oliver turned back to Vivian. "Are you all right?"

"Yes. Nothing hurt but my dignity—and you know how little I have of that." Vivian grabbed his arm and pulled him to the side as another tavern patron reeled backward toward him.

Oliver took Vivian's hand and hauled her away from the tavern. "I think it is time for us to depart."

They strode quickly down the block and turned the corner, heading toward Oliver's carriage, which was parked unobtrusively down the side street. As they walked, a man and woman came into view at the next intersection. The woman carried a small dog that squirmed and wriggled, then jumped out of her arms and headed straight toward them.

"Good God! Pirate!" To Oliver's amazement, the dog made a flying leap, and Oliver automatically caught him.

"That's Cam!" Vivian exclaimed in a dumbfounded voice. "And my brother!"

Camellia and Gregory, who had come dashing after the dog, came to a sudden halt, staring at them.

"Cousin Oliver?" Camellia asked.

"Oh, dear." Gregory sighed in a resigned way. "Stewkesbury, I know you've every right to be furious, but—" He stopped and peered at Oliver's companion. "Vivian?" His voice and eyebrows rose dramatically.

For a moment, all four of them simply stared at one another; then everyone burst into a torrent of questions and explanations. One word, however, jumped out of the babble.

"Dead!" Oliver repeated, staring at Camellia, then swiveling to look at Gregory for confirmation. "Did you just say you found someone dead?"

Vivian drew in her breath sharply.

"Yes! That's what I've been saying!" Camellia exclaimed. "We found Cosmo, and he's dead!" She half turned, gesturing behind her.

"Your stepfather?" Oliver stared. "What happened? How—never mind. Just show me."

They started back the way Gregory and Camellia had come, pausing long enough for Oliver to grab a lantern from his coachman, still sitting placidly waiting for him. As they walked, the story of her evening came out in fits and starts from Camellia, her story added to now and then by Gregory. Oliver remained grimly silent.

They reached the narrow, dilapidated building and started up the stairs. This time the lantern provided ample light to see their surroundings, but the view was not improved. And the stench was just as bad. Vivian placed her hand over her nose and mouth, breathing shallowly. When they reached the room, Gregory opened the door and stepped inside, followed by Oliver. Pirate jumped lightly down from Oliver's arms and renewed his explorations.

Vivian remained by the door with Camellia, but even at this distance, it was clear that the man on the floor had breathed his last. Vivian's stomach roiled, and she turned away queasily.

"The devil!" she heard Oliver say, and then her brother's low voice as he pointed out the murder weapon.

"I'll inform my Runner," Oliver said. "And return here with him. But first let's get the ladies home." He turned a hard look at Camellia. "Where you belong, I might add, Cousin."

"I had to come," Camellia protested. "I had to do something. And look at Vivian. You brought her here, and she's wearing boy's clothes." Her look at Vivian's attire was envious.

"I am not Lady Vivian's guardian, thank heaven. And you are not getting out of this that easily, Camellia. You endangered your life by coming here alone."

"Gregory was with me."

"Only by accident, if I understand your story correctly." Oliver turned toward the other man. "Thank you, Seyre, for looking out for her."

"Well, if that isn't the most unfair thing I've ever heard!" Camellia gasped. "You ring a peal over me and you thank him!"

"You are the one who came up with the scheme, and *he* came along only to keep you safe. That makes a great deal of difference." Oliver turned back to the room and snapped his fingers at the dog. "Come, Pirate."

The dog obediently trotted to him. Oliver walked over to Vivian and, taking her arm, steered her toward the staircase. "Are you all right?" he asked in a low voice.

Vivian nodded. "I'm sorry. I should be more stoic. It is just . . . I have never seen a dead body before. I mean, well, except in a casket. All that blood! Someone must have hated him very much."

"I suspect a number of people did. I had little liking for the man myself. However, I think that for some people it doesn't take hatred or much of any emotion at all to kill a man."

"That's even worse." Vivian shivered, and Oliver curled his arm around her.

"There's a traveling rug in the carriage. You'll be warm soon."

She smiled up at him. "Thank you." She lowered her voice to a whisper. "But perhaps you'd better remove your arm; it might look a trifle odd."

Oliver started guiltily and dropped his arm. "Sorry." He cast a glance back toward Gregory. "I'm not sure how to explain this to your brother."

"There's no need to," Vivian told him firmly. "I am not accountable to my brother, as Gregory himself would tell you. He's most progressive in his thinking. Besides, he's the most unflappable man alive." She paused, then said, "Don't be too hard on Camellia. I am sure she is just as shaken as I am."

"Perhaps. One hopes it will curb her tendency to jump into danger, at least somewhat."

"I imagine so. It will certainly have a restraining effect on me."

Oliver glanced at her. "Really? Are you saying you're willing to leave this matter alone and let my Runner look into it?"

"Of course." Vivian nodded. "I'm quite capable of being reasonable, Oliver. It's one thing to visit gambling dens and masquerade in taverns and speculate on who might be stealing things. That is all rather fun and exciting. But murder is an entirely different matter. Besides, as you said, a Runner is surely better equipped to handle this situation than we are."

Oliver relaxed. "I am greatly relieved." He turned back to look at his cousin and Gregory, walking behind them. "What about you, Camellia? Will you promise to let the Runner take care of this and not go investigating on your own?"

Camellia nodded. "I don't know how I'd go about doing

anything, anyway. I have no idea who Cosmo was afraid of—or if that was even who killed him."

"One thing I don't understand," Gregory said thoughtfully. "Why do you *have* a Runner, anyway?"

"Yes." Camellia perked up a little. "And why were the two of you here tonight? Dressed like that?"

"We were investigating a series of jewel thefts." Stewkesbury explained as briefly as possible the events leading up to their expedition this evening.

"But jewels were what Cosmo was wanting from me." Camellia's voice rose in excitement. "He wanted to steal the Talbot jewels."

"That fact struck me when you said it." Oliver nodded.

They had reached the carriage, and the group fell silent for a moment while getting into the vehicle. But as soon as they were settled in their seats, Gregory started the conversation again.

"Do you think the two incidents are related? This murder and the jewel thefts?"

"It seems likely to me. Clearly, from what we have learned, there is a ring of professional thieves operating, and their prime target is jewelry. The only difference seems to be the method by which the jewels are taken—some by burglarizing a house, others by simply grabbing it from people on the street. Cosmo apparently had promised someone to get jewelry from Camellia's relatives, which would lead one to believe that Cosmo was involved with these same thieves."

"Do you think it was the leader who murdered him?" Camellia asked. "I know that Cosmo was well able to anger a number of people, but he was clearly frightened of this man who wanted the jewels from him."

"I would say that he is the most obvious choice," Gregory

spoke up. "But from what you said, Stewkesbury, there seems to be a chain of command. There are the lowliest ones, who actually do the stealing, and they turn their ill-gotten gains over to someone higher, such as the man you questioned tonight."

"That's true." Vivian nodded. "This man Cosmo could have been frightened of the intermediary or the head of the ring, I suppose. Either could have killed him."

"Whichever it was, if the Runner can find him, they can break the ring. Get the names of the others out of him. He'll turn over the rest of them if he thinks he can keep his life that way."

They continued to talk about the thefts until the carriage rolled to a stop in front of Carlyle Hall. Oliver and Camellia came inside with Gregory and Vivian so that Oliver could write a note to the Bow Street Runner asking him to meet Oliver at Stewkesbury House. After that, he planned to take Camellia home, pick up the Runner, and take him to Cosmo's body. Gregory decided that he would accompany Oliver on the gruesome errand, and so Vivian turned to say good-night to the others.

When she reached Camellia, Vivian paused, then said, "Cam, I don't understand. Why didn't you just tell Stewkesbury what your stepfather was threatening? Why didn't you tell me?" Vivian could not entirely conceal the note of hurt in her voice. "I would have helped you. Did you think I would not?"

"Oh, no!" Camellia cried, distressed. "It wasn't that. I knew you would help. You've been the best of friends. It was just . . ." She shook her head. "I don't know. I was ashamed, I guess, that he was even my stepfather. I didn't want anyone to know. I didn't want you or Stewkesbury to have to be involved in anything concerning Cosmo. And I—" She cast a slightly wary glance at Oliver before she said reluctantly, "I was afraid you might believe him, Cousin Oliver. Or at least wonder if what he said might be true."

"Camellia!" Oliver looked shocked. "How can you think that? I thought I had made it quite clear that I accepted you and your sisters as my cousins."

"Yes, but . . . it would be so odd, you see, for a man to claim someone as his daughter if she wasn't. People would be bound to wonder if it wasn't true."

"I don't listen to what people 'wonder.' "

"Yes, I know. But there were the other things—I could see that you might be suspicious. Others would be; there would be talk. I didn't want to embroil you in a scandal."

"Any scandal would have died quickly," Oliver assured her. "If I say you are my cousin, who would argue?"

Camellia looked at him squarely. "But do you truly believe it? Despite my birth records and everything?"

Oliver gazed back at her just as steadily. "Yes. I believe you. Records do burn. Not every Talbot has black hair. And if you had known my grandfather, I think there are aspects of your personality that you would have known were very like one Talbot, at least."

"I'm like your grandfather?" She stared.

"In some ways. He was a very stubborn, self-sufficient man." Oliver smiled slightly. "In any case, I know you. And I know your sisters. You all say you are their sister. I know that none of you would lie about that."

Tears welled in Camellia's eyes. "Oh." She blinked them away determinedly and gave him a small smile. "Well, that's all right, then."

Vivian smiled as she looked from Camellia to Oliver. That, she thought, was what made Oliver the consummate gentleman that he was. It was not his old and prestigious title, nor that he could trace his ancestors back to 1066. It was not even his punctiliously correct manners or knowledge of society's rules. No, what made him a gentleman, a nobleman in the truest sense of the word, was what she had just witnessed—Oliver's inherent sense of right and wrong, his unerring ability to steer the best path through any situation. Most of all, it was his kindness, the openheartedness that had impelled him to take in four orphaned girls—not just to provide for them in the minimal way that his peers would expect of him as the Earl of Stewkesbury, but to see to their happiness as well as their welfare, to make them truly a welcome part of his family.

Vivian could feel her own throat closing up a little with tears. Oliver was, truly, the best of men. And she knew suddenly, looking at him now, that this was not just a passing affair, a matter of passion. Oliver was everything she wanted in a man, and she was perilously close to falling in love with him. Indeed, she found she already had.

Chapter 20

Vivian kept a determinedly pleasant expression on her face as she listened to Lady Prym and wished for at least the tenth time that they had not already made plans to go to the theater tonight. She had not slept well since the night they had discovered Cosmo Glass's body. The first night she had been unable to go to sleep until she had heard Gregory return to the house. Last night, as she and Gregory had come home from a deadly dull musicale at Mrs. Cavanaugh's, she had had the most peculiar feeling of being watched when she stepped out of her carriage. She had looked all around and seen no one, but the whole thing had given her the shivers, and she had slept poorly, waking to every sudden noise.

She had considered quite seriously sending her regrets to Eve and staying home to go to bed early. It would have been the sensible thing to do. But she told herself that she could not let the earl think her nerves had been so adversely affected by the events the other night. She was made of sterner stuff. However, Vivian knew, deep down, that the real reason she'd decided to attend the theater with Eve and Fitz was that Oliver would be with them, and she wanted to see him.

It was quite foolish, she told herself, that she apparently

could not go two days without seeing the man. She had always been so independent, so heart-whole. Yet now here she was, missing Oliver whenever he was not around, wondering where he was and what he was doing. Yes, finding Cosmo's body had been disturbing, but Vivian had also been quite certain that if only Oliver had been there, sleeping in her bed, she would have slept soundly.

Tonight as soon as she saw him, her tiredness had vanished in an instant. Much as she enjoyed feeling that way, that her emotions were so tied to Oliver was rather frightening. Her happiness had never depended on any man before, and she could not help but wonder what would happen when Oliver was no longer with her.

That day would come. Vivian had no illusions about that. She might be falling in love with the man—God forbid, perhaps she already was in love with him. But they had no chance of a future. Oliver most definitely did not feel the same way about her, and there was no chance of his asking her to marry him. Indeed, she would not marry him if she had the chance. However much her feelings might have become engaged, she was no fool. She was ill-suited for marriage. And she and Oliver were even more ill-suited for each other.

Such thoughts had cast something of a pall over the evening despite her pleasure at being with Oliver. Then, to make things worse, Lady Parkington and the maddening Dora were at the theater. Lady Parkington had seen them and managed to catch Eve's eye and wave. Eve had let out a low groan as she politely but unenthusiastically smiled back.

"Oh, dear, she caught me," Eve murmured. She glanced over at Camellia, sitting beside Gregory at the other end of the row. "I did not see her until too late. Now she is certain to visit us between acts."

"It isn't your fault," Vivian had assured Eve. "Once she

saw us, we were doomed to a visit. Lady Parkington is not the sort to wait for even the slightest invitation."

For the first intermission, they had had to endure her ladyship's and Dora's company and their untiring efforts to maneuver Gregory into talking to the girl. Fortunately Fitz, safely off the marriage market, stepped in to occupy Dora's time, engaging in the sort of light, meaningless flirtation at which he so excelled, and Gregory, positioned between Camellia and the wall, managed not to utter a word beyond a greeting and a good-bye to either Dora or her mother.

When they left, Vivian had hoped that the worst was over, but now, here was Lady Prym ruining the second entr' acte with her recounting of Mrs. Cavanaugh's musicale the evening before. It had been boring enough the first time around, Vivian thought, without having to go through it again.

Vivian breathed a sigh of relief when Lady Stillkirk, who accompanied Lady Prym, moved in to shift the conversation. "That is all very well, but you have not yet touched on the most exciting news," Lady Stillkirk told her friend, glancing around the theater box to make sure everyone's eyes were on her. "Miss Belinda Cavanaugh received a proposal at the end of the evening—and from a most eligible *parti.*" She paused, casting them a look of triumph.

"A brave man indeed if he could still tie his fate to hers after enduring that evening," Fitz commented wryly, having also had the misfortune of attending the musicale.

Vivian stifled a laugh, but Lady Prym's next words wiped all trace of humor from her mind. "Ah, well, Lady Stillkirk, love seems to be in the air these days, after all." She leaned forward to tap the earl lightly on the arm with her fan, saying archly, "You have been dancing attendance on Lady Vivian for weeks now, my lord. One wonders if one might not soon hear a happy announcement from Marchester."

Vivian stared at the woman in shock, and her tongue seemed to cleave to the roof of her mouth. Eve cast a quick glance of apology at Vivian. Only Oliver seemed able to reply.

He let his eyebrows drift upward in a cool look of condescension and drawled, "Indeed, madam? I imagine you would have to inquire of the duke about that."

Vivian recovered her voice and let out a light laugh. "My dear Lady Prym, I fear you are much mistaken. I am helping my friend Mrs. Talbot with Stewkesbury's cousin's first Season." Vivian cast a smiling glance at Eve. "It hardly seemed fair for a newlywed to shoulder the entire responsibility of bringing out a young girl. Poor Stewkesbury has been forced to accompany us. I am sure the poor man finds it dull beyond measure."

"Nonsense, Lady Vivian, how could any man find escorting two lovely ladies dull?" Oliver responded, his voice achieving exactly the right tone of boredom to signify a denial for courtesy's sake only.

Vivian could see the hesitation on Lady Prym's face, the sudden niggling doubt that perhaps her source of gossip was wrong. Fitz seized the moment to pay Lady Prym an extravagant compliment on her dress, and the woman's attention was diverted. Vivian could not bring herself to look at Oliver. Doubtless he was displeased—and, moreover, he would regard it as proof that they should be more circumspect.

If people were beginning to suspect something between them, then probably the wiser course would be to spend less time together. Of course, now that they were turning their mystery entirely over to the Runner, there would be fewer reasons for them to be thrown together. It was amazing, Vivian thought, how often the most sensible course was also the least palatable.

The two ladies departed after a few more minutes, and the play began again. Vivian relaxed into her seat, glad to be out from under scrutiny for a time. After the play, she was forced to wait, for her brother and Camellia seemed in no hurry to leave, but finally they exchanged their good-byes with the others in their party, and Vivian and Gregory climbed into their carriage to go home. At first, they were silent, but she felt his eyes upon her, studying her.

Finally he said, "Lady Prym—"

Vivian interrupted him with an inelegant snort of disapproval. "Lady Prym is a fool."

"That and more," Gregory agreed mildly. "But I couldn't help but think, Stewkesbury has been around a good deal lately."

"Well, you and he are friends, are you not?"

"I don't think it is me he wishes to see. You and he spend a great deal of time together."

Vivian shrugged. "I might point out that you and Camellia Bascombe spend a great deal of time together, too."

"Yes, but the thing is . . . I think I love Camellia."

His reply brought Vivian straight up in her seat. "What? Really? Gregory . . . are you sure? You have not known her long."

"I know. But the first time I saw her, even before I knew who she was, I felt—I'm not sure what, as if someone had reached right into my chest and grabbed my heart. I know I am not very experienced, but neither am I a fool. You know I am not a romantic sort. I am a man of science, not poetry. But I have met a number of other young women, and never did I feel for them what I feel for Camellia. She's like no one I know. Open and refreshing. Different. I think about her all the time."

Vivian simply looked at him, not sure what to say. She liked Camellia very much, and she could not think of anyone she would more want as her brother's wife. But she had no idea if Camellia returned Gregory's affections. She had talked to Camellia little lately, and she had seen her with Gregory only a few times. Camellia seemed to like Gregory; she talked with him animatedly. But Vivian had seen in her little of the flirtatiousness of a young girl who was interested in a man. On the other hand, Vivian was not sure that Camellia had that flirtatious quality in her.

Gregory must have sensed the sorts of thoughts that were whirling around in her mind. "Do not worry, Viv. I know that the odds are against me. I don't expect her to fall in love with me. I am not handsome enough or exciting enough for Camellia. I'm sure no one would think we would suit. But I cannot change how I feel about her."

"You are very handsome, and any woman who did not think so would be most foolish!"

He chuckled. "Spoken like a loyal sister. But I know what I am—bookish, unromantic, not the kind of man who appeals to young women. And the irony of it is that the one thing that usually draws women to me like flies to honey is something Camellia doesn't care a fig about—my title."

"Perhaps that is one of the things that appeals to you about her. You know that whatever she feels about you, it is for you yourself and not some title or land or wealth. And who is to say that the two of you would not suit? You both love to ride. You enjoy living in the country. Neither of you likes parties or making calls or any of the *ton*-ish sorts of things."

"That scarcely seems the basis for a marriage, does it?"

"I would think it's more than a good many couples have. Think about the man who falls in love with Dora Parkington for her sweet and girlish ways, only to find that it was all cold calculation."

Gregory smiled. "No need to threaten me with such

horrors. I would like to think that if Camellia comes to know me better, she might feel something stronger for me. But I fear I'm deceiving myself. We are quite different. She is so vivid, all fire and passion, straight like an arrow to the heart of what she wants. And I am the puttering, meandering thinker, always questioning, planning. Dull."

"You are not dull." Vivian leaned across the carriage and took her brother's hands. "Stop saying such things. I have clearly been too wrapped up in my own doings. I have not paid enough attention to you or Camellia. I will talk to her, spend time with her, and see if I can gather some sense of how she feels about you."

"Do not push her, Vivian." He sounded alarmed.

"Gregory, dear, give me some credit. I will be as subtle as a butterfly." She settled back in her seat and fell silent.

She could not help but think of her own relationship with Oliver and how very different they were. Was her brother right, that two people so different could not find happiness? A common ground? She and Oliver, she thought, had the opposite relationship to that of Cam and Gregory. Her brother and Camellia were friends, but he feared that there was no attraction between them. With Vivian and Oliver, it was all attraction, but they were not compatible. It was all heat, with nothing solid beneath it. Such a relationship could not last; surely it was only illusory. But if it was illusory, why did it hurt so much when she told herself she must see him less?

When they reached their home, Vivian went straight up to her room. She was tired and ready for sleep, and she wanted, quite frankly, to stop thinking. Her maid helped her out of her clothes and into a nightgown, then took down her hair and brushed it out. It was a relief, as it always was, to shake out her hair, and the rhythmic strokes of the brush through it soothed and relaxed her. When her maid slipped out of the room, Vivian climbed into bed and snuggled down into the soft mattress. This night, finally, she fell quickly and deeply asleep.

She awoke with a snap, pulled abruptly out of her sleep, and for an instant, she was lost. Darkness was all around her, only the faintest bit of light around the edges of the draperies. Something was around her neck, choking off her breath. She struggled and the hard thing around her neck tightened. She realized, coming fully awake, that she was in her bed and someone was there with her, seated on the bed behind her. He had lifted her up and wrapped his arm around her neck.

"Where is it?" a hoarse whisper rasped in her ear. "What have you done with it?"

She shook her head. His forearm pressed harder into her throat. A moment later she felt the sharp prick of something on the side of her throat beneath her ear, and she knew he held a knife to her. At the same time the arm loosened enough for her to breathe.

"Scream, and I'll cut you," the harsh, low voice went on. "Now, tell me, what did you do with it?"

"I don't know what you're talking about!" Tears of fright welled in Vivian's eyes, and she blinked them away.

"You took it. I know you did. I saw you there. You have it. Now give it to me or I'll slice your throat right here."

Vivian steadied herself. What was he talking about, where had he seen her? She had to think. She had to outwit him. "If you slice my throat, you'll never get it."

"But no one will know."

She could not let him believe that killing her would rid him of his problem. Vivian summoned up a derisive laugh. "More fool you. If you have lost something, it was not I who took it." She had to keep him talking, make him concentrate on something besides threatening her. "*I* didn't take anything. I haven't the slightest idea what you're looking for." She tensed, waiting.

"Stewkesbury!" the voice exclaimed, and she could feel his body relax, the hand that held the knife dropping away from her neck. She had been waiting for that moment, and she reared up and back with all her strength, and she shrieked her brother's name at the top of her voice.

She felt the crown of her head connect hard with the man's chin, and she heard the sharp clack of his teeth slamming together, followed by a startled cry of pain. His grip loosened, and she lunged in the opposite direction, off the bed and straight for her door, screaming. The room was dark, but she knew it like the back of her hand, and she veered off course, turning to her right and grabbing the water pitcher that sat beside the washbowl. Her hand closed around the handle and she whirled, all in one motion, as her attacker came off the bed after her. She released the pitcher and it flew straight at him, catching him solidly in the chest and splashing water all over him.

He reeled back as she headed once more for the door. She heard a door crashing open and footsteps in the hallway. The intruder apparently heard them, as well, for instead of pursuing her, he turned and ran for the window. Vivian opened her door, and Gregory charged in just as the intruder nimbly slipped out the window.

"Vivian!" Gregory looked around and caught sight of the man disappearing. He ran for the window and leaned out, looking down. "The devil! Where did he go?"

"I suspect he clambered down that brick column between your bedroom and mine. It has enough decorations and outcroppings to give a good climber handholds." Vivian turned and lit a candle with fingers that trembled.

Gregory turned and started toward the door, but Vivian reached out and took his arm. "No, don't bother. You'll never catch him now."

Gregory hesitated, looking for a moment like their father in one of his more bullish moods, but then he relaxed. "No doubt you're right. Bloody hell! Who was that? What was he doing here? Did he hurt you?"

He peered at his sister in the dim light.

Vivian shook her head. "Other than frightening me half to death, no, he did not hurt me. I have no idea who he was. But he wanted something he thought I had."

"What was it?"

Vivian shrugged. "I have no idea. He never said. But we have to get dressed and go to Oliver."

Her brother stared at her, dumbfounded. "Stewkesbury? Now? It's the middle of the night."

"That doesn't matter. To get him to let go of me, I intimated that while I didn't have this something, someone else did. And he said, 'Stewkesbury!' So obviously he thinks that if I don't have it, Oliver does. He'll go after Oliver next. He may be going there right now. We have to warn Stewkesbury."

Gregory looked as if he had a hundred other questions burning to be released, but he was smart and practical enough not to give voice to them. Insead he nodded and left the room.

Fifteen minutes later, brother and sister were downstairs, dressed and cloaked, ready to leave. Seyre had had the foresight to ring for a servant, whom he had sent round to the mews, and though Vivian chafed at waiting the extra five minues until their carriage had pulled up in front of the house, Gregory insisted upon it.

"You have just been attacked by someone who is still out there, free to do so again. You are not going out unless it's in a closed carriage, no matter how nearby Stewkesbury House may be."

Vivian hated to wait, but she could not argue with her brother's reasoning. As soon as the vehicle pulled up, she climbed into it, and when they stopped in front of Oliver's house a few minutes later, she whipped open the carriage door and jumped down, not waiting for the step to be pulled out. Trotting up the front steps, she rang a sharp tattoo on the brass door knocker, repeating it as Gregory joined her on the stoop.

A footman finally opened the door, blinking the sleep from his eyes and still buttoning his livery. "My lord? My lady?" He gaped at them in sleepy confusion.

Vivian pushed past him into the entryway, saying, "I have to see Lord Stewkesbury. It's vitally important."

"Best run up and give him the message," Seyre advised the servant as he followed his sister inside. "She'll only keep after you or go up to pound on his door herself."

His words moved the servant to action, but the man had made it only halfway up the stairs when Oliver appeared at the top. His hair was mussed from sleep, his shirt hanging loose outside his breeches, but his eyes were sharp, the sleep already banished from them.

"Vivian!" He ran down the stairs. "What is it? Are you all right?" He reached her and took both her hands in his, only then glancing at Gregory. "Seyre. What's happened?"

"I'm not entirely certain," Gregory replied, turning toward his sister.

"I have put you in danger. I'm sorry, Oliver; I didn't mean to do it. That is, I meant to deflect him, but I didn't realize he would assume you had it."

"Deflect who? Had what?" Oliver frowned, his hands instinctively tightening on Vivian's.

"What's going on?" Camellia's voice came from the stairs,

and the three in the hall turned to see her standing there, a candle in her hand. Her hair hung in a long golden braid over her shoulder, and her dressing gown was wrapped around her, held closed by her other hand. Her eyes were heavy and slumberous, as if she'd just been pulled from her bed.

Vivian heard her brother's sharp inhalation beside her, and she thought wryly that if his heart had not already been lost, it was now.

Camellia hurried down the rest of the steps, her dressing gown fluttering around her legs, opening to reveal flashes of the thin white cotton nightgown beneath it. Vivian noticed that it was Gregory Camellia went to stand beside, not her cousin or her friend, and Vivian filed that bit of information away for further examination later. Perhaps the situation was not as hopeless as her brother believed.

Fitz came into view on the stairs, with Eve beside him, her fair hair unbound and hanging like spun silver and gold over her shoulders, her hand clasped in her husband's.

"Lady Vivian. Seyre." Fitz grinned in his usual way. "So glad you decided to drop by."

"Hush, Fitz," Eve reprimanded softly, her forehead creased in concern. "Vivian, what's wrong?"

"Lady Vivian is about to tell us," Oliver said, taking Vivian's elbow. "I suggest we all move into the drawing room to hear it." He turned toward the footman. "Jameson, I believe tea might be in order."

The group relocated to the drawing room, decorated at some briefly whimsical moment in the past in chinoiserie. Teak dragons climbed the wooden columns to the mantel and bared their teeth at the ends of sofas and chairs upholstered in red patterned damask.

"Eve, I thought you would have banished the dragons by now," Vivian commented as she settled into a chair.

Her friend chuckled. "No, it is Stewkesbury's house, love. We are simply moving out."

"The danger I believe you mentioned, Vivian?" Stewkesbury reminded in a mild voice. "What you didn't mean to deflect on me but did?"

"Vivian was attacked tonight," Gregory told him.

Oliver went still and straight, his mouth tightening into a hard, thin line as a chorus of whos and whats and wheres broke out all around.

"I was asleep," Vivian said. "I woke up, and a man had his arm around my neck choking me."

"The devil!" Fitz burst out, and Oliver's face turned grimmer.

"Did he hurt you?" Oliver asked.

Vivian shook her head. "Not really. He frightened me half to death. He had a knife to my throat, and he asked me where it was."

"Where what was?" Gregory asked. "I don't understand."

"Neither did I. I told him I didn't know what he was talking about, but he insisted that I had something and he wanted it back. I tried to get him talking, hoping he would loosen his grasp and give me a chance to get away. So I told him he was a fool."

Oliver winced. "Vivian . . . the man had a knife to your throat."

"Yes, well, but when I said I hadn't the slightest idea what he was talking about and if it was taken, it was someone else who took it, then he said, 'Stewkesbury!' That was when he relaxed and lowered the knife, and I was able to hit him."

"Hah!" Fitz let out a crack of laughter. "You planted him a facer? Well done, Vivian."

"Well, no, I couldn't hit him with my fist. I rammed my head into his chin. But it did hurt him; I heard his teeth snap together." Vivian smiled a little at the memory. "I yelled for Gregory, and he came running, and the man went out the window."

"I was too late to catch him," Gregory said with regret. "I didn't even get a proper look at the villain."

"Nor did I," Vivian said, staving off the question she saw coming on Oliver's face. "He was behind me and the room was dark."

"But who—?" Oliver frowned. "Obviously for his mind to leap to me, you and I must have been together when this thing was taken."

Vivian nodded. "I think it must have been that fellow in the tavern, the one we followed outside. You did punch him. Several times."

"Yes, but I didn't take anything from him. Except perhaps his pride."

Fitz spoke. "Perhaps he simply lost this . . . thing, whatever it was, while you were fighting. And he assumed you took it."

"Yes, but if he and Stewkesbury were fighting, wouldn't he assume Stewkesbury was responsible from the beginning? Why would he come after Vivian?" Eve pointed out reasonably.

"Maybe it's the murderer," Gregory said quietly, and all the others looked at him, the room suddenly silent.

Oliver nodded. "A murderer would seem a more ruthless sort, the kind who is willing to break into a house and threaten one. But what the devil would he think Vivian has? The murder weapon? We left it there; the Runner has it now. And how could that damage him anyway? There's no way a plain iron candleholder would lead to the man who murdered Glass."

"And how does he know Vivian is involved?" Gregory asked.

"He saw us, if he was the man we passed going to

Cosmo's," Camellia put in. "Maybe he thinks we could identify him." She slumped back in her chair. "Only Vivian wasn't with us then. It would be Gregory and me he wanted."

"And we didn't take anything from him," Gregory added.

"None of us did, for that matter." Oliver glanced around at the others. "Did we?"

All three of his companions shook their heads.

"Obviously he thinks we did, and that's what important. Whether it's the murderer or the man from the tavern or someone entirely different—" Oliver paused and looked at Vivian. "Perhaps that chap from the gambling den, the dealer—"

"The gambling den?" Fitz burst out. "The tavern? Is this really you, Oliver, or has someone taken your place?"

Oliver shot his brother a glowering look. "Whoever it was," he said firmly, "and whatever he thinks we have, he's obviously determined to get it."

"I know. I'm so sorry, Oliver." Vivian sent him an apologetic glance. "It was the only thing I could think of to say."

He shook his head. "Don't worry about it. You getting away from him was all that was important. Besides, it will work out perfectly. Now we know that he will come here to find what he's missing."

"You're going to set a trap?" Fitz guessed.

"Exactly. I doubt he will show up tonight. More likely it will be tomorrow. But I'll have the footmen all on alert. When he breaks in, whatever time he chooses"—a distinctly feral grin touched Oliver's lips—"I'll be waiting for him."

Chapter 21

Oliver took a final look around at the butler, four footmen, and two grooms gathered in the servants' dining room. The butler had been entrusted with a musket, and the rest of the men were the largest and most muscular of the servants. Hooper was admittedly not an expert shot, but Fitz had assured him that the musket would stop anything at close range so long as one aimed for the large target of the intruder's torso. The men, even the imperturbable Hooper, seemed excited at the thought of the evening that lay in front of them. The chance of stopping a burglar held far more allure than their usual cleaning and early bedtime.

"Well, men, stay on the alert," Oliver told them. "I hope to be home by one o'clock, and then Mr. Talbot and I will take over." He glanced toward Fitz, who lounged by the open door. Turning back, Oliver looked at the two grooms. "Jarvis, Bates. Make sure you are well hidden in the yard. I don't want to give any hint that we expect a visitor."

"No, me lord." Jarvis nodded.

"Very well." Oliver nodded briskly at the men and left the room.

Oliver glanced over at Fitz as he fell into step beside him. "I'd much prefer not to go to this party."

"But then you wouldn't get to dance with Lady Vivian." Fitz grinned. "Anyway, it's important to appear to keep to our normal routine, just in case this chap is watching the house. We don't want him to realize that we're aware of his interest in you; if he did, he might not try anything tonight."

"What if he comes while we're gone?"

Fitz shrugged. "Well, you'll have captured him, then. And Hooper won't do anything but hold him till you arrive. You'll still get to draw the chap's cork."

"And what makes you think I want to fight him?"

Fitz snorted. "Don't try to gammon me. I know you too well. I saw that light in your eyes last night. You're itching for a mill."

A faint smile touched Stewkesbury's lips. "Perhaps I would like to teach the fellow a lesson in manners."

"You mean you'd like to beat him bloody for putting a hand on Lady Vivian."

"Of course I would. Any gentleman would feel the same way."

"Doesn't mean any gentleman would be as ready to act on it. Face it, Ol, you're a changed man since you've been dangling after Lady Vivian."

"What?" Oliver cast an alarmed glance at his younger brother. "Nonsense. I'm not dangling after anyone."

"Of course not. You just suddenly have discovered your great love of balls and routs and the opera."

"I have always liked opera."

"Mm-hm." Fitz's bright blue eyes danced. "And the rest?"

"Very well. I have come to enjoy Lady Vivian's company."

"Then she's no longer a hoyden?"

"I didn't say that." The earl grinned. "She's still an absolute romp of a girl. But she's a diamond of the first water, as well. And I think I have discovered that I enjoy a bit of adventure in my life now and then. Maybe I am a changed man. Even I hardly know what I'll do next."

"Well!" Fitz's eyebrows rose and he came to a full stop. "I can scarce believe my ears."

Oliver grimaced. "Oh, stop playing the fool, Fitz. Come along, we must not keep the ladies waiting." Oliver strode toward the entryway, with his brother trailing thoughtfully after him.

The ladies in question were standing in Camellia's room, with Camellia craning her head to catch a look at her back in the mirror. "Does this sash look right? Is the bow crooked?"

Eve smiled to herself as she stepped forward to retie the bow in question. "There. Now it's perfect. And *you* look perfect. Expecting to see Lord Seyre at the party?"

"No. Well, perhaps. What if I was?" Camellia turned to regard her with a rather mutinous air.

"Nothing." Eve smiled, holding her hands palms up in a peaceful gesture. "There is nothing wrong with wanting to look your best for the marquess."

"I am not trying to look good for him." Camellia scowled. "And I wish you wouldn't call him that."

"But that is his title."

"I know. But I hate it."

"His title? Well, the good thing is that the title will be different one day. He'll be a duke."

Camellia let out a groan. "That will be even worse." Camellia sighed. "I know, I know, only I would think that. But he is so little like that . . ."

"Like what?"

"A lord. A duke. Even Oliver—I mean, he's nice once you get used to him, but you never forget that Oliver is a lord. He has that look, that way of talking—as if he expects everyone to obey him. And, of course, they do." Camellia paused, then added candidly, "Except for Fitz or Vivian, but they are different."

"As is Seyre."

"Yes." Camellia's gray eyes began to sparkle. "Gregory is easy to talk to, just like an ordinary person—like you or my sisters or Fitz. He doesn't think he's better than everyone else even though he's far smarter than most people. He talks about interesting things, not his family or his club or his clothes. He . . . he doesn't look at me as if I'm bizarre or tell me that I shouldn't say things or do things. He said I looked like a Valkyrie that time I galloped in the park. Do you know he wasn't upset that I was carrying a gun the other night—and a knife? He just asked if he could have one when it began to look dangerous. And he doesn't care for Dora Parkington in the slightest."

Eve laughed. "That is certainly a sign of superior taste."

"That's what I think."

"He's rather handsome, too."

"Yes, isn't he?" Camellia smiled at Eve approvingly, as if she had confirmed something. "I hear girls talk about him all the time, about his title and his estate and how much wealth he has or what a good catch he is. They hardly ever mention that he's handsome. But he has the most wonderful green eyes, and he looks at you the whole time you're talking, as if he's really interested in everything you say. And his hair is thick and has that little hint of red in it, like mahogany."

"He has nice shoulders, too, for a scholar."

Camellia smiled. "That's because he rides so much. He told me he would like to put me up on one of his mares back at Marchester. He hopes that I will come visit Vivian there sometimes. That would be splendid, don't you think?"

"I do indeed." Eve glanced at her again, then said

carefully, "Camellia, it seems to me that you might have feelings for Lord Seyre."

Camellia tightened all over. "What do you mean?"

Eve smiled. "You know what I mean—an interest in him as a man. As a husband, perhaps."

"No." Camellia gave a brittle little laugh and turned away, strolling over to her bed to pick up her gloves and cloak. "Don't be silly. I wouldn't—he wouldn't—"

"I am not so sure on either count."

"No. It's ridiculous. Absurd." Camellia draped the blue cloak over her arm and turned to the other woman, making a comic face. "Can you imagine me as a duchess?"

"I can imagine you as Seyre's wife."

Camellia shook her head. "I think sometimes that he is interested in me, that he might even want to ask me to marry him. But that's probably because I'm inexperienced and naïve. Everyone says I am. No doubt I mistake his liking for more than it is. He has never tried to do anything . . . you know, to press his suit."

"He is a gentleman."

"But he is a man as well." Camellia cast Eve a searching glance. "You cannot tell me that Fitz never—"

Eve chuckled, a blush rising in her cheeks. "No. I would not tell you such a bald-faced lie. But I think not all gentlemen are as confident as Fitzhugh. Or as flirtatious. Seyre is himself, not Fitz or any other man. You just finished extolling his differences."

"I know. But I also know that even if he did like me or want to be with me, it isn't possible. Not really. I've learned enough about England and the *ton* to know that. A nobleman doesn't marry for love, or at least not usually. Certainly not someone who is going to be a duke. They have all sorts of duties. They have to marry the right sort of person with the right sort of family."

"The Talbot family is as good as any in the realm," Eve protested. "Your cousin is an earl."

Camellia quirked an eyebrow at her. "It's not the family that's the problem; it's the woman. They marry the sort of woman who doesn't ever create a scandal. Or say the wrong thing."

"Poor Gregory. You are condemning him to a boring life."

"I'm sure he doesn't like the idea of it. But he will do what's expected of him. What he has been raised to do. I think perhaps that is why he never goes beyond a glance or a smile or a certain look with me. He knows that he won't marry, can't marry, against his family."

"I have known Seyre's father almost my entire life," Eve told her. "I can assure you that he is not a man who stands on tradition; I do not believe he would try to force Seyre to marry against his wishes. I know Gregory, too. He seems mild, but he has, in nearly every way I can think of, done exactly as he pleased all his life. You were right in saying he doesn't act like a duke. Why would he choose a wife like a duke?"

Hope flashed for an instant in Camellia's eyes, but then she shook her head and said a little wistfully, "No, it's impossible. Come, we should join Oliver and Fitz. No doubt they are growing impatient."

With that, she swept out the door, and Eve had little choice but to follow.

Vivian glanced around the room again, surreptitiously looking for an indication that Oliver and his family had arrived. She had been on edge all day, thinking about her unwelcome visitor the night before and wondering what would happen tonight. Would the man try to enter Stewkesbury's house while Oliver and his family were out?

Or would he creep inside in the middle of the night, as he had with her? Vivian felt sure that Oliver would be waiting for him if it was the latter—and probably Fitz and Camellia, as well! Vivian wished that she could be there with Oliver. She would like to see her assailant's face when Oliver sprang the trap on him.

Vivian smiled to herself at that thought and turned to stroll along the edge of the crowd. She was halfway to the door into the corridor when a footman came toward her and bowed, extending a folded and sealed piece of paper.

"My lady. I was asked to give you this."

Oliver! Vivian took the note eagerly and broke the seal, opening it. She felt a brief rush of disappointment when she saw the familiar hand of Lady Mainwaring and realized that the note did not come from Oliver. In the next instant, however, it occurred to her how odd it was for Lady Kitty to be sending her a note in the middle of a party, and she edged closer to one of the wall sconces so that she could make out the spidery handwriting:

> *Dearest Vivian,*
> *Forgive me for this interruption to your evening, but I have learned the most Dreadful News. I must talk to you. I am in my carriage outside. It is of the Utmost Importance. I cannot think what to do.*
> *Yrs.,*
> *K*

Wesley! Vivian's suspicions burst into full bloom as soon as she read the letter. Kitty had discovered something "dreadful," and, knowing Kitty, such alarm was not likely to be centered on something outside her own circle of interest. No, "dreadful" news meant something that wounded Kitty or someone close to her. For her to have driven over to pull

Vivian from a party, the news must be both immediate and extremely upsetting. Given the matter that had occupied Vivian's mind for the past few hours, she jumped to the obvious conclusion: Wesley Kilbothan was involved in the jewel thefts.

Vivian had suspected as much from the moment he had so easily recovered Kitty's brooch. It seemed clear to her now that Kitty must have heard something or seen something that had made her doubt the man. Looking down at the note and the thin, even shaky, writing, Vivian could not help but think that Lady Kitty might well be frightened as well as unhappy. What if she had found out not just that Wesley was a thief? What if she had learned that he was the man who had murdered Cosmo Glass?

Vivian's hand clenched around the note, crumpling it, and she hurried for the door. She did not bother to look for a servant and ask for her cloak. It was too chilly outside for her thin dress, but she could not wait for a footman to locate her cloak and bring it to her. She had thought last night that something had been faintly familiar about the man who had attacked her from behind. It had been too nebulous a thing to put her finger on—a tone in his voice? A faint scent? She had nearly decided that she had simply imagined the feeling.

But what if it had been Wesley Kilbothan who had held the knife to her throat? Someone she knew yet did not know well enough to identify if she could not see him? Her friend could be in real, grave danger. Vivian's only thought was get to Kitty and hear her story. She would persuade her to return to Carlyle Hall, where she and Gregory could protect her.

"Vivian!"

She glanced across the entryway and saw Eve and Camellia. They had just entered, apparently, and were taking off their cloaks. Fitz and Oliver were off to their right, already deep in a discussion with Sir Kerry Harborough. Vivian crossed quickly to Camellia and took her hand, pulling her aside.

"May I borrow your cloak?" she asked in a low voice as Camellia untied the garment in question.

"Of course." Camellia's brows rose in question, but she slid the cloak off her shoulders and handed it to Vivian. "Why? Where are you going?"

"Outside, to talk to Lady Kitty. She's in her carriage waiting for me. I'll explain later." Vivian whipped the cloak on over her dress and tied it, leaning closer to say, "Gregory has been looking for you all evening. He's just inside the assembly room by the potted plant, utterly bored."

Vivian smiled and slipped away. She went out the door and looked down the street. She spotted Lady Mainwaring's elegant, old carriage standing near the end of the block. As she started down the steps, Mrs. Dentwater was coming up, and the woman greeted her effusively, linking her arm chummily through Vivian's and chattering away. It took Vivian several minutes and a promise to come to her house for dinner next Thursday to get away from the woman. As she turned away, Vivian pulled up the hood of the cloak as far as she could so that it would be difficult to see her face. She was glad she had done so when she started along the broad sidewalk and saw Lady Parkington and her daughter Dora coming toward her. Vivian ducked her head so that her face was not visible at all and moved over to the edge of the sidewalk, walking with swift purpose. She thought she heard an indrawn breath as she passed the women, but she kept her eyes determinedly on her feet as she walked.

Once she was past them, she glanced up and saw that the door to Kitty's carriage stood open, waiting for her, and she hurried to it. Swinging up into the carriage, she closed the door, then turned back to Lady Kitty. To her astonishment, a man, not Kitty, sat on the seat, watching her.

"Mr. Brookman!" She gaped at the jeweler in bewilderment.

After a cry and a snap of a whip, suddenly the horses took off, throwing Vivian onto the seat beside him.

Dora Parkington turned her head to look at the woman who had just walked past them. She was certain that it was Camellia Bascombe. Dora had seen Camellia wear that vivid blue cloak more than once. The pale blue braid that edged the hood and hem made the cloak distinctive. Dora had felt a stab of envy the first time she had seen Camellia wearing it, knowing that she herself would have looked so much better in it than the blond Camellia. The color would have been stunning against her black hair and pale skin and would have deepened the blue of her eyes. Moreover, she would have known how to drape the hood so that it complemented her looks, not pulling it so far forward that one couldn't even see her face.

Of course, perhaps that was exactly what Miss Bascombe intended. Dora watched as Camellia walked straight up to the carriage and climbed into it. Dora sucked in her breath in a delighted gasp. She was even more elated when the carriage then took off immediately, the horses and vehicle clattering loudly into the night.

"Dora!"

She turned to see her mother waiting for her, frowning at Dora's dawdling. Grinning, Dora scurried after her. Her mother's mood would certainly change when she heard this tidbit.

Moments later, the two of them walked up the steps, ready to begin. Several people were bunched in the large entry hall in front of them, handing their outerwear to servants and preparing to greet Lady Cumberton.

Raising her voice slightly as they took their place behind

the others, Dora said, "But, Mama, I am sure it was Miss Bascombe."

Her mother clucked her tongue, then said, "Goodness, child, you must have been mistaken. Miss Bascombe would not have been running off to get in a carriage alone!"

All around them, the noise level dropped perceptibly, and Dora could almost feel the people around her leaning in to better hear her words. Ignoring her audience, she went on breathlessly, "But, Mama, that is the thing—she was not alone. There was a man in the carriage waiting for her."

After her words, utter silence fell all around them. Lady Parkington glanced about, as if she had just now noticed all the people turning to stare at them.

"Oh!" Lady Parkington's hand fluttered up to her cheek in dismay. "Oh, my. Dora! See what you have done! Surely you are mistaken. It couldn't have been Miss Bascombe."

"Oh." Dora looked around her, wide-eyed, then glanced down, quickly covering her cheeks with her hands as if embarrassed, pressing hard to bring up a "blush." "Mama, indeed, I would not want to do that." Her voice faltered, and she let her hands drop to reveal her girlishly reddened cheeks. "Perhaps . . ." She brightened, and her voice grew stronger. "Perhaps it was not she. There must be another girl who has a blue cloak like that with the braid all around the hood."

A look of even more consternation crossed her mother's face. "Oh, dear. Um, yes, of course, that must be it." She pasted on a bright smile. "There is doubtless another guest with a cloak like Miss Bascombe's. How silly of you to be so fooled."

"Yes, indeed." Dora looked elated at having come up with this explanation. She had to look down again, though, to hide the triumph in her eyes as voices rose around them in excited murmurs.

Dora could hear Camellia's name being whispered as she

handed off her cloak and moved to the line to be presented to her host and hostess. As she and her mother moved on from the receiving line, she found it slow going, for she was stopped time and again and asked if Camellia Bascombe had really ridden off in a carriage with a man.

"Oh, no," Dora protested, wide-eyed. "I must have been mistaken. After all, she had the hood of her cloak pulled so far forward that I could not see her face. I am sure Mama must be right, and there was another woman here wearing a cloak just like hers. You must not think that it was Miss Bascombe. I would be so heartbroken if anything I said made anyone gossip about her. I am convinced that it was not Camellia Bascombe."

"What was not Camellia Bascombe?" said a flat voice a few feet away from them.

Dora looked up, and her mouth dropped open in astonishment. For there was Camellia herself, and standing right beside her was Lord Seyre. Dora opened her mouth and closed it, unable to speak.

Camellia glanced around and her brows drew together. "What have you been saying, Miss Parkington? I'd like to hear it."

Someone to Dora's left hastened to say, " 'Twas nothing. Miss Parkington merely saw someone wearing a cloak just like yours a few minutes ago."

"Oh." Camellia's frown cleared. "That must have been Lady Vivian. I lent her my cloak." She stopped, glancing at the faces that had suddenly turned to stone around her. "What's the matter? What's wrong?"

A few people eyed Seyre nervously, but most looked everywhere but at him. Then whispers began to buzz. Camellia, eyes flashing, took a step forward and grabbed Dora by the arm. "What were you saying? Tell me! What lies have you been spreading?"

"I wasn't lying!" Dora retorted, stung. "I saw her!"

"You saw her what?" Now Seyre came closer, and Dora looked around, her face a study in desperation.

"I—I'm sure it was nothing, Lord Seyre." Dora widened her eyes, trying to force tears into them. "I was probably mistaken about the cloak."

"Tell me what you saw," Seyre said through clenched teeth, looming over her. "What happened to my sister?"

"I don't know!" Dora wailed, no longer having to force the tears, which were flooding out wretchedly now. "She got in a carriage with a man and left!"

"A man!" Camellia exclaimed. "Now I know you're lying. Seyre, it's nothing." She laid a calming hand on Gregory's arm. "It was not a man. It was that friend of hers. Kitty. She told me she was going out to talk to Kitty, and she asked to borrow my cloak."

"Lady Mainwaring?" Seyre relaxed with a smile. "Oh, of course." He cast a look of contempt at Dora. "It might be advisable to think next time, Miss Parkington, before you start spreading lies about someone."

"I wasn't lying!" Dora cried, outraged past the point of good sense. "It *was* a man. I saw him in there when we walked past the carriage. There wasn't a woman in it, only a man!"

Lord Seyre took a step back, and his face suddenly drained of all color. He looked over at Camellia, who stared back at him in equal dismay. "Gregory, no, do you think—"

"That it was a ruse? Yes!"

"We have to get Oliver!" Camellia took off at a sprint for the other room.

Vivian straightened up in her seat and turned to face Brookman. "What are you doing here? Where's Kitty?"

"I imagine that Lady Mainwaring is where she usually

can be found—at some party or club, gambling. It wasn't hard for Kilbothan to get the carriage; she'll never know. And he's been able to copy her handwriting for some time now."

Her mind raced, the pieces of the puzzle falling into place. "You and Kilbothan are stealing the jewels! Both of you run the ring!"

"Kilbothan!" Brookman made a contemptuous flick of his wrist, as though dismissing the man. "He's an employee, nothing more. I am the one in charge."

Vivian nodded. "It makes sense. You don't have to sell the jewelry at reduced prices to jewelers or pawnbrokers. You can take the jewels from the settings and reset them in the pieces you sell. Have them recut if need be. You can even melt down the gold and silver to use again."

"Waste not, want not." A thin smile curved Brookman's lips. "I was even able to sell some of the reset stones back to their original owners. There was a certain wonderful irony in that." Some of Vivian's disgust at his words must have shown on her face, for the smile dropped from his lips and he snapped, "You were happy enough to buy my jewels, my lady."

"You sold me stolen jewels? Is the Scots Green stolen, too?"

"Presumably it was stolen several times throughout its history, but I had nothing to do with its theft. It came through the usual channels of jewel merchants just as I told you. And, no, none of your jewels were stolen—except for diamond chips or something of that like. You were far too knowledgeable, as well as too influential, to sell you stolen goods—or to take them from you. I intended to use your patronage to make me the favorite of the *ton*. If you had recognized one of the stolen pieces in something I'd sold to you, then where would I have been?"

"Precisely where you are now, it seems to me," Vivian retorted.

He sighed in that same rather arch manner that was so different from the way he had always spoken to Vivian before. It was almost like seeing an entirely different man. He even looked somehow different. As soon as she had the thought, Vivian realized where the change lay—Brookman was no longer dressed in the plain, serviceable sort of suit he wore at his business. His jacket and breeches, his shirt, even his neckcloth were of the best-quality material and cut. His hair was artfully styled. Gold fobs dangled from his watch chain, and emeralds gleamed at his cuffs and in the stickpin of his neckcloth. He was dressed like a gentleman of fashion and leisure, and the helpful, just-short-of-obsequious demeanor he used in his shop was gone. He could have passed for any young gentlemen of the upper class.

"Yes, I hate losing your business," Brookman admitted in response to Vivian's last words. "I tried my best to keep you from finding out. Even gave Kilbothan back that brooch in the hopes that it would make you drop the matter."

"I am surprised you still possessed it."

He shrugged. "It was such a valuable piece in its present form. I hated to recut the central diamond; it wouldn't have been worth as much. But it was too recognizable to sell the gem, even in a different setting. I couldn't make up my mind."

"I don't understand why you did it." Vivian looked at him, disgust mingling with puzzlement. "You have such talent. You are an artist. You've already had success. In the years to come you would have only had more."

"I enjoy designing the pieces. But that's not enough money. Not the life I want. Bowing and flattering, effacing myself to people utterly lacking in taste or talent. Putting my beautiful works on the neck of some old hag . . . making rings for a buffoon to toss to some light o' love as a parting gift. Dressing like a bloody shopkeeper because that is what's expected of me. You're right—I am an artist. And I quickly saw that in order to be treated with the respect I deserved, in order to be free to design what I pleased, I would need a great deal more money than I made in that store. At first, it was just a little extra money, being able to make a larger profit from a necklace or a pair of earrings because I didn't have to buy the jewels. But I quickly saw that I could get far more jewelry than I could use, so I began selling to others. That is when I began to make real money."

Vivian shook her head. "I don't understand. Kidnapping me makes no sense. I had no idea that you were involved until you showed yourself tonight."

"Yes, I saw that when you got into the carriage. You truly do not have it." He heaved a sigh. "That means Stewkesbury is the one who picked it up. Or one of those other two—and though they wouldn't realize its importance, sooner or later they'd be bound to show it to you or the earl or someone who could see the significance of it, and then I would be finished. But now that I have you, Stewkesbury will give it to me in exchange."

"What is it you're looking for? Why is it so important? Stewkesbury and I will know who you are and what you did. You'll be imprisoned!" Vivian stopped, sucking in her breath sharply. "Unless—you mean to kill us all."

"I thought of that." His voice was horrifyingly nonchalant. "But I decided that it would be far too messy and dangerous. Getting rid of a mercenary little thief like Glass is one thing; killing an earl and a duke's daughter is a different matter entirely. God knows, I might have to do away with the other two as well, and that would mean doing away with a marquess. No, I shall have to disappear—change my name, my appearance, perhaps even live on the Continent for a few years. But I've money enough to do it now. As long as Stewkesbury gives me what I want, there'll be nothing to connect me to the murder of Cosmo Glass. The murder charge is all that is important."

"But Stewkesbury doesn't have it!"

"One of you four does. Maybe no one else has admitted it. Obviously no one's realized what it means. But I searched Glass's place after you left, and it was not there. One of you took it."

"No one took it!" Vivian exclaimed in frustration. "Why won't you listen to me? We didn't find anything at Glass's place."

Brookman's eyes narrowed, and his face turned cold. "You had better hope that one of them did. Because if they didn't, then I can be tied to his murder and I'll have no choice but to kill you all and flee."

Vivian could only stare at Brookman as an icy cold swept over her.

His expression changed, becoming once again the light, faintly sardonic face he had worn throughout the ride. "Ah, here we are."

Vivian turned to the window as the coach slowed and came to a stop. They were pulling up in front of Brookman's shop.

"Now, we'll just go inside," he went on pleasantly. "And I'll send a note around to Stewkesbury telling him how to recover you. It won't be long, and hopefully you won't be too uncomfortable."

Vivian lunged for the door handle, screaming at the top of her lungs. Brookman was quick, however, and stronger than she would have imagined. He grabbed her around the waist, pinning her arms to her sides, and hauled her back against him, clamping his other hand over her mouth to stifle her screams. Vivian continued to struggle, kicking and trying to bite his hand, but he held on just as fiercely. After a few moments, the door to the carriage opened, and Wesley Kilbothan appeared.

"For Christ's sake, shut her up!" he growled. He climbed inside, closing the door behind him, and pulled out a small, leather-wrapped roll. His hand slashed down toward Vivian's temple in a swift stroke.

Pain crashed in her head, and everything went black.

Chapter 22

Oliver knew the instant he saw Camellia's face. *Something has happened to Vivian.* A hard, cold lump formed in the pit of his stomach, and he closed the gap between him and Camellia in two quick strides.

"What is it? Where's Vivian?"

Camellia looked startled, but she said only, "I don't know. She told me she was going out to talk to Kitty, but Dora Parkington insists that she got into a carriage with a man and that the carriage left."

"Bloody hell! After last night, why would she meet someone by herself?"

"She got a note from Lady Kitty. She had it in her hand."

"We must be certain that Miss Parkington isn't making this up in order to appear interesting. And we'll look outside to make sure Vivian isn't sitting out there in Lady Kitty's carriage."

"I'll find Lady Kitty," Fitz said. He and Eve had come up behind Oliver and had caught the gist of their conversation. "Perhaps Kitty had some crisis that Vivian went to help her with."

Oliver nodded. "As soon as we talk to Miss Parkington, we'll go home. Meet us there."

It did not take long for Oliver's terse, cold questioning to have Dora Parkington crying again and swearing that she had seen a man and only a man in the carriage the woman in Camellia's cloak had entered. Oliver, along with Camellia, Gregory, and Eve then walked up and down the block, looking into all the carriages lined up there. None of them contained Vivian. Leaving the Carlyle carriage at the curb in front of the Cumbertons' house in case Lady Vivian returned to the party, they got into Stewkesbury's carriage and drove to his home, where they gathered in Oliver's study.

No one could seem to sit down, at least for more than an instant. Gregory stood, staring sightlessly down into the fireplace, his face drawn. Camellia went to stand beside him and slipped her hand into his. Gregory offered her a faint smile in return. Both of them turned back to Oliver, who was pacing up and down the length of the room. His face was set, his eyes dark and cold as a winter sea.

"It has to be the man from last night. It has to! Who else would abduct her?"

"But wouldn't Vivian have known if the note was not written by her friend?" Eve asked.

"Does Vivian know the woman's hand that well?" Oliver turned to Seyre. "Would you know her handwriting?"

Gregory shrugged. "I wouldn't. But Lady Kitty was closer to Vivian. They've corresponded for years, ever since she and the duke parted."

"Then it was forged," Oliver responded. "Or someone else wrote a note, saying they were writing it for Lady Kitty, that she was too distraught."

"I suppose she might have gone if she received such a note." Gregory turned to Camellia. "Did she specifically say that Kitty had written the note?"

"I don't remember!" Camellia's face knotted in distress. "I've been wracking my brain, but I can't recall the exact words. It was just a quick thing, a few words as she put on my cloak. I'm certain that she said she was going out to talk to Kitty in her carriage. But I'm not sure anymore if she even said that there was a note or I just assumed that because I saw the paper in her hand."

"It's all right." Gregory squeezed her hand comfortingly. "There was no reason for you to pay attention to what she said. You had no way of knowing."

"But I shouldn't have let Vivian walk out by herself!" Camellia's eyes filled with tears. "I didn't even think that it might be a trick. I should have been more careful. More alert."

"We all should have." Oliver's voice was heavy with regret. "If I had only gone there earlier . . ."

"We cannot sit here indulging ourselves in should-haves," Eve said crisply. "It doesn't help. What we need to do is figure out who took her and why."

"And, most of all, where she is now," Oliver added. "You're right. If the note was a forgery, then it seems to me that the likeliest suspect would be that poet that Vivian said Lady Kitty had taken in."

"Kilbothan," Gregory said darkly. "I'm sure he's taking advantage of Lady Mainwaring. I can believe he's learned to copy her handwriting. He could have supplemented the money she freely gave him with an extra bank draft or two. But it's a little hard for me to imagine him killing someone or abducting Vivian."

Oliver looked bleak. "I have absolutely no idea who else it could be."

"Let's look at it from the other end," Gregory said. "I have to wonder why this fellow is so concerned with whatever he thinks we have. What would be worth exposing himself this way? Vivian will see him. She will know who he is and can have him arrested."

"If he lets her go," Oliver said, and everyone in the room looked at him in horror. "That's why we have to get her back. We cannot rely on this man to be fair or kind. If this is the same one who attacked her last night, we have to ask, why did he take her? Why didn't he come here? Why not attack me?"

"Because he hopes to force you to tell him," Eve said. "Perhaps he even realizes you may have a trap laid for him. It would not take much imagination to guess that Vivian warned you about him. He might have assumed you would be armed against him, waiting for him to break in here."

"But if he stole Vivian, he could make me give him whatever he asked for," Oliver concluded. "You're right. I would give it to him in a second . . . if I only had some clue what it was."

"It must be something that could identify him," Gregory said. "Something that, if found, would show that he'd been in Glass's room."

Oliver nodded. "An engraved watch, say, or a distinctive ring."

"Exactly."

"That makes sense. Did you see anything like that in Glass's room?"

Gregory and Camellia were silent, thinking, but after a moment both of them shook their heads.

"Perhaps someone else took it," Camellia suggested. "If all four of us know that we didn't take it, and it's gone, the only answer is that someone else did. Maybe after Gregory and I left the room, someone sneaked in there and took it."

"I suppose someone could have," Oliver began reluctantly. He went utterly still. "My God," he breathed. "There *was* someone else there. Someone who delights in taking things."

He swung around and charged out of the room. The others looked after him in baffled silence. Then Camellia clapped her hands together and let out a whoop. "Pirate!"

They found the earl on his hands and knees in the space beneath the backstairs. He crawled around, checking under the dog's blanket and in every nook and cranny. Pirate stood watching him with great interest, wagging his tail. Eve, who had thought to bring a candle from the other room, bent down to bring light to the small, dark space.

A glint of metal at the edge of an old boot caught Oliver's eye, and he pounced on it. "My God." He sat back on his heels, staring at the object.

"What is that?" Camellia asked.

"It's a jeweler's loupe." Oliver's face was grim as he exited from the dog's hiding place. "And I have a very good idea whose."

He held it close to Eve's candle, turning it so that the silver ring around it glinted. Something was engraved on the silver.

"GDB," he said, his lip curling up in a smile that was chilling. "It's Brookman's loupe."

"Brookman?" Gregory gaped at him. "Vivian's jeweler?"

Oliver nodded grimly. "I'm certain of it. I was there when he handed it to her to look at a necklace. It's quite distinctive; it has his initials here on the silver band. See?" He held it out to Gregory. "He must have had it with him when he went to Glass's, and during the fight it fell out of his pocket. He knew it would identify him beyond any doubt. That is why he was so anxious to retrieve it."

"But why?" Camellia asked. "If Vivian had had the loupe, she would have already known who he was. Why bother to get it back?"

Oliver shrugged. "I don't suppose criminals are always logical."

"He could hope that she hadn't really examined the thing yet and so didn't know the truth," Gregory offered. "Besides, as long as the loupe was gone, there wouldn't have been any proof. Even with Lady Vivian's word or yours, the Crown's case would be weak without the loupe itself."

"It doesn't matter now." Oliver's hand closed into a fist around the loupe, and he set his jaw, his eyes cold and glittering. "I know where Vivian is."

He thrust the loupe into his jacket pocket as he strode toward the door. The others followed him, including Pirate, his nails clicking merrily on the marble floor of the entryway. They had not quite reached the front door when it opened and Fitz came in. His face was grim, and he shook his head.

"I went to Lady Kitty's. She wasn't there—nor the carriage. The servants said she'd gone to Bunting's in the coach, and when I reached the club, her carriage was there. I talked to the coachman, who swore he'd taken Lady Kitty to Bunting's and had waited for her the whole time. But there was clearly something smoky about the situation. The horses were heated; they obviously hadn't been just standing about. It didn't take long before the driver admitted that after he dropped Lady Kitty off, Kilbothan tipped him a yellow boy to lend him the carriage. He swore that he had no idea where the fellow went with the vehicle. He just whiled away the time in a tavern, and Kilbothan took his driving coat and the carriage. I believed him. Unfortunately, Kilbothan was not there, and I haven't the slightest idea how to find him."

"So Kilbothan was in on it, too," Gregory exclaimed.

"Too?" Fitz asked.

"I'll explain in the carriage," Oliver said, starting toward the door.

"Let me get my pistols," Fitz said. "They just might come in handy."

"You're right." Camellia turned and started toward the stairs with him. "I'll get mine."

"Wait. No. Camellia, you ladies are staying here."

Eve and Camellia looked at him with expressions almost identical in their obstinacy.

"Don't be such a . . . a *lord*." Camellia's tone turned the word into an insult. "You know I'm the best shot here except Fitz."

"I think we've both proven we are not going to fall to pieces in a crisis," Eve pointed out. "And there's something to be said for sheer numbers. This man is not going to think he can get away with harming Vivian in front of *all* of us."

"Don't waste time arguing." Fitz tossed back the advice to his brother as he trotted up the stairs.

Oliver sighed. "Very well. It would be good to be armed. But hurry."

In only minutes both Fitz and Camellia were back. Camellia had pulled on the dark cloak she had worn the night of Glass's murder, and her pocket once again sagged with the weight of her pistol. They made their way out to the carriage in front and climbed in. Pirate dashed out with them and sprang up into the carriage before anyone else.

Oliver cast the dog a jaundiced glance, but said only, "I suppose you might as well go. You got us into this mess, after all."

The others climbed in, and though it was a tight fit, they managed it. They made good time through the almost deserted streets, and the coach pulled up, as Oliver had instructed, half a block away from the jeweler's store. They walked quickly and quietly the rest of the way.

"Seyre, I think it's best he see only you," Oliver whispered as they grew close. Gregory nodded and went to stand in front of the door while Fitz and Oliver took their places on either side of the door, out of sight. Eve and Camellia lined up behind them.

Gregory took a breath, then rapped loudly on the door.

Vivian came slowly awake. Her head ached abominably, and she recognized nothing around her. It didn't take her long to realize that she was lying on a bed in a room she didn't know, that she was gagged and bound, and that her bound wrists were attached by a short length of rope to one of the four posts of the bed.

Fear flooded her, and she began to struggle. The rope cut painfully into her wrists, but she managed to pull and wriggle her way up to a sitting position. She looked around the room. It was a small but tastefully furnished bedroom—and completely foreign to her.

Memories flooded back in—the note from Kitty, the carriage and Brookman, Kilbothan. Brookman had taken her back to his shop; she had seen that much before that wretched Kilbothan knocked her in the head. This bedroom was probably part of the jeweler's living quarters above his store. Many shopkeepers lived above their work.

She sat for a moment, letting her head clear. Brookman was going to use her to lure Oliver here, and if Oliver didn't have whatever Brookman wanted, the man planned to kill them both. She had to get out of here and warn Oliver. She scooted across the bed to the post where the end of her rope was tied. If she could just undo the knot, though her wrists would still be bound, she would be able to untie the bonds at her ankles and get rid of her gag as well. Unfortunately, the knot was securely tied, and her fingers had grown cold and numb from being bound. After several minutes of fumbling with the rope, she was forced to acknowledge that she was unlikely to untie the knot like this. She leaned her head against the bedpost, willing herself to think.

Her hair ornament! She had pinned a decoration in her

hair this evening—a cunning thing made with jet bangles and a black feather. It had looked quite dashing against her red hair, she thought, but the important thing now was that it had been too heavy for the hair comb attached to it, so she had secured it with an onyx-topped hatpin. It was not, perhaps, quite as lethal as some hatpins she had seen, but the shaft of the pin was at least three inches long, and the little onyx knob on the top gave it a grip. She could use it to defend herself if it came down to that, and she might be able to use it to work the knot loose.

It took a bit of contortion to reach the decoration, but finally she pulled out the pin. She slipped the pin into the knot and began to wiggle it. Her hands, she found, grew even more numb from holding them up to do the slow and wearying work at the knot. Gradually, however, the thing began to loosen. In just a few more minutes, she thought, the rope would ease enough for her to work her forefinger into the knot.

Suddenly a loud rapping came from somewhere below. Vivian's head shot up and her numbed fingers dropped the hatpin. Frustratingly, it lay on the counterpane just beyond the reach of her bound hands. But she was too elated by the knocks on the door below to worry about that. Somehow Oliver must have figured out that Brookman had kidnapped her!

Of course it could be someone else, but it seemed unlikely at this time of night. And even if it was a stranger, he might rescue her—if only she could make him hear her. Vivian began to scream, but the gag muffled the sound effectively. She raised her feet from the floor and slammed them back down as hard as she could over and over. Then she turned and began to kick her feet against the wall.

Downstairs the knocking began again, even more insistently. "Brookman!"

Was that Gregory's voice? Vivian's heart leapt in her throat, and she hammered her feet against the wall as hard as she could, cursing the rope that bound her to the bed. She heard men's voices outside in the hallway, followed by receding footsteps. A moment later, the door to the bedroom was flung open, and Wesley Kilbothan rushed in.

"Stop that!" he hissed, closing the door behind him and hurrying over to her.

Vivian ignored him, still beating her feet on the wall. He whipped a knife out of his pocket, and she froze, certain that he was about to stab her with it. Instead he sawed through the rope connecting her to the bedpost. Relief washed through Vivian. She turned, snatching up the hatpin from where it had fallen, and twisted, jabbing with all her strength at Kilbothan's chest. The man flinched away, turning enough to take the hit in his upper arm. The pin plunged into the knob, and he let out a shout of pain.

"You bitch!" He pulled back his fist and punched her in the jaw.

For the second time this evening, Vivian lapsed into unconsciousness.

"Who's there?" A man's voice came from behind the closed door.

"Mr. Brookman?" Gregory managed to keep his voice lower and calmer than he felt. "Could you open the door? I need to talk to you."

"It's quite late. Come back tomorrow."

"No! Please, open the door. It's Lord Seyre, Lady Vivian Carlyle's brother." Swallowing, he made his voice sound as pleading and uncertain as he could. "Something's happened to Vivian. She's vanished and . . . and I think it might be the thieves Vivian talked to you about."

"How terrible! But, really, I don't know what I can do."

"If I could just talk to you—I know Vivian discussed it with you. I told her not to get involved in such things, but she's always so headstrong. I thought if you could tell me what you'd told her, I might be able to figure it out. Please!" Gregory waited a moment, then said, more forcefully, "Open up the door! I refuse to leave until I talk to you, even if I have to stand here and pound on your door all night."

Beside him, Oliver turned and looked at the nearest store window. If Brookman didn't open the door in the next few seconds, he would have to kick in the window and go in that way. But just then, the door opened a crack, revealing a slice of the jeweler's face.

"Are you alone?"

Gregory flung himself against the door, sending the other man staggering backward, and he rushed inside, quickly followed by Oliver and Fitz. Camellia and Eve squeezed in after them, the dog on their heels.

"Here! I say! What do you think you're doing?" Brookman huffed, tugging his jacket straight and looking indignant.

"Where is she?" Oliver growled, grabbing the other man by the lapels of his jacket and shaking him. "Where the bloody hell is she?"

"I don't know what you're talking about!" the jeweler flared.

"The hell you don't!" Oliver smashed his fist into Brookman's face and followed it with a jab to his stomach. "You want to tell me now?"

The jeweler folded, going down to his knees on the floor. Pirate growled at the man, his lips pulling back from his teeth. The door into the rear of the store burst open, and Wesley Kilbothan strode into the showroom, pistol raised. Fitz turned and squeezed off a shot, and the gun flew out of the other man's hand. Kilbothan let out a cry and grabbed his hand. He started toward Fitz, murder on his face.

"Stop!" Camellia cried out, her word followed by the deadly click of a pistol's hammer.

Kilbothan froze and swung his head toward Camellia. He narrowed his eyes in assessment.

"Don't think that she won't shoot just because she's a woman," Fitz told him lightly. "Besides, as it happens, I have a set of pistols."

Kilbothan swiveled back and found Fitz training a second gun on him.

"I suggest you go sit down on that stool," Fitz continued, waggling the gun toward the stool behind the counter.

With a sneer, the other man did as he ordered, flopping down on the high stool and glaring at Fitz, his arms crossed over his chest. "She's not here. No matter how many times you hit Brookman here, he won't tell you where she is. He can't; he doesn't know."

Oliver, paying no attention to the drama going on around him, reached down and hauled the jeweler to his feet. "Where is she?"

"I don't know what you're talking about," Brookman gasped. "I'd never hurt Lady Vivian. She's my best customer."

"I know about the loupe." Oliver reached in his pocket and pulled it out, holding it up so the man could see. "There's no use lying. You'll only make things worse for yourself by hurting Lady Vivian."

Brookman grabbed for the loupe, but Oliver jerked it back out of his reach. Brookman looked at him cagily. "Perhaps a trade might be in order?"

Oliver looked as though he might hit the man again, but he set his jaw, visibly bringing himself under control. "I think a search of your shop is in order."

He took Brookman's arm and whirled him around, shoving him toward the door into the rear of the shop. Fitz stayed behind, his gun trained on Kilbothan, as Oliver, Gregory, and Camellia followed Brookman into the back of the store. Pirate trotted after them. Oliver kept a firm grip on Brookman's arm while Camellia and Gregory searched the office and workroom. When they found nothing, they marched up the stairs. Room by room, they went through it, ending up finally in the bedroom.

"You see?" Brookman asked somewhat plaintively. "She's not here. Now, if you were to give me back my property, I might—"

"I'll put the bloody thing in your casket with you if you don't tell me where Vivian is right now!" Oliver roared, doubling his fist.

"Oliver!" Gregory, who had wandered over to the bed, bent down and picked up something. "Look at this." He held out a strand of fiber. "Doesn't this look like a bit of rope?"

"Really, gentlemen, this is beyond everything!" Brookman began, then jumped at the sound of a sharp bark behind him.

"Pirate, hush!" Camellia said automatically.

Oliver, however, swung around and looked at the dog. Pirate was standing facing a blank wall across from the bed. His rear end was wriggling, his stump of a tail wagging. He let out another bark or two before he trotted over to the wall and sat down in front of it, lifting a paw to scratch at the wall.

"Here." Oliver all but threw Brookman to Gregory and strode over to where the dog sat.

The other three watched Oliver as he rapped his knuckles against the wall in several spots, then ran his fingers lightly over it. "There's a crack here. I think this wall is hollow." He swung back to Brookman. "There's a hidden space here, isn't there? Open it."

"I don't know what you're talking about."

Oliver turned to Camellia. "Did you happen to bring your knife this time as well?"

Camellia reached into her pocket and wordlessly extended the knife in its scabbard. Oliver took it, whipping out the small but lethal-looking weapon from its case. Striding over to Brookman, he took him from Gregory's grasp and shoved him hard against the wall, twisting his arm painfully up behind his back to hold the man still.

"Now." Oliver's voice was emotionless and implacable. He raised the knife, laying the point just beneath the other man's eye. "Tell me where the catch is to open that hidden door, or I am going to take you to pieces, bit by bit, starting with your eyes."

Brookman began to tremble so hard that the point of the knife pierced his skin a little and blood began to trickle down his cheek. "B-behind the wardrobe. Waist high. There's an indention; just stick your finger in it and pull."

Oliver released him and returned to the wall, where Pirate sat patiently, reaching up now and then to scratch at the plaster. Oliver slid his hand behind the wardrobe until he found the indention, then pulled. A lever popped out, and a section of the wall opened. Vivian lay on her side in the narrow room, her hands and feet bound. Another small section of rope, obviously cut, lay on the floor beside her, along with a hatpin.

"Vivian!" Oliver went down on one knee beside her limp form, lifting her up. "Wake up. My love, are you—"

She turned her head, her eyes still closed, and let out a little sigh. A red, abraded spot was on the side of her face that had been turned away from them. It was already beginning to swell. Higher up, beside her temple, was another reddened swelling.

Oliver whipped his head around, murder in his eyes. "You hit her!"

"No! No!" Brookman gibbered, cringing away as far as he could with Gregory's hand clamped around his arm. "It wasn't me! It was Kilbothan!"

"Oliver?" Vivian murmured.

He turned back. Vivian's eyes fluttered open.

"Oliver!" she said again, and smiled faintly. "You found me."

"Of course I found you. Did you think I wouldn't?"

"I was a bit worried."

His laugh was shaky. "It's all right now. You're safe." He bent to press his lips to her forehead and murmured, "I'll take you home, love."

Chapter 23

Vivian leaned closer to the mirror above her vanity table, turning her head for the best view of her bruises. As bruises went, she thought, they were magnificent. A bluish purple stain spread across her cheekbone, with a distinct line of dark purple beneath her eye. The bruise at her temple reached down so that the two almost met, giving it the look of one continuous mark. All around the bruise and down that side of her face almost to her jawline, her skin was swollen, giving her a faintly lopsided look.

She looked, she thought, as if she had been in a mill. Of course, she supposed that she had been. She poked tentatively at the bruise and was rewarded with a twinge of pain. Not as sensitive as it had been yesterday morning, however, so there was hope.

The bruise gave her an eminently reasonable excuse for not going to Admiral and Lady Wendover's ball tonight. No one would expect one of the leading beauties of the *ton* to appear at a major function looking as if she had gone a few rounds at Gentleman Jackson's Boxing Saloon. It had also given her a perfect reason for staying in her room and not going down to greet Oliver when he came to call yesterday and today. She could not, she told herself, bear to let the man she loved see her like this.

But that, she knew, was not the real reason she wouldn't see Oliver—or, rather, like one of those intricate puzzle boxes, the true cause of her discomfort and confusion was hidden within that reason. She could not bear to face Oliver *because* he was the man she loved. For days she had been tiptoeing around the idea, her mind skittering away from the truth whenever her emotions brought it to the forefront. But the other night, when Oliver had pulled her out of the dreadful little closet, when he had wrapped his arms around her and told her she was safe, all her defenses had simply melted away. Her whole being had been filled with love.

It had been wonderful. There was no denying that. She had lain in a blissful daze in his arms as they drove home. Snuggled against his chest, his strength and warmth all around her, the rumble of his voice beneath her ear, the steady beat of his heart, she had known that he did not need to take her anywhere. She was already home.

However, the next morning, when she woke up, she had realized how dreadful her situation really was. Far more painful than her bruises was the knowledge that she loved a man who did not love her—who would never love her. Oh, yes, he had called her "love" when he discovered her—and he had proven more than once that he desired her. But a careless word spoken in the heat of the moment was not a true indicator of his feelings. And passion was not the same thing as love.

Vivian was not the sort of woman with whom Oliver would fall in love. She was flighty, impulsive, rebellious, careless of others' opinions of her, and given to thoughts and behaviors that went against what was accepted. In short, she was the opposite of Oliver. While she might have fallen in love with Oliver despite all those things, Oliver was far too reasonable and practical a man to make the same mistake.

He wanted a woman who matched him in outlook, taste, and intellect. He had told her so. A sedate and settled woman—tactful and modest, with a firm moral sense. Definitely *not* someone whom he regarded as a hoyden—and who had proven the instability of her moral fiber by entering into an affair. It wouldn't matter that the affair had been with Oliver himself or that she could not now imagine doing such a thing with anyone but him. Men, in her experience, did not think that way, especially someone as staid as the Earl of Stewkesbury.

The sad truth was that Vivian did not know what to do or what to say to Oliver. How could she see him, knowing how she felt about him, and not give herself away? How could she continue in this affair, loving him without being loved in return? She had set out the rules, had blithely been sure she was uninterested in love or marriage. She had insisted on an affair without entanglements.

Now she wanted to break all those rules. She didn't want to see him whenever they could manage it without anyone's knowing. She didn't want to pretend in public that they were simply friends, with nothing romantic between them. She wanted to be with him all the time, to see him at the breakfast table, to feel him lying beside her in bed at night, to laugh and talk and share their lives. She wanted, in short, to be married to him.

It was impossible. Unthinkable. Vivian knew that. But it was also unthinkable to simply keep on with their affair, knowing how everything had changed. Neither could she bear the thought of cutting herself loose from him, ending their affair and not seeing him again. Every avenue that presented itself to her led only to heartbreak. So she had simply refused to face it, taking to her bed and telling the maid that she did not feel well enough to see Lord Stewkesbury.

It had been cowardly, and it had made her so lonely that she had wound up crying into her pillow anyway, which was, she told herself, unbearably foolish.

It was also cowardly, she knew, to use her bruises as an excuse for avoiding gossip. But she was doing that as well. She had realized yesterday that no one had called upon her all day long except for Oliver, Eve, and Camellia. It was most unusual, especially given that her disappearance at the Cumbertons' party had been announced to one and all by Dora Parkington. Vivian would have expected to have had several gossip-loving women of her acquaintance dropping in to find out exactly what had happened.

Since they hadn't, she concluded it must mean that she had finally done something so outrageous that she was in disgrace with the beau monde. It had taken some doing, but she had wormed the truth out of Eve and Cam today when they came to visit her again. Vivian's escapade had become a major scandal. Not only had Vivian left the party alone in the company of a man, but she had also spent a good part of the evening alone in the man's living quarters. Worst of all, that man was not even a gentleman, but a person engaged in trade.

"The vultures!" Camellia had exclaimed, her cheeks flushed with anger. "I told them that you had been abducted! It wasn't as if you'd chosen to do it. And Lady Penhurst said that only made it worse, that you wouldn't have gotten into the situation if you weren't always putting yourself into precarious situations."

"I suppose she's right about that," Vivian had said with a shrug and a smile. "What can one do? That's the way people are."

Inside, however, she could not feel quite so unaffected by the matter. Vivian had flouted convention for years, and she had never gotten into serious trouble for it. She supposed that she had come to feel that she could do what she wanted with impunity. She had shrugged off Oliver's warnings of what could happen, believing him to be too fussy, too staid. But he had been right. Vivian had finally gone beyond the bounds of what the *ton* would accept, even if she was a duke's daughter.

She could not help but wonder what would have happened if she had gone to the Wendover ball tonight. There would have been talk, of course—a great deal of it. She would have had to face down whispers and sideways glances and looks of barely contained glee from those who had long wished to see Lady Vivian finally get her comeuppance. Was it possible that she might even be given the cut direct?

It was a sobering thought. If someone had told Vivian a few days ago that this would happen, she would have laughed and said it didn't matter. But it did matter. She would not enjoy being ostracized by her peers. Lady Kitty's fate would not be one she looked forward to. She liked the whirl of parties and dinners and social calls. She loved to dance, to wear beautiful clothes and jewels. She enjoyed the way she lived. It was more than a little frightening to think of losing it.

Perhaps she should have been more careful. Perhaps she should—

Vivian stopped and looked at her image in the mirror. What was she thinking? Yes, perhaps she should have been more careful—not only about the stolen jewels, but also with her heart. But did she really regret what she had done? Should she not have looked for the jewel thieves? Did she wish she had not fallen in love with Oliver?

Of course not. It might cause her more pain than she had ever before experienced, but she would not have given up what had happened with her and Oliver for any amount of peace. Nor would she have refused to help Lady Kitty, either that first day or the other night. Maybe she should have been more careful, but she had helped expose a ring of thieves and a murderer. Wasn't that more important than being whispered about?

And what, she asked herself, was she doing sitting here hiding from those who were attacking her? If they wanted to say something about her, then let them say it to her face. If she was going to lose out on love, she was certainly not about to just surrender.

Squaring her shoulders, Vivian considered her somewhat battered image in the mirror. She had never backed down from a fight before, and she wasn't about to start now. Jumping up, she strode over to the bellpull and rang for her maid.

When the girl came rushing in a few minutes later, Vivian had already discarded her dressing gown and was brushing out her hair. "Get out a dress for me, Sally. I am going to a party."

Camellia circled the floor in Gregory's arms. She loved dancing as long as Gregory was her partner. Parties, too, were much more enjoyable when he was there. She smiled up at him, then felt a little guilty about her own happiness.

"I'm sorry Vivian isn't here," she said. "Is she feeling any better?"

"I think so. Her bruises look worse, but she assured me that she was not in as much pain. I was actually a bit surprised she didn't insist on accompanying me tonight. She hates to miss a ball."

"It might be because everyone's being so hateful about what she did." Camellia cast a dark glance around the room. "I nearly told Lady Kirkpatrick to shut up tonight when she said something about Vivian, but Eve pinched my arm, so I didn't." Camellia grinned as she went on, "Then

Eve delivered a perfectly acidic comment about something in Lady Kirkpatrick's past. I didn't understand what it was, precisely, but it certainly made Lady Kirkpatrick go quiet."

Gregory chuckled. "Good for her."

"I hate it. People are being so unfair to Vivian."

"You're a loyal friend." He smiled down at her. "But don't worry. Once she's back to herself, Vivian will take care of them. I've never known her to be bested by anyone yet. You'll see. Pretty soon, they'll be eating out of her hand again."

The music wound to a close, and they started off the floor. Gregory led Camellia toward the door. "I have something I wanted to say to you."

Camellia glanced at him, surprised. "All right."

"Alone." They emerged in the hallway, and he glanced around before whisking Camellia down the corridor. He caught sight of the library and smiled. "Ah, here's the perfect place."

"The perfect place for what?" Camellia asked as she followed him into the room.

"We first met in the library at the Carrs'."

"I remember." She grinned. "When you tried to pretend you weren't an almost-duke."

"I didn't," he protested, then saw the smile on her face and relaxed. "All right. I admit that I am an almost-duke. And as such, it's quite important, you know, for me to have an almost-duchess."

Camellia frowned, pulling her hand from his. "What do you mean? What are you saying? You—you need to find a proper girl to marry?"

"I've already found her." He reached out and took her hand back. "I know I'm probably speaking much too soon, and you don't have to give me a definite answer if you'd rather not. I just want to know if there's a hope, if there's any possibility that one day you could see your way to . . . that is to say, that you might consider my suit." Camellia stared at him, and a blush started in his cheeks. "I know I've rushed this. But I—I have no idea if you like me at all, at least in that way."

"In what way?" Camellia looked at him intently. "Gregory, what are you saying?"

"I'm asking you to marry me." He waited, his face tense, watching hers.

"Gregory! Are you serious? But . . . but . . . you haven't thought! I'm not right for a duchess."

"You're right for my duchess."

"But—I don't know how to do any of those things I'd be supposed to. I'd be sure to say or do something wrong. You know I would."

"I don't do any of the things a duke is supposed to," he pointed out. "And it doesn't matter if you get the precedence wrong at a dinner party or talk to someone that a duchess would ignore. I don't care about any of those things. All that matters, all I care about, is how you feel about me. Because, you see, I'm frightfully in love with you. I don't want to think about what my life would be without you. So if you aren't sure, then just don't say no, please. If you think you could get used to the idea or grow to like me, I can wait, and we can have this conversation another time. You see—"

Camellia let out a laugh and threw her arms around Gregory's neck. "Oh, Gregory, sometimes you offer entirely too many options. I'm not the sort of girl to wait and think, you know. I know how I feel. Yes, I'll marry you. I love you."

"Really?" He looked at her in delighted amazement. "Because I think I've loved you from the first moment I saw you."

"I can't say that. But I knew I loved you that night you walked me over to see Cosmo, when I told you what I was doing—and you didn't try to dissuade me or tell me that I was rash or making a mistake or any of those things that people always say. You just said all right. And walked along with me. And I knew that you were the first man who'd seen me for what I was—and still liked me."

"I can't imagine seeing you for what you are and not liking you. Not loving you." Gregory looped his arms loosely around her waist.

"You see? You're doing it again." Camellia smiled and went up on her toes to kiss him.

Some moments later they pulled apart, startled by the sound of footsteps running down the hall. They half-turned toward the doorway as a girl darted into the room. Her face was red, her eyes bright with anger.

"Oh!" She came to a sudden halt, gaping at them. She clapped her hands over her face, and a moment later she let out a little sob.

Camellia and Gregory cast a puzzled glance at each other.

Dora dropped her hands from her face. Her expression of rage had been replaced with one of heartbreaking sorrow. "My life is ruined!"

"I cannot see how *your* life is ruined," Camellia replied unfeelingly. "It was Lady Vivian's reputation you tried to stain."

"Lady Lindley just called me a horrid little gossip!" Dora exclaimed with a flash of her earlier temper, but then she looked down, squeezing her hands together. "And I did not mean to harm Lady Vivian at all. I pray you will believe me, Lord Seyre."

She raised her head, her hands clasped prayerfully together, and looked beseechingly at Gregory. Tears pooled in her large blue eyes, trembling, about to spill over.

"Oh, I believe you," Gregory replied in a voice so cold

Camellia hardly recognized it as his. "It was Miss Bascombe whose reputation you hoped to ruin. 'Twas your misfortune that it was my sister who had worn Miss Bascombe's cloak . . . instead of my fiancée."

"What?"

Camellia pressed her lips together to hold back the laughter that threatened to bubble up at the other girl's stunned expression.

"You-your fiancée?" Dora repeated, her voice dying away on the last word.

"Yes. I have just asked Miss Bascombe to do me the honor of marrying me. And I am happy to say that she has accepted."

"No. You can't mean it." Dora turned to Camellia, her face tightening in fury and disbelief. "You! I can't believe it! *You* are going to be the Duchess of Marchester?"

"I am going to be Gregory's *wife,*" Camellia smiled. "And that, Miss Parkington, is the difference between you and me."

"Good evening, Miss Parkington." Gregory nodded faintly at the girl and offered his arm to Camellia. "Shall we return to the others, my dear?"

"I'd love to." Camellia looked up at him, a glorious smile spreading across her face.

The two of them walked out of the room without a backward glance at Miss Parkington.

When Lady Vivian walked into the ball, a susurration of shock and excitement ran through the crowd. She stood for a moment, her head regally high, before she started across the room. Whispers rose around her, but she paid them no mind. Vivian wasn't sure where she was going. She hoped she would soon see a safe harbor such as Eve and Fitz, but until then, she would concentrate on appearing sublimely unconcerned about the gossip swirling around her.

Lady Arminter looked directly at Vivian as Vivian approached her, then turned pointedly away. Vivian hesitated for a second before she continued on her way, her face as smooth and passionless as marble. Lady Wendover came fluttering up to her.

"Lady Vivian." Lady Wendover glanced around uncertainly. "How are you? I mean, uh . . ." Her eyes flickered to the bruises on Vivian's face and quickly away. "That is, are you certain you feel well enough to be here? Surely you should stay in bed for a few days, after your, um, ordeal."

"Trying to get rid of me?" Vivian asked in an amused tone.

"No, of course not. Always an honor . . . it's just that . . . well, so soon after . . ."

"What's she's trying to say, Vivian," said a firm voice, Lady Euphronia, Oliver's aunt, as she stepped up to join the conversation, "is that you should exercise a measure of good sense and go home. Things will die down after a while, but in the meantime, you're better off staying away. You're exposing Lady Wendover and everyone who knows you to unnecessary distress."

"*I* am subjecting *you* to distress?" Vivian asked, her eyes flashing.

"Yes." Euphronia leaned in closer, lowering her voice to a hiss. "When you make yourself the object of scandal, it affects more than just you. What about your friend Mrs. Talbot and Fitz? What about that Bascombe girl? She will have a hard enough time making it though the Season without you tainting her with your scandal."

"Aunt Euphronia!" A male voice sliced through Euphronia's words, strong and clear. "I am sure Miss Bascombe would be pleased to hear that you are so concerned about her Season, but I really think it would be better all around if you didn't say anything else."

Vivian's gaze went past the other woman to where Oliver stood, his eyes hard as stone and his mouth set in a straight, tight line. Joy rushed up in her.

Beside her, Lady Euphronia swelled up like a pigeon and started to address her nephew, but he fixed her with his gaze and said, "No. Don't embarrass yourself, Aunt."

His gaze swept from his aunt to Lady Wendover to Lady Arminter, falling on all the others in between. "I might remind everyone here that Lady Vivian was injured two nights ago in the course of trying to apprehend a criminal," he went on. "A murderer, in fact. She is guilty of nothing but helping a friend and keeping a number of you from being victimized further. She was hurt; she could have been killed. And all because she has a kind heart and a belief in doing good. That is where she differs from most of you." He ignored the chorus of shocked gasps. "Now . . . if any of you have anything to say about Lady Vivian's character, I suggest you say it to me. Here and now."

He paused again and looked all around. Every pair of eyes in the room was riveted to him. "Because in the future, Lady Vivian is going to be Lady Stewkesbury. My wife." In the stunned silence that followed, he extended his hand to Vivian. "My dear, may I have this dance?"

Vivian took his hand, too stunned to say anything, and let him lead her onto the dance floor. The waltz was already playing, but Oliver whirled Vivian into the circling dancers with ease. Dozens of questions tumbled around in her head, but a waltz, especially one done under the watchful eyes of every occupant of the room, was neither the time nor place for a serious conversation. When the dance ended, Stewkesbury held out his arm to Vivian and escorted her off the floor.

"Oliver . . . ," she began, but he shook his head.

"I think it is good time for a promenade," he told her. "Don't you?"

"Oliver, we must talk."

"And we shall, in a moment."

The moment turned into minutes, then an hour. They made their way slowly around the room, Oliver nodding to everyone he knew and stopping to talk with many of them—whether the person looked eager to speak to him or not. No one dared offend the Earl of Stewkesbury, and at every possible occasion, it seemed, Oliver brought the name of Vivian's father or brother into the conversation. One could almost see the thaw spreading around the room. The longer Vivian was by Oliver's side, the more the tension in her eased. He had just made her task of returning to the good graces of the *ton* a great deal easier, and she could not but love him all the more for it.

But she could not let him ruin his own future for the sake of her reputation.

Vivian did not have a chance to talk to Oliver until a long while later, when they'd finished their circumnavigation of the room and stopped to talk with Eve and Fitz. Eve enveloped Vivian in a hug and stood with her arm looped around Vivian's waist as the four of them made idle chatter. Before long, Camellia and Gregory joined them. Camellia was sparkling, and Gregory looked somehow smug, satisfied, and relieved, all at once. Matters must have progressed rather well with the two, Vivian thought, and wondered if it had gone as far as a marriage proposal. She cast an inquiring glance at her brother, and he blushed and grinned. She knew that Seyre must have asked and been accepted.

The idea was enough to make her want to laugh aloud—just imagine the stir it would make for all the Bascombe girls—that unrefined, troublesome quartet from America—

to make excellent matches before the end of their first Season. And think of Camellia, the wildest of them all, marrying the highest-ranking catch of the entire *ton*!

The thought was enough to carry her for the next few minutes, but after a time, weariness began to sink in on her. Oliver, who had been chatting with his brother, turned to Vivian, putting a supportive hand beneath her elbow.

"Tired?" he asked, bending his head toward her.

She nodded. "A little. I think I will go home now. But, Oliver . . . we must talk."

"Of course. I'll see you home."

They took their leave of the others, and Oliver escorted her to her carriage, climbing in beside her. As soon as the carriage door was shut, he curled his arm around her shoulders, pulling her against him. Vivian went with him, resting her head upon his shoulder. It felt so right, so natural and good, that tears sprang into her eyes.

"Oh, Oliver . . ."

"Hush, now, just rest." He turned his head a little to kiss her forehead. "Are you in much pain?"

She started to shake her head, then said, "A bit. I'm afraid I'm not accustomed to being punched."

"I should have hit him a few more times," Oliver said darkly.

"It wasn't he who hit me, actually."

"He was responsible. Wish I'd hit the other, too, though. Still, Fitz told me you got some of your own in. He said the fellow's coat had blood on it where someone stabbed him with a hatpin."

Vivian's lips curved up in satisfaction. "True. I wish I had had a longer pin."

"So do I. If you intend to continue in this way, perhaps you ought to carry a knife strapped to your leg like Camellia."

Vivian laughed. "I'm not planning on breaking up any more rings of criminals, thank you."

"I have found that one's plans have little to do with the matter."

They reached her house and walked inside. When they were seated on the sofa in the smaller drawing room, he took her hand and raised it to his lips, kissing the knuckles, then said, "Very well, Vivian. Now . . . let's talk."

He looked at her, waiting, and suddenly Vivian found it difficult to say anything. Her throat clogged with tears, and she had to wait a moment and swallow.

Finally, not looking at him, she began, "You are a very good and kind gentleman to do what you did for me tonight. I am very grateful."

"I don't want your gratitude," he responded, his voice almost rough.

"Perhaps not, but you have it anyway." She paused and raised her head to fix him with her gaze. "Do you realize what you've done? How do you plan to get out of this engagement?"

"I have no plans to do so."

"Oliver!" Vivian could feel the tears battling against the backs of her eyelids, but she refused to give way. "I will not let you sacrifice your life to keep me from suffering a little social discomfort."

"I am not sacrificing my life." He took both her hands in his. "I am sorry that I did not ask you before I announced it. I would not have forced it upon you like that if I had had any other choice. But when Aunt Euphronia began braying like an ass, I could not just stand by."

Vivian chuckled softly at the description of his aunt. "But you do not want to marry me. I know you don't." She cast a droll look at him. "You have told me more than once that you do not."

"Whatever I may have said, I was a fool. Vivian . . ." He stood up, pulling her to her feet, and took her by the arms, staring down intently into her eyes. "I love you."

"Oh!" Vivian could not stifle a little cry, and she covered her mouth with her hand, her eyes filling with so many tears that she could not hold them back.

"This makes you cry?" he asked, his voice caught somewhere between laughter and frustration. "Vivian, is the thought that abhorrent to you? Can you not bear to be married to me?"

"No! Oh, no!" She reached up to curve her hand against his cheek. "There is nothing abhorrent about you to me. Nothing. But I—you—oh, Oliver, how could it ever work between us? We are so different. I would drive you mad within a week; you have said so yourself. I am impulsive and emotional and—"

He stopped her words with his mouth. After a long moment, he lifted his head and said, "You are also beautiful and kind and generous and the most . . . fun I have ever had in my entire life. Yes, we're different, but it doesn't mean we cannot get along. We've managed to do it so far, haven't we?"

"But we've been in the grip of irrational lust!"

"I have the feeling that I shall be in the grip of irrational lust as long as I am around you, my love. And our differences match rather well. I keep you from flying off in too mad starts. And you keep me from being deadly dull." He paused, then said soberly, "It doesn't matter how different we are. The fact is that my life is meaningless without you."

"Oh, Oliver!" She began to cry again.

"There. I've done what I thought was impossible. I've turned you into a watering pot." He pulled her to him gently and stroked his hand down her head and back. "Just tell me one thing, Vivian. That's all that matters. Do you love me?"

"Yes, oh, yes! I love you more than anything in the whole world."

He stepped back a little and crooked his forefinger under her chin, lifting her head. "And I love you. And in the end, my beautiful, mad, magnificent hoyden, that is all that matters."

He bent his head and kissed her.

Turn the page for a peek at

the first two delicious Willowmere romances . . .

A LADY NEVER TELLS

and

A GENTLEMAN ALWAYS REMEMBERS

now available from Pocket Books.

And look for Candace Camp's new Regency series,

"The Legend of St. Dwynwen," beginning with

A WINTER SCANDAL

coming this fall!

A Lady Never Tells

London, 1824

Mary Bascombe was scared. She had been frightened before—one could not have grown up in a new and dangerous land and not have faced something that set one's heart to beating double-time. But this wasn't like the time they had seen the bear nosing around their mother's clothesline. Or even like the way her heart had leapt into her throat the day her stepfather had grabbed her arm and pulled her against him, his breath reeking of alcohol. Then she had known what to do—how to back slowly and quietly into the house and load the pistol, or how to stomp down hard on Cosmo's instep so that he released her with a howl of pain.

No, this was an entirely new sensation. She was in a strange city filled with strange people, and she had absolutely no idea what to do next. She felt . . . lost.

Mary took another glance around her at the bustling docks. She had never seen so much noise and activity or so many people in one place in her life. She had thought the docks in Philadelphia were busy, but that was nothing compared to London. All around them were piles of goods, with stevedores loading and unloading them, and people hurrying about, all seemingly with someplace to be and little time to get there.

There were no women. The few whom she had seen disembark from ships had been whisked away in carriages with their male companions. Indeed, all the passengers from their own ship were long gone, only she and her sisters still standing here in a forlorn group beside their small pile of luggage. The shadows were beginning to lengthen; it would not be long until night began to fall. And though Mary might be a naïve American cast adrift in London, she was smart enough to know that the London docks at night were no place for four young women alone.

They could not stay here. Unless a carriage happened by soon, they would be forced to pick up their bags and walk into the narrow, dingy streets beyond the docks. Mary glanced uncertainly around her. Several of the men loading the ships had been casting their eyes toward Mary and her sisters for some time. Now, as her gaze fell on one of them, he gave her a bold grin. Mary stiffened, returning her most freezing look, and pivoted away slowly and deliberately.

She studied her three sisters—Rose, the next oldest to Mary and the acknowledged beauty of the family, with her limpid blue eyes and thick black hair; Camellia, whose gray eyes were, as always, no-nonsense and alert, her dark gold hair efficiently braided and wrapped into a knot at the crown of her head; and Lily, the youngest and most like their father, with her light brown, sun-streaked hair and gray-green eyes.

All three girls gazed back at Mary with a steadfast trust that only made the icy knot in her stomach clench tighter. Her sisters were counting on her to take care of them, just as Mama had counted on her to get the girls away from their stepfather's house after their mother's death and across the ocean to London, to the safety and security of their grandfather's home. Mary had managed the first part of it. But all of that, she knew, would be for naught if she failed now. She had to get her sisters someplace safe and proper for the night, and then she had to face a grandfather none of them had ever met—the man who had tossed out his own daughter for defying his wishes—and convince him to take in that same daughter's children. Instinctively, Mary clutched her slender stitched-leather satchel closer to her chest.

At that moment, a figure came hurtling toward them and careened into Mary, sending her sprawling to the ground. For an instant, she was too startled to move or even to think. Then she realized that her hands were empty. *Her satchel!* Frantically, she glanced around her. It wasn't there.

"My case! He stole our papers!" Mary bounded to her feet and swung around, spying the running figure. "Stop! Thief!"

Pausing only long enough to cast a look at Rose and point to the luggage, Mary lifted her skirts and took off running after the man. Rose, interpreting her sister's look with the ease of years of familiarity, went to stand next to their bags, but Lily and Camellia were hot on Mary's heels. Mary ran faster than she had ever run, her heart pounding with terror. Everything important to them was in that case—everything that could prove their honesty to a disbelieving relative. Without those papers, they had no hope; they would be stranded here in a huge, horrid, completely strange town with nowhere to go and no one to ask for help. She had to get the satchel back!

Her sisters were right behind her; indeed, Camellia, the swiftest of them all, had almost caught up with her. But the wiry thief who had taken her case was faster than any of them. As they rounded a corner, she spied him half a block ahead, and realized, with a wrenching despair, that they could not catch him.

A few yards beyond the thief, two men stood outside a door, chatting. In a last, desperate effort, Mary screamed, "Stop him! Thief!"

The two men turned and looked at her, but they made no move toward the man, and Mary knew with a sinking heart that her sisters' future was disappearing before her eyes.

Sir Royce Winslow strolled out of the gambling hell, giving his gold-headed cane a casual twirl before he set its tip on the ground. A handsome man in his early thirties, with blond hair and green eyes, he was not the sort one expected to see emerging from a dockside gaming establishment. His broad shoulders were encased in a coat of blue superfine so elegantly cut that it could only have been made by Weston, just as the polished Hessians on his feet were clearly the work of Hoby. The fitted fawn trousers and white shirt, the starched and intricately tied cravat, the plain gold watch chain and fobs all bespoke a man of refinement and wealth—and one far too knowing to have been caught in the kind of place frequented, as his brother Fitz would say, by "sharps and flats."

"Well, Gordon, you've led me on another merry chase," Sir Royce said, turning to the man who had followed him out the door.

His companion, a man barely out of his teens, looked a trifle abashed at the comment. Unlike Sir Royce's, Gordon's clothes evinced the unmistakable extremes of style and color that branded him a fop. "And I would never have taken it into my head to wear that yellow coat."

"But it's all the crack!" Gordon exclaimed.

However, his companion was no longer listening to him. Sir Royce's attention had been caught by the sight of a man tearing down the street toward them, clutching a small leather satchel. What was even more arresting was that running after him was a young woman in a blue frock, her dark brown hair loose and streaming out behind her and her gown hiked up almost to her knees, exposing slender stocking-clad legs. Behind her were two more young women, running with equal fervor, bonnets dangling by their ribbons or tumbling off altogether, their faces flushed.

"Stop him!" the woman in the lead shouted. "Thief!"

Royce gazed at the scene in some amazement. Then, as the thief drew almost abreast of him, he casually thrust his cane out, neatly catching the runner's feet and sending him tumbling to the ground. The man landed with a thud and the case went flying from his hands, skidding across the street and coming to a stop against a lamppost.

Cursing, the runner tried to scramble to his feet, but Royce planted a foot on his back and firmly pressed him down.

"Gordon, fetch that leather satchel, will you? There's a good lad."

Gordon was gaping at the thief, twisting and flailing around under Sir Royce's booted foot, but at the older man's words, he picked up the case, weaving only slightly.

"Thank you!" The woman at the head of the pack trotted up to them and stopped, panting. The other two pulled up beside her, and for a moment the two men and three women gazed at each other with considerable interest.

They were, Sir Royce thought, a veritable bevy of beauties, even flushed and disheveled as they were, but it was the one in front who intrigued him most. Her hair was a deep chocolate brown and her eyes an entrancing mingling of blue and green that made him long to draw closer to determine the precise color. There was a firm set to her chin that, along with her generous mouth and prominent cheekbones, gave her face an unmistakable strength. Moreover, that mouth had a delectably plump bottom lip with a most alluring little crease down the center of it. It was, he thought, impossible to see those lips and not think of kissing them.

"You are most welcome," Sir Royce replied, pulling his booted foot off the miscreant's back in order to execute a bow.

The thief took advantage of this gesture to spring to his feet and run, but Royce's hand lashed out and caught him by his collar. He glanced inquiringly at the women.

"Do you want to press charges? Should we take him to a magistrate?"

"No." The first woman shook her head. "As long as I have my case back, that is all that matters."

"Very well." Sir Royce looked at the man he held in his grip. "Fortunately, the lady has a kind heart. You may not be so lucky next time."

He released the thief, who scrambled away and vanished around a corner, and turned back to the group of young women. "Pray, allow me to introduce myself—Sir Royce Winslow, at your service. And this young chap is my cousin, Mr. Harrington."

"I am Mary Bascombe," the young woman replied without hesitation. "And these are my sisters Camellia and Lily."

"Appropriately so, for you make a lovely bouquet."

Mary Bascombe responded to this flattery with a roll of her eyes. "My mother had an exceeding fondness for flowers, I fear."

"Then tell me, Miss Bascombe, how did it happen that you are not named for a flower?"

"Oh, but I am," she responded, smiling, and a charming dimple popped into her cheek. "My name is actually Marigold." She watched him struggle to come up with a polite response, and chuckled. "Don't worry. You need not pretend it isn't horrid. That is why I go by Mary. But . . ." She shrugged. "I suppose it could have been worse. Mother could have named me Mugwort or Delphinium."

Royce chuckled, growing more intrigued by the instant. The girls were all lovely, and Mary, at least, spoke as perfect English as any lady—even though there was a certain odd accent he could not quite place. Looking at their fresh, appealing faces or hearing her speech, he would have presumed that she and her sisters were young gentlewomen. But their clothes were not anything that a young lady would wear, even one just up from the country. The dresses and hairstyles were plain and several years out of date, as though the sisters had never seen a fashion book. But, more than that, the girls behaved with the most astonishing lack of decorum.

There was no sign of an older female chaperoning them. And they had just gone running through the streets with no regard for their appearance or the fact that their bonnets had come off. Then they had stood here, regarding him straightforwardly with never a blush or averted gaze or a giggle, as if it were perfectly ordinary to converse with strange men. Of course, they could hardly be expected to follow the dictum of not speaking to a man without having been properly introduced, given the way they had met. But no well-bred young lady would have casually offered up her name to a stranger even if he had helped her. And she certainly would not have volunteered the girls' first names as Mary Bascombe had just cheerfully done. Nor would she have commented in that unrestrained way regarding her mother's naming them. Most of all—what in the world were they doing down here by the docks?

"Are you—Americans?" he asked abruptly.

Mary laughed. "Yes. How did you know?"

"A lucky guess," he replied with a faint smile.

Mary smiled back, and her face flooded with light. Royce's hand tightened involuntarily on the handle of his cane, and he forgot what he had been about to say.

Mary, too, seemed suddenly at a loss for words, and she glanced away, color rising in her cheeks. Her hands went to her hair, as though she had suddenly realized its tumbled-down state, and she fumbled to repin it.

"I—oh, dear, I seem to have lost my hat." She glanced around.

"If I may be so bold, Miss Bascombe. You and your sisters are—well, this is not a very savory area, I fear. Are you by chance lost?"

"No." Mary straightened her shoulders and returned his gaze. "We aren't lost."

Behind her, one of her sisters let out an inelegant snort. "No, just stranded."

"Stranded?"

"We got off the ship this afternoon," explained the youngest-looking of the Bascombe sisters, turning large gray-green eyes on him. Her voice lowered dramatically. "We are all alone here, and we haven't any idea where to go. You see—"

"Lily!" Mary cut in sharply. "I am sure that Mr. Winslow isn't interested in hearing our tale." She turned to Sir Royce. "Now, if you will be so kind as to hand back our case, we will be on our way."

"Sir Royce," he corrected her gently.

"What?"

"My name. 'Tis Sir Royce, not Mr. Winslow. And I will be happy to return your case." He plucked it from Gordon's clasp and handed it to Mary but kept hold of it, saying, "However, I cannot simply walk away and leave three young ladies alone in this disreputable part of the city."

"It is all right, really," Mary argued.

"I insist. I will escort you to . . ." He paused significantly.

"An inn," Mary said firmly, and tugged the case from his hand. Her chin went up a little. "Indeed, we are most grateful for your help, sir. If you will but direct us toward an appropriate inn, we shall not bother you anymore."

Sir Royce bowed to her, schooling his face to hide his amusement. Her words were a dismissal as much as a thanks, he knew. Well, he thought, Miss Mary Bascombe might find dismissing him was easier said than done.

A Gentleman Always Remembers

Fitz stood still for a long moment after the woman ran away, staring after her in amazement. Sudden flight was not normally the feminine reaction to his name. At thirty-two years of age, Fitzhugh Talbot was one of the most eligible bachelors in England. He was the younger half brother of the Earl of Stewkesbury, and though his mother's family was not nearly as aristocratic as his father's, the money that she and her father had left Fitz more than made up for that minor flaw. These factors alone would have made him well liked by maidens and marriage-minded mothers alike, but he had also been blessed with an engaging personality, a wicked smile, and a face to make angels swoon.

Indeed, it would take a determined soul to find anyone who disliked Fitz Talbot. Though he was clearly not a dandy, his dress was impeccable, and whatever he wore was improved by hanging on his slender, broad-shouldered body. He was known to be one of the best shots in the country, and though he was not quite the rider his brother the earl was, he had excellent form. And though he was not a bruiser, no one would refuse his help in a mill. Such qualities made him popular with the males of the *ton*, but his skill on the dance floor and in conversation made him equally well liked by London hostesses.

There was, in short, only one thing that kept Fitz from being the perfect match: his complete and utter disinterest in marrying. However, that was not considered a serious impediment by most of the mothers in search of a husband for their daughters, all of whom were sure that their child would be the one girl who could make Fitzhugh Talbot drop his skittish attitude toward the married state. As a consequence, Fitz's name was usually greeted with smiles ranging from coy to calculating.

It was *not* met with a noise somewhere between a gasp and a shriek and taking to one's heels. Still, Fitz thought, he did like a challenge, especially one with a cloud of pale golden hair and eyes the gray-blue of a stormy sea.

When he reached the road, he swung up into the saddle and turned his stallion once again in the direction of the village. He did not urge the animal to hurry; Fitz was content to move at a slow place, lost in his thoughts. He had been willing enough when his brother Oliver asked him to fetch the new chaperone for their cousins. Fitz was often bored sitting about in the country, and the week or two until Mary Bascombe's wedding had stretched out before him, filled with the sort of plans that provided infinite entertainment for women and left him looking for the nearest door. So he had not minded the trip, especially since he had decided to ride Baxley's Heart, his newest acquisition from Tattersall's, in addition to taking the carriage. That way, he could escort the doubtlessly dull middle-aged widow back to Willowmere without having to actually spend all his time riding in the coach with her.

But suddenly the trip had acquired far more interest for him. His plan to return to Willowmere the following day now struck him as a poor choice. There was not, after all, any need for the girls' chaperone to be at Willowmere immediately. What with Cousin Charlotte as well as Lady Vivian overseeing the wedding preparations, there was more than adequate oversight of his cousins.

Fitz could put up at the inn for a few days and look around the village for his "water nymph." First he would pay a call at the vicarage to meet the widow and tell her that they would be leaving in a few days. He might have to pay another courtesy visit to the vicarage in a day or two, but other than that, he would be free to spend his time in a light flirtation—perhaps even more.

Fitz's avoidance of marriage did not indicate any desire to avoid women. Though he was too careful in his relationships to be called a rake, he was definitely a man who enjoyed the company of women. And after all, he had been immured in the country for a month without any female companionship . . . at least, of the sort he was wont to enjoy in London. But this naiad offered a wealth of possibilities.

He thought of the girl's slender white legs, exposed by the dress she had hiked up and tied out of the way . . . the pale pink of her lips and the answering flare of color in her cheeks . . . the soft mounds of her breasts swaying beneath her dress as she hopped from rock to rock . . . the glorious tumble of pale curls, glinting in the sun, that had pulled free from her upswept hair.

Yes, definitely, he wanted more than flirtation.

He considered how to go about finding her. He could, of course, describe her to someone like the local tavern keeper and come up with a name, but that would scarcely be discreet. And Fitz was always discreet.

He supposed that she could be a servant sent to tend the boy. However, her dress, speech, and manner were all those of a lady. On the other hand, one hardly expected to find a lady splashing about like that in a stream. And who was the child with her? Could the boy have been hers? There was, he thought, a certain resemblance. But surely she was too young to have a child of seven or eight, which was what he had judged the lad to be. Fitz would have thought that she was no more than in her early twenties. But perhaps she was older than she appeared. There were mothers who romped with their children; he had seen Charlotte doing so with her brood of rapscallions.

Perhaps she was the lad's governess—though in his experience governesses were rarely either so lovely or so lighthearted. Or maybe she was the personal maid of the boy's mother. Personal maids were more likely to have acquired the speech patterns of their mistresses than lower servants, and they also frequently wore their mistresses hand-me-downs.

None of these speculations, however, put him any closer to discovering the girl again. She had hinted that he might come across her walking through town, so perhaps she regularly took a stroll. Still, he could scarcely spend his entire day stalking up and down the streets of the village.

Lost in these musings, Fitz was on the edge of the village almost before he knew it. Indeed, he had almost ridden past the church before he realized where he was. Reining in his horse, he looked at the squat old square-towered church. A cemetery lay to one side of it; Fitz had gone past it without a glance. On the other side of the church was a two-story home, obviously much newer than the church but built of the same gray stone. This, he felt sure, would be the vicarage.

It was a rather grim-looking place, and he could not help but hope, for his cousins' sake, that the widow who resided there was not of the same nature as the house. He thought for a moment of riding past it, but a moment's thought put that idea to rest. In a village this size, it would be bound to get back to the residents of the vicarage that a stranger was in town, and they would feel slighted that he had not come first to meet them. Fitz knew that many deemed him an irresponsible sort, more interested in pursuing his own pleasure than others' ideas of his duty, but it was never said that he ignored the social niceties.

Besides, he thought, with a little lift of his spirits, as he swung down off his horse, he would have an excellent reason to keep his visit short, since he needed to get his animal stabled and find himself a room. Brushing off the dust of the road, he strode up to the front door and knocked. The summons was quickly answered by a parlor maid, who goggled at him as if she'd never seen a gentleman before, but when he told her that he wished to speak to Mrs. Hawthorne and handed her his card, the girl whisked him efficiently down the hall into the parlor.

A moment later a woman of narrow face and form entered the room. Her dark brown hair fell in tight curls on either side of her face, with the rest drawn back under a white cap. Her face was etched with the sort of severe lines of disapproval that made it difficult to guess her age, but the paucity of gray streaks in her hair made him put her on the younger edge of middle age. She had on a gown of dark blue jaconet with a white muslin fichu worn over her shoulders and crossed to knot at her breasts.

Fitz's heart fell as he watched her walk toward him. Poor cousins! He had the feeling that the girls had merely traded one martinet for another, and it surprised him that the lively Lady Vivian would have recommended such a woman. However, he kept his face schooled to a pleasant expression and executed a bow.

"Mr. Fitzhugh Talbot, ma'am, at your service. Do I have the honor of addressing Mrs. Bruce Hawthorne?"

"I am Mrs. Childe," she told him. "Mrs. Hawthorne is my husband's daughter."

"A pleasure to meet you, madam." He took the hand she extended to him and smiled warmly down at her. "Clearly you must have married from the schoolroom. You are far too young to be anyone's stepmother."

The tight expression on her face eased, and color sprang into her cheeks. She smiled somewhat coyly. "'Tis most kind of you to say so, sir."

"I am the Earl of Stewkesbury's brother," he went on. "And I am here to escort Mrs. Hawthorne to Willowmere. I believe he wrote to her regarding the matter."

"Yes, of course. I have sent a servant to tell Mrs. Hawthorne that you have arrived."

She gestured toward the sofa, and Fitz sat down, relieved to learn that at least his American cousins had escaped living with this woman—and that he would not have to endure two days of traveling with her.

Mrs. Childe took a seat across from Fitz, her spine as straight as the chair back, which she did not touch, and inquired formally after his trip. They made polite small talk for a few moments before there was the sound of hurrying footsteps in the hallway. A moment later a tall, slender woman dressed in a gown as severe and dark as Mrs. Childe's, her blond hair pulled back and twisted into a tight knot at the crown of her head, stepped into the room.

Fitz shot to his feet, his customary aplomb for once deserting him. There was no mistaking the woman despite the complete change in her attire. The tightly restrained hair was the same pale [illegible] sea.

The middl[illegible] t, his water nymph.